SIEGEL   Siegel, Andy.

F   Suzy's case.

JUL   2012

$26.00   **32026002428958**

DATE			
11/13	2c	8cob	8/12

FOREST PARK PUBLIC LIBRARY

BAKER & TAYLOR

SUZY'S
A NOVEL

CASE

ANDY SIEGEL

SCRIBNER
New York   London   Toronto   Sydney   New Delhi

SCRIBNER
A Division of Simon & Schuster, Inc.
1230 Avenue of the Americas
New York, NY 10020

First Scribner hardcover edition July 2012

SCRIBNER and design are registered trademarks of The Gale Group, Inc., used under license by Simon & Schuster, Inc., the publisher of this work.

For information about special discounts for bulk purchases, please contact Simon & Schuster Special Sales at 1-866-506-1949 or business@simonandschuster.com.

The Simon & Schuster Speakers Bureau can bring authors to your live event. For more information or to book an event contact the Simon & Schuster Speakers Bureau at 1-866-248-3049 or visit our website at www.simonspeakers.com.

Designed by Renata Di Biase

Manufactured in the United States of America

1   3   5   7   9   10   8   6   4   2

ISBN 978-1-4516-5878-1
ISBN 978-1-4516-5880-4 (ebook)

I dedicate this book to my clients. In an instance of negligent conduct, your lives have been tragically changed forever. The brave way that you have dealt with your unfortunate tribulations has inspired this work.

Although Suzy's Case is meant to be entertaining, I am well aware there is nothing humorous about being the victim of personal injury or medical malpractice.

When a story begins "Little Suzy," you know some messed-up stuff is about to happen to an innocent kid. I understand that nobody wants to read about the suffering of a child, but in my line of work the chronicle always begins with an unfortunate event.

Hang in there. The ride begins soon after.

SUZY'S CASE

THE UNFORTUNATE EVENT

Little Suzy is lying in a Brooklyn hospital bed fevered and weakened. If her temperature were heating a pot you'd hear the high-pitched tone of a whistling teakettle. That's why her six-year-old frame is on top of the dingy white sheets and not under them.

If her lungs were a train engine you'd hear *puff, puff . . . chug, chug* with the internal dialogue of her autonomic nervous system repeating, *I think I can . . . I think I can.*

Her heart, meanwhile, is in tachycardia, thumping *boom-boom, boom-boom, boom-boom,* nearly twice its normal rate.

Whistle, puff, puff, chug, chug, boom-boom. Whistle, puff, puff, chug, chug, boom-boom. Not good.

Since the arrival of her mother two hours ago, Suzy's vitals have picked up their rhythmic tempo. Again, not good. But there's nothing a mother can do in this situation, even one as dedicated and resourceful as June Williams. She has no choice but to watch and wait, sitting there in the standard-issue bedside chair. Sitting, watching, and waiting go against the grain of her take-charge personality, but, like most of us, June defers to the expertise of the medical professionals.

Suzy pops forward jackknife-style at the hips, expelling a deep "cough-cough" with lung rales inconsistent with her childish appearance. You'd think she'd dragged two packs a day for thirty years by the sound of it. She finishes by clearing her throat with a softer, more age-appropriate "uhum-hum" while patting her chest, so as to say, "It hurts here." Her head drops to the pillow, yet she flashes a smile at her mother.

The kind Caribbean nurse at Suzy's bedside turns to June. "No worries," she consoles as she softly dabs Suzy's clammy forehead. The medical term for the beads of sweat collecting on her light brown skin is diaphoresis. "Them doctors mons be making their rounds now. De'll be here soon. Your Suzy be's just a little hot. No worries."

June looks her in the eye and nods with the sincerity of a mother's appreciation. "Okay. Thank you, nurse."

The woman performs one last caring dab so as to say, "There now," then gives Suzy and June a serene, comforting smile as she leaves the room.

June moves from the chair onto the bed and snuggles up to her daughter. Suzy takes her hand. "Don't worry, Mommy, I'm fine. Like the nurse said, I'm just hot."

"You're the best little girl a mother could ask for." They share a smile, acknowledging how fortunate they are to have each other, then tighten the cuddle.

"You'll feel more relaxed if I read to you, Mom," Suzy suggests, pointing to the table. "Reach over and hand me that book."

The warmth of happiness comes upon June's face as she feels her daughter's concern. Suzy shines brightness on overcast days. June often wonders how a child of her tender years could have such maturity and caring presence. In kindergarten the teacher had called Suzy her "little helper" because of the way she looked out for less independent classmates.

"Hold on, Mom, we're going for a ride!" Suzy warns, smiling. "I'm gonna press this button and the head of the bed is going to come up even higher." They giggle together as the bed buzzes and vibrates on the rise. "Cool, huh? Right, Mom?"

June looks at her daughter with a blend of adoration and admiration.

"Now put your head on my chest," Suzy tells her. "And listen to this story. It's a good one. It's called *Old Yeller*. That nurse from Jamaica brought it from the library when I told her how much I loved dogs. The librarian gave it to her. Can you believe this place has a library?

With a librarian? It's on the second floor. And you know, Jamaica's an island in the Caribbean. Now before I begin, I just want your promise that we can get a dog as soon as I leave here, so say 'I promise.' "

"We'll discuss it when you're discharged."

Suzy's having none of that. "Say 'I promise,' Mom?" she responds, in an insisting tone.

"I promise," June replies, giving in. She rests her head on Suzy's chest. It's burning hot. She hears the wheezing sound of labored breathing, with rapid respirations like the beats of Suzy's stressed little heart. Everything that's happening right now scares her. She raises her head to check her daughter's face. Their eyes meet and Suzy perfectly reads her mother's look of concern.

"What's the matter, Mom?"

"It's your heart. It sounds like it's beating so fast."

"That's because it is. Now listen to the story," she says, dismissing her mother's worry. "It's my new favorite, even though I'm not done yet." Suzy holds the book out, displaying the cover. "You see that dog, Mom? That's Old Yeller. That dog chased an angry mother bear away."

Suzy turns to the first page. Just as she's about to read, a group of doctors shuffles into the room, six in all, entering by order of medical rank. One is an experienced doctor, while the five others are residents. The group approaches and the attending doctor, in a commanding voice, addresses June. "Good morning. I'm Dr. Gino Valenti. I'm one of the staff hematologists taking care of your daughter. Chief of the department, I might add."

June has never seen or met this Dr. Valenti before. Dr. Richard Wise has been the hematologist assigned to Suzy's care since her admission three days ago, though she doesn't think much of him. June has good instincts for most things and takes an instant liking to Dr. Valenti. He's tall, in his midsixties, with a full head of silvery hair, a Kirk Douglas chin, and the air of knowing precisely what he's doing.

"Oh, I'm glad you're here," June anxiously replies. "Suzy's all sweaty and her heart sounds like a drum solo from a halftime band. And she's breathing really quickly, too, but with difficulty if you listen close."

"That doesn't sound good. No one made me aware. Let's have a look."

June stands off the bed, without letting go of Suzy's small hand. This causes *Old Yeller* to slip and fall to the floor, landing at the feet of Dr. Valenti. "One of my favorites," Valenti says as he bends down, picks up the book, and hands it to one of the residents. "A real classic."

Suzy is pleased by the comments and smiles at him. "I'm halfway through and Yeller is some special dog. I hope the book has a happy ending."

Valenti smiles back, says, "Yes, well . . . ," and takes a step closer as the residents fan themselves out like a poker hand at the foot of the bed. "Good morning. I'm one of your doctors. Like I told your mother, I'm a hematologist. That means—"

Suzy politely breaks in. "I know, Dr. Valenti. A hematologist is a doctor who specializes in disorders of the blood, like my disease. If you're one of my doctors, then how come I've never met you before?"

"Well, you got the hematology definition exactly right, and I feel it's my loss that we've never met before this moment." Dr. Valenti pauses and studies her. "Now, how are you feeling this morning?"

"Just like my mom told you, hot and sweaty, and if my heart were a dog it would be a greyhound. That's a racing dog, you know. I love dogs and I'm getting one when I leave here."

"I love dogs, too. Now—"

"Sorry for cutting you off again, but are you a pediatric hematologist who takes care of kids like me or just a regular one?"

"That's a very intelligent question, Suzy. I'm a regular one."

"What happened to Dr. Wise, who saw me the last two days? He's a pediatric hematologist, you know, but no offense."

Dr. Valenti shakes his head in appreciation of her moxie. He glances at the residents, lifting a brow, then back to her. "No offense taken. He had to take a personal day today, but he told me all about you, Suzy. Are you okay with me treating you this morning?"

"Sure. We like the same books and you seem like you know what you're doing."

The residents share a common chuckle, making their presence felt for the first time. As Valenti's smile disappears he directs his attention to one of them. "Dr. Hassan, take a look at that chart and tell me what you see happening here."

The resident puts his clipboard down and begins to reach for Suzy's medical record hanging on the end-of-bed patient chart holder.

"Hassan," Valenti barks, with an annoyed look on his face, "never put your clipboard down on a patient's bed. It's invasive, rude, and discourteous."

Hassan quickly picks it up, then takes Suzy's chart off the holder and begins flipping through it with all eyes on him. A moment later, he speaks.

"The patient's temperature has been spiking throughout the night and her pulse rate shows a pattern of continued elevation, Dr. Valenti."

"Hassan," Valenti demands with an annoyed look on his face, "hand me that chart. This sweet little girl has a name and it's Suzy." Valenti pauses and looks down at Suzy, who grins. "When talking about a patient in her presence, use her name. Don't depersonalize her by using the term *the patient*. Are we clear, Dr. Hassan?"

"Yes, sir."

Dr. Valenti flips through the chart with a studious eye, then hands it to the resident still holding *Old Yeller*. "Dr. Gold," he says to a different one, "when I'm done listening to Suzy's heart, I'm going to ask you the significance of the chart findings Hassan told us about relative to Suzy's disease. I'm giving you a head start on this one, so begin formulating your answer. For the rest of you, you'll be filling in the gaps of Dr. Gold's response."

Dr. Valenti takes the stethoscope, which had been draped around his neck old-school-style, and plugs it into his ears. He leans over, softly places it on Suzy's chest, and moves it about while listening intently. "Now take a few deep breaths for me, Suzy," he directs. She does. Dr. Valenti stands up and unplugs. All eyes are on him. He's formulating.

"One second," he says, then walks to the door and looks out. First left, nothing. Then right. "Nurse!" he calls in a firm voice. "Oh, nurse! Yes, I'm talking to you. Please come over here for a moment."

From the hall the sound of slowly approaching footsteps is heard, then a nurse can be seen crossing the six-inch gap made between the right side of the doorframe and the well-built body of Dr. Valenti.

"I'm sorry, I don't know your name," he says. "You must be new around here. I'm Dr. Gino Valenti, just like the tag says. Nurse, please bring a heart monitor to this room right away and hook Suzy up to it."

"Yes, doctor sir, mon, right ahway," the nurse replies in a lilting island accent. Dr. Valenti may not have recognized her, but June and Suzy know who she is.

He struts confidently back to the bedside. "Nothing to worry about," he says. "I just want to monitor your heart rate more closely, Suzy. Would that be okay with you?"

"I guess," she answers with hesitation. "Is a heart monitor the clip thing you put on my finger?"

"No, Suzy, that's something different that basically measures your pulse rate. What I want to use is a cardiac monitor, which evaluates your heart directly. So, is that okay with you?"

"I never had that done before. How are you going to do that? Will it hurt?"

"No, it's not going to hurt."

"How does it work?"

"Well, technically speaking, the nurse is going to place something like stickers on your chest that are really called electrode patches. Then she's going to connect plastic-coated wires to those patches, which are called lead wires, and plug the other end of those wires into a cable coming from the machine."

"How does that monitor my heart?"

Valenti looks at June. "She's a real pip, isn't she?"

"That's my baby," June says. "She's going to be the first African-American female president."

Valenti grins, then turns back to Suzy. "The way it works is the electrode patches pick up the tiny electric current made by your heart muscle during a heartbeat and it is transmitted by the wires to the machine, which is really just a recording instrument that prints out a graphic tracing of the electric current generated by your heart. Got it?"

"Got it," Suzy confirms.

"I know *you* understand, Suzy. That 'got it' was for Dr. Gold over here." Another chuckle circulates at the foot of the bed. "Now, Suzy, I'm going to step outside with your mother and these doctors and have an adult conversation. All right?"

"That's fine with me, Dr. Valenti. I know you're going to tell her the bad stuff you don't want me to hear. My mom will want to know everything, so don't hold back." She gives Valenti an endearing smile. "Just say it like it is."

Dr. Valenti makes a "you're quite the precocious kid, aren't you" nod. "Thank you, Suzy. We'll be right back."

Once outside the room, he leans against the wall facing June. The residents keep their same positions in the horseshoe, now around them. "That's a remarkable little girl you have there, Mrs. Williams," Dr. Valenti comments.

"It's Ms. Williams, and yes, she's something special. But she can never get a break from her disease."

Before Valenti responds, the group's attention is distracted by a loud noise. It's a continuous *click-click* sound with a split second between the double clicks. Approaching from down the hall is the Caribbean nurse wheeling a cardiac-monitoring machine with a broken wheel. As she slowly nears, pushing the machine, the clicking sound becomes louder. She reaches the group, stops, and so do the *click-click*s. She's breathing heavily, very heavily. She leans over and rests her hands on her thighs just above her knees, tugging at her whites. Her position resembles that of the guy at the foul line late in the game waiting for the basketball from the ref so he can tie things up. The residents have inverted their horseshoe circling the nurse and watch as she sucks air to catch her breath.

She takes one last big inhale as she uses her hands to push off her thighs, then stands up. "Oh, I be tired, mon," she gasps. "Had to go all da way to da basement to get dis here machine, ya know. Not a one available on dis here floor, mind ya. Da basement I be tellin ya, it be far, far away. Here you go, doctor sir, mon." She turns to walk away.

"Nurse," Dr. Valenti says in a stern voice, "my instructions were for you to hook up that child in there. Could you please do that?"

"Me, doctor sir, mon?"

"Yes, you, nurse, thank you."

"Ya, mon, doctor sir," and she *click-click*s the machine into Suzy's room.

Dr. Valenti turns back to June and, with a comforting look, continues. "Ms. Williams, everything is just fine right now. Suzy's having some mild complications associated with her blood disorder, a little more serious than the ones that gave rise to her prior three admissions. There's nothing to worry about. I promise. In a girl her age, this kind of thing will come and go. When she gets older, she'll be at risk for more serious complications, but like I said, for now she'll be fine. Would you mind waiting here a moment while I pull these residents to the side for some instruction?"

"You mean you're going to talk about the bad stuff?"

"Now I see where Suzy gets it from, Ms. Williams. But no, like I said, at her age the complications from a crisis are relatively minor when treated. Suzy's going to live a healthy and productive life. She'll be giving you grandchildren whom you'll be visiting one day at the White House during her presidency. I'm just going to do a little Q and A with my students. Okay?"

"Okay."

Valenti and his residents shuffle a few steps to the left until they're out of June's earshot. "Okay, Gold," Dr. Valenti queries, "can you tell us why I'm placing that wonderful little girl in there on a heart monitor?"

"To monitor her heart?"

"Very good, Gold. No doubt you'll be discovering a cure for the common cold by the time you've completed our program." Valenti turns to the next resident. "Dr. Guthrie, you've been quiet as usual. How are things this morning?"

"F-fine," stutters Dr. Guthrie.

"Don't be so nervous, Dr. Guthrie. Nobody likes a nervous doctor. Now, can you tell Dr. Gold and the rest of us why I just ordered a heart monitor? And please give us an answer incorporating the relevant information particular to Suzy's condition."

"Yes, sir," Dr. Guthrie replies in a hesitant voice, not comfortable being the center of attention. "Suzy has sickle cell disease, which is an inherited blood disorder in which red blood cells are abnormally shaped. Instead of the RBCs being round, they're distorted to the elongated shape of a sickle. A sickle is basically the shape of the letter *C*. Unlike round RBCs, which move easily through the body's small blood vessels, the pointed and stiff sickle-shaped cells have a tendency to get stuck in these tiny capillaries. This can cause a sickle cell crisis which, technically speaking, is a vaso-occlusive crisis. *Vaso,* meaning vascular, and *occlusive,* meaning the inside of the vessel is blocked. So a sickle cell crisis is when the sickle-shaped cells obstruct the capillaries restricting blood flow to an organ. The lack of blood flow, known as ischemia, results in the deprivation of oxygen and can lead to organ damage. A sickle cell crisis can cause varying symptoms of pain to different parts of the body, depending upon where the vascular occlusion is."

"Very good, Guthrie. Anything else you want to add?"

Dr. Guthrie nods. "The worst type of a sickle cell crisis is a sickle cell stroke to the brain. This is when the rigid sickle cells block the tiny brain vessels and the patient strokes out from the ischemia. Suzy doesn't appear to be in this type of crisis, but, like all sickle cell patients, she's at risk for developing a sickle cell stroke. The type of sickle cell crisis Suzy's in is known as an acute chest crisis. This is caused by the trapping of the sickle-shaped red blood cells in her lungs, which obstruct the normal exchange of oxygen. The signs and symptoms of this are the exact ones Suzy is now exhibiting. She has difficulty breathing, is coughing, and has chest pains. When Suzy arrived here, she only had an elevated fever, which is generally the first indication that a child is going into crisis. So, Ms. Williams responsibly got her daughter here in a timely manner. Suzy's constellation of symptoms, however, evidences a worsening of her condition, putting her in a full-blown acute chest sickle cell crisis."

"Dr. Guthrie," Valenti interjects, "very good, but the question was why I ordered the monitor."

"Yes, of course," she responds, but before continuing she looks worriedly over to June, to the doorway of Suzy's room, then slowly turns back to the group. "Without having listened to Suzy's heart, I believe you ordered the heart monitor because her heart is beating faster than normal. Tachycardia can be an early sign of pulmonary congestion, when the sickle-shaped cells block the arteries that bring blood to the lungs. This causes the heart to beat more quickly as a compensatory measure in an effort to get more oxygen to the lungs. Like a heart attack, where the heart muscle is deprived of oxygen, the lungs can have a similar type of attack if they are deprived of oxygen, called a pulmonary infarction. A pulmonary infarction leads to a cardiopulmonary arrest, where both the heart and lungs stop functioning. An acute chest crisis that progresses into a cardiopulmonary arrest is the most common cause of death in sickle cell patients, so I believe you want to monitor Suzy's heart to keep a watchful eye out for this."

"Excellent, Dr. Guthrie. That was a textbook answer. I'm so pleased you switched your residency program from cardiology to hematology. You're a born hematologist. Now let's go back to Ms. Williams. It's rude to keep her waiting there alone for too long." The group shuffles back over.

Dr. Valenti faces June. "Ms. Williams, as I said, Suzy is going to be just fine. I'm going to put her on oxygen, which should help her breathe easier, and change her oral antibiotics to intravenous, upping her dose. I'm going to give her some fluids and medicine to dilate, or open, her lungs, which should also help with the breathing. I'm actually a little surprised Dr. Wise didn't order these things earlier. It's standard practice, but he's the pediatric hematology expert, not I. I'll make a note to discuss it with him."

"Why isn't my baby getting the standard care?" June asks testily.

"Dr. Wise is a good doctor, one of the best pediatric hematologists around. Maybe it's because Suzy's symptoms have only recently taken a turn for the worse, but I don't know. As I said, I'll discuss it with him, but for now, no harm done. I can assure you of that. If things don't improve, which I expect they will, then I'll order a chest X-ray to look for a lung infiltrate."

At that very moment, a loud shrieking scream blasts out from the room. It is Little Suzy. The echo of her cry can be heard throughout the entire floor and maybe the ones above and below. It's followed by the accented screams of the nurse. "Help! Oh me God! Help me, doctor sir, mon! Help! Help me, God!"

June pops off the wall and barrels through the residents, knocking Dr. Gold to the floor. Dr. Valenti follows, high-stepping over Gold. All but one of the residents run around Gold into the room. The shy Dr. Guthrie freezes in place, incapable of meeting the demands of the evident medical emergency.

Upon entering the room, June and Dr. Valenti abruptly stop in their tracks at the horrid sight before them.

Suzy's neck and upper back are freakishly arched off the bed. Her hair is standing on end and she's shaking and convulsing uncontrollably, like the girl in *The Exorcist*. Her foaming mouth is wide open with no tongue in sight and her eyes have rolled back inside her head, with only the whites showing.

"Help me, mon!" the nurse screams, breaking the petrified silence from the corner a few feet away where she's kneeling and using the heart monitor for cover. "Doctor sir, help me, mon!"

Valenti grabs a resident by his shoulders and speaks to him in a firm and controlled voice. "Call a code. Call a code. She's in arrest. Get a code team here. Go now. Get a crash cart in here now!" The resident runs out.

Valenti swiftly moves to Suzy and presses her shoulders, forcing her jerking body down to the bed. He looks back and sees June standing there, her hands covering her mouth in shock and disbelief.

"Get her out of here! Get her out now!" Valenti demands as he struggles to keep Suzy's jerking body pinned to the bed.

Dr. Gold, now up from the floor, rushes over to June Williams. "Come, come. You don't need to see this," he tells her. "Come outside the room. Dr. Valenti will take care of it. You don't need to see this. Come with me." He guides June out with comfort and compassion as she instinctively resists.

Suzy is convulsing, her neck vaulted back unnaturally. Dr. Valenti rips the electrode patch with the lead wire off Suzy's chest, tossing it backward. It slides along the tile floor toward the corner, underneath the cart, coming to rest between the thighs of the nurse, now kneeling in prayer.

Suzy abruptly stops her uncontrolled shaking, falling to the bed in apparent cessation of life. Valenti begins pounding the chest of her motionless body, attempting to jump-start the child's heart so hard that ribs are surely being broken.

"Come on, come on, Suzy! Stay with us!" Valenti pleads, trying to beat the life back into her. He seals her mouth with his, gives a blow, causing Suzy's chest to rise. This coincides with further "Help me, God, mons" coming from the corner behind the machine as the residents watch their mentor try to resuscitate the limp child.

The crude, barbaric-seeming chest pounding, alternating with mouth-to-mouth, continues for three more minutes until rushing footsteps are heard. A team of doctors hurries into the room wheeling a crash cart. Now it's time for the advances of modern medicine to have a shot at saving the child.

The code team leader picks up the paddles. "Clear!" he yells, then presses them against Suzy's chest, delivering a defibrillation shock that pops up her body. The nonlethal dose of therapeutic electrocution has no effect, so he again yells, "Clear!" and delivers a second charge. He steps back and looks at Suzy's chest. "Ambu-bag her! Ambu-bag her!" Another code team responder secures a mechanical ventilation device over Suzy's face and starts forcing air in her by squeezing the bulb.

The lead doctor puts his left arm under Suzy's upper back and his right under her knees and lifts her limp body, cradling her in his arms. He quickly turns and dashes for the door with his second-in-command running alongside, bagging her.

They exit the room, heading past June. She's sitting on the floor with her back against the wall and her head in her hands in the exact place where Dr. Valenti had promised everything would be all right. June doesn't notice as her near-lifeless daughter is whisked away by the dynamic duo of code team responders. She's in shock and, by the looks of things, so is the motionless Dr. Guthrie, who is standing where she was when those double clicks were first heard coming down the hall. She watches the code doctors turn the corner, eyes hollow, in disbelief of what just happened.

'm standing near the corner of Twenty-Fifth and Madison on this bright sunny morning staring at the Beaux Arts–style courthouse just down the block, where it all started for me: the Appellate Division, First Department. The place where I was sworn in and admitted to the practice of law in the state of New York.

I never imagined it would also be the place where the practice of law could end for me, too.

As I wait for *my* attorney to arrive, so we can deal with certain allegations made against me, I see the street cart vendor who sold me a hot dog fifteen minutes after I took the lawyer's oath. That was eighteen years ago. He's stationed in the exact same place, at the curb in front of the courthouse steps. He looks exactly the same, too, just older with salt-and-pepper hair. Me, I've put on a few and now I buzz-cut close to my scalp what's left of my hair, riding the cusp between fashionable and just another bald guy.

I take in the structure of that mighty courthouse, a New York City landmark. The front facade is dominated by an imposing triangular portico supported by six Corinthian columns. The message sent is *Don't mess with the law.* But this particular building is more than just a courthouse that houses appeals, motions, and client complaints against their attorneys. It's an elegant blending of art and architecture, and I count no fewer than twenty-five sculptured marble figures. They're all over the place, on the steps, next to the columns, up on the roof—allegorical figures such as Peace, Justice, Wisdom, and figures in legal history such as Confucius, Justinian, and Moses.

But one is missing. There should be a sculpture of a Herculean figure near the arched entry doors with a large marble erection in his masturbating hand because some of the lawyers forced to show up here by client complaint against them are just being jerked off because of a bad case result. A legal outcome that was inevitable the moment the client committed the act requiring him to seek counsel in the first place.

Me, I'm guilty of the charge. Unethical Conduct.

At least I admit it.

My lawyer arrives no time too soon, because you never want to be seen standing in the vicinity of this building on Friday mornings, the day when the Disciplinary Committee conducts hearings stemming from serious unethical conduct alleged by the client. The purpose of the committee is to protect the public by ensuring attorney adherence to the ethical standards codified in the Rules of Professional Conduct, "The Rules." That's why I insisted on meeting my attorney near the corner.

We go in and take our place. My case is the first one up so we take our seats at the table in front of the judge's bench instead of in the audience with the other attorneys who will walk out of here today with either a sense of relief or professional destruction.

The three judges for today's proceeding take forever to make it from the side door to their seats up on the platform. The Disciplinary Committee disciplines attorneys whom they find have committed professional misconduct toward their clients in violation of The Rules. What I'm talking about is the authority to take away your license to practice law. Permanently.

Now the disciplinary judge sitting between the two other grouches stirs. "Will respondent Wyler stand up?" he commands in a crusty voice. I hate being called by my last name alone. First alone, fine. First and last, that's okay, too. "Mr. Wyler," perfectly acceptable. But last alone . . .

"That's you," my lawyer whispers out of the corner of his mouth. "And what are you doing there? Get your hand out of your pocket."

"Sorry, these guys make my balls itch."

"Stand up."

"How do you respond to the complaint against you?" It's Judge Howell, the one in the middle, asking the questions.

"You mean the one from my client?" I answer. "The guy convicted of murder now serving a life sentence without parole? The fellow that also raped and killed a different man at Rikers while waiting for his murder trial to commence for the first guy he did in?"

"Yes, that complaint."

"The one brought against me to this most judicious and fair council, the judges of the Office of Professional Conduct, claiming I handled his slip-and-fall case in a less than professional manner?"

Howell grimaces. "Yes, counselor."

"The one where my client swears he slipped and fell on a broken sidewalk while passing a construction site here in New York and where defense counsel came forward with videotape evidence that my client was actually perpetrating an armed robbery in a McDonald's in Oakland, California, on the very same day, thus making the occurrence of his accident impossible? That complainant?"

"Yes, counselor," Judge Howell responds firmly, "that complainant. Now how do you plead?"

"Judge Howell," I say, "I thought my lawyer here responded to that complaint, but I'll tell you anyway. My personal code of conduct compelled me to allow my client's fraudulent case to be dismissed by the trial court. But, I might add, only after my motion to be relieved as his lawyer was denied by the very same Supreme Court judge. Didn't my attorney tell you all this in his written response?"

"That's what his formal response on your behalf says, accompanied by a disclaimer that it was against his legal advice."

"Well, I haven't changed my position. I'm guilty as charged."

"Do you understand this admission violates the ethical standards of the Code of Professional Conduct requiring you to represent your client in a zealous manner?"

"Define *zealous*."

"Don't test me, counselor!" Judge Howell bellows.

"Your Honor, if you're suggesting *zealous* means to aid and abet in the perpetration of insurance fraud, then yes, I violated the oath to represent my client in a zealous manner."

"I didn't say *zealous* meant that, counselor."

"Well, Your Honor, the only way I could have defeated the defendant's motion to dismiss his case would've been to put in an affidavit by my client with a statement of fact I knew to be false. You're aware of the facts of my client's underlying case, Your Honor?"

"I'm well aware of the particular circumstances of your client's case, counselor."

"Great, then do the right thing here. With all due respect, Your Honor, I have two appointments I have to get to, so let's decide my destiny, shall we?"

"You understand your admission requires that I sanction you?" he states in question form.

"Understood. Sanction away. I'd rather get sanctioned than take dirty money to pay for my wife's tennis lessons, even if her new pro costs double and speaks with a sexy Argentinean accent."

"You are hereby sanctioned in the sum of twenty-five dollars and the complaint is otherwise dismissed," Judge Howell declares.

"Thanks, Your Honor. I appreciate that the punishment is fitting to my violation."

"You know this is the fourth complaint against you in the last two years by one of your clients."

"With more due respect to this honorable court, may I take the liberty in correcting you, Your Honor?"

"Go on," Judge Howell says in an unreceptive tone.

"It's the fourth complaint against me by one of my clients who became my client after I took over the injury practice of Henry Benson, the famous criminal lawyer. You know the venerable Mr. Benson, don't you, Your Honor?"

"Who doesn't?" Judge Howell sighs. "I stand corrected, counselor. It's the fourth complaint against you by one of Mr. Benson's clients."

"Your Honor, I'm going to meet him after I leave here to pick up a new case." I pause. "So there's a remote possibility you may be seeing me again."

Judge Howell shakes his head disapprovingly. "I hope not, counselor, and I caution you to be careful when dealing with Mr. Benson's clients. You know, I was a criminal judge for forty years before they retired me to this place and I've presided over a number of Mr. Benson's criminals . . . I mean clients."

"Thanks for your concern," I reply. "My understanding from Mr. Benson, regarding this new case, is that it involves a little girl, brain damaged as a result of what sounds like the injudicious monitoring of her sickle cell disease, not one of his criminal clients, which is why I say remote."

I turn to leave.

"One moment, counselor." It's Judge Piccone, the one to the left of Judge Howell.

Damn. What's this guy got to say? He isn't my assigned judge. The only reason he's sitting in is so we won't have to repeat the proceeding in the event the pacemakers of the other two fail before a decision can be made.

I turn back around.

"Counselor, you'd better hope I won't be the one determining your punishment in the future," Piccone declares. "Both you and Mr. Benson will then have a problem. He shouldn't be taking cases that don't have merit, but if he does it becomes your obligation to represent the client zealously, something you obviously have a problem with . . ."

I agree. Nonetheless, a retort is invited by the nature of his sentence-ending pause. "So that's the way it's going to be, Your Honor? The trial court prevents me from quitting a phony case. A case that rightfully gets dismissed, at the risk of my losing my license, and this is how a member of the committee that rules on ethics thanks me?"

"That's right," Judge Piccone replies. "I'm against cases without merit and against those involved."

"I'm against them, too. Isn't that the reason why I'm here today?"

I turn to my lawyer. "Let's get out of here before I pop off at this pseudorighteous shit flake."

"Did you use a profanity toward me, counselor?"

"No, Your Honor, I asked my lawyer if he was going to the White House clambake. He's very political." Piccone gives me a skeptical stare.

I break the pause by giving him two finger snaps, Jerry Springer–style, and turn to go. The last I see, his gaze is still fixed on me.

Piccone was known as a defendant-oriented judge when he sat on the bench, the kind of guy who would never know, unless it happened to him, the devastation and detriment that occurs to the injured and their families when insurance companies defend indefensible cases, thus withholding for years the money the plaintiffs deserve in a circumstance where life was permanently altered in an instant of reckless conduct.

My lawyer and I recommence our exit journey. "Don't be such a wiseass," he warns.

"How could anyone blame me for putting forth the truth of the matter?"

"You know the truth carries little weight in legal proceedings."

"I know, but my life philosophy is 'The truth will set you free.' We're walking, aren't we?"

We head down the stone steps of the Appellate Division. "Just stay out of trouble," he cautions. "You've got an unbelievable practice going. Attorneys from all over the city still send you their injury cases *despite* your involvement with Benson."

"If I keep winning, they'll keep sending. It's all about results." I point to the cart vendor. "You want some street meat? Some people think Papaya King on Eighty-Sixth and Third has the best dog in the city, but they got nothing on this guy. He grills, no dirty water, and they're kosher."

He looks to the vendor, who just blew his nose in a paper napkin. "I'll pass."

"Suit yourself. I feel compelled to eat a couple every time I leave that building as a tribute to continued licensure." He grins. "Listen,

I got to hop. I have to meet Henry to pick up that case I told Judge Howell about." I salute my lawyer good-bye saying, "God bless America," then pick up my commemorative dogs. I turn from the cart with my two grilled beauties, mustard and kraut, to flag a cab.

What I see is too good. Even more tasty than what is in my hand. I can't believe it. Adam Hellman is stepping out of a limo. I hate that asshole. He's a showboat plaintiff's attorney who gives our profession a bad name. I mean, who takes a limo to a disciplinary hearing? He's a snake, too. He stole not one but two clients of mine by paying them off to switch attorneys. He's leaning on the open door, gabbing into the limo. I bend down to see he's talking with a young hottie all diamonded up. I can see the sparkles from here. A new girlfriend, no doubt, his having been divorced four times. I quickstep over. He doesn't see my approach. I stop a foot behind him, holding my dogs to the side, out of harm's way. I take a deep breath.

"Adam!" I scream at the top of my lungs. He flies up into the air and almost falls upon landing between the elevation of curb and street. It feels good to startle the crap out of a guy like that. He gathers his balance and turns to me with a confused look on his face. A look that says, *Why did you startle the crap out of me like that?* So I accommodate. In my most excited of utterances.

"You missed your hearing before the committee!" I yell out, causing alarm to infiltrate his nervous system. He turns white. He struggles to swallow the lump that just gathered in his throat. "They disbarred you!" I shout. "Summarily! For nonappearance!"

"What! What!" he responds, in disbelief. "What did you just say, Wyler?" Called by my last name again. I hate that.

"You heard me, man," I state, taking a moment to bend down and flash the dogs at the hottie in the back so as to ask, *Want one?* Her brow rises with interest. Cool. She wants to bite my wiener. I stand to finish what I started. "You've been disbarred, man! Get in there!" I say, pointing to the courthouse. He takes off like a sprinter up the steps, falling three times and leaving a shoe behind before disappearing into the structure. I give a shrug, then casually slip into the backseat of the limo next to the hottie. I shut the door and lean forward.

"James," I say, talking to the limo driver, "I'm a friend of Adam's. Could you run me downtown to the Village, please? I think he'll be a while." The driver puts the stretch into gear and pulls away from the curb. I turn to my left and undertake a quick profile. Blonde, light blue eyes, twentysomething, boobs out and about—she must be Eastern European. "Ivonka?" I ask.

"No. My name is not Ivonka," she responds, with a hard Russian accent. "It's Ivonna."

"My bad, Ivonna. Are you Adam's new girlfriend?"

"Maybe," she answers, holding her hand out in front of her, looking at the jewels on her flared fingers, then adjusts one of her very expensive rings.

"Listen," I say, with the rusty reflexes of a married man and the joy of having just stuck one to Adam, "if things don't turn out too good back in there, I'm around town, honey. I don't got a full head of hair like your boy, but skin is in, baby girl." She looks at me like I'm some kind of idiot. I definitely make better opening statements in front of a jury where I'm given a fact pattern to work with.

Five seconds later, after telling her my first name and then making an offering where something was lost in translation, I find myself stepping out of the limo, evicted. Before shutting the door I plead my case, as lawyers do.

"I was talking about a hot dog, *that* wiener, and my *name* is Tug. I wasn't asking you to—"

"Shut door! Pig!"

The Money, the Whole Money, and Nothing But the Money, So Help Me God

I hop a cab. "Boca Coca Java Mundo Coffee Expressions, please, on Bleecker Street." The cabbie gives me an inspecting look through his rearview. "Yeah, I know, buddy, I'm not hip enough to be hanging out there, but I got business to do and the guy I'm meeting is completing the second decade of his midlife crisis." He ignores me, assuming he understood, starts the meter, and slowly pulls away from the curb, which I greatly appreciate, hating herky-jerky takeoffs.

Boca Coca Java Mundo is a supercool downtown coffeehouse. It's a social networking mecca and subculture to itself. The most beautiful and free-spirited young people in the city gather to peck on their laptops and socialize while sipping five-dollar coffees with eight-word descriptions. It's the ultimate of trendy daytime environments, and I'm sure the old fellas will stick out more than I'd like. I'll be arriving early so I'll grab us a table in the corner.

I enter Boca Coca, which I haven't been to in fifteen years. I stopped coming to *this* Boca when I started going to the other, in Florida, where my in-laws live.

On first glance, everything looks the same. The extralarge purple couches with orange and gold throw pillows are randomly scattered about just as I remember. The rich-looking, purple-stained, floor-to-ceiling wood shelving still runs the perimeter, stocked with hot-chocolate powders and coffee beans from around the world and hundreds of one-pound purple coffee bags containing their traditional blend.

Everything is the same except for one thing—an oversized purple-and-orange lounge chair in the center of the place occupied by none other than Henry Benson.

That chair was never there and it's placed, or should I say displaced, in a highly visual location. It screams, *Look at me,* so I'm not surprised Henry has claimed it as his purple-and-orange throne, drawing the attention due a king.

So much for the corner table.

Henry Benson is a high-profile New York City criminal attorney who was forced to give up his injury practice by his professional insurance carrier because of a civil litigation "misadventure." He committed malpractice in open court in front of his client. He still defends penal prosecutions, but now Henry refers his injured criminals seeking money damages to me.

He chose me—a complete stranger—to take over his civil practice because his bigwig best friend, Dominic Keller, the self-proclaimed "king of all injury attorneys," innocently told him he thought I was a phenom in the courtroom. The nonnegotiable deal was that I take all or none of Benson's twenty-one injured criminals, based solely on his short verbal description of each case. And we split the fees fifty-fifty. Oh yeah, the other reason he chose me to handle his injured criminals was so he could tell his best friend, Dominic, to go fuck off, without actually telling him. It's the case of *Ego v. Ego.*

Forrest Gump would say a Henry Benson case is like a box of chocolates; you never know what you're going to get. Each Benson case never really is what Benson's verbal describes it to be or even what it appears to be after review of the file. Each comes with some built-in wrinkle and unapparent twist that offers the prior warning of a land mine you just stepped on.

That said, the thing you do know about a box of chocolates is that each piece of candy comes with a chocolate-coated covering. And, the thing you know with Henry's injured criminals—or HICs, as I've affectionately termed them—is that each HIC is a *bona fide criminal who has been tried, convicted, and jailed for his felonious conduct.*

Before Benson singled me out to take over his HICs, I was making a good clean living. My maxim was, No one case is worth losing your license, your career, your self-respect, and the respect of others.

My own clients had relatively pure and straightforward injury cases with none of the potential for blowing up in my face, and none were convicted felons. I was gaining recognition in the legal community as an up-and-coming plaintiff's lawyer, and attorneys from all over the city were sending me their medical malpractice and general negligence cases. My practice was moving forward steadily, but unfortunately, my expenses were growing and my efforts weren't exactly yielding retirement dough.

So, despite hating anything to do with moral turpitude—which includes persons of perpetual criminal disposition with injury claims—I accepted Henry's deal for the money, the whole money, and nothing but the money, so help me God. On the first case alone, just weeks after receiving all the HIC files, I made a bundle with very little effort.

Since taking over Henry's injury clients I've identified four fake cases. That makes nearly 25 percent of the whole. For those, I moved to be relieved as counsel, basing my application on attorney-client irreconcilable differences, because it's an ethical violation to come straight-out and tell the judge that your client's a fraud. You go figure that ethics code out. The Rules, yeah, right.

On two of these four cases, relief was granted by the judge. On the other two, permission was denied, and I had to continue representing two plaintiffs I knew to be attempting fraud. For one, I have an offer of settlement to the tune of seventy-five thousand dollars, which sum my client has rejected against my legal advice. He wants an even hundred. I restated to him in the clearest terms my legal wisdom: hogs get slaughtered. The other case had been dismissed as a result of my intentional malpractice, which had landed me in front of the Disciplinary Committee this morning. That brings us up-to-date . . .

. . . well, except for the fact that three HICs have threatened me with bodily harm, and on a fourth occasion, I had to wrestle my letter opener out of the murderous hands of a convicted killer attempting to repeat his offense. In any event, these are the basic costs involved in being an HIC lawyer in the city that never sleeps.

I take in Henry's stately appearance before I approach. Just under six feet, in his early sixties, Henry Benson is slender and seemingly in good shape. He shaves what remains of his hair with a number 1 clipper giving him the look of military strength. He has a strong jaw, large ears, and a warrior's Roman nose disproportionate to his smallish head, but altogether he's a very good-looking man. He's wearing cowboy boots, as always, with his blue pinstripe suit—which doesn't work for me since I know he's from Brooklyn. The one thing you can't take away from Henry is his presence. It's strong, masculine, and authoritative, and everyone gets it.

He signals me to come with a firm wave and, as I approach his table, he looks over and around me to anybody and everybody. He wants to see who's noticing him, which, of course, is status quo for a narcissistic egomaniac. I dismiss the thought of bowing, deciding instead to greet him standing tall.

"Hi, Henry. I just got out of court on one of your cases."

"How much did we make?"

"We didn't make. It was a Disciplinary Committee hearing. I lost. It cost me twenty-five on the sanction and four thousand in legal bills."

"Take half out of this." He hands me one of the four file folders that are sitting on the floor. It's different, newer looking than the other three.

I sit down with the folder in the skimpy chair waiting for me. "Am I going to get a verbal now?"

"I've trained you well. Before I begin, do you want a Mega Boca Coca Java Mundo decaf skim latte?"

"No, I'm good."

"Very well then. What's that on your lapel?"

"Mustard and kraut backlash. I tried to slip some hottie the dog."

He lifts a confused brow, then begins. "The case I just handed you is Betty and Bert Beecher. It's a medical malpractice case I just settled for six hundred thousand dollars. Since I can't practice civil law anymore, I naturally resolved the matter in claim. No formal lawsuit was brought, but I did allow the insurance company to take Betty and Bert's preaction statements under oath."

"Henry, I thought—"

Henry, angry, stops me cold. "What did I tell you about interrupting?"

"Never do it."

"Correct. Now, listen. You'll have no questions when I'm done. You're going to earn your fee if you can get Bert Beecher to sign off on the proposed settlement. It was Betty who was injured as a result of some cosmetic surgery she had on her face—chin, nose, brow lift, lips, eyelids. The perimenopausal fab five. At the start of the procedure the surgeon placed hard plastic protective lenses in her eyes for intraoperative shielding. You know, so nothing got in her eyes. These were inserted after Betty was under the effects of anesthesia so she had no idea she had a foreign body covering her baby blues. At the end of the procedures, the surgeon forgot to take out these nonporous cornea shields and she was discharged home with them in, stuck to her eyeballs. She had no clue about the shields because her eyes were swollen shut from the eye job itself, or so she thought. After ten calls to the surgeon over four days, he finally took a minute out of his busy surgical schedule to see her. He immediately identified the problem and had to remove the shields, stat, so he strapped her down to his exam table, then jabbed forceps in her eyes, ripping the shields out. I say ripping, because they became glued to her corneas from the lack of moisture. The malpractice took place about six months ago and she's got permanently scratched corneas. The problem is, Bert, her good-for-nothing ex-husband, is insisting he get half the client share of the money for his claim for loss of services on behalf of the uninjured spouse."

Henry stops talking, and more than a nanosecond later, I inquire, "If I ask you a question now, will I be cutting you off?"

"No," Henry explains. "I paused in excess of the acceptable break time between sentences, so a question is fair game."

"Why am I getting the case if it's already settled for digits like that? That's a big number for scratched corneas."

"Bert knows I can't practice civil law anymore. He knows I can't institute a formal legal proceeding because of the problem I had and he's using that as leverage against me. Bert says either I get his ex-wife to give him half her recovery as payment for his claim or make up the difference out of my fee. I don't take kindly to ultimatums, especially from a Louisiana hick like him." A hick HIC, I think to myself, that's too funny. If Henry only knew. He continues.

"I told Betty I was referring the matter to you. I explained to her that you'd start the formal lawsuit by serving a summons and complaint on the surgeon and see it through to conclusion to ensure she gets the client's share of the money to the exclusion of her extorting ex-husband. If it goes to a jury, Bert won't get a penny, not with his rap sheet, which happens to include a criminal conviction for attempted murder. So, if you can get him to sign off, you pocket half the fee for doing nothing. A gift. If not, you'll have to work on the case, knowing it's a guaranteed payday because I was already offered six hundred thousand in response to my claim letter to the insurance carrier. That's your verbal. Have fun. And don't underestimate Bert, he's smarter than he looks. By the way, if your interruption earlier was to say you thought I couldn't practice civil law anymore, I'll have you know that settling a case in claim by writing a simple letter is not considered the formal practice of law according to how I interpret the applicable regulations. You need to file suit for your conduct to be considered the practice of law."

Henry reaches down and picks up one of the other three folders, which I assume is the sickle cell case. It's not skinny like Beecher's file. It's thick and heavy, like the other two remaining on the floor. As I take it, I note the date of accident penned on the outside of the folder. With that date of loss, way before Henry and I ever met, I should've gotten this file when I got the rest of the HIC cases. Our deal was a take-all-or-take-none proposition, meaning I'll give you my big-dollar cases but you must also take the crappy ones. So obviously, Henry had held this one out, putting a dagger through the heart of our deal. That ain't right.

But what's more significant about this date of loss is that it is six years ago. This lawsuit should be over and done with by now. It's a stale case and there's always a reason for that, and there's always a disgruntled client because of the unreasonable wait.

Anyway, I'll never forget his words when I asked him if he wanted to put our agreement in writing. "A guy like me, with clients like mine, doesn't need a piece of paper to enforce a deal," he'd said then. "I trust you. You trust me. That's the only thing we have to lose here." Yeah, right. I'm angry but say nothing, not a word. I mean, he's giving me a gift on the Beecher case that's worth no less than a hundred grand in my pocket and he's handing over the one he'd been holding out on me. I guess I'm ahead of the game. It's just his attitude toward trust that bothers me.

"This is the Suzy Williams file," Henry says, "the girl who sustained brain damage from her sickle cell disease when she was six."

"Right, the one you told me about."

"Yes, the one I told you about."

"I'm listening. No interruptions, I promise."

"Yes, the verbal. Well, uh, the verbal on this case is there is no case."

"I thought you told me they mismanaged her condition in the hospital."

"Yeah, that's what I told you."

"So, what changed?"

"Defense counsel served me with a motion to dismiss the case, so I had to pay for an expert medical review. My expert said no case. There's a memo in the file from my expert doctor, attached to the defendant's motion for summary judgment seeking dismissal."

"What am I missing here? Are you telling me you didn't have the case reviewed by a qualified medical expert *before* you started the lawsuit to avoid this exact scenario?" I pause, giving him time to respond. Nothing. "Henry, you know that rule ensures you don't sue a doctor or hospital that doesn't deserve it and, more important, so that you don't give the injured client false hope of recovery."

"Don't bother me with details," Henry says dismissively. "You know I don't like details. Just handle things . . . somehow."

"By 'somehow' are you suggesting I make a cross-motion to the court requesting that you be relieved as counsel?" He kind of looks up toward the gold ceiling with a "that's not such a bad idea" expression, then brings his head down and deadeyes me with force and authority.

"You're their lawyer now. And by 'their' I mean the injured child, whose name is Suzy, and her mother, June. Since you're their lawyer and my good name is on the legal documents, just get us relieved as counsel as gracefully as possible."

"I'm on it, Henry. No worries," I offer confidently.

"Good, now get out of here. I'm having a get-together with a young Asian girl I met on Match.com. She kept giving me the wink, so I thought I'd give her the opportunity to give me more. Now get going."

"On my way, Henry." He immediately starts looking over and around me to anybody and everybody the way he did on my approach. Two steps into my escape, I hear Henry.

"And one more thing." I pivot one-eighty on my wing tips.

"Listening, sir," I reply, playing into his ego.

"I saw the way you looked at the Williams file when I handed it to you," Henry continues, "the date of loss, that is. It *was* a holdout. I was handling the case the day you received delivery of the rest of my files and I held this one out." Henry pauses and waits for a response. I don't accommodate him. When he realizes this, he fills in the gap. "This little girl was a child prodigy who became a spastic quadriplegic with severe brain damage as a result of what happened in that hospital. She's badly brain damaged, permanent feeding tube and all. So I thought they'd be throwing the money at me. You and I both know the money follows the injury in an emotional case like this. I didn't know you could end up like her from sickle cell, without somebody doing something wrong. I appreciate your not calling it to my attention, the holdout status of the case, that is. And yes, on this one I was practicing law. Thanks for saying nothing about that, too."

Surprised to hear Henry say the word *I* before the word *appreciate,* I flash him the Beecher file and a smile. "And I appreciate you giving me half the fee on this settled case."

As my cab cruises through the six-block stretch that constitutes Fourth Avenue, the forgotten way, before it turns into Park Avenue, the famous way, I think to myself maybe one day Henry will find it in himself to say "I'm sorry," and how I'm glad I didn't make an issue about the Williams holdout since it's a turndown anyway. The hardest thing for a lawyer to learn is to know when not to talk. The second thing I and my fellow attorneys are most guilty of is talking too much but saying too little.

The trouble is that it's a serious no-no in the state of New York to commence a medical malpractice case without first obtaining an affidavit of merit from a duly licensed physician. In my mind such a failure is just as bad as bringing a fraudulent claim altogether, and so now it's time to begin dealing with the dilemma Henry has thrust me into.

An attorney in New York must obtain court approval to withdraw as counsel once litigation has commenced. Getting court approval to withdraw from a noninfant case is a fifty-fifty proposition, the court's logic being that if there wasn't a legit case to begin with you shouldn't have brought suit. That means: live with your error and associated expenses until the jury throws you out. Infants, on the other hand, are technically wards of the court. Getting court approval to drop an infant's case, where the judge has an obligation to protect the child, is even more difficult. Once you proceed to factor in the tender age of Suzy Williams at the time of her injury and her brain damage, withdrawing as counsel gets harder still. Then add to the equation the fact that the attorney was supposed to obtain an affidavit of merit vouching that malpractice had been committed prior to starting the suit in the first place and you have a case that is nearly impossible to withdraw from as counsel. Thanks, Henry, and I'm not done yet. The problem continues.

In my application to be relieved as counsel, I'll be required to give the court an affidavit from a medical expert stating that the case lacks merit. This will raise the question of who the doctor was who opined the case had merit before the lawsuit was commenced and therein lies the conundrum; there was no affidavit of merit in this case in the first place.

The worst part is that you have to serve your papers requesting the court's permission to withdraw on the client. So when you go to court to plead your cause, you have to argue right in front of your client why you don't want to be his or her attorney any longer. If and when the judge denies your motion, you then have to continue being the client's attorney in a situation where the client no longer has any faith in you. Great.

Benson's put me in a fucked-up situation, being the attorney of record for Suzy Williams as I now am. I'll have to find a really creative legal or medical argument to get out of this one.

On the flip side, Suzy Williams is a brain-damaged child and obviously not an HIC. I won't have to worry about being threatened, stabbed, or otherwise assaulted and battered, at least by Suzy, although I'm sure I'll find out at some point along the way who the criminal is who's connected to the Williams family and therefore landed Little Suzy in the legal hands of my distinguished colleague, Henry Benson.

The cabbie interrupts my train of thought. "Where did you say you were going?"

"I didn't. I just said uptown," I reply, then pause.

"Would you like to give me an address?" the driver responds.

"Lenox Hill Hospital," I tell him. I have other problems, too. Only, I know how the next one will end.

You Look Good in That Suit

I enter Lenox Hill Hospital on East Seventy-Seventh and casually walk past the two guards toward the elevator bank. Over the years I've become an expert in legal matters, in medicine, and especially on liars and their lying habits. I've also become an expert on entering hospitals without being stopped by security or having to wait in line to get a visitor's pass. It's part of the craft of being a successful personal injury attorney.

I go up to the surgical ICU and wash my hands before entering, just like the sign instructs. "Where's my mommy?" I ask the nurse who's keeping a beady eye on my every move.

Her look is skeptical, a clear rebuff to my innocent attempt at humor. "Come this way," she orders. As we walk down the hall, she starts issuing the usual laundry list of the dos and don'ts, such as don't get too close to the hospital bed, don't disturb the patient, keep away from the medical equipment, etc. Maximum care means maximum regs. I cut the lecture short.

"I've been through the drill, nurse. Many times. I promise I know the rules."

She stops walking. Turning to me, she puts her hands on her hips and attacks. "I don't care what you think you know. You listen to me. It's my job, understand?"

I back off. "Yes, yes. Sorry." She shakes her head, then continues leading me to the room where my mother lies recovering from her incredibly serious cancer operation.

Before I enter, my sidekick reiterates an order in a firm tone. "Don't disturb her. She's in and out of consciousness at this point. She needs her rest."

"Okay," I say meekly. But the nurse, instead of dismissing herself, just stands there giving me an unfriendly look, which I really don't think I deserve. We have nothing left to say, and so I break the silence. "Anything else?"

"No, nothing. Just don't bother her."

"Thank you, nurse, I assure you I won't." She looks me over, hesitant about leaving me alone with my own mother.

Mom is lying propped up with tubes and monitors everywhere. Her eyes are closed and she looks peaceful. The oxygen mask covering her face reminds me of the scene from *Blue Velvet* where Dennis Hopper does the asphyxiation thing just before he's about to have sex. Jesus, even with my own mother clinging to life before my very eyes, I inexplicably make this association. I repulse myself sometimes.

At least I admit it.

I've played my role in this hospital scene many times during my mother's twenty-year battle. It started with breast cancer and now metastatic ovarian has been added to the cell-destroying mix. The thing is, she's never looked this lifeless. I quietly approach and inspect the mechanicals. There's an IV drip line connected to a Flowmaster fluid monitor and a bundle of plastic-coated cardiac monitor lead wires emerging from beneath her sheets. The wires run into a single plastic housing that is connected to some cable. For whatever reason, this connection has some separation and I feel compelled to push the two pieces together to close the quarter-inch gap. I reach over, grabbing it, and just as I do, my new best friend enters the room.

"What are you doing back there? Trying to kill her?" Nurse Hostile screams. "Call security! Someone call security!"

"Relax, relax," I say. "I thought the monitor cable looked a little loose. Everything's under control. I was just—"

"Out of the room! Now!"

Ten minutes later, after my mother's been evaluated by a doctor, for no good reason, her watchdog comes out.

"You can go back in now, but it's against my better judgment," she scolds. "Keep quiet. I mean it! She's one day post-op and needs her rest. And don't touch anything again. Got it?"

"Got it, nurse. Sorry about before." I go in and sit on the far side of the room nowhere near Mom. There are two visitor chairs, for some reason, and I'm sitting in the one directly across from the foot of her bed. Mom's still resting peacefully in a state of unconsciousness. Or so I hope.

After fifteen minutes of sitting, watching, and waiting for her to open her eyes, I decide to check out one of the Suzy Williams files, simply from curiosity. I pull out the defendant's motion to dismiss, with Henry's expert review memo clipped to it, just like he said. I take the memo off and put it under the motion, which I intend to read first.

The attorneys defending both the Brooklyn Catholic Hospital and Dr. Richard Wise are my old friends Goldman & Goldberg. I used to have a lot of cases with them as defense counsel, but we haven't had any contact now for a while. I call them my friends because after I beat both of them—Goldman *and* Goldberg, in different cases, each by jury verdict—they started sending me the plaintiffs' cases they couldn't handle because of interest conflicts with the medical insurance carriers paying their bills. In the field of medical malpractice litigation you can't wear both hats. You either sue doctors or defend them, period. Reason being, the carriers don't want to pay attorneys to defend their insureds if they're just going to turn around and sue one of them.

I chose to represent the victims of medical malpractice because my mother never should've ended up this way. There was a two-year delay in diagnosing her breast cancer, taking her from completely curable to years of otherwise unnecessary pain, suffering, and insidious yet life-prolonging medical treatments and operations. A wretched battle that didn't need to be fought and that will soon be lost.

In any event, the papers indicate that the firm's name is now Goldman, Goldberg & McGillicuddy. Where have I heard that name before? I check out the attorney's affirmation in support of the motion to dismiss and see it's been written by one Winnie McGillicuddy. I don't know her, but wonder if she's as cute as her name sounds. My mind wanders and I recall McGillicuddy is the maiden name of Lucy Ricardo from the *I Love Lucy* show.

I see the motion is returnable next Friday, one week from today. Thanks again, Henry, for waiting until the last possible moment to put me in a bind. It's crunch time, considering I'm currently in the middle of a trial. I also note the judge assigned to the Williams case is Leslie Schneider, who's way too stingy about giving adjournments. Be ready or be dismissed. The worst part about appearing before Judge Schneider is her voice. I think I even settled a case a few bucks short just so I wouldn't have to spend a week in her courtroom listening to that nerve-pinching whine.

I skip reading what Winnie McGillicuddy has to say, pass over the voluminous medicals, and go right to the medical expert affidavit in support of the motion to dismiss. I figure it's attached as exhibit A— and I'm right. I don't recognize this expert's name, but the fact that defense counsel included the expert's name in the first place gives the motion credibility. That's because in New York lawyers are permitted to withhold the identity of an expert in a medical malpractice case.

In sum and substance, defendant's expert says that Suzy was admitted suffering from the onset of a sickle cell crisis and acutely took a turn for the worse, suffering a cardiopulmonary arrest with a concurrent sickle cell stroke, both being known complications of her disease. The conclusion is that the management of her condition was appropriate, that sickle cell strokes cannot be foreseen, are unpreventable, and cannot be associated with medical malpractice. Suzy's stroke is responsible for her brain-damaged condition and the concurrent cardiopulmonary arrest also contributed thereto. The end. Very clear and logical. If this is accurate, then Henry was a real ass for bringing suit—and I'm going to look like a bigger one trying to get us out of it.

I find our expert's typewritten memo. It says, basically, the same thing. I read the handwritten notes accompanying it, looking for some morsel of merit, but it just confirms the memo. Nonetheless, before I seek to get out of a case with a multimillion-dollar injury, I feel it's in my best interest, and the best interests of my clients, whom I don't even know, to pay a visit to this expert I've inherited. That would be one Dr. Laura Smith, and I never heard of her before, either.

I look up from the papers and see Mom's still out. Her vitals are stable, according to the monitoring devices, so why not just make the call now? I dial Dr. Smith's number and a man picks up on the first ring. "Smith Sickle Cell Pediatric Care Center, Steven Smith, director, speaking. How may I help you?"

"Hello. This is the attorney for the plaintiff on the Suzy Williams matter. I'd like to set up an appointment to see Dr. Smith, please."

"My wife, I mean Dr. Smith, has a very busy schedule," Steven Smith replies. "Could we do it next month?"

"How's Monday look for you?"

He snorts. "Is it really that important?"

"Yes, it is."

"Then come Monday anytime you want," he says, "because no time is good. But I must advise you I'll have to charge a flat fee of five hundred dollars for the expedited appointment. Then there's the standard fee of seven hundred fifty dollars per hour of time. Plus, I'll also have to charge you for time lost from Dr. Smith's normal patient schedule, so that's another five hundred. Therefore, if you choose to show up on Monday, you won't be seeing Dr. Smith unless you hand me a check for one thousand seven hundred and fifty dollars for the first hour of her time. And if I'm not mistaken, didn't she already review and reject that case?"

"That is correct," I reply. "See you Monday." *Click.*

"Greedy fuck," I say aloud just as my mother opens her eyes. Oops. She looks at me and, for certain, knows who I am. She slowly raises her right arm, giving me the international beckoning signal. I get up from my chair and approach with extreme caution. I move to the head of her bed and she points to her oxygen mask.

"Do you want to say something, Mom?" She nods and points to the mask again. "Do you want me to take that off?" She slowly nods again, so I gently lift it away from her face. She beckons again and so I move in closer, but not too close out of fear for my nursing nemesis.

"You look good in that suit," she says softly.

"Thanks, Mom, I appreciate that." She squints at my lapel.

"Is that a mustard stain?"

"Yeah, Mom, it is."

"Doesn't *she* send your clothing to the dry cleaner?"

"Mom, if by 'she' you mean my wife, then yes, Tyler does." Mom cringes and it's not because of pain. She gathers strength. Here we go.

"Tug, my son, every time you say her name I have less and less respect for that woman. How does a girl named Tyler allow herself to marry a man named Wyler? It's ridiculous, Tyler Wyler. And together you two sound even more cartoonish, Tug and Tyler Wyler. Such stupidity. She knew you were going to be a success and that's why she married you to live with such a name." She motions for her mask to be put back on. Two deep breaths. I ignore her comments and attempt to change the subject from my wife and marriage.

"So, Mom, how do you feel?" Mask off.

"Like I got hit by a wrecking ball from a crane gone wild, died, donated my organs, only to wake up from the dead to see my son's wife isn't taking care of him properly. A lawyer's suit is part of his stock-in-trade. It shouldn't have a stain on it, mustard, no less."

Mask on. She takes three big inhales and wants it off again, so I comply. She continues. "But we both know my organs are not acceptable for donation and that wife of yours is too busy with her tennis and spending your hard-earned money to slip your clothing into a dry-cleaning bag and place it outside under the portico of that beautiful home you built for her so your cleaner can pick it up. Other than that, I feel *fine*." Mask on again. That last rant took the steam out of her, but I can't leave it alone.

"Mom, I love Tyler. All marriages have stuff." Mask off.

"Never close the door to other women. You must always talk to other women—you promised, a son's promise to his mother." Mask on.

"I do, don't worry, I talk to them. But I'm good with Tyler." Mask off.

"Dump her."

She points to the guest chair motioning for me to sit down. She's exhausted from her part of our exchange. She takes three large in-hales, then her lids close shut.

I spend the next hour sitting there. She opens and closes her eyes every so often as our pal the nurse periodically checks on us. Then, with her signaling again to remove the oxygen mask, I stand up and comply, positioning my ear so I can hear within a whisper's reach. At that moment the nurse appears at the doorway and stomps in. "What are you doing?" she barks. "Why is her mask off? Why are you so close to her?"

"My mom wants to tell me something," I plead.

"Make it quick. I'm watching you."

I turn back to the bed. "What, Mom? What is it?"

My mother, even with great effort, can manage nothing more than a whisper.

"Did you dump her yet?"

Two days have passed since I visited Mom, and I keep seeing that oxygen mask of hers in my mind's eye. Still, if she hadn't asked me to dump my wife, I know I'd be worrying about her more.

The weekend distracted me. I had a romantic encounter with Tyler Friday night, having told her I settled a big case instead of revealing I was in front of the Disciplinary Committee. I spent the day Saturday admitting defeat in every tiff I intentionally started with her as an approach to foreplay, since I can't resolve cases over the weekend. But the highlight was playing basketball in the driveway with my three kids all day both days. Now it's Monday and back to business.

With my truck in the shop, I'm taking my weekend car to see the expert, Dr. Laura Smith. It's a 1976 Cadillac Eldorado convertible, wide whites and all. But I'm not too happy about driving it from the burbs of upper Westchester to Brooklyn because it could also use some time in the shop.

"Tyler," I call out before leaving, "remember you have to keep an eye on Otis to make sure he doesn't get that funnel thing off his neck and rip his stitches out." Otis is my eighty-five-pound Labradoodle. He looks like a doggy reggae star with his dreadlocks. Yesterday he cut his paw pad chasing a squirrel through a thorny rosebush and had to have it stitched up.

"I'm not watching Otis," she yells back from somewhere upstairs,

"I have my tennis team practice this morning, which I guess I could take him to, but then I have to go to the mall in the afternoon. So I can't do it."

"But the vet said to keep an eye on him," I yell, "and I've got to meet a doctor on a potentially *large* case out in Brooklyn," I say, lying, to initiate the foreplay process at the start of the week. "Can't you skip the mall?"

"Nope," Tyler screams. "He's your dog. You watch him."

So I have a choice to make. Take her on or else take the customary path of least resistance. I choose a middle-of-the-road approach, hoping to appeal to her slim sense of reason. "Do you really *have* to go to the mall today?" I ask. "Would it be *possible* for you to go tomorrow when the housekeeper's here so she could keep tabs on Otis?"

"No can do. Got to go to the mall today."

"You *got* to? Are you firm on that one hundred percent?" I call out, getting tired of all the yelling and ready to surrender.

"Look," Tyler yells, "I'm getting waxed today. Rita's only working one day this week and today is it. The week after, I'll be bleeding like a wounded lamb and I don't feel comfortable getting waxed when I'm on my period. And for certain I'm not waiting three weeks to get this done 'cause the grass on the infield is growing."

"Couldn't you find a different groundskeeper?"

"Not an option. Rita's actually from Brazil. Do you know how hard it is to find a hair-removal therapist to give you a Brazilian who's actually *from* Brazil?"

Hair-removal therapist? "Okay," I yell, "I'll take Otis." Otis tilts his head and lifts his ears upon hearing his name. "Come on, Otis, my man. You're going to see what it's like to be a lawyer."

We enter the garage and he jumps in the front of the Eldo. "In the back, Otis," I command, four times. He just stares at me with those expressive eyes of his and that goofy big white funnel around his neck. "Okay, okay, Otis, shotgun it is."

I pump the gas pedal four times, then turn the key. The engine ignites and the massive five-hundred-cubic-inch purrs to a hum.

An instant later, vintage music begins blasting from the aftermarket sound system I had installed back when I thought loud music was cool. Blaring out over and over again is the verse "roller coaster of love (Say what)" from the Ohio Players song.

I finally head down the driveway after accepting my CD player is stuck and explaining to Otis we're going topless because the convertible motor is broken. Before reaching my entry gate I realize I left my lawyer bag in the house. I back up to the garage, where my wife's in the process of pulling out. There's not enough room for her to pass so I block her in and get out of the Eldo, leaving it running.

"Move that piece of shit!" Tyler screams. "I've got an early tennis practice!"

"One moment, honey. I forgot something."

"Hurry up!" La Comandante orders as I enter the house.

Before walking back out, I open up the only drawer in my seven-thousand-square-foot home I can call my own and take out one of the cigars stored in a ziplock plastic bag with indelible marker writing that reads: HUMIDOR. I sniff it, cut the butt, stick it in my mouth, then go back out while stuffing the ziplock in the side of my bag.

"Hurry up already!" Tyler growls as I stroll past.

I continue at a pace that will annoy the hell out of her.

"Turn that music down!" she yells as I reach the Eldo. "I can hear it all the way over here. What are you trying to be? Some kind of gangsta?" she screams in a spine-piercing pitch. It has the equivalent effect of what one must feel during a lumbar puncture that accidentally lances a nerve root.

I get in and take a few moments to light my cigar. "Move already!" Tyler calls out her window, honking her horn. I give her the international sign for "I can't hear you" by pointing to my ears, at the same time exhaling a big puff from my mild and smooth Avo. Yeah, I'm being an ass, but so what? I just realized, after all these years, it's part of the marital contract and I'm way behind on the deal.

I grab the shift and happen to look up before changing gears. I see the Eldo reflecting off the glossy finish of her fancy Benz. Her side panel is acting like a mirror, and it's one of those rare times where one's given the chance to take a momentary and unintended visual inventory.

I can clearly see the reflection of my license plate, which reads: SILVRADO. I see that massive Eldorado chrome bumper and distinctive front grille. I see the signature crest-and-wreath hood ornament and the superlong silver-colored hood with its custom black double pinstriping. Behind the windshield and steering wheel I see some balding asshole smoking a big stogie next to a funky black dog in need of a haircut with a large white funnel around its neck, evidencing a recent visit to an overpriced vet.

Some guys look cool smoking cigars and some guys look like they're trying to look cool. I'm the latter.

At least I admit it.

Think Humpty Dumpty

As I drive across the Brooklyn Bridge I accept "roller coaster of love" will forever be etched in my mind. It was catchy when I turned out of my driveway, but after two thousand verse repeats . . .

I come straight off the bridge onto Adams Street, taking the long way to my destination because I insist on passing Brooklyn Law School, my alma mater. A half mile later, I'm the first car stopped at the red light at the corner of Joralemon Street with the Supreme Court to my right and BLS in front of me. I'm next to the curb and on the sidewalk are three attractive law students carrying those red law books. The girl with the curves heads over so I put the passenger window down, thinking how early spring is my favorite time of year to admire women as they transition their clothing.

"Oh my God," she says, staring at Otis, "that dog is so cute. Can I pet him?"

"Sure." She reaches in, slightly bending, and scratches under his chin. Her tank top floats down and open, so now the ancient question arises. When a girl wears an inviting shirt that showcases her gifts, early in the season while a nip is still in the air, put on no doubt to attract the attention of her male counterparts—pork bait—am I supposed to look?

"What happened to him?" she asks, focused on Otis.

"Cut his paw, stitches," I answer, noting a pile of résumés jutting out from under the cover of her law book. "What year are you in?"

"Second," she says, without looking over.

"I went to BLS," I offer, trying to connect.

"Really? What kind of law do you practice?" She still hasn't looked away from my dog, scratching him intensely, arm back and forth causing things to jiggle, wiggle, joggle.

Before I get a chance to answer, some guy on the sidewalk yells out, "Cool car," giving me the thumbs-up. I say, "Thanks," then turn back to my intern candidate.

"Personal injury and medical malpractice, specializing in HIC cases."

"That's interesting," she answers, now working his neck.

"And I happen to be interviewing law students for a summer position." I thought that would induce her, but no dice. Given her reluctance to look at me, I feel it's safe to sneak a peek from the perfect angle she has provided. I almost feel like it's my duty as a man to check out the goods, so I do. Ah yes, they are lovely. I look up after a quick glance and finally we are eye to eye. She smiles. I smile back. She has beautiful, expressive green eyes and I can tell she's about to express herself.

"Asshole!"

"No, I just glanced for a—"

"You were peeping the whole time!"

"No, not the whole time, just—"

"Uh!" She storms away, back to her friends.

Well, that answers that ancient question. You'd think, being a law student, she would've asked me what an HIC case was, anyway. The follow-up questions are the most important ones. I can't have someone like that working for me.

The rest of my journey, left on Atlantic Avenue, onto Flatbush, then taking side streets to my destination near Prospect Park, went without a hitch. Tallying the number of thumbs-ups the Eldo gets has become sort of a counting game for the kids and me. Eleven is the total for this trip, a big number, all since coming off the bridge. Brooklynites possess a certain spirit of understanding for this old relic, something most of my neighbors up in Westchester just don't get.

I noted that the defendant, Brooklyn Catholic Hospital, the institution sued in Suzy's case, is just three blocks away from my expert's medical building. I find this fact curious.

I park in the lot underneath the medical building and take out from my bag the black marker I'd grabbed from my drawer with the cigars. "Hold still, Otis!" I plead as I write on the funnel in capital block letters, SEEING-EYE DOG IN TRAINING. I walk up to street level, and in the front door of the Smith Pavilion, with Otis on a short leash, instructor-style. Three steps in I see a security-type guy twenty feet away and closing in.

"Sit," I direct, and Otis complies. "Good boy," I say, pretending to give him a treat, creating the illusion of positive reinforcement.

I look up and see the guy is ten feet away.

"Come!" I order, and walk away from him. "Heel!" I command in a loud voice in an effort to further perpetuate my charade.

"Hold on there!" demands the guard.

"Otis, sit! Good boy," I say as Otis complies. "Yes, sir?"

"You can't bring that dog in here," he states smugly, apparently convinced of his authority.

"Sure I can. It's part of his training."

"I can read what you wrote on that plastic thing, but you're not fooling me. Besides, you left out the DO NOT PET part. I'll need to see an official document," he continues, "if you want me to believe you."

"I'd like to show it to you," I say in a playful voice, "but unfortunately, my dog ate it, which is going to cost him four more weeks of training."

"You're not getting in." He's turning testy.

"Officer," I say, knowing he'll like my use of a title, "I could give you another bullshit excuse as to why I've got my dog with me here today, but the truth is my wife needs to get her bush waxed this afternoon so I had to take him to make sure he doesn't bite out his stitches."

He smiles. "Why didn't you say so in the first place? Go right in. This is a minimum-wage gig anyway. They're real stingy with the dollar around here."

"Thank you, officer," I say, slipping him a twenty. To which he responds, "Nice dog you got there."

I take the elevator to the fourth floor. I walk down the hall to a set of metal doors that read SMITH PEDIATRIC HEMATOLOGY. On the other side is the reception area. I enter and approach. There to greet me, sitting in what looks like a specially built chair to elevate short people, is an unusual-looking man.

The word *achondroplasia* pops into my head. That's the medical term for a common form of dwarfism in which the trunk is of average stature while the limbs are disproportionately short. However, this guy's definitely not a dwarf. What he is is too tall to be one, and yet too short for a normal person, so caught somewhere between these two worlds. There's only a hint of extremity disproportion, with his most distinctive feature his egg-shaped body. Think Humpty Dumpty.

His face is covered by a well-trimmed, prematurely gray beard and mustache. He wears those round Harry Potter glasses, only his are metal. With his bow tie and vest, he presents older than he is, but there's no way, in fact, that he's more than thirty-five.

He looks like he's expecting me. But not Otis. His name tag reads: STEVEN SMITH, DIRECTOR.

"Good morning, Mr. Smith, I'm—"

"You're the attorney," he cuts in. He extends his hand for what I assume is going to be a handshake. "Check, please."

"Yes, of course," I say, handing it to him.

He inspects it. "Would you mind dotting the *i* and crossing the *t* better?"

"My bad. I flunked penmanship in third grade and never made it up." He looks at me impatiently. I oblige without further comment. He inspects the check again, folds it in half, and places it in his shirt pocket just underneath the vest. "How did you get in here with that dog?"

"The guard was throwing out some loud, unruly drifter when I entered and didn't see me. He really takes his job seriously."

Smith throws me a suspicious look. "You're early. Be mindful of your dog and take a seat in the waiting area." I do exactly that.

There are ten or so young children there, presumably with sickle cell disease. They run over and begin petting Otis before I can even sit down. A few of the parents belatedly yell, "Ask if you can pet the dog first!" as I signal it's okay.

"Kids, this is Otis," I explain. "He loves little children." The remark provokes grins. "He loves them so much he ate a little boy for breakfast this morning."

Two kids jump back. "No way! You're lying!"

"Yes, I am," I admit. "You guys can pet him all you want. I'm going over there to make a phone call. Stay, Otis!" I command. Otis gives a "what are you doing to me?" look. He's unhappy with his babysitting detail.

I walk over to a row of windows, knowing it's the only place I may get reception on the floor, to check in with Lily, my trusty paralegal, clerk, secretary, calendar person, and personal assistant. She's been with me for ten years, ever since she was nineteen. She gets more beautiful every day, which is great. But she's also a little abusive from time to time. Correction: most of the time, these days. Which isn't so great. Like trick candy laced with cayenne.

Lily answers. "Law Office. Please hold," she says. I hate that. I've instructed her numerous times to find out if the caller is a new case prior to putting him on hold. If it's a new case, then everything *else* has to hold—not the call. Would *you* hire a lawyer if you were put on hold at the instant of first contact? It's even worse when the caller's in serious pain and it's taken a big effort to get to the phone to make the call in the first place. Christ, I've got to wait for some stupid doctor to malpractice somebody or for an inattentive driver to run somebody down to generate new business. I don't want to risk losing a case over a rude greeting. "Please hold," my ass. Full-service sympathy's the name of the game. I hate having to correct Lily because she doesn't take criticism well, but business is business. I'll have to go back over with her what proper phone etiquette is composed of. She now comes on the line again.

"Can I help you?"

"Yeah, it's me. I thought we discussed—"

"Hold, please."

Two minutes later, she's there again.

"What do you want?" she asks.

"First of all, how about a little respect for the boss?"

"Don't be so sensitive. What do you want? I'm busy."

"I'm not the sensitive one. Anyway, when you answer—"

"Hold."

In one minute she picks back up.

"Okay. What do you want?"

"When a call comes in," I begin, "and before you put the caller on hold—"

"Hold again. Be right back."

Thirty-seven seconds later, she returns.

"I'm back. What's up?"

"Please stop putting me on hold."

"Well, the phone keeps ringing and you always tell me to find out if it's a new case before putting the caller on hold. What do you want from me? Do you want me to baby you or do you want me to pick up the phone and see if it's a giant new case? Okay? If the answer's pick up the phone, then what's this 'before you put the caller on hold' stuff?"

"Never mind. Were those other calls new cases?"

"No. It was my babysitter calling me for my arroz con pollo recipe. She's making dinner for the first time tonight. I told her she has to learn how to cook Latino or to find another job. I hate being a single parent sometimes. Now, what do you want before she calls back?"

"Call up Bert Beecher and confirm my appointment with him for one o'clock today."

"Is that the HIC who's trying to shake his wife down for half her settlement you sent me the email on?"

"Yeah. That's the guy."

"Scumbag. I want to know what criminal offense he committed before I talk to him. I hate Benson and I hate his injured criminals."

"Kindly direct your hatred elsewhere. We're going to make a lot of money off his HICs. We already have."

"I'm sorry, there must be something wrong with the connection. I thought you used the word *we* when referring to money being made. I haven't made anything. You have."

"I gave you a bonus, as I recall, on a few of the big ones, didn't I?"

"Big whoop. I deserved every penny for having to deal with all of those . . . *criminales.*"

"Don't start going native on me now. I know what that means. Just relax. Call Beecher up and make sure he comes in at one."

"Not until you tell me what he did."

"I recall Henry telling me that Bert Beecher was a violent guy. He was convicted for attempted murder, so don't get into it with him. Just confirm the appointment I made over the weekend. Then call June Williams and confirm my three o'clock with her. Tell her to bring in Suzy. I want to meet that poor little girl before I throw her under the bus. We most likely will be rejecting her case, but don't tell June. I'll have to finesse it. Speak to you later."

"Before you hang up, I'm letting you know that I'm buying some air fresheners for this place, the expensive kind that you have to plug in, which you'll have to reimburse me for. It's finally beginning to reek in here. Now, what kind of criminal is June Williams?"

"I don't know. Henry's verbal didn't say." *Click.* That was her click, not mine.

I go back to where the kids are petting Otis and find him lying on his back with his paws up in the air. His new best friends are mauling him with love. "Look what I taught him," one boy says. He starts scratching the dog's belly, causing Otis's right hind leg to twitch. "That's a great trick," I say. "Thanks for teaching him."

The C Word

A moment later, Smith walks over. "The doctor will see you now. Follow me." Otis and I trail after him down the hall. In the office he ushers us into, the first thing I notice is a barren wall embedded with empty picture hooks. It's an eyesore, especially for a guy whose mother is an art dealer, and who's been taught never to leave an empty hook on the wall. The next thing I notice is Dr. Laura Smith, standing just a few feet away.

She's tall, skinny, and very ordinary-looking. Her hair's up in a bun, which doesn't seem to be such a good idea as it somehow accentuates her long, thin nose. Frankly, she's nearly a dead ringer for Popeye's beloved Olive Oyl, but in hospital whites.

"Come in, come in," she greets Otis and me in a hesitant tone. "I'm Dr. Smith. The kids call me Dr. Laura, so you can, too." She speaks in what I'd describe as modified baby talk. I guess being around kids all day may have influenced her, but it's no less annoying for it. "That's an unusual-looking dog you've got there. What kind is it?"

"His father was an apricot poodle and his mother was a yellow Labrador retriever."

"Yellow Lab, you say?"

"Yes, yellow Lab." The information strikes her for some reason.

"But he's black except for his red beard."

"You never can predict what Mother Nature's going to do genetically."

"That's not entirely true. The case you happen to be here on is a prime example. Sickle cell disease is inherited from parents in much the same way as eye color."

"I stand corrected, Doctor," I reply in the spirit of a courtroom litigator, and we share a smile.

"Let's have a seat, shall we?" Dr. Laura says. I take my customary position on the opposite side of my expert's desk. She turns toward the door. "Steven, if it's okay with you, you can go now. I can handle this."

I turn my head toward the entry and conclude Smith has stationed himself just outside the door. I would've never realized this if his wife hadn't addressed him. He takes a step in. "Why don't I stay and listen?"

"You're the director," Dr. Laura tells him. "If you want to stay, then stay. It's your prerogative."

He looks over at me and then down at Otis. "No, I've got some billing to do. That's all right."

Dr. Laura begins to respond, but what she's saying to her husband is going right by me. I'm distracted by what I see on the floor underneath the picture hooks.

Leaning face against the wall are what I assume to be her medical diplomas, which obviously were taken down for some reason. This reminds me that I'll have to get a copy of her résumé, something doctors seem to prefer calling their curriculum vitae. Her CV will contain a detailed description of her medical education, training, and background. I'll need to attach it to my papers as an exhibit to be relieved as Suzy's lawyer if I can't salvage things here.

"I'll be up front," I hear Smith announce.

Dr. Laura turns to me. "How can I help you? I thought I was pretty clear to Mr. Benson concerning my feelings about this case."

"The reason I insisted on seeing you is because before I tell this family they have no case, I want to be sure you're sure there is no case."

"I see, but I can assure you there is no case."

"For whatever reason, this lawsuit has been pending for nearly six years. That means for six years the Williams family has been of the belief that there is, in fact, a case—that malpractice caused this little girl's injuries."

"Why has the case been going on for so long?" she asks.

"I can't answer that right now. All I can tell you is I only got involved recently and I'm certain shit's going to hit the fan when I tell the mother there's no case." I notice Dr. Laura grimace when I say "shit," and so I look repentant. "What I've learned in this business is that mothers of injured kids are more concerned with righting a wrong than with the financial aspects, although both are important.

Subconsciously, they want vindication that what happened to their child was not their fault, and that can only occur if fault is established as someone else's. Acts of God are generally not good enough because mothers still feel responsible for the genetic basis for the injury. Mrs. Williams is going to want to hear what she's been led to believe with the institution of this lawsuit, which is that something else is at fault for Suzy's condition besides her own DNA. Why don't you tell me in the strongest of ways why there's no case, so I can overcome the mother's expected resistance."

She gives me a firm and understanding nod, the way one does when they know exactly what they're going to say. "In simple terms, this unfortunate little girl was admitted to the hospital in an early stage of acute chest syndrome. Her red blood cells began forming clumps in her lungs and one of these clots broke off, making its way into the vessels of her brain. Once the tiny vessel in her head became blocked, that area of her brain was deprived of oxygenated blood and she stroked out. Her acute chest syndrome also took its natural progression, preventing her sickle cell clot–filled lungs from getting air— and so they stopped functioning. Once her lungs stopped functioning, the rest of the organs in her body couldn't get oxygen, either, inclusive of her heart, and that suffered arrest, too. It was a terrible tragedy, but not the fault of any doctor."

"She had been in the hospital for three days. Couldn't anything have been done to prevent this?"

"Things were done. In this situation, you give supportive care and hope the crisis will pass, as most do in patients her age. The morning of the event, her condition took a turn for the worse and a Dr. Valenti ordered the appropriate care. There's some issue having to do with why oxygen wasn't ordered earlier, but it would've made no difference. She also had a positive blood culture on admission showing she was suffering from septicemia, which I'm sure you know is a blood infection. I guess she could have been placed on IV antibiotics instead of oral, but that's a judgment call, not malpractice. Nothing could have prevented this unfortunate complication. Suzy had an acute attack that was unpreventable. Yes, a terrible complication."

Now, whenever I hear the word *complication* spoken by a physician in a medical-legal setting, what I see right away in my mind's eye is Pinocchio's nose. In other words, the doctor's fibbing. The term *complication* points a way out of his malpractice. The C word usually makes its appearance at doctors' depositions under oath. Some of my favorites are: "Yes, I amputated the wrong foot. It was mismarked preoperatively. It's a rare but known complication of the procedure." Or "Yes, several lap pads were left inside your twenty-two-year-old client after her cesarean section. It's true that she'll never be able to get pregnant again because we had to remove her uterus, but as you know, these things are a risk and complication of the procedure." And when the defendant doctor uses the word *risk* in conjunction with the word *complication,* it usually means the fuckup was of major proportions.

Here, however, Dr. Laura is *my* expert. She's on *my* side—the side of truth and justice. The side of the injured malpractice victim, not the doctor or hospital that was sued. I rarely hear my expert use the C word because my cases are peppered with merit. Peppered, I tell you. That is, they were before I became an HIC attorney.

"Dr. Laura," I ask, "are you saying that Suzy suffered from four different complications from her sickle cell condition?"

"The cardio and pulmonary arrests do have a relation to one another," she avers, "but the septicemia and stroke are mutually exclusive. Technically, you could say there were four separate complications."

"Is this a common occurrence?"

"The answer would have to be no, especially in a child this age."

"Thank you for your time, doctor. I know now what I need to say to the mother to have her understand the situation. I'll be preparing an affidavit for you to sign that memorializes your opinions, and will be part of my motion to the court to be relieved as counsel. I'll need a copy of your CV so I can incorporate your qualifications into the affidavit."

"Certainly. I'm sorry things couldn't turn out better for you and that unfortunate little girl."

"Thanks for your time, but I have to tell you the pricing was completely unreasonable." I get up, as does Otis.

"You'll have to speak to Steven about that. He's the director and in charge of all matters financial in nature. I don't even know what he charged you for these fifteen minutes we've spent together."

"Would it surprise you if I told you close to eighteen hundred dollars?"

"I guess no, it wouldn't surprise me," she admits. "I agree it's unreasonable, but unfortunately, I have no control over the situation." I don't like their clinic's, or her husband's, billing practices, but I do like her, maybe because I was addicted to Popeye growing up. "If you need anything else or if something new comes about that you believe may change my opinion, call me," she offers. "But based on what we have here, I see no case."

We shake hands good-bye. "Is that the steps of Borough Hall?" I ask, pointing to a photo of her and Steven showcased on her desk.

"Why, yes. Yes it is. That was our wedding day."

"It's a great photo of you two," I say, mustering up every ounce of sincerity within my body.

"We eloped. That's why we're not wearing wedding attire."

"Very romantic." As I walk out of the door I belly-bump right into Steven Smith, knocking my large frame firmly into him. He begins to pitch backward with his feet stuck underneath.

"Oh, I'm so sorry," I say.

He sighs, looking aggrieved. I'm afraid he's going to charge me a penalty.

"Were you standing out here the whole time?" I ask him.

"Of course not!" he snaps.

"Are you sure?"

"Of course I'm sure," he responds, defensively. "What are you suggesting?"

"Me? I'm not suggesting anything, but the fact that your feet were planted squarely when we made contact was suggestive, that's why I asked."

pump and turn, sparking the Eldo to purr and the music to blast. I don't know how or why, but a different song is playing.

I leave the lot, smoking another cigar to the blasting and repeated tune of "Play That Funky Music" by Wild Cherry. After driving a few miles, I find myself the first car at a red light on Clarkson Avenue, right in front of Kings County Hospital. Crossing the street before me is a black youth in a full leg cast, hip to toe. He's got a mile-high Afro, seventies-style. I can tell his injury is fresh from the bright white color of his cast and the awkward way he's negotiating his crutches. My bet is he was just discharged.

Interesting.

Mile High is with two friends. Both have dreads like Otis, neither with funnel. They're making fun of their injured friend as he struggles with the sticks. The three stop near the front of the Eldo. "Yo, cool ride," Mile High yells to me.

"Thanks. Who fucked you up?" I point to his leg.

Mile High hobbles over to the driver's side as I put down my window. "Yo, check out the Rasta dog," he calls to his friends.

"What happened?" I ask.

"Got taken out by a limo up in Harlem in front of the Apollo the other night."

"Who's your lawyer?"

"Got five cards in my pocket. One of them."

"Get in the car. I'm your lawyer. I'll take you to my office."

"You Jewish?" he asks.

I respond to his question with a question, like any normal Jewish lawyer would. "What do you think?"

He smiles. "Cool."

By this time the light has changed to green and the traffic behind is honking as Mile High hobbles around the front of my car to get in on the passenger side. "In the back, Otis," I command. This time he obeys, knowing we're going to have company.

"Yo, I'm coming," one of his buddies says as he opens the passenger door. "Me, too," chimes in the second. They both get in the back, forcing Otis behind me. Otis doesn't like the seating arrangement so he jumps over the guy next to him and takes the center seat. Mile High gets in the front and shuts the door. Otis jumps back into the front between us, startling Mile High.

I make the introduction. "This is Otis. He's friendly and been a victim of black dog discrimination his whole life." The boys laugh.

"What's up, my man Otis?" Mile High says. It's amazing how many people say that when they meet him.

I start driving to my office on Park Avenue South at Twenty-Ninth Street with my new crew loudly singing, "Play that funky music, white boy . . ." They're attempting to draw public attention and succeed. I weave the Eldo in and out of traffic, as best the Eldo can weave, attempting to make all the greens. I'm trying to avoid the spectacle of waiting at a red light with my attention-hungry passengers. Luckily, no other car in the world can cause traffic to divide like the Eldo and I make it all the way into Manhattan without stopping.

Just before we enter the garage, my crew is putting the finishing touches on their new gangsta-style sample of "White Boy."

I enter the underground garage and resourcefully pull up to the sign that says PULL TO HERE. "Play that funky music, white boy" is echoing throughout the garage, yet is actually outdone by the screams of my trio. They've completely transformed this classic into a catchy sample, beat box and all.

Oscar, my garage guy, appears entertained by my entourage. He opens my door and Otis vaults over my lap and out, causing Oscar to jump back. Otis shakes his funnel head and sneezes. "Hey there, easy, boy," Oscar says, his hands making a "no closer" gesture. "I don't like big black dogs," he remarks.

I look over to my crew. "There you go," I say. "Black dog discrimination." I turn back to my garage guy. "Oscar, meet Otis. He's a licker not a biter."

Oscar gives Otis a cautious pet. "What's up, my man Otis?"

The boys and I walk out of the garage and begin our slow journey to my office, two blocks away. Going up the ramp, I realize it was insensitive of me not to drop Mile High off in front of my building, but truth be told, I didn't want him out of my watchful eye and risk losing the case after getting him this far. At least I admit it.

As we approach my building, there's an old lady with three dogs coming from the other direction. Otis sees them and gives a slight tug. "Okay, Otis," I tell him. "You can meet some city dogs if you want. But I got to warn you, they're much more advanced and sophisticated than your typical canine from the boonies."

As we hit the entrance to my building, I turn and say, "Yo, go up to the seventh floor and wait in my reception area. My dog needs to take care of some business." I realize at this moment I didn't even ask that kid or his companions their names. All I saw was a bright white cast, dollar signs, and a mile-high 'fro. More insensitivity. They enter and I continue past, with Otis tugging forward.

The old woman has two bulldogs and a boxer, all with stubby tails wagging in excitement. Our dogs make contact in front of Deli-De-Lite, and it's an ass-sniffing bonanza. Their owner's a cross between a bag lady and a Rockefeller. Disheveled with ratty old clothing and poor oral hygiene, she nonetheless sports diamond earrings, a big diamond ring, and chunky diamond bracelets.

I recognize all of the pieces as contemporary Tiffany, having seen them in the catalog my wife likes to leave in our bathroom magazine rack. Every time she dog-ears a page for something she intends to buy,

I rip it out ultracarefully so its absence can't be detected. I check out the way-too-expensive price of whatever item she's taken a fancy to, then fold the page and wipe my ass with it. I accept the discomfort inflicted by the sharp paper edge as preferable to the ache induced by the diminishment of my bank account, finding extra joy in the flush.

I smile at Mrs. Bagafeller as our animals get acquainted. She smiles back. I can tell she's real hip. We watch them sniff away. "Nothing like the smell of fresh doggy ass," I observe.

She widens her smile. "So true, young man. So true. Wouldn't life be easier if it was socially acceptable to approach a nice young woman you found attractive and go right to the sniff without all the discomfort involved in initiating conversation?"

I widen my smile, too. "That's the way it should be. It would take the awkwardness right out of the equation."

"Yes," she replies. "Talking only gets in the way. If things don't smell right, why waste time?"

"I can see you have a lot of wisdom stored up in that head of yours."

"As you get older, you realize what's important."

"So share some of that wisdom before we go our separate ways."

"That's easy. If you can't sniff the duff of the one you love, then sniff the one you're with."

"Would it be all right if I quoted you someday?"

Her dogs pull her toward an approaching mixed breed. "Please be my guest, young man."

Not Marital Property

After eating two beef jerkies in front of Deli-De-Lite, I make my way up to my office. I have a Park Avenue address, but my space is no grand digs. I'm a solo practitioner so my needs are one giant impressive windowed corner office for me, a secretarial station for Lily, and a conference room where I can conduct depositions of all the friendly people I've sued.

I've occupied this space since I hung my shingle, first as a tenant of some fading law firm in a windowless closet-sized office and now as the leaseholder. At three thousand square feet, it's way too big for my practice, yet too run-down for lawyers of any worth to share. So, my current subtenants, who occupy most of the space, are a small group of individuals in the publishing and e-commerce industries. They publish a newsmagazine for the medical marijuana community called *TOKE*. They are a direct competitor of *HIGH TIMES* and a perfect fit for me.

I tolerate their herb-smelling runners that float in and out for apparent transactional purposes and they tolerate my HICs. Kind of a mutual admiration society of killers and deadheads. Besides, where else could you find tenants who pay most of the rent and insist on the anonymity of not having their name on the front door? As I reach for the knob I take in the new scent in the hall, fresh blooming roses. Lily. The paralegal, not the flower.

I enter to see my new crew is huddled in the corner of my reception, seeming uneasy. I look to the opposite corner and see a behemoth from the bayou occupying half the entry couch. If I had to venture a guess on professions, I'd say Swamp Thing wrestler. Conservatively, six foot five and three hundred pounds.

It takes no longer than an instant to notice he's acting strange, murderously strange. It's what he is doing with his right hand. In it is a handgrip exerciser. It's the kind with a metal coiled spring resistance mechanism atop black plastic handgrips that you squeeze together. Only, this one is special. It's custom-made.

The extralarge handgrips are pitted steel and have lucky charms affixed to the ends of each one. Jutting off one side is a shiny dagger. The other handgrip has a hollow-eyed steel skull with a vertical slot where its nose should be. With a large bayou beast hand covered with thick tufts of hair, Swamp Thing slowly squeezes the handgrips together, causing the dagger to move toward and pierce the skull through the slot with the pointed tip shooting out the back. He holds it together for six, seven, maybe eight seconds, then releases. We watch as he does another rep with his forearm swelling into full flex. He's fixated on it as the dagger penetrates, fantasizing, I suspect.

Time to say hello to one of Henry's injured criminals and my new HIC client.

"Bert Beecher?" I ask. He looks up for the first time.

"Yeah, that's me." He gives Mile High and pals an unfriendly stare—real unfriendly, like inciting-a-riot unfriendly. They huddle closer.

Bert looks at Otis. "Nice mutt," he says, which is not intended as a compliment.

"Mr. Beecher," I tell him, "I'll be with you in a moment. Wait right here, please." I turn to the trio. "You guys with me."

I open what I call the "spy door" that separates reception from my internal office and walk five steps down the hall. "Now go in here," I direct as I open the door to my conference room and put on the lights. "My paralegal, Lily, will be right in to take your information and have you sign some documents," I say to Mile High. "She's really good-looking and I expect you and these two to be on your best behavior. We cool?"

"We cool," Mile High confirms, then pauses. I don't like the feel of it. It's the type of pause someone gives when they intend to do the reverse of what they just promised.

"What's your name anyway?" I ask him, thinking I should apologize for not asking him sooner.

"I was wondering when you were going to ask. Barton Jackson the Third," Mile High responds.

Oops. Too late. I restate my concern. "I mean it, now, Barton Jackson the Third—best behavior."

"Yeah," Mile High says too quickly.

I don't like it. He's playing with me. I need to keep this going until he reveals himself. "In a few moments," I explain, "a twenty-nine-year-old dark-haired, dark-skinned, dark-eyed, saucy PR beauty who's almost six feet tall, slender, with a ten body, who walks with grace, elegance, and a booty call is going to come through that door. If I'm not mistaken, Lily's going to be wearing hip-hugging, wrinkle-free pants that showcase her smoking ass. Can you still be on your best behavior?"

"Yeah, yeah. We cool." Mile High pauses significantly again. He doesn't know it's significant, but it is. I detect a lip quiver, like he's not serious about what he said, then suddenly, he breaks out in laughter and gives in. "Okay, all right. I won't play no games on your girl. You found me out. She's gonna get all our respect. Now, how we gettin' back to Brooklyn?"

I take a hundred out. "Lily will be instructed to give you this if she feels you respected her. It should be enough to get you home in a cab."

Mile High grins. "Thanks." We both know he'll be pocketing the hundred and taking the number 4 train home and I'm fine with that. No harm in giving a little spending money to the recently discharged. "What's with that psycho killer?" he asks me.

"I don't know. I never met him before, but I'm pretty sure he's an ignorant racist from the swamp. Pay no attention to guys like him. Nothing good can come from it."

"Where can I get some of that cherry bud I'm smelling?" he asks. "That's African Buzz. I know that scent. That air freshener ain't throwing me off."

"I don't know what you're talking about." Deny, deny, deny.

I leave, closing the door behind me, and walk back toward the reception area to fetch Bert Beecher. Before I open I sneak a peak at Bert through the window panel, making sure he can't see me. That's why I call it the spy door. He's dressed in a blue flannel work shirt, sleeves rolled up and unbuttoned and open to a stained white T-shirt. My guess would be all-you-can-eat ribs. His big stomach is hanging over his belt, resting on his thighs, and he's got loosely laced work boots on, with the bottom of his grimy jeans tucked behind the tongue. He's just sitting there slowly choking to death that handgrip exerciser, intently watching his hand motion with pleasure.

He's got a full head of unkempt dirty brown hair, and that alone makes me hate this guy. What the hell does a monster like that need good hair for, anyway? Bert's nose looks like it's been smashed down a few times and he has thirty-six-hour scruff covering his face. Oddly, he's carrying a men's Gucci bag. It's the classic tan color with the G insignia pattern and signature green-bordered red stripe. Maybe he's their alligator skin supplier.

I open the door. "Mr. Beecher!" I call out.

He follows. As we pass Lily's station, I say, "There's a new sign-up waiting for you in the conference room. The kid got run over up in Harlem in front of the Apollo Theater."

"Is it an HIC?"

"No, it's a direct matter, no referring attorney. Sign it up." I continue with Bert and Otis into my office.

"Have a seat," I tell him, patting the back of one of my guest chairs with an inviting gesture. I take a seat on the other side of my large bird's-eye maple desk.

Before I get a word out, Bert Beecher speaks. "What's an HIC?"

I respond with a lie. "Heavy Injury Case," I say, accompanying it with the kind of smile that surfaces on your face when you've entertained yourself with the lie you've just spoken.

"Then why'd you tell her it was a direct matter without an attorney referring the kid to you the way Benson sent Betty over here?"

My smile disappears.

"No reason," I say, skirting the issue. I make note of his acumen. Henry did warn me. Swamp Thing leaves it alone, after a pause. Or maybe he just filed it away. "Mr. Beecher, as you know, your wife formally changed attorneys from Henry Benson and I'm now her trial counsel."

"Yeah?"

"As you also already know, her case was conditionally settled by Mr. Benson for six hundred thousand dollars for both claims, hers and yours."

"Yeah?"

"Well, we can't effectuate the settlement without your cooperation."

"That I know. And—"

"And your wife, who was the injured party, has authorized me to offer you five percent of the client's share, in order to get this case resolved. It's the standard amount for a claim like yours."

"Yeah?"

"I've asked you here today hoping to obtain your cooperation so we can finalize the settlement."

"Yeah?" Beecher repeats.

"That's about it. I need you to sign a general release reflecting your consent to accept five percent, which I would suggest is reasonable under the circumstances."

"Fine, but tack a zero on after the five. I want half the money just like the law says." I pause. *Just like the law says,* I repeat in my mind. What is this guy talking about? I tilt my head and look him in the face, seeking a clue.

His nose is smashed down and to his right. That must have been some punch. Bert's upper lip, with its blood-filled cracks, is irregular near the center where a tiny scar crawls up to under his nose, evidencing a surgically repaired cleft palate. Dirt fills the creases coming off the corners of his eyes, which are squinting in emphasis of his point. He's giving me the mean face, with his head cocked to the side. I look down at his hand and he has that exerciser vise-gripped closed.

"I don't think that's going to happen."

"Then there's nothing left to talk about. I'm leaving."

"Mr. Beecher, please don't go. I think we should play this out a little more and see if we can resolve things favorably for everyone."

"What's there to resolve? My ex can't get the money unless I sign off, and I'm not signing off unless I get half. I know Betty needs the money and she's gonna get desperate, so I'll wait her out. Besides, I know the divorce law says each person gets half the money, right? Why should I take less?"

I nod in understanding of his misunderstanding. "I see where you're coming from now, Mr. Beecher. I think you may have a mix-up about the law here."

"Yeah? How so?" Get ready for a dose of reality, Bert. It's back to the swamp for you.

"Despite you two being legally married at the time she was malpracticed, money from an injury lawsuit is not marital property subject to the equitable-distribution divorce laws of New York. You're not entitled to half of that money. In fact, you're not entitled to a penny of it. That money is for the injury Betty sustained to her corneas as a result of the surgeon forgetting to remove the eye shields at the end of her surgery. The law sees it as compensation to make the injured party whole again. It's not viewed as income that would be subject to a split like you're suggesting. Your wife doesn't even have to pay taxes on it for that very same reason."

"Tell that to someone else. I want half. That's what the law says. Half. Especially now that I know she don't have to pay no taxes on it, even though she don't pay no taxes anyway."

"Is that your final word on this topic?"

"Half." We enter into a Mexican standoff pause.

I give in first. Time to change direction. "Okay, since we can't re-solve things, let's fully discuss the nature of your claim, just so there are no surprises during the course of the lawsuit or at trial."

"Go ahead, I'm listening."

"I represent both you and your wife since, again, you two were le-gally married at the time she was injured. My job is to get your wife fairly compensated for her injuries and you fairly compensated for your loss concerning how you were affected by her injuries. I have an obligation to both of you individually, as my clients—and I will never compromise one in favor of the other."

Beecher smiles. "I'm happy to hear that. Now you're talking." He takes the wrist strap off his hairy hand and places his Gucci bag on the floor. Good, harmonious conduct suggesting he's going to stay a while.

"As the husband of the injured person, you're entitled to be com-pensated for the loss of your wife's services for the time period mea-suring from the date of the incident up until the day that you two split. According to the file, that was six months. So I'll argue to the jury that you sustained a loss for that period of time."

"Sounds fine to me."

"It might sound fine to you, but the type of injury your wife sus-tained is, in fact, not typically the kind of injury a husband would lose his wife's services from."

Beecher gives me a quizzical look. "What do you mean by 'services'?"

"A claim for loss of services on behalf of the noninjured spouse," I explain, "is for things the injured was prevented from doing around the home and the disruption of the quantity and quality of the intimate or sexual marital relationship."

Beecher grins broadly. "Then I have a big claim here. Sex sucked after this operation. I want half, like the law says, or we go to trial."

I refrain from correcting Bert on his continued misstatement of law, knowing it will get me nowhere. A Zen master would call it "accepting what is." A good lawyer would call it "mistake of the law is no defense"—you do the crime, you do the time. "Mr. Beecher, your wife had a nose job, a chin implant, her lips enlarged, her brow lifted, and her eyelids done during the procedure. Basically, a facial rehab."

"Figures," Bert cuts in, "I had to marry a piece of trash that cares about how she looks. That costs bucks, you know."

"Anyway," I continue, "Betty was left with scratches to the corneas of her eyes. This compromises the ability for tears to spread evenly resulting in a condition known as dry eyes, which she successfully treats with eye lubricants. It's my opinion—and I stress, it's only my opinion—that a jury is going to struggle with giving you money for a compromise to your sex life because Betty's eyes are dry. However, I could be wrong."

"I want half," Beecher repeats, mantra-like.

"I understand. So let's continue with how this will play out in court. First of all, when you're on the witness stand the judge is to your right and the jury is to your left, just like you see on television during a courtroom scene. Know what I mean?"

"I don't watch television."

"I'm sure sometime in your life you've seen a courtroom scene on TV."

"Like I said," Beecher replies testily, "I don't watch TV."

"Well, just like in the movies, then. Like the trial scene in *My Cousin Vinny* or *A Few Good Men*."

"I don't go to the movies, either."

"Mr. Beecher, certainly at least one time in your life you've seen a courtroom drama play out on television or in the movies?"

"Never."

"Never ever?"

"Never ever, ever."

"Interesting."

"Interesting?" Beecher asks. "Why interesting?"

"Whenever someone says 'never' to something, bells just go off in my head like an alarm, signaling to me someone's being less than candid." Maybe I shouldn't have said that.

"You calling me a liar?" Beecher threatens. No maybes about it.

Otis, who's been lying quietly to my left, jumps to his feet. I give him a "good boy" pat. "Down, Otis!" I command. He lies back again, but continues to keep a watchful eye on Bert.

"Please settle down, you're making Otis nervous. Of course I'm not calling you a liar. You're my client and I believe everything you say. Just understand that the judge is to your right and the jury is to your left just like they were during your attempted murder trial."

"Oh, is that what you mean? Why didn't you say so?" He grins at me as if I were his entertainment.

"Now, let's turn to the testimony forming the basis of your claim. I read your prelawsuit deposition under oath and I also read Betty's medical records. I found direct conflicts between the two."

"There you go again, calling me a liar."

"No I'm not," I quickly retort.

"Yes you are!" he yells in a firm voice, hand exerciser closed, popping up from the chair with intent to cause serious bodily harm. I instinctively jump up from my seat as Otis whips to his feet and lets out a serious warning growl. Bert looks to the dog, then back at me. A moment ago he put his Gucci bag down in peace and now we're up and ready to brawl. I got beads of sweat collecting on my shiny dome, knowing it's near impossible for me to look tough given the pattern of my baldness. It's moments like this I wish I had gone skinhead instead of buzz cut.

Something's got to give.

He looks back at Otis, whose lips are now retracted, showing his teeth, giving a low-pitched snarl. "I've had enough of this legal mumbo jumbo." Bert picks up his Gucci, turns, and leaves, stomping out, going back to the swamp.

I plop to my chair in relief. I look over at man's best friend. He's licking his balls like nothing happened. I wish I could do that. Not lick my balls, but move past a conflict like it never happened.

A minute after Bert Beecher leaves, I get a buzz from Lily. "Your three o'clock is here early. What do you want me to do with them?"

"Once Bert Beecher clears the office, send in the Williams family. How did things go with the sign-up and his friends?"

"They were nice boys. Very respectful."

I like that Mile High. I can see him as a community leader one day. Good thing I'm getting in on the ground floor. Guys like him were born to be a good source of referrals for lawyers like me.

When I'm about to meet a client for the first time, I usually want to look my best. So right about now I should be wiping the moisture off my scalp to dull the shine. Flossing, too, and taking a swig of mouthwash. On the other hand, I'm rejecting this case, so I don't really care about how I present. Instead, I embrace my balding status by whisking the moisture away by running my hand over my head; tongue-suck the processed beef particles from my uppers like an unfortunate soul trying to dislodge secondhand chicken parts scored from the KFC parking lot garbage bin; cup my hands together while orally delivering and nasally inhaling a hot breath, making a mental note not to breathe on Mrs. Williams. This taken care of, I relax in a slouch, like the rest of the schlubs in my profession.

Yes, now I'm ready to throw Little Suzy Williams farther under the bus.

Sch-weet, Dog, and Vegas

A moment later, Mrs. Williams looks around my door and leans in. "Be right there!" she calls, then disappears just as quickly.

Holy shit! She's fucking gorgeous! Like, the most beautiful face I've ever seen.

She's a light-skinned black woman with large, round, expressive blue eyes and bottomless dimples between her high cheekbones and low, soft jawline. If I saw it correctly, her tiny nose is ever so slightly turned up and it's adorable. And the shape of her face, it's like a gently curving heart that comes to a natural point at her lovely chin.

I scramble around searching for my plastic floss picks. Shit! The bag's empty, so I slam the drawer shut and open the one above it. I fish around and pull out a large paper clip that's most likely been a bottom dweller since I got the desk eighteen years ago. I bend the metal arm out, then hold the mirror up and quickly pick out the jerky particles stuck between my teeth, hoping the new object of my carnal desires doesn't walk in on me. Next I grab a tiny bottle of Listerine for a quick freshen. After spitting into my wastebasket, I strike my favorite new-client pose. Crap! My shiny head! I take the arm of my suit and buff it dry, then reassume the pose. I twine my fingers together, resting the fleshy butt of my hands on my desk and making sure my cuff is riding high, to call attention to my gold watch. Okay, I stop to acknowledge how insecure and superficial I am for needing to have my watch show. I sit up straight and suck in my gut.

Mrs. Williams is so good-looking I feel I got to take the pose to a higher level, so I suck in my cheeks and push out my jaw, hoping to highlight my facial bone structure. I take a deep breath and say to myself, *Loser.*

A moment later, a pair of red leather boots secured in the leg braces of an old-style wheelchair comes rolling around my doorframe. Inside the boots are thin light brown legs, and from what I can see they are atrophied and contorted. This lower extremity mess belongs to Suzy Williams. The cinnamon-colored toy poodle resting on her bony little lap is adorable, somehow giving balance to the visual.

As her mother wheels Suzy forward, I realize I forgot to move one of my chairs out of the way as I customarily do when I know a client is going to be wheeled into my office. The obstructive chair causes Mrs. Williams to slow down, so I break my unseen pose and leap from my seat. I pull one of the two chairs to the side and she wheels Suzy forward a few more feet, then locks the wheels.

"Sch-weet," Suzy says as the motion ceases and she's parked.

Mrs. Williams and I are two feet from each other, and she smells vanilla delicious. She's near six feet, has Halle Berry's perfect complexion, and yes, I saw correctly that tiny little nose is slightly turned up. Her superlong eyelashes are covered with gobs of that stuff women use to make them appear thicker and longer. On someone else such excess would look ridiculous, but on June it's merely glamorous. Her eyes open and close like shutters, and each slow blink suggests innocence in a carnal kind of way, if that makes any sense. "I truly apologize," I say. "It was insensitive of me not to have moved this chair out of the way in anticipation of your arrival."

She looks into my eyes, melting me with her dreamy baby blues. I make a mental note to myself that blue eyes on a light-skinned black woman are one hot combo. "That's not a problem, it happens all the time," she says in a soft sexy voice.

Now I really feel horrible, having been told I'm just as insensitive as the rest of society, even if I know that wasn't her intent. I wonder if I would've forgotten to move the chair if I were keeping Suzy's case or knew how sexy June Williams was beforehand. On second thought, I definitely wouldn't have forgotten.

Otis gets up and walks around from behind my desk to see what's happening. "Sch-weet Dog, sch-weet Dog, sch-weet Dog," Suzy says excitedly, and begins swaying her upper body back and forth with minimal trunk control. Otis moves toward Suzy and her little poodle, his tail wagging. He rests his funnel head on Suzy's bony lap and the poodle starts licking his big black nose. Suzy seems entertained. "Sch-weet."

"Mrs. Williams . . ." I start.

"It's Ms.," she cuts in, "but please call me June."

I nod, and after the appropriate postcorrection pause time, start again. "June, what does 'sch-weet' mean?"

"Sch-weet," she explains, "is Suzy's way of saying she's good, happy, or, basically, that things are sweet with her."

"How much speech does she have?"

"Three words: *sch-weet, Dog* with a capital *D* because that's her dog's name"—she gives the little pup a gentle pat on its head—"and *Vegas.*"

"*Sch-weet, Dog,* and *Vegas?* As in Las Vegas?"

"Exactly. There's a component to her brain damage affecting certain ocular centers that are stimulated by bright flashing lights. To you and me, flashing lights are a distracting alert signal, but in Suzy's case, they make her feel calm and relaxed. She likes to watch television in the dark and the Las Vegas tourism commercials show lots of flashing neon lights in them, which she loves, so, somehow, she learned the word *Vegas.*"

"Incredible."

"Yes, it is. Watch." She opens her extralarge red leather bag, which matches her own red boots, and reaches in. She comes out with a plastic toy. It's a round, clear globe attached to a red plastic handle with a black button. She leans over, butt out, and puts it in front of Suzy, who's staring up at the ceiling. "Suzy, look," June says. "Suzy, look here. Suzy, look."

Suzy moves her unfocused gaze to the toy. "Vegas, Vegas, sch-weet, Vegas." June presses the button and multicolored lights start spinning around and around inside the globe. Suzy stares and is mesmerized by the spinning lights almost to the level of a conscious sedation. Me, I'm mesmerized by June Williams's perfect little bottom, hanging out there just right. As I look at June, I imagine all the ways I could take advantage of her vulnerable position.

I hear "Excuse me, excuse me" and realize I've spent the last few moments in a state of conscious sedation of my own. I didn't even realize June leaned back up, now looking at me.

"I'm sorry, I was just thinking of something." I move back around the desk and slowly sit down, thinking she just busted me checking her out. It's time to turn my attention to Suzy.

A Mother Knows These Things

June Williams's daughter's formal diagnoses are vast and diverse. The main one that covers everything I see sitting before me is severe cerebral palsy and spastic quadriplegia. Cerebral palsy is essentially damage to the motor control centers of the brain, compromising voluntary movement. It has also seriously compromised her intellectual development, keeping her functioning at a two-year-old level. Spastic quadriplegia means Suzy is nonfunctional from her neck down, but she has a significant amount of nerve sparing that allows her to flap her arms about in a spastic manner. Suzy can hardly swallow and her head rocks, and since this makes eating a problem, she has a gastric tube sewed into her stomach for nutrition as Henry had mentioned. Her arms are skin-and-bone appendages contorted and twisted into flipper-like shapes from tendon contractures. I could go on and on but . . .

If Suzy's case had merit, I'd make millions with this injury, and that appalling thought is what separates attorneys in my business from the rest of society. I disgust even myself for thinking it, but that's just the work I happen to do. The bigger the injury, the bigger the attorney fee, the better my marriage. At least I admit it.

"Ms. Williams . . ."

She interrupts again. "Please, please, I asked that you call me June."

"Okay, June. And you can call me Tug."

"Oh, I don't think so," she responds, like I said something naughty. "I'll call you Mr. Wyler."

"No, please, that's too formal, please, call me Tug."

"I can't do that, call my lawyer Tug. I tell you what," she says, looking like she's got a bright idea, "I'll just call you Wyler, with no Mr."

Anyone else, no, but . . . "Sounds great to me."

"Good. Now let's get busy. I have a lot on my plate and I'm counting on you to help me clear it." She smiles. I melt.

I like June Williams. She's gorgeous, intelligent, and witty. She calls things the way she sees them without a filter, which is a complete turn-on. I hope she has an interest in me, too, but I have to break it to her.

"I have some bad news."

"I'm listening. Give it to me straight."

"There's no case."

"No case where?"

"No case here. Suzy's got no case."

June knits her brow. "You must be mistaken. This lawsuit's been going on six years already. Look at her and tell me there's no case."

"I understand how long this case has been pending, and sometimes in this business that can happen for a reason or for none at all. I just don't know the explanation in this case yet. And I see the unfortunate condition of your daughter right before my eyes, but that doesn't change anything. You've got no case."

There's a long pause. The kind of pause used to think things over. The pause, I have to tell you, is definitely underexamined as a communication tool.

"Explain it to me," June demands. "Explain how this lawsuit came to be started and why it's been around for so long if there was no case to begin with." Sarcastically, she continues. "I'm listening. I can't wait to hear about it. Go ahead, Wyler."

I take advantage of a pause myself. "In a case like this you need a doctor, a medical expert, to come forward and say another doctor committed malpractice. Without imputing any wrongdoing to Mr. Benson, I'll say he started this suit in your best interest, thinking that the case had merit and that he would be able to pick up an expert along the way. It's not uncommon for attorneys to do that. Recently, the attorneys for the defendants asked the court to throw Suzy's case out. It's called—"

"I know what it's called," June interrupts. "A motion to dismiss. A motion for summary judgment. I'm familiar with legal procedure. So, are you saying that Henry had the case reviewed by an expert for the first time only after they made their motion to dismiss and it was at this time he first came to realize Suzy has no case?"

"That's exactly what I'm saying." After waiting for a few moments to pass, to allow June the dignity of her anger, I continue. "Our options are either you voluntarily discontinue the lawsuit with the judge's permission or else I make a cross-motion to have Henry Benson and myself relieved as counsel since there's no good-faith basis on which to go forward. Otherwise, the defendant's motion to dismiss goes in unopposed and the judge throws out the case. The outcome is the same, regardless."

She shakes her head in disbelief. "Then how did Suzy end up this way?"

"I hate to use these words, but what happened to Suzy was a risk and complication of her sickle cell condition and it's documented in her hospital records. This is the unanimous opinion of the subsequent treating doctors who have no connection to this lawsuit, the defendant's expert, and also our reviewing expert. The event would have occurred even if the guy in *House* was her doctor."

"Who?" June asks.

"Never mind. What I mean to say is that the outcome would have been the same in the best hands that modern medicine could have offered. Unfortunately, Suzy had numerous complications from her sickle cell crisis."

June pauses before she responds. I can't identify the intent of the pause, but before I can figure it out she speaks. "I see you're buying."

"Buying what?"

"You're buying their sell. They're trying to convince you Suzy's disease is the cause of this and you've bought it. Was our expert at the hospital when this happened?" June asks.

"Of course not."

"I *was*, Tug." She hammered that statement. The tension's thick. "I don't know who or what, but somebody did something wrong. A mother knows these things. You got a mother?"

"Yes, June. I have a mother."

"Ask her. She'll tell you about a mother's intuition. A mother knows when someone harms her baby . . . and somebody wronged my Suzy. I'm certain. I was there."

"I understand you're upset about this news, but that's not going to change things. There's no case. It was an act of God."

June looks mulish. "I don't have your education and I don't have your smarts, Tug, but I know what I know and I know what I don't know and I know someone did something bad to my Suzy."

June's choice of words shocks me. The message is clear. I have to further investigate this case. June was there and she knows what she knows, and I can't turn my back on that. That's the principle guiding how I live my life. Besides, she's calling me Tug now. Progress.

"June, I accept what you've just said. I don't know what I can do with it at this point, but I definitely accept it. I'll look into things further, only I'm not optimistic."

"Just look further," she encourages. "That's all I'm asking. If there's no case, then there's no case, and I'll accept responsibility for this."

I knew it. I'd better address her guilt right now. "June, what are you talking about? Suzy's condition is not your fault, not by any measure. Like I said, this would've happened in the best of medical hands."

"No. I don't believe that," she says, softening like a wilting flower. Puddles gather in her expressive blue eyes. She takes a deep collecting breath. "Either they did something wrong or I didn't act quickly enough when I saw my baby suffering that morning with her heart beating so fast."

"That's not true. You must believe me. It's not uncommon for a mother to feel responsible for an outcome like this under such circumstances, but I assure you it's just groundless guilt, not fact. Leave it alone, guilt is for the guilty."

"It's me or them," she says, as if it's a matter of fact. "So where do we go from here?"

"As you know, this Wednesday Suzy is scheduled to see a doctor designated by the attorneys for the people we sued to evaluate her condition. It's called an independent medical exam, or IME, although there's nothing independent about it. The doctor works for the defendants. This was arranged before they made their motion to dismiss. I was going to cancel the appointment, but now, you just go ahead and take her there. Besides, if I can somehow make a case, Suzy'd have to go for this exam anyway. If there's no case, then no harm done. I'll call the court and ask Judge Schneider for an adjournment on the motion. I should get some time since I can argue there was a change of attorney and I just received the file. Hopefully, I'll figure out some theory of recovery in the interim."

"That's a plan, Tug, old boy," June says merrily, like we're back on track. "What time are you meeting us at the doctor's office?"

"June, that's not necessary," I say, repeating "old boy" in my head, damn. "You don't need me there. In a case like this, defendants generally don't dispute the severity of the injuries and I'm surprised they even asked for an exam. Just one look at Suzy tells the whole story. They're disputing the liability, meaning that they didn't do anything wrong to cause Suzy's condition. Nothing's going to happen at the IME that in any way relates to the issue of liability or fault so you don't need me to accompany you."

"See you there," June says, ignoring me. "You're the one telling me 'no case,' so you're going to be there. It's the least you can do under the circumstances."

"But I'm in the middle of a trial right now," I plead. "I was only able to meet you today because the judge told us he had an emergency special proceeding that came up. I'll be back in court tomorrow and the case I'm litigating may last until the end of the week, so it'll be impossible for me to get to Suzy's IME on Wednesday."

"If you're as good as Henry Benson says, then your case will be over by Wednesday, I'm sure."

"June—"

"No excuses. I'll see you at the IME. Come on, Suzy. I need some lunch and you need your feeding tube filled."

June gets up, unlocks the wheels, and spins Suzy around toward the door. "Sch-weet!" she blurts, stimulated by the motion, as Dog, the toy poodle, balances herself on Suzy's lap. When June takes a few steps forward, I check out her smoking ass again. June's perfectly shaped bottom moves in rhythmic form with each step. Foot plant right, wiggle left. Nice.

Just as she reaches the door, June whips around. She makes no mention of the level of my eyes, but definitely takes note. She points to a picture of a woman in a black party dress on the corner of my desk. "That your wife?"

"Yes, it is," I reply proudly.

"She's sexy. She treat you right?"

That's a complicated question. "Yeah, she treats me all right."

She slowly nods, the way one does when formulating judgment. "I hope you're more convincing in court."

She turns and wheels Suzy and Dog out.

My first thought once she's gone is whether June is trying to use my obvious appreciation of her good looks as a lure to keep me plugging away at Suzy's case. My second thought is who cares because I can't remember the last time I felt so alive, the testosterone flowing through my vessels. Sch-weet.

Thirty seconds after June and Suzy's departure, Lily marches in. "What kind of HIC was Mrs. Williams? A prostitute?"

"I don't know who the criminal is affiliated with the Williams family, but based on my first impression, I highly doubt it's her, and it's 'Ms.' Williams."

"She was gorgeous."

"Yes, she was. I think I'm attracted to her."

"Well, she's definitely attracted to you."

"How do you know?"

"On her way out, she was talking to her poor little girl. I heard her say 'Suzy, your new lawyer's got it going on, but he ain't getting out of this case so fast.' That's what I came in to tell you."

I need to collect my thoughts. It figures this would happen in the worst of possible scenarios, a child's case with a massive injury I have to withdraw from. Yet with a single-parent hot mom. If I fool around with June, then drop Suzy's case, the retaliation could be disastrous, both personally and professionally. Also, I remember there being something in The Rules about not humping your client and I don't want to end up in front of the Disciplinary Committee for that. Last, I'm pretty sure there was a similar provision in my wedding vows.

My silence catches a look of disapproval from Lily. "You're married, remember?"

"I'm aware of that, Lily, but I can fantasize, can't I?"

"No," she informs me. "That's cheating."

"Lily, that's not cheating. That's normal, or else the divorce rate would be near one hundred percent."

Lily gives me the "you're a cheater and I'm a loyal Puerto Rican" look. "Why do we have to get out of the case? Suzy's as bad as we've ever had. Is someone lying or making something up to make a case where none exists?"

"Not this time, and one thing's for sure: June and Suzy are as honest as honest can be. Besides, it's a lot harder to fabricate a medical malpractice case than it is your typical slip-trip-and-fall injury case."

"Why's that?"

"In a malpractice case," I explain, "the facts giving rise to the claim are generally documented in the medical records, eliminating the possibility of the patient creating a false set of circumstances. Besides, in this instance, Suzy was only six at the time of malpractice and too young to victimize herself in a fake case. It may be the first Benson case we've handled that has no twist to it."

"Like you say, when you're handling an HIC case, it ain't over till your Fat Aunt Sandy sings. I got to go. My sitter burnt up our dinner, so I got to make a new one. Bye."

"Travel safe, Lily," I say as she runway turns and leaves my office. My first thought while finally having a moment alone, a selfish one: if I'm going to bone June, assuming she'd have me, and assuming I had it in me to act on such an opportunity, I better do it before I tell her there's no case—if that's how things turn out—because there's no way she'll bang after. I can't believe how self-centered I can be, thinking about a sexual interlude at a time when I'm on the verge of possibly ruining someone's life. I think I just turned myself off. At least I admit it.

As I gather my things to leave, one thought in particular keeps popping in and out of my head, which is June's belief about Suzy's braindamaged condition. Having such a child is a sad enough situation, but if the mom wrongfully thinks she's responsible for the damage, things are that much worse. Her individual existence is stifled by overriding and unjustified guilt, and she's fixated on caregiving to the mutual exclusion of life around her. The family unit often breaks down and what's left is a brain-damaged child and a nonfunctional, emotionally damaged mother.

So the question now arises. Can June Williams be liberated from her emotional jailing or am I about to take away her chances of freedom? June's belief that the hospital wronged her daughter has given her hope of vindication over all these years. June will never be the same if she has to accept that the hospital did nothing wrong. Her hope will be lost and her guilt will be permanent. If the hospital didn't cause Suzy's brain damage, ipso facto, she did.

5

O f course we're coming to Boca for the holidays," I hear my wife say as I step down the back staircase into our upscale country-style kitchen.

"I'm not going to Boca!" I holler. So much for having a peaceful morning.

"Shut up, you idiot," she scolds as I pull a chair out from our "antique" farm table that cost me double for its custom manufacture. "My mother's on speaker."

"Why didn't you say so," I respond. "I—am—not—going—to—Boca!"

"Is that Tug I hear?" my mother-in-law screams, mistakenly thinking you have to yell to be heard on speaker.

"Yes, Mom," answers my wife. "Don't listen to him."

"Why not? I'm happy he wants to come to Boca."

"No! I'm not going to Boca!"

"Wonderful, see you soon. I have to go. I don't want to be late for mah-jongg." Tyler clicks the phone off, then turns to me, angered. "What's your problem?"

"Me, I got no problem. I just don't want to go to Boca and stay with your parents. I paid my dues. Fifteen years straight. It's time for a change. Why don't we go to some Arabic-speaking country for the Jewish holidays, that's got to be less torturing than Boca."

"Well, I'm going, and so are the kids. And my parents expect to see you, so you're going, too. It would be embarrassing for them to explain to everybody at the club why you're not there. People will talk."

"I'm not interested in appearances. I'm not going."

"Yes you are."

"No I'm not."

"Yes you are."

"Nope."

"Yep."

"No way."

"Yes way."

"Uh-uh."

"Uh-huh. Yes you are!"

"I are not!"

"Bet?" she says, breaking up the back-and-forth childishness, but only slightly.

"Yeah, I'll bet."

She puts her hands on her hips, the way a woman does when she's about to make things conclusive. "You're going to Boca for the holidays. And that's final!"

Cornbread Connie

On my Metro-North train ride to Grand Central I ponder my wife's parting words. The last time she said, "That's final," I had to resolve five cases before getting any play. That took six weeks, and every time I told her about a settlement, she asked me how much the fee was as if keeping a tally to some fixed amount she had set in her mind before she would let me in. And I can't believe I started a fight with her on a Tuesday, I must be going crazy. Boca, here I come.

I take the 4 train from Grand Central and my destination is the Borough Hall stop in downtown Brooklyn. Standing in the center of the car is a homeless subway preacher orating his holy beliefs. He's an unkempt, rumpled, messy black man in his midforties. His mission is clear.

"It's the woman that has the fruit that tempts the man," he says in a nasal high-pitched voice. "If they had no fruit, there'd be no temptation. That sweet, succulent fruit of temptation is juicy on the outside, but seeded with evil on the inside. Can I have an amen from the congregation, yeah-ya."

"Amen," responds a guy who looks down on his luck. He glances around to notice that eyes are now on him, embarrassed for being the only one of thirty riders to speak out. The women in the car are dispersing away from the center, making sure their pocketbooks are closed and shirts buttoned high.

"Be careful, my fellow men," the reverend continues, in gospel form, "for no good can come from tasting the sweet fruit of temptation, the fruit from the vines of the punany no-no bush. The sweet fruit women use to tempt their mens, to influence their mens, to manipulate their mens, and to rule their mens. Stay away from the punany no-no bush, stay away from the forbidden fruit of temptation. It will control your life, yeah-ya."

An instant later, we come out of the tunnel that runs under the East River, brakes screech the train to a jolting stop, and the subway doors open. The crowd hustles out as New Yorkers do, and I slip the orator a fiver, saying, "Amen, my brother. Would you consider sermonizing a group of worshippers in need of your words for the holidays down in Boca?"

I step off the train, then negotiate an underground maze with the other rat racers and come up the stairs into a large, open square. In front of me is another building from the 1800s with columns supporting a triangular pediment. I can't get away from these structures. Borough Hall was built as Brooklyn's city hall containing the offices of the mayor, the city council, and it had a courtroom and a jail—an all-in-one building of city government. Now it houses the borough president, but I've never seen anyone go into that place. What I often see is exactly what I saw on Dr. Laura's desk—newly married couples photographing their special moment on the impressive entry steps, memorializing the day that will forever change their lives.

To my right is my destination, Brooklyn's Supreme Court, the building I drove by the other day on my way to meet my soon-to-be ex-expert. I'm in the middle of a trial and the defendants are putting on their expert radiologist this morning. This witness will make or break my case.

I arrive at court early and go up to the fourth floor to wait for things to heat up. With any luck, I'll settle this case today after cross-examining the radiologist, who also is the last witness in the case. I sit on one of the hard wooden benches that line the corridor just outside Judge Dixon's courtroom.

I open my bag and take out what I've prepared, my outline for my cross-examination. It's headed "CROSS-ASSASSINATION: RADIOLOGIST FOR THE BAD GUYS."

As a rule, there's no way to effectively cross-examine radiologists on what they say they see on X-rays. They come to court and say, "This film is a picture, and this is what I see." End of story. The more you try to get a radiologist to change his interpretation, the worse the testimony gets for you. It gives them the opportunity to repeatedly pound their findings into the jury's head. Thus, you have to embrace what they say they see, lulling them into a false sense of security, then proceed with the execution you have planned.

The case on trial is the Connie Cortez matter, another HIC case. It's the first Henry Benson referral I've actually had to take to trial. It's a hit-in-the-rear automobile accident that took place four years ago, where Connie sustained a brain injury resulting in the loss of her senses of smell and taste. In Supreme Court, Kings County, such a case is litigated in two separate phases. In the first half of a bifurcated trial, the jury decides who's at fault for causing the accident. If the defendant is found responsible in whole or in part, then a second trial is held with the same jury to determine the extent of monetary damages for the injuries claimed.

In the first part of the trial, the defendant, who's the spoiled-brat daughter of a federal court judge, contended that at the time of the accident, my client, Connie Cortez, was not a passenger in the car being driven by her husband but rather a "jump-in" extortionist attempting to perpetrate a fraud upon the court. The term has its roots in the realm of bus accidents, where a person claiming injuries was not on the bus at the time of the accident but rather "jumped in" after the accident occurred.

This defense was based on the fact that Connie Cortez was not at the scene when the police arrived. Her name did not appear on the police report, no ambulance was called or came to the scene, and she did not seek emergency room treatment.

I was not happy about being involved in a case against the daughter of a prestigious federal court judge where the only issue for the jury to determine was whether or not my client was committing insurance fraud. But such is life when you get involved with an HIC.

My key witness to rebut these allegations was one Maddy Hernandez, the Cortez family babysitter. Maddy testified that on the date of the accident, Connie Cortez showed up at her home as she usually did to drop off her nine-year-old daughter, Melissa. On this day, however, Connie had a large bump and bloody cut in the hairline of her forehead and told Maddy she'd just been in a car accident a half block away.

The jury obviously believed Connie Cortez and Maddy, which is why I'm here today on the damages part of the trial.

Last week I put on my neurologist to prove the claim that Connie struck her head as a result of the impact, sustaining a subdural hematoma and brain contusion in the area of her frontal lobe, which resulted in a complete loss of her senses of smell and taste. My neurologist interpreted the brain MRI and circled an area of blackness on the film representing the contusion.

My ass is getting numb from the pressure of the hard bench so I get up and begin my precross, pacing down the long courthouse hall. I see Maddy walking toward me, carrying a brown paper lunch bag. "*Hola,* Maddy,*" I say. "*¿Qué tal?* I don't need you here anymore. The jury believed us, and we won that part of the case last week."

"Oh, I know. *Qué bueno.* But I want to watch. It's very exciting."

As I'm about to respond I see Connie Cortez coming toward me with her daughter in tow. I wait until she pulls up. "Look who we have here as a spectator today, Connie, Maddy."

"I know. She insisted on coming," Connie replies. "She'll sit in the back with my daughter and won't interfere. I hope that's okay."

"Let me mull it over for a second."

I hear the courtroom door unlock from the inside and the heavy wooden structure opens with a distinctive high-pitched metal-on-metal squeak. The court officer assigned to Judge Dixon's room sticks his head out. "Hey, youse guys, we're open for business," he says with a Brooklyn brogue. "Mr. Wyler, someone called here for you this morning."

"Who?" I ask.

"She wouldn't say." Then he disappears back behind the squeaky door.

I turn to my Latin trio. "Maddy, I don't think it's a good idea if you come inside since you told the jurors you were only Connie's babysitter and not really her friend. If the jury sees you here today, when there's no legal reason for you to be here, they might infer the testimony you gave last week was really motivated by friendship. If they make that inference they may second-guess their verdict on liability and compromise their verdict on damages, giving Connie less money than they otherwise would have given her, and I don't want that to happen. I know it may sound strange to you, but you never know what a jury is thinking. So it's better if you stay out here with Connie's daughter."

"Oh, I get chu," Maddy responds. "I stay outside."

Inside the courtroom, I sit at the end of the trial table closest to the jury box and Connie sits in the first row of seats closest to the jury. Ten minutes later, the defense counsel arrives with his people. He takes his place at the far side of the trial table, away from the jury box, his expert radiologist takes a seat right behind him in the first row of seats, and the moneyman from the insurance company who's been monitoring the trial sits in the back row, far side.

"What's up?" I say to defense counsel in a calm, cheery voice.

"Nothing, Wyler," defense counsel snorts. "This doctor's going to sink your case."

"Okay," I respond, unimpressed. "You got a couple of poppy seeds stuck in your teeth and a gob of cream cheese on your tie. You mind if I ask your expert a question?"

Defense counsel takes his finger out of his mouth. "Is it about this case in any way, shape, or form, Wyler?"

"Not at all. And please, call me Tug."

"Go ahead then, but I'll be listening."

"Thanks, and there's still a big seed caught between your two front teeth." He gives me a smirk. He has no idea what's coming.

I turn back to the radiologist. "Good morning, Doctor. I hope your trip here was a pleasant one."

"Good morning," the doctor replies. "My trip here was pleasant. Thank you for asking."

"Not at all. Being in court can be stressful in and of itself, and the last thing you want to have to start your day is a messy commute."

"I couldn't agree with you more."

"Doctor, on my way here this morning I was reading some medical literature on an unrelated matter and I came across a term I'm unfamiliar with. Do you think you could give me a medical definition for the word if I told it to you?"

"Maybe. What's the word?"

"The word is orchiectomy."

The doctor smiles knowingly. "Yes, that word pertains to an operation where the surgeon takes off one or both of a man's testicles."

"Thanks, Doc." I turn back around seemingly satisfied with his superior store of knowledge.

Defense counsel spends two hours on his direct examination of the radiologist. In sum and substance, the radiologist testifies that the MRI does show evidence of a brain lesion in the frontal lobe, but that the cause, or etiology, of it is remote in time. That, in his expert opinion, Connie Cortez must have sustained some form of head trauma when she was a little girl by falling off the bed or some other traumatic event of the sort that happens to infants and young children. He stated with a reasonable degree of medical certainty that this lesion is in no way from the accident that gave rise to this lawsuit.

Defense counsel sits down and Judge Dixon looks at me wearily. "Counselor, do you need a break before your cross-examination?" That's the question judges ask when they think you need time to recover after a witness kills your case. Dixon has just heard testimony that, in the absence of my cross-examination, seems destined to send me and Connie Cortez packing *sin dinero*.

"Judge," I state for all to hear, "if this witness or a member of the jury needs a break, then let's break. Otherwise, I'm ready to cross-examine the doctor."

Judge Dixon inquires, "Does anybody need a break?" All heads shake in the negative, and he looks back at me. "He's your witness, Mr. Wyler."

As I begin to stand up I hear that distinctive high-pitched squeak and jerk my head toward the source, as do the judge, the jury, the court officer, the court clerk, the insurance guy, and the defense counsel. The big wooden door slowly opens and in walks June Williams. Surprise, surprise. She takes care to close the door quietly behind her. We make brief look-away eye contact just before she sits down.

Judge Dixon addresses June. "Excuse me, miss, do you have any connection with this lawsuit?"

"No, sir," June answers. "I'm just a student of the law and would like to observe this trial if that's okay with Your Honor." She looks the part in a dark blue pantsuit with a gray pinstripe.

"You're more than welcome to stay, then. Civil trials are a matter of public record."

"Thank you, Your Honor."

"If you have any questions after this is over, I would be more than happy to answer them in my chambers."

"Thank you, Your Honor. I'll let you know."

Judge Dixon addresses me. "He's your witness, counselor."

I get up. "Your Honor, would you mind if I questioned by standing in front of this table?"

"Stand wherever you want, Mr. Wyler."

"Thank you, Your Honor." I move around the trial table. I look at the radiologist, we lock eyes, I smirk, he nervously wipes his forehead. My cross begins appearing on my laptop's screen in real time because it's plugged into the court reporter's steno machine. As I do my thing, my questions and his answers would read like this:

Q: Good morning, Doctor.

A: Good morning.

Q: We met a little earlier, did we not, before you took the witness stand?

A: Yes, we did. Right here in this courtroom.

Q: You were nice enough to answer a question I had regarding a certain medical definition unrelated to this case.

A: Yes, I was.

Q: I'd like to thank you for being kind enough to help me out, given that you are coming into this courtroom today against the interests of my client.

A: Not a problem at all.

Q: Now, I think you and I are going to agree on everything here. Would that be okay with you?

A: That would be fine with me.

Q: Then let's start agreeing, shall we?

A: Fine.

Q: If I understand your testimony properly, it is your position that there is, in fact, a brain lesion on that MRI, correct?

A: Correct.

Q: No issue for these jurors, then—we all agree Connie has a brain lesion, correct?

A: Correct.

Q: The location of that brain lesion is in the inferior frontal lobe, correct?

A: Correct.

Q: Structures in that area of the frontal lobe translate taste and smell, correct?

A: Correct.

Q: A lesion like the one we see on the MRI can be responsible for the loss of the sense of smell, correct?

A: Yes it can, but sometimes there can be no problems.

Q: Be patient, Doctor, we'll get to that.

A: Okay.

Q: When there's a loss of sense of smell, everything tastes like cardboard, correct?

A: Correct.

Q: The joys of eating are gone, correct?

A: Correct.

Q: Now, it's your position that this brain lesion is not from the accident of four years ago, but rather from some head trauma Connie must have sustained as an infant, correct?

A: Correct.

Q: Can we agree it would be improper for this jury to give Connie money for injuries that are unrelated to this accident?

A: Well, I'm not a lawyer, but it's common sense that she should only get money for injuries that are causally related to this accident.

Q: I couldn't agree with you more, Doctor. So far you and I have agreed on everything, correct?

A: Correct.

Q: Doctor, let's assume you are right that this brain lesion occurred when Connie was a child, okay?

A: Okay.

Q: Doctor, you of course have heard the terms *asymptomatic* and *quiescent* as they relate to brain lesions just like the one you see on Connie's brain MRI?

A: Yes, of course I have.

Q: Tell the jurors what this means, in your own words, Doctor.

A: Someone can have a head trauma, develop a brain lesion like the one we see in Connie's films, but never have any signs, symptoms, or complaints related to its presence.

Q: In other words, Doctor, someone can have a brain lesion in the exact location we see in Connie's films and never have even one single complaint or even know it's there, correct?

A: Correct.

Q: Now, Doctor, can we also agree that the
    presence of an asymptomatic and quiescent brain
    lesion predisposes a person to sustaining a
    greater injury from a subsequent trauma than a
    person with a healthy brain?

A: That's true, too.

Q: Doctor, have you seen any medical records
    inclusive of doctors' office records or
    hospital records that in any way indicated that
    Connie Cortez had no sense of smell or taste
    prior to this accident?

A: No, I have not.

Q: So, Doctor, let's see if we can put this all
    together for the jurors from your perspective,
    shall we?

A: Okay.

Q: Can we agree that from your perspective
    Connie Cortez, prior to the accident, had a
    frontal brain lesion that was asymptomatic
    and quiescent, predisposed her to injury, and
    she had full sense of smell and full sense of
    taste, agreed?

A: Agreed.

Q: Since this is your opinion, you must also be of
    the opinion that the trauma from this accident
    must've aggravated this quiet condition and
    been a substantial factor in causing Connie's
    brain lesion to become symptomatic and causing
    her to lose her senses of smell and taste,
    agreed?

A: Agreed.

Q: No further questions, Doctor.

As I walk back to my chair I pretend-cough. Not just any kind of cough, but the fake cough-cough clearly signaling a secret message. As I do so, I say under my breath, but loud enough to be heard by defense counsel, "Orchiectomy, cough-cough; orchiectomy, cough-cough." His face turns beet red. I look up at the doctor before sitting down and can tell he just realized he was the unwitting patient of a courtroom nut-ectomy.

Before my duff hits the chair, I hear *bang, bang, bang*. I look up to see Judge Dixon smashing his gavel on the top of his bench. "Both counsel, in the back to my chambers. Doctor, you wait here. Officer, take the jury into the jury room." These orders set everyone into motion—that is, everyone except for June, whom the insurance guy just passed on his way out to the hall to report the new developments to the higher-up money guys at his office.

We get into the back and Judge Dixon immediately takes off his judicial robes and hangs them up. He's wearing suspenders, button-style. He sits down at his desk, with defense counsel and me seated across from him. He looks at defense counsel. "Go get that insurance guy in here now," he orders. My adversary hops to it. Dixon and I just look at each other as we sit there. It's improper for us to have an ex parte conversation, but I know he's itching to say something to me. He appears angry.

While we wait I can't help but notice a long bundle of hair jutting out of Judge Dixon's nose. I can't believe I never noticed it before now. Why wouldn't he clip that? It's, like, an inch out from the rim of his right nostril and clumped together.

"What are you staring at, counselor?" Judge Dixon asks curtly.

"Oh, nothing, judge. Not really focused on anything in particular."

"I see." He begins to twirl his nasal hair between his thumb and finger. I get it now.

Moments later, my adversary returns with Money Man.

"Sit down," Judge Dixon commands. I look over at Money and see he's got a smidgen of sauerkraut on his suit lapel. It seems these defense guys are sloppy eaters, but more important, it means the hot dog vendor in front of the courthouse is an early riser. Seeing the stain triggers my hunger for a dirty-water dog, which I intend to get just after I settle this case.

Judge Dixon looks at me. "You plan that?" he asks.

"I had an outline with two points on it."

"That wouldn't have happened if I had prepared the witness. You're a lucky man I took to the bench."

"I feel lucky about that, Your Honor."

Judge Dixon turns to defense counsel and Money. "You know he can't lose now, right?"

"Well—" defense counsel sputters.

"No 'well' about it. He can't lose. His doctor said the accident caused a new brain lesion resulting in the loss of the senses of smell and taste, and your doctor says the accident caused an aggravation of an old asymptomatic brain lesion resulting in the loss of the senses of smell and taste. Game over. The accident caused the loss of the senses of smell and taste. Now that you've played, it's time to pay. I have no alternative but to instruct the jury in my damage charge that they must accept as a matter of law that the accident caused the injury."

We spend the next thirty minutes negotiating a settlement in Judge Dixon's chambers for nine hundred and fifty thousand dollars. For most of that time I am considering whether I'll order a dog or one of those fat spicy sausages when I get out of there. I decide if it is going to be a dog I'll get it with mustard and kraut. If it's a sausage I'll get it with mustard and smothered with onions. The judge brings back the court reporter, I bring back Connie Cortez, and we put the settlement on the record.

Afterward, Connie and I walk into the courtroom from the judge's chambers. The only person still there is June, right where we left her. She stands up. "So? What happened back there?"

I look at Connie. "Connie Cortez, this is June Williams. What you two have in common is that both of you came to me from Henry Benson." They shake hands. "Connie, it's your settlement, so if you want to discuss it with June that's fine with me but it's not my place."

Connie turns to June and begins jumping up and down in excitement. "*Dios mío, Dios mío.* I getting so much money." They hug like they've known each other forever. Connie goes on to tell her how much and what she intends to do with all her money. This can't be good.

On our way out of the courtroom I turn to June. "How did you find me?"

"Yesterday there was a piece of paper with the heading 'Verdict Sheet' sitting on the edge of your desk, so I looked at who the judge was. I called the court this morning to verify and here I am."

"I see." That was resourceful.

I hold open the big, squeaky door for us all and we make our way out. Sitting on a bench ten feet away from the courtroom door is Maddy with Melissa. Connie runs over and hugs her daughter and Maddy. They start shrieking in rapid-fire Spanish, just like Ricky Ricardo when he's excited with Lucy. This reminds me of Winnie McGillicuddy's pending motion to dismiss Suzy's case. I understand enough to know Connie told them about the big money and that she intends to buy a condo in San Juan overlooking the water. I love water views, too. June and I sit down on the bench and wait for them to finish their celebration.

"Thank you so much," Connie says to me, finally.

"Just doing my job, Connie. You deserve the money. Not being able to smell or taste anything is a horrendous injury. I'm glad we settled it because talking about all the foods you can no longer enjoy made me hungry."

"Oh, you hungry, *abogado*?" Maddy asks. "I got something." She reaches into her little sack and takes out a perfectly square golden piece of cornbread with real corn kernels baked right in. They stick out from the sides, causing my mouth to water. "Here, *abogado*. You eat this. I bake it myself last night."

I reach for it. "Thank you. It looks so good I can't wait to taste it." I turn it from side to side, deciding where to take the first bite.

I bring it to my nose for a whiff. It smells buttery-corn scrumptious. As I open my mouth, I hear Connie, still brimming with the excitement of the settlement in her voice. "You're going to love that cornbread!" she exclaims. "I had two pieces last night fresh out of the oven. It tastes just as good as it smells."

6

June and I leave the Supreme Court building together. We don't say a word and we don't look at each other. We just walk side by side down the courthouse steps right up to the hot dog cart. "What can I get you two?" the vendor asks.

"Two dogs, please," I reply. "One with mustard and kraut and one with . . . June, how do you take your dog?"

She looks at the vendor. "I'll take a sausage, yellow and dirty."

"You got it, lady," he says. We take our foil-wrapped lunch and go over to the benches that line the walkway in front of the courthouse and sit.

We begin eating in silence. I finish mine and look over at June. She catches my stare. "Yeah? Can I help you?"

"I was thinking of getting that earlier. It smells good with those onions."

"It tastes just as good as it smells, counselor." Then she gives me the "you know exactly what I mean" pause.

"Yeah. Cornbread Connie. Who knew?"

"That's fucked-up. You're thinking of dropping Suzy's case, which I know is real, but you go to court on Connie's, which is fake, and get her close to a million dollars."

"June, had I known she was faking I would've gotten out of it. Do you think I'd knowingly litigate in open court a fake case against the daughter of a federal judge?"

"Say what you want. I still think it's fucked-up."

She looks away and pushes the end piece of sausage into her mouth with authority, to punctuate her sentence. Some onion sticks to the corner of her mouth and I give her the international signal for "You got some stuff on your face." She nods and takes care of it, licking her finger in a way I find . . . distracting. She's stretching it out on purpose. And she knows I know.

At the distinct roar of an approaching car, June looks up. "There's my ride. See you tomorrow." She stands and walks casually to an old black Impala that's just pulled up to the curb. The paint and chrome are mirror finish, and there's a discernable difference in the street noise level once the engine is turned off. Before I'm done taking an inventory of the car, a giant-sized black man gets out of the driver's side, walks around the front, and opens the door for June. She gets in and he shuts the door like a true gentleman. He walks back around the nose, gets in, and ignites the engine, which rumbles like a well-tuned race car. I hear it shift into gear as it rockets away with a screech, leaving a tiny cloud of smoke. The license plate reads: THEFIDGE.

I sit on that bench for two more hours. I eat two dirty sausages as I reflect on the morning's events. I just pocketed over a hundred and fifty thousand dollars on a fake case, and I can't say a thing to anybody in an effort to cleanse my soul without breaching my oath of confidentiality, losing my license, and risking a beating from an HIC. Connie's scam was a secret to me until she admitted enjoying the cornbread. Before that, I was merely representing my client in a zealous manner, in conformity with The Rules, guaranteed to make Disciplinary Committee Judge Piccone proud. This is messed up. They should revise The Rules to cover real-life situations, because the etched-in-stone canons of ethics they contain just don't work when it comes to preserving the integrity of the system.

I get up to make my journey back to the office. I can't wait to litigate a Benson case with actual merit. I'm going to make a fortune.

Subject to Cancellation

On my subway ride I decide I'm not doing any work when I get back to the office. Instead, I'm going to find a new primary care doctor on my health plan because based on how I feel right now, I'm going to need some drug therapy to quiet my nerves. Unfortunately, my old doctor just lost his license for injudiciously prescribing narcotic medications, which was the reason I chose him in the first place. In any event, I haven't had a comprehensive physical examination in over three years, so I'm definitely due.

I walk in the office and see Lily. "Do you have that book of doctors that are on our health plan?"

"Of course. Why? Are you finally going to see a doctor for a medical reason, not just to get your pills?"

"Just give me the book." She does. "Did you call Judge Schneider and get an adjournment on the Williams motion?"

"I called her, and she gave you two weeks."

I go into my office and open up the directory to the listing of primary care doctors. I start looking for ones within five blocks so I can walk there. I call the first geographically desirable doctor and the receptionist answers. "Hello, Dr. Abel's office. This is Jean, can I help you?"

"Hi, is Dr. Abel accepting new primary care patients?"

"Yes, he is."

"Does he have any availability tomorrow afternoon?"

"If you hadn't called this very minute, you'd have had to wait three months, but I just had a cancellation. See you at three."

"Three is fine, but before I take the appointment, can I ask you something?"

"Sure. What do you need to know?"

"How tall is Dr. Abel?"

"Hmm. That's a strange question, but if you must know he's about six foot two."

"I see. Forget about it. Thanks anyway." *Click.*

I make nine more calls using every bit of my charm before I'm able to find a doctor shorter than five foot six inches tall within walking distance who can squeeze me in tomorrow afternoon.

It's been a long day so I head directly home, seeking some comfort and security. Upon my arrival my wife meets me a few feet from the front door. "Good, you're early. Change the lightbulbs in the garage," she commands.

"Yes, dear."

"Go out and pick up some dog food."

"Yes, dear."

"And go plunge Penelope's toilet."

"Yes, dear."

So much for comfort and security. And, "yes, dear" translated from *pussy-whipped* means "shove it." But I have to keep in mind that it is Tuesday night.

When I've completed the list, I enter the kitchen, where my children are seated around our oversized farm table eating pizza. As I walk in, they abruptly stop whatever they were doing, but I make no mention of their suspicious conduct. I grab the back of a chair with the intention of sitting and the kids start laughing.

"What's so funny, guys?" I ask.

"Nothing, Dad," Brooks and Connor chime. Penelope continues to laugh even harder. I sit down and all three start cracking up uncontrollably.

"Come on, let me in on it. What's so funny?"

All respond with greater hilarity. "Nothing, Dad."

Just as I'm about to ask again, I feel something moist underneath me, so I pop myself up out of the chair. I look to the source and eyeball a pile of pizza sausage stuck to my butt. The kids are laughing hysterically.

"Very funny, guys," I say, which amplifies their laughter. "Why was there a pile of sausage on this chair?"

Brooks, my nine-year-old and eldest, speaks for the group. "Mom ordered the pizza from a new place and we don't like their sausage. It's too chewy. So we were playing sausage basketball and using the chair as our hoop."

"Nice. You know the Old Marcolina never would have let you get away with that." Marcolina was our old housekeeper and our young children have chosen to call her recent replacement "the New Marcolina" for the time being.

"We know. That's why we like the New Marcolina better," Penelope, my six-year-old, explains.

As I'm cleaning the sausage off my pants, I hear my cell phone start to ring. I run to the mudroom dropping sausage on the floor, ensuring at least one more "yes, dear" if I don't clean it up before she sees it. I can't afford another "yes, dear," because like I said, it's Tuesday night, and based on how the day started with the Boca fiasco, I'm already behind the eight ball.

By the time I get to the charging station, the phone has stopped ringing. I look at the call history and it reads: PRIVATE CALLER, which can suck for me. I may've just lost a really big case and I'll never know it. I begin to walk back into the kitchen and my phone rings again. I quick-turn. "Hello?"

"Hi. I'm sorry to bother you but this is really irritating me."

I recognize the voice. "June? June Williams?"

"Yeah, it's me. I'm really mad and upset."

"How did you get my cell number?"

"I happened to see it posted above Lily's desk when she was giving me the address where I have to meet you tomorrow for Suzy's medical exam by the defendant's doctor. The numbers were easy to remember, so I did."

"Kudos to you for your resourcefulness and memory, but try only to call it for emergencies."

"This is an emergency. I've been waiting years on this case and my lawyer's telling me he may be deserting me."

"I'm not deserting you. I told you I was going to investigate things further. Listen, June, now is not the time or place to be discussing this. We'll talk about it tomorrow."

"You bet your ass we will," June states heatedly. "The Fidge said if you don't want to move forward on my case he'll handle the situation, find me an attorney . . ."

I interrupt. "Who's the Fidge? The guy who picked you up from court today?"

"No, that was Trace. He's the Fidge's driver, close personal friend, business associate, and right-hand man."

"Okay. Well, is the Fidge a lawyer?"

"No, he's not a lawyer, but he knows how to handle problems that come up in the community. You can always count on the Fidge. Anyway, you can't go around handling fake cases like that Connie Cortez's while dropping real cases involving little children like Suzy."

"Listen, June," I say in a firm tone. "I don't know what to make of Connie Cortez. All the doctors agreed she has a brain lesion, and that fact takes it out of the realm of a fake case. I'm sorry, but I got to go now. I have to clean a sausage mess from the floor before my wife comes down. I'll see you tomorrow and we'll talk about everything, including the Fidge." I hang up.

I can't really blame June for feeling the way she feels, but I don't have time to think about that now. I got to clean up the sausage stat or the night will be ruined.

You see, this evening is Tuesday Night Hand Job. It's a regularly scheduled event just like *Monday Night Football*. But unlike football, Tuesday Night Hand Job only occurs on every *other* Tuesday, and is subject to cancellation for a variety of reasons, known and unknown, without prior notice. And I have to be on my best behavior for the rest of the evening, because just after we were married it was Tuesday Night Blow Job, and there're no downgrades from here.

I wait until I know Tyler has changed, washed up, gotten into bed, played her iPad games, read her magazines, and is ready to reach for the light switch. If I enter our bedroom before that moment my longing gawk turns her off and can jeopardize things. Standing outside our door I hear some papers rustling, my signal it's time to make a move. I enter and stand before her as she lies in bed. Tyler is absolutely beautiful. Big brown eyes, high cheekbones, luscious lips, strong jaw, and a body that could kill. I mean, why not, she works that five-foot-nine frame out six hours a day doing various activities. I have the one-two planned, and the one has to be executed before I get into bed.

"Hi, honey," I say, in a kind tone despite my lame sweet-talking abilities. "I'm really sorry about this morning. I just want to say I'm looking forward to going to Boca for the holidays and seeing your parents. I even spoke with a man of religion on the train about it this morning."

"Oh good," she responds, "I'm glad you came around. It'll be fun."

"Yes. Fun. It'll be fun," I repeat mindlessly. I get into bed and slide near her. She turns toward me. We are face-to-face and she smiles. Time for the two punch in this evening's foreplay repertoire.

"Honey, guess what? I settled a monster case today."

"Oh, really. How big are we talking?"

"Nine hundred and fifty thousand." I smile, beaming with achievement.

"Wow. That is big," she responds enthusiastically. Cool, I'm getting the HJ. I feel the blood rushing to where it has to go. "Is the fee all yours?" The blood slows.

"Half, it's an HIC case, one of Henry's injured criminals." I'd tell her about the fraud, but I don't want to get involved in a diverting exchange.

"That's still a big fee." Blood flowing furiously again, my boy is on the rise. She turns away and reaches for her light switch. What the . . . what the . . . ? It's hand job first, light switch second. That's the routine. I disrupt her reach.

"Honey!"

She halts, a bit startled, and turns back to me. "What's up, Tug? Why'd you 'honey' me like that?" Maybe she doesn't realize today is Tuesday Night Hand Job.

"I said I'm sorry about this morning . . . I'm going to Boca . . . I settled a big case today, and . . . it happens to be Tuesday night."

"Oh, yes, I didn't realize," she says in an apologetic tone. "I must have lost track of the days. So it *is*, Tuesday. Give me a sec." Departing from the normal custom, she turns away and reaches again as I roll onto my back. I prefer this in the dark anyway and Tyler's the one who insists on lights to aid in her cleanup duties. She flicks the switch off and I reposition myself just right. I'm ready, but she's stalling on the rollback.

"Honey," I say, gently nudging, giving her sensual shoulder a soft touch. She motions, slightly, to start her rollback, then—

"I had to play two tiebreakers today. My opponent was one of those tennis players who kept hitting it to my backhand, every shot, over and over again, and we had long rallies, each and every point. I hit backhand after backhand after backhand, all afternoon."

"So what are you saying?"

"I'm all stroked out. You're on your own tonight, Tug."

7

The sign on the door reads: DR. LEONARD HARPER. He's a specialist in pediatric neurology. The best in the city, five years straight, according to *New York* magazine, which does an annual issue featuring the top doctors in town. He's the guy doing the physical exam on Suzy, the so-called independent medical one. Most IME doctors are medical whores for the defense bar, who are handsomely paid to conclude that the injured plaintiff has made a complete recovery, but this guy's a real doctor. I expect he'll confirm Suzy's pathetic condition without reservation and pin her disability on sickle cell complications.

Before going in, I have to shake off my salty feelings from the cancellation of TNHJ last evening. I mean, it wasn't like I was going for the forbidden fruit from the punany no-no bush, we're talking hand job. I take a deep breath and say to myself, *Accept what is.*

I enter and find June waiting in reception with Little Suzy and Dog. They're wearing matching off-white pants with tan and red plaid tops. I realize they were dressed identically on Monday, too. How'd I miss that one? June stands and approaches. She's got another big leather bag, this time tan-colored, which matches her hot boots. I guess that's her look.

She seems annoyed. "'Bout time."

I look at my fancy stainless and realize I should've worn my gold watch with this shirt-and-tie combo. What a loser I am. Not for wearing the wrong watch, but for giving it one second of thought. "June, I'm five minutes early."

"It's common courtesy to arrive fifteen minutes prior to a scheduled medical appointment."

"Says who?"

"Says every single medical receptionist I've ever had contact with and that would be quite a few. So you're ten minutes late."

"Sorry. Let's try to move past this."

"Oh, I'm past it, yo."

"June," I point out, "that's the first time you've used slang."

"Well, you better hope you don't hear it again. When I get mad I can't control the ghetto in me."

"Then don't get mad."

"I know this is just another case for you, Mr. Big-Time Lawyer, but this is my life and Suzy's life, and you're about to turn them upside down." She gives me the stare. The emotions are love and hate. I'd love to get some of her, and maybe she hates me.

We're in a bad place and we're only two days in. I'm pretty sure it's my fault, so I need to change things. "You know something? You're right," I tell her. "I've been insensitive to your situation and I promise it won't happen again. I can't promise you I'll continue with Suzy's case, but I do promise to handle whatever time I have left in this matter with compassion and sensitivity."

"That's acceptable. Now check in. We're being rude." I feel good about this interaction but question my own integrity. Was I taking the path of least resistance, or did I really mean what I said?

Every Scar Has a Story

We quickly find ourselves in an exam room. A moment later, a very distinguished elderly man walks in and looks at us. "Hello, I'm Dr. Leonard Harper and this must be Suzy," he says, caressing her face with his soft old hand.

The tactile stimulation brings a smile to Suzy's face. "Sch-weet," she says.

"You're the sweet one, darling," Dr. Harper responds. He turns to June. "I'll need you to disrobe this adorable little girl and put her in the gown hanging behind the door. I'll be back in five minutes." He leaves the room.

When Dr. Harper refers to Suzy as "adorable" I realize I don't even know what she looks like, the particulars of her appearance. I thought I was going to get out of the case, so registering her appearance in my office never crossed my mind. I hadn't even realized she and June had been wearing matching outfits, for God's sake. All I saw was a mangled little girl with a bad brain injury. I assessed her for value and felt what a waste of a catastrophic injury it was not to make any money from. There was no humanity involved. June's clearly justified in feeling the way she does and I realize my attitude was the cause. I now know I really didn't mean what I said to June a few moments ago about compassion and sensitivity. The way Dr. Harper interacted with Suzy as a person rather than as an income source made me see my insincerity. From this point forward I pledge commitment to this cause in the most sensitive of ways, case or no case. I look to June.

"I'll wait outside, June."

"No, you stay. You need to see what they did to my baby."

June picks up the pup. "Here, hold Dog," she says to me. "She needs to be on somebody's lap." I pet Dog as June takes off Suzy's clothing in that wheelchair, with the child seemingly unaware of her environment. I say seemingly because there's no real medical way to verify how much children like her are aware of something lawyers like me would love to know when assessing monetary damages. And something I'd like to know just from a human perspective. Suzy's shoes and pants came off easily, but June has to struggle to get her shirt off with her contorted arms flapping. "Come on now, Suzy," June coaxes. "Mommy has to take it off."

"Does she always struggle like that when you're trying to take her shirt off?" I ask.

"Always. She's embarrassed about her scar."

"She's what?"

June restates her words in a slow, deliberate manner. "She's embarrassed about her scar, just like a normal person would be." When June finally wrestles the shirt off her arms, Suzy immediately, and in the most spastic of ways, folds her arms across her chest like she's covering something up. "See, I told you. She doesn't want you to see her scar. I know she has the brain of an infant, but she's self-conscious about her scar. I can't explain it."

I look at Suzy. She's struggling to keep her uncontrollable arms folded in one place. They're shaking back and forth but she manages to keep covered the area she wants to hide from us. It's the most cerebral behavior I've witnessed thus far. "June," I ask, "what's the scar from?"

"When they resuscitated her on the day this all happened, they used those defib paddles on her chest and it left her with a scar."

"That can happen," I explain. "Defib paddles can burn the skin. But generally they don't leave a permanent scar."

"In this case they had to use adult-sized paddles since they were the only ones available. I was told it saved her life but left her with bad scarring."

"Would you mind if I took a look at it?"

"I don't mind, but I think Suzy will."

"Can you open her arms so I can see? I'm curious."

"I'll try." June gently grasps Suzy by her wrists. She begins to resist, causing June to coax, "Come on, baby, let your soon-to-be ex-lawyer see that scar." She attempts to pry open her daughter's arms. Suzy grunts and snorts as the two struggle. "Come on, baby. Please open those arms," June urges, but to no avail.

"June. Stop. Please." June lets go of Suzy and their arm wrestle ends in a draw. "Can I have a crack at it?"

June starts laughing. "Oh, sure. Go right ahead, Mr. Sensitivity."

I kneel down on one knee on the right side of Suzy's wheelchair. That's the side her head is cocked to from the tension of the fibrous adhesions that have developed in the soft tissues of her neck area. I'm in the traditional "will you marry me" position and I'm looking up at

Suzy's twitching face. It's my first close-up, and I can tell by her features she must have been a beautiful girl. I say "must have been" because you have to block out the tongue protrusion, crossed eyes, mild drooling, and general overall look of a brain injury to access her beauty.

I speak to her in a mellow whisper. "Hey, Suzy. I know you can hear me. Maybe not understand me, but I know you can hear me. I want to apologize to you for acting like such a schmuck. *Schmuck* is a Yiddish word that means 'stupid person.' You see, I figured I was gonna turn down your case, which is basically what I'm still gonna do, so I depersonalized you. That was wrong and I am sorry." Her trembling has lessened a little bit and she seems interested in what I have to say, although I'm relatively certain she can't understand one single word. But you never know.

I continue softly. "Suzy, as long as I'm coming forward with my own shortcomings, I'll have to also admit the only reason I came here today is because your mom has a smoking tight ass and I've already fantasized about her in a very carnal way." I look up at June and she gives me the response I was hoping for, a smile. I take Suzy's rigid contorted hand into mine. "Suzy, if you let me move your arms open so I can see your scar your mom over here is going to think I have some special powers. If she thinks that, I truly believe it will increase my chances of getting a little romance sooner rather than later." I look up at June and her smile broadens. But I imagine she knows I'm just being playful, not serious. I think.

I whisper some more. "So, I'm going to slowly move your arms open and I don't want you to resist because I could use a little stimulation in my life at this point. I know that's selfish, again, but at least I admit it. Most people are in denial of their faults."

I slowly open Suzy's arms. The only resistance I feel is involuntary from the contractures that plague the musculature of her entire upper limbs. Otherwise, Suzy appears to be relaxed and fully compliant. As I open her arms, it feels really weird because nothing is moving naturally the way it's supposed to. Every joint seems frozen. As I apply more force I get more resistance of the kind you feel stretching out a rubber band. I continue to open her arms outward slowly, and it reminds me of those enormous curtains parting to begin a Broadway show.

I finally get to see the scar my little client is so ashamed of. It's a round scar on her chest, left of center. Suzy's skin was not just charred as you would expect from the shock of defibrillation paddles; it was excessively burned. Also, its contour is inconsistent with the shape of defib paddles as I know them to be, and so a question occurs to me. Why just one geometrically shaped scar? I look up, and Suzy is watching me eyeball her scar like she knows something. Then, all of the sudden, we make eye contact. Sustained eye contact. We have connected the most we ever will. She knows something, and this is the best she can do to get her message across. Weird.

Her scar reminds me of a time when my wife went to pick up a half-eaten Tootsie Roll off our kitchen floor. "What's the matter with you kids? You're a bunch of slobs!" La Comandante yelled. She picked it up and held it out. "I want to know who left this Tootsie Roll on the floor."

My son, Connor, looked up from his handheld gaming device. "Mom, dat ain't no Tootsie Roll."

My wife put it up to her nose for the smell test. "What is it?"

"A dried-up piece of cat shit Otis ate out of the litter box," Connor casually informed her.

From my kneeling position, I now say to June, "Dat ain't no defibulation paddle scar."

"Then what's it from?"

"I'm not sure what it is. I'm just sure what it's not. When Dr. Harper comes back I'll try to get him to give us his opinion. You keep quiet about it. Let me do the lawyering." She nods. I place Suzy's arms back over the scar. "Thank you, Suzy," I say. June moves in and puts the gown on her daughter.

Two raps sound, and Dr. Harper enters, acknowledging each of us with a nod. He begins the routine exam on Suzy as she's seated in her wheelchair, her arms folded. He seems to have a way with her, so I'm eager to see what happens when he goes to pull her arms apart. He makes his move and Suzy resists as expected, adding a few grunts to the mix. Dr. Harper turns to us. "Does she always do this?"

June responds, "Always."

"Why?" he asks.

"Because she's sensitive about her paddle scar," June blurts out before I get a chance to form an answer that will elicit Dr. Harper's opinion about the scar. So much for lawyering.

Dr. Harper shrugs slightly. "I have to evaluate her upper body. How can we get her arms open and robe off?"

"Doc, I'll help you out here," I offer. I kneel down to make my second proposal and start whispering again for Suzy's ear only. "Listen, Suzy, I got to get this guy's opinion as to what that scar is on your chest. It may also further my efforts to get inside your mommy's panties, although I'm not sure I have it in me to cheat on my wife. But I did promise my mother, who is pretty sick, I would always be open to other women, yet I seem to get in my own way when it comes to closing the deal. Anyway, please unfold your arms for me. Please, Suzy. Your mom already blew it with her big mouth, so let me play my lawyer game." Suzy lets me open her arms, and Dr. Harper steps in to take down her robe. He listens to her heartbeat with his stethoscope and does a few finger thuds on her chest and abdomen. I pose my question. "Dr. Harper, how did she get that scar from a defib paddle?"

"That's not a paddle scar," he states, "that scar is from a defibrillation patch."

"What's that?" I ask.

"There are generally two ways to deliver a therapeutic dose of electrical energy by defibrillation in a hospital setting to reestablish the heart's normal sinus rhythm. One is by use of a metal paddle known as a resuscitation electrode with an insulated handle that the physician manually holds in place on the patient's skin in the chest area while a shock or a series of shocks are delivered. This is the method the medical television shows like to glorify because it's very dramatic when the doctor yells 'Clear!' then shocks the patient." He takes his stethoscope out of his ears. "The other type of resuscitation electrodes are designed as adhesive pads or patches that are applied to the patient's chest wall on one end and to a defibrillator machine at the other. No one has to yell 'Clear' because of the direct contact. This form is generally used on patients being monitored and at risk for a cardiac event by the very same machine that delivers the resuscitation shock."

"Isn't defibrillation achieved by delivering the electric current with the axis of the heart situated directly between the two resuscitation electrodes?" I ask.

"That's exactly right."

"Why, then, is there only one scar?"

"I'm certain there's a reasonable explanation," Harper says sternly, "but I haven't been asked to review any records in this matter and I'm not a cardiologist. I was just asked to perform an IME on this child, and I might add they're throwing away their money. Anyone can see Suzy's clearly a spastic quadriplegic. We're done here. You can get her dressed now." As Dr. Harper begins to leave the room, he turns back to us. "I'm sorry about the condition of your daughter, Mrs. Williams. Complications from a sickle cell crisis can be devastating, as you are well aware. Good day."

June's only response is one of a corrective nature. "It's Ms. Williams, Doctor." I can tell from her tone she's holding in the ghetto girl. June watches the door close behind him and then turns to me. "Oh no. No, no, no."

"June," I tell her, "stay in control."

"Oh, don't worry. I'm in control. He's wrong."

"I'm listening."

"Suzy was defibbed with paddles, not with patches. This I'm certain of."

"How?"

"First, by the sound of things going on in that room."

"Sound?"

"Yes, the sound," June states firmly. "They ordered me out of the room, but I sat down just at the edge of the doorway and could hear everything that was going on in there. They wheeled a special cart by me into the room. A crash cart. What I heard after that was someone yelling, 'Clear!' just like Harper said. You hear me?"

"I hear ya. Go on."

"After they carried Suzy off to another part of the hospital, I just sat there outside her room, leaning up against the wall with my head in my hands for what seemed like an eternity. This lady stayed there and comforted me for a while, but I didn't look up even once and she finally let me be. The first time I picked my head up was when some men in orange uniforms looking like maintenance workers came to Suzy's room and wheeled out the two carts."

"Two crash carts?"

"No. One was a cart with a broken wheel that made a *click-click* sound with a heart monitor on it that Dr. Valenti had ordered and the other was the crash cart. They wheeled them right past me and the crash cart had paddles on it. I saw them."

"That's pretty clear evidence," I say. "I'm with you on this, June. I won't be applying to the court to be relieved as Suzy's lawyer until I can make some sense out of that scar. Something's not right. Every scar has a story and I'm going to figure out the story behind Suzy's."

June grabs my cheeks, smooshing up my lips with her hand just like my nana did when I was a kid. She'd say how cute I was, giving an extrahard squeeze for emphasis. June now looks me in the eye, with an added squeeze of her own, and says, "Now that's a good lawyer." As she releases her kung fu grip, I feel the warmth of blood rushing back into my face.

Unexpectedly, she reaches into her tan bag and extracts a video-tape. Suzy sees it. "Sch-weet, sch-weet, sch-weet," she says excitedly as Dog tries to balance herself on her tilting lap.

"What's that?"

"It's Suzy's fifth birthday party. I don't want you to think my daughter's only what you see here. She's a lot more. Suzy may not be on the outside the girl you'll see on this tape, but that same girl is inside of her." June hands me the tape, which causes Suzy to start bucking back and forth in defiance. June looks at her. "Don't worry, baby. We'll get it back. I just want your lawyer to see who you were." June turns to me. "Guard this tape with your life. I don't have a copy and Suzy insists on watching it every evening before going to sleep."

"It's safe with me. Don't worry," I assure her. I bend down to Suzy. "Don't you worry, either, Suzy." After dressing her, June starts to wheel Suzy toward the door. "June," I call.

She stops and turns. "Yes?"

"How did you become one of Henry Benson's clients? I mean, how do you know him?"

"I didn't know him. My husband did."

"How did your husband know Henry Benson?"

"Henry was my husband's lawyer."

"Criminal?"

"Very," June replies.

"What were the charges against him?"

"A better question is, what *weren't* the charges against him? My husband was a bad man. Very bad."

"Why do you say he *was* a bad man? Has he changed?"

"You could say that."

"In what way?"

"Well, he's no longer with us."

"I'm sorry to hear that."

"Don't be. We're all a lot safer without him around."

"You know best. Look, I got to go. I have a doctor's appointment of my own."

"Good luck at your doctor."

"Thanks."

I leave the building. Parked at the curb is that old black car again with the deep-sounding idle and the license plate that reads: THEFIDGE. It's a 1962 Impala SS with the distinctive bubble top and all the right badges. I look in as I walk by but can see only a shadow of a person through the smoked windows. After walking a block or so, I hear in the distance that same distinctive burnout sound I heard when the Impala peeled away from the courthouse curb.

Linking and Connecting

I walk through the door of my new doctor's office with Suzy's party video in hand. The only person in the waiting area is a twentysomething hot tamale. She's sporting a colorful Pucci print top, fashion-forward jeans, and casual Prada flats. Last year's. Her one lapse is the outdated Kieselstein-Cord belt, the one with the sterling silver buckle in the form of an alligator. It was a status symbol back in the 1980s. At least on Long Island it was.

Despite my inclination, I make eye contact with the receptionist instead. "Hi, I'm the doctor's three o'clock."

She hands me a clipboard. "Fill this out, please."

I look straight down at my clipboard and begin entering my personal information. From the peripheral vision of my peripheral vision I can see Tamale checking me out as I pretend not to notice. A few minutes go by and I realize I have to engage her because once she's called in for her appointment she's gone forever. So I decide to make creative use of my medical form.

"Name," I say out loud, then start scribbling on the clipboard. "Date of birth," I say aloud, leaning down to write again. My sixth sense tells me she's turned her head in my direction. Perfect. I pause, and straighten up. "Social security number," I remark as I jot some more. She's still looking at the guy talking to himself. "Sex," I say aloud, tilting my head in her direction for the very first time. When our eyes lock, I resume my monologue in an especially husky tone. "Most definitely, but never on the first date."

She laughs out loud, and I know she's my kind of girl. When you're hot, you're hot. I know it's unlikely I'd ever commit an act of marital treason against my wife, but if I did it could only be with someone who has a sophisticated fourth-grade sense of humor like mine. "Come here often?" I ask.

Tamale bites. "Sure do. Do you?"

"This is my first time. Is the doctor gentle?"

"That's an interesting question, but yes, he's very gentle. Why, what are you here for? Oh, I'm sorry. I know better than to ask that question."

"No, I don't mind. I believe in open and honest communication. I'm here for my genital herpes. I'm having a massive flare-up. How about you? What are you here for? Or shouldn't I ask?"

"No, I don't mind, either. My vagina schvitzes every time I ride the subway. I think it's the vibrations. It's very embarrassing when it seeps through to my clothing."

"Oh, I've heard of that before. Subway Schvitzing Vagina Disorder, or SSVD. I'm sorry to hear you have it, but it's better than the other kinds of VD. I thought SSVD only affected Jewish girls."

"I'm half Jewish; my mom. She's a schvitzer, too. It's a hereditary disorder."

"Those hereditary disorders can be a disaster. I'm a lawyer and represent a little girl who appears to have had a severe complication from her hereditary disease, but I'm less convinced of that now than I was about an hour ago."

"Well, SSVD doesn't have any severe complications, I'm happy to report, and I'm sorry to hear about that little girl and also about your herpes." Tamale pauses for a second. It's the type of pause when the pauser is deciding whether to take the conversation to the next level or end it.

Tamale goes for it. She asks, "So, what are you really here for?"

"I'm a little embarrassed to tell you, but I'm consulting the doctor for a penile reduction." A loud bang comes from behind the reception window like someone fell off a chair. We both look in the direction of the sound, but no one's there. We smile. I shrug my shoulders. "How about you? What are you really here for?"

"Well, I'm a little embarrassed, too. I'm consulting for a vaginal rejuvenation."

"At your age!" I exclaim. "Wow. They're doing that younger and younger these days. My wife had her crumbling cookie rejuvenated on the day she gave birth to our third child."

"Really?"

"No, not really. I mean, it was a modified rejuvenation. I slipped her OB/GYN a fifty for an extra stitch as he was suturing up her episiotomy cut to tighten things up."

"Is that all it cost?"

"Actually, it's fifty per stitch, so it cost me two fifty cash."

Suddenly, we both start laughing. Then Tamale goes for a more serious tone. "So now I have two questions for you. Are you really married with kids and what are you really here for?"

"Yes, I'm really married with kids and I'm here to get drugs. My previous doctor was nice enough to overprescribe drugs for me, but unfortunately, he lost his license for overprescribing drugs. It's a good news–bad news story."

"What kind of drugs?" Tamale wonders.

"Prescription medications, the good kind. Have those answers changed things between us?"

Before she gets a chance to answer, the door next to reception opens inward and my new doctor, Dr. Vargas, walks out. He's a tiny guy, exactly as I preselected when making the calls. He looks at me. "Are you my new patient?"

"Yes, I am."

"I see you've met my daughter," he says, then turns to Tamale. "This gentleman is my last patient, Lisa. Did you tell your mother I was taking you shopping after school today?"

"Yes, Daddy."

Shopping after school? Mommy? Daddy? Jesus.

Dr. Vargas turns back to me. "Right this way." I comply, continuing to be a little confused about Tamale and her life experiences. We enter an exam room. "What can I do for you?" Dr. Vargas asks.

"I need an annual exam. It's been awhile. I should also be right up front with you, I'm looking for drugs."

"If drugs are medically indicated, I don't have a problem with that, but first we have to do a comprehensive exam and evaluation."

"Consider me a compliant patient, Doctor."

"Take everything off but your underwear." I do. He draws blood, weighs me, listens to my heart, and performs several other routine exams. "You're at the age where it's standard practice to begin check-ing the prostate for enlargement."

"I know that, Doctor."

"The prostate," he explains, "is checked by a physician performing a digital rectal exam."

"I know that, too."

Dr. Vargas walks over to his supplies cabinet and speaks with his back toward me. "I'll need you to turn on your side." I hear the snapping sound of a latex-free rubber glove making its way onto his hand. I roll to my side and hear the telltale sound of K-Y Jelly being squeezed out of a near-empty container. Dr. Vargas moves behind me. "I hope this won't be too uncomfortable for you."

"I'm counting on it not being. I went through a sophisticated screening process and chose you based on your expected hand size."

"Really?" He makes his move.

"Your daughter was right," I say after the deed has been done. "You're a gentle man."

As Dr. Vargas snaps off the rubber glove, he begins to extol his daughter's many virtues. "She's a wonderful girl. Beautiful and in the top of her class. She's going to go to NYU next year. She wants to stay around town."

"Great," I say, thinking to myself I hope no ass like me has a con-versation with my daughter at that age like the one I just had with his. What kind of idiot am I? At least that explains her receptiveness, lack of life experience.

"Now, we have one last thing to do here. I'm going to perform an EKG. Have you ever had one done before?"

"Actually, no, I haven't. I know I'm past due."

"You certainly are, so we're going to get a baseline on your heart pattern in case you ever have trouble in the future. I'm going to send in my tech to perform the study and we'll talk in my office afterward about your pharmacological desires."

"See you in a few," I reply.

Into my exam room a few minutes later walks Marta, as her name tag informs me. "Good afternoon," she says. "I'm here to perform an

EKG to make sure your ticker is tocking right. It shouldn't take too long. Now lie flat on your back, and relax. I do all the work."

I comply, allowing her to do her thing, but the relaxing part ends as soon as Marta displays a round white object. "This is an electrode patch," she tells me. It instantly triggers a replay of what Dr. Harper said during Suzy's IME.

Marta's patch is the same size and shape as the scar on Suzy's chest. She moves over me and places it on my chest in the same location as Suzy's scar. Marta continues to put four more electrode patches on my upper body—one on each arm and two more on my chest as I make copious mental notes every step of the way. All five patches that she applies have little receptor holes elevated up off the bull's-eye of the patch. Marta then inserts into these receptors the metal prong-like ends of plastic-coated lead wires. After that she plugs the other end of the lead wires into a piece of plastic housing and plugs that into a cord leading into the cardiac monitor.

"Marta," I ask, "does this shock me? Will I feel anything?"

Marta laughs. "No. These patches merely obtain information from the electrical activity of your heart and send it through the lead wires to the machine for interpretation. That old machine isn't sending anything to your heart. Now, let me finish this test."

"Why are you calling that machine old?"

"Because it is. Nowadays we use simple snap-on caps to connect the lead wires to the patches, not these antiquated prong things, but Dr. Vargas doesn't want to spend the cash for the upgrade yet." So Suzy's machine may have been outdated, too. After Marta's done, she says, "Get dressed and then go into the doctor's office, which is two doors down on your right."

"Will do."

I enter the doctor's office. "Please, sit down," Dr. Vargas says. "I went over your questionnaire and have some follow-up."

"Shoot," I respond.

"What kind of lawyer are you?"

"Does it matter?"

"No."

"Then I'm a malpractice lawyer. I sue physicians like yourself who practice medicine outside of the parameters of good and accepted medical standards, customs, and practices."

"Good for you," Dr. Vargas replies. "I see so much malpractice in my hospital affiliations and most of it just gets swept under the rug. Physicians are supposed to come forth with their errors but none ever do. It's all about burying the mistakes at the expense of the patient."

"I couldn't agree with you more, Doctor. Most physicians don't share your point of view."

"Those would be the ones to watch out for." We share a pause, a smile, and a nod. "I also noted you've been on a variety of medications in the past to help you lose weight. Stay away from those. I would suggest as a start to order your meals in from one of those programs."

"Duly noted. Now can we talk about my drugs?"

"What are you looking for? Oxycodone?"

"Doc," I assure him, "I got a lot of dependencies, but semisynthetic opioid analgesics is not one of them. I just want a little Xanax now and then to take the edge off."

"Will ten milligrams do?"

"Twenty-five would do better."

"Fifteen."

"Deal."

On my way out Tamale is sitting just where I left her. "Have fun shopping with your dad," I say.

"That's it?"

"What else is left but a cordial good-bye?"

"I thought we had a connection. You're different."

"No doubt we connected, but I thought you were much older. Our moons are in different phases. Timing is everything, and I'm obviously losing track of it, given my cluelessness about your age."

"Forget about it. It happens all the time," she assures me. I offer a mature smile.

In the elevator down from Dr. Vargas's office my mind is going in multiple directions, linking and connecting the events of the last few days. I make a mental numeration that breaks down like this:

1. This morning I saw a round scar on Little Suzy's chest Dr. Harper claimed was a defib patch scar, despite June's insistence that paddles had been used. This afternoon an identically shaped electrode patch was applied to the exact same spot on my chest for purposes of cardiac monitoring, in the same way, basically, that my mother's heart was being monitored in ICU, with a similar device.

2. I selected Dr. Vargas based on my estimation of his hand size because modern medicine still hasn't managed to invent a scan for the prostate. And it turns out that he's one of the rare doctors critical of the medical community for covering up such malpractice as he sees routinely in hospital settings.

3. I represent a little girl who was injured in a hospital setting and the only explanation I have for her condition is the always suspect *C* word, *complication.*

On my first step onto the sidewalk I take out my phone and hit a speed-dial key. One ring later, Lily picks up. "Law Office. Can I help you?"

"It's me."

"Hi, me, what do *you* want?" she says in a snippy voice.

"Babysitter issues?"

"As always. Now what do you want?"

"Please pull out the hospital chart for the admission of Suzy Williams when she sustained her injury and leave it on my chair before you go."

"You mean you can't pull some medicals out of a file for yourself?"

"No. I could, but I'm asking you to do it so I don't have to search for anything when I get back. Am I asking too much?"

"It's not that you're asking too much, it's just that you could do it yourself."

"Just put the Williams file on my chair before you leave and I'll pull the records out myself."

"So you want me to move the Williams file from the corner of your desk and put it on your chair?"

"Never mind."

"Bert Beecher called three times for you in the last few minutes and is anxious to talk. I told him you'd call him back. You want his cell?"

"I'll call him when I get back. I'm on my way now."

I have no idea why I stay married to my wife and keep Lily as my paralegal. These two women have the kind of strength most men wish they had and continually use it to push me around. I must possess some kind of genetic disorder that makes me attracted to tough women who don't seem all that interested in making life easier for me. Maybe I have SOMBS—Step On My Balls Syndrome, a condition that causes the women I love to keep my nuts under foot pressure. The fact of the matter is that Lily's right in this instance. At least I admit it.

walk the few blocks back to my office, clutching the videotape. My plan is to view it, look at the records, then go home. About twenty feet from my building my peripheral identifies a large object coming from my right carrying a man's Gucci handbag. Bert Beecher.

He casually walks over in a nonthreatening manner from the heap he'd been leaning on, illegally parked at the curb, and angles in front of me so as to break my stride. "I was going to call you when I got upstairs," I tell him. "What's up, Bert?"

"I want to know what those things are you said were in conflict with my claim between the statement I gave under oath and Betty's medical records. And I want to know now."

"Bert, that's a great idea, but there's a lot to discuss. Why don't we make an appointment instead of you stalking around in front of my building waiting for me to return?"

"An appointment. That's a good idea. I'd like to make an appointment right now to see you right now. How's that?"

"I'm a little busy right now." I flash him the tape so as to say, "I got to watch this."

"Porn?" he asks.

"No, Bert, it's not pornography. It's a videotape of one of my clients and I'm committed to watching it and going over the medical records pertaining to it right now."

Bert smiles, but it's not the happy kind. It's the type of smile someone gives you just before they inform you that you have an unexpected change in plan. Without choice. "Fine," he says. "You can do that after we talk."

I take the sidewalk of least resistance. I give him the international hand gesture for "after you."

In the elevator up I switch the tape into my left hand and wipe my sweaty right palm on my pant leg. I take a look at the label for the first time. It features colorful yellow and orange flowers with green stems drawn in Magic Marker around the entire edge, acting as a frame to the inscription. In a child's handwriting in red marker it reads: MY 5TH BIRTHDAY PARTY. Suzy must have personalized the label at some point after her party and before her injury.

My left palm is sweaty now so I switch the tape back. I look at my palm and it's smeared with yellow, orange, green, and red marker. This guy makes me nervous.

As we enter my office suite Lily is speeding out. "Got to go," she says. "I'll make it up. Bye." She vanishes into the elevator we just left.

It's All in the Records, Bert

"Come on, Bert," I tell him, "we've got some serious talking to do." He follows me into my office. It's just him and me. My drug-running ten-ants from *TOKE* magazine are even gone, having fled the country this week for their annual junket to Amsterdam to restock supplies. I don't like it, but at least I've got the desk between us. "Now do you remember what you said about your sex life with Betty when you gave oral testimony under oath?"

"Of course I do. That's when I told them how my sex life sucked with my wife because of that doctor leaving those lenses in her eyes."

"Correct. You were very emphatic about the intimacy compromise from what I read in the transcript."

"That's right. Sex sucked after the surgery and it was great before."

"That would be the perfect scenario to get you money from a jury for your claim, and it appears you knew exactly that prior to giving testimony."

"That's right. I discussed it with Benson before the questioning."

"I figured you were in the prep bubble with Henry because your testimony read like it was scripted. Great sex before, shitty sex after. It read contrived especially because any juror who's married is going to know the truth anyway."

"What do you mean by that?"

"A truthful answer would've been 'sex was okay with my wife before the surgery and a little less than okay after.'" Bert gets my point. I continue. "Now we must deal with how defense counsel is going to cross-examine you on this. They will attempt to have the jury believe your sex life with Betty sucked, as you've termed it, prior to the date of the malpractice, and that nothing about her dry eyes had any effect on your already sucky sex life."

Beecher starts laughing. "How the fuck they going to do that? They weren't in my bedroom and Betty ain't going to say anything different."

"She already has."

Beecher starts slowly motioning his right hand open, then closed. Violently. Murderously. Only at this moment, there's no handgrip exerciser in it. "What the fuck you talking about?" he asks crossly.

"Her medicals, Bert. Her gynecological records that predate her eye injury say something different and it's all going to come out in court. How your wife felt about having sex with you and your aptitude as a lover *before* her dry eyes." I pull some medicals out of the file Henry gave me. "These are her records right here." I wave them in Bert's face from a safe distance. If he doesn't agree to 5 percent after what's about to happen next, then he'll deserve the 50 as compensation for his public humiliation.

"Let me see those," he angrily demands.

"I'm sorry, but I can't do that."

Beecher has started to approach rage status. "You can and you will. Now let me see them!" He gets up with obvious intent.

"Sit back down, Bert," I direct in a firm voice to disguise my fright, wishing Otis were here. Beecher tilts his head to the right and gives me the evil stare. Things are tense, but then he slowly sits back down. "I can't and I won't show you these records because of attorney-client privilege, so please don't ask again. I must tell you I feel threatened by your conduct. It's probably not a good thing to do that to the guy who's trying to get you money. Besides, I'm uncertain if I'm a 'fight or flight' guy and I don't want to find out against you."

"A pussy like you is a flight guy," he replies with a hint of challenge.

"Bert, we have a situation here, and it's not between you and me. Let's not complicate things with personal attacks."

He doesn't respond so I take the opportunity to have a little internal dialogue. I say to myself, *I hate Bert Beecher. He's a bad guy who's trying to shake down his wife for money he's not entitled to. He needs to be shown he can't go around bullying everybody. He needs his face rubbed in the reality of you can't always get what you want—and I'm going to take satisfaction in doing it. Yeah, you want to see your wife's records? Then you can see them, fucker.*

I focus on him again. "Are you the kind of guy who can keep a secret, Bert? I mean, if I show you Betty's records, could you keep it between us guys?"

"I'm a lot of things, but I ain't no stoolie. Secrets are my specialty."

"Heck, I'll show you her records, then. Would you mind if I came around this big desk separating us and sat next to you?"

"No, I don't mind. Just let me see them."

"Coming right up." I move around and sit in the chair next to him. I put the records down in front of both of us and open them up. "Can you see good, Bert?"

"Perfect."

"Excellent. I don't want you to miss anything. Apparently, Betty made some complaints to her gynecologist that are inconsistent with a great sex life before the malpractice."

"I doubt that."

"I understand. That's a natural reaction, but I'm pretty sure the truth of the matter is she hated having sex with you."

Beecher starts turning red. "I totally doubt that," he grumbles angrily.

I point to the chart. "Look at this entry right here. Over a year before the malpractice it reads, and I'll quote: 'I hate having sex with my husband.' See?" I point with emphasis to the chart again. "It says 'I hate having sex with my husband' right here." I start tapping on the entry with my finger. Beecher looks but has no response.

I go on. "Let me show you something else. Over the next three-month period, your wife submitted to a battery of tests in an effort to ascertain if there was an organic basis for her hating to have sex with you. That means they evaluated things such as the size of her vagina, its moisture content, whether or not it had any bacterial organisms, anatomic abnormalities, such as a variation in its shape that would contribute to her having complaints of pain during sex, and other things that would explain why she couldn't stand having sex with you. They concluded nothing was wrong with her organically, meaning her equipment was completely normal. Are you with me on this, Bert?"

No response.

"They also took a medical history from her," I continue. "She said you were the first person whom she ever hated having sex with. Let me show you. See?" I hammer my finger into the chart. Beecher looks at the record and says nothing at first, then takes a stab at reason.

"If she did complain of pain while having sex with me, which I'm sure she didn't, despite what those records say, then maybe my package was too big for her. Yeah, that was it. My package is too big."

"That would be the first thing I'd say in my own defense. Good for you. You're thinking like a lawyer with a big dick, Bert. Now I have to go out for a minute. Look through these records while I'm gone. There's some other stuff in there, too. They got a lot of info on you and your penis for cross-examination. I'll be right back." I exit my office, leaving Bert looking all rattled. I head for the elevator.

I go down to the lobby and walk out with a purpose. Snacks. I go next door into Deli-De-Lite to pick up some beef jerky and a big bag of popcorn to munch on during the second act of the Bert Beecher show. Since they're out of jerky I go for the beef stick. Okay, two beef sticks. One hot and one teriyaki.

I go back upstairs and sit down next to Bert, who's using his finger to read the records, one word at a time. "Beef stick?" I offer, tilting one in his direction.

"I don't eat that shit."

After demolishing both sticks while watching Bert try to make sense of the handwritten doctor's entries, I take out the large bag of popcorn. Beecher looks up. "Popcorn?" I offer.

"Yeah. I'll take some of that." His monster-sized hand barely makes it into the open bag. He comes out with half the popcorn. Figures—half, his favorite percentage.

As he swallows a handful, I start in. "Where were we? Oh yeah, you were saying your package was too big. That's something her doctors definitely considered." I slide the records back so they're between us, then turn a few pages. "Yes, here it is." I point to what looks like a multiple-choice question. Bert leans over to see. "Look at these three questions in large print," I say. "The first question instructs, 'Circle one,' and reads: 'I consider my partner's penis small, medium, or large.' Betty circled the word *small*. See, right here? She circled the word *small*. See it right here? Is that the way she makes a circle, Bert? Is that her circle right there around the word *small*?"

Beecher says nothing, but clearly he's agitated.

I could stop. But I don't. "The next question reads: 'I would describe the thickness of my partner's penis as thin, medium, or thick.' Your wife circled the word *thin*. See it right here? Are you looking where I'm pointing, Bert? It says 'thin' right here. See it?" Beecher says nothing, his complexion reddening.

I carry on. "The next question states: 'When making love to my partner, I reach an orgasm never, some of the time, or always.' Betty circled the word *never*. See it? Right here. 'Never.' It's right here." Beecher is just about at a boil. Perfect. I turn the page. "Look at this entry, Bert. It reads: 'Patient states her partner would measure less than four inches when aroused, ruling out a mechanical basis for her pain from her slightly anteverted uterus.'"

Bert, now steaming, keeps his head down. Looking at the record, he says nothing.

"According to the impression on the next page," I say, "their conclusion was your wife has a psychosomatic disorder relative to having sex with you."

"What's that? Something's wrong with her, right?"

"Um, no. That means since there wasn't anything abnormal with either of you physically, the only explanation was the way she felt about you. In effect, Betty hated you and hated having sex with you, so her subconscious conjured up some nonsense pain response associated with your intimacy. Let me show you, right here next to the word *impression*. See?" Beecher looks and says nothing. His eyes are now bloodshot, presumably from elevated pressure.

"Since you want money for a loss suffered to the quality of the marital intimacy," I tell him, "and since these records generated before the malpractice say things inconsistent with this claim, the jury will hear it all, as it goes to your credibility. I also might add these gynecological records indicate your wife tested positive for venereal disease on two separate occasions prior to the malpractice. There's actually a quote that reads: 'My husband gave me VD,' as a presenting complaint on one of these visits. See? Look right here for yourself."

Beecher looks and becomes belligerent, defensive, and attacking all at once. "She was the one who gave me the VD!" After his outburst, Bert looks both deflated and defeated. It seems he has learned the lesson I set out to teach him. I just sit, watch, wait, and continue to eat popcorn in the stillness of the moment, curious to hear what he has to say next.

Finally, after about a minute, Bert speaks up. "Listen," he says, "I knew about these entries. They're wrong. In fact, Betty wrote a letter asking the doctor to correct her record."

"Really? That's helpful. We need to get a copy of that letter because the doctor didn't make it a part of her permanent chart."

"I'll get it from Betty and if she don't got a copy I'll make her write it again, yeah, that's what I'll do."

"So long as you deal with her in a civil manner, that would be fine."

"You saying I ain't civil?" he challenges.

"Not at all, Bert, not at all. But I'd suggest the five percent is very acceptable in light of these entries. I mean, it's all in the records, Bert, and I'd hate to see this stuff come out in court. Those VD entries offer the jury the option to give you nothing, and we're not talking about the schvitzing kind of VD either."

"The what kind?" Bert asks.

"Nothing, Bert," I respond, underestimating him again.

"I need to think about this shit. You're supposed to be my lawyer and you're fucking forcing me to take, like, nothing while Betty gets it all."

"Listen, Bert. I'm new to this case and these entries have been in existence long before I ever got involved. Don't shoot the messenger."

"Shooting's not my style," he says, getting up in a huff.

I look up at him as he's standing over me. "I'll need you to sign these documents should you decide to take the five percent." I slide the general release and spousal release agreements I had Lily prepare in front of him. "Here. Take them home with you and read them. I'll answer any questions you have. What it all boils down to is you'll take five percent in full satisfaction of your claim. No rush. Just think it over. I'm here."

Bert grabs the documents and crumples them the way one does when taking anger out on paper. "Fucker, this shit ain't over," he grumbles, then stomps out.

I Love You, Too, Baby

I open my bird's-eye-maple built-in and my TV/VCR combo unit awaits me. I thought I'd never use it again after the advent of the CD, but that just goes to show you. I hit the power button and slip in the tape of Suzy's fifth birthday party. I think this is the first tape I've ever played in my office that wasn't a video surveillance of one of my clients exchanged by defense counsel, showing the HIC performing some activity they testified under oath they could not do.

The tape begins to play. Suzy is standing in front of a tree in what looks like a public park. She's an obviously delightful little girl. She has pigtails with yellow bows that match her yellow party dress. She's still got all her tiny white perfectly aligned baby teeth. She's standing there as if waiting for something fun to happen. All her expressions exhibit excitement, anticipation, and exuberance. It's hard to believe I'm looking at the same disabled, deformed child I just left back at Dr. Harper's office.

After ten seconds, Suzy speaks in an adorable voice. "Is it on, Mom?" She's gazing straight at the camera.

June's voice responds. "It's running, honey. Take it away."

"Thanks, Mom. Hi, y'all. I'm Suzy Williams and today is my birthday. I'm five years old and we're having a party to celebrate. I made my mom have it right here in Prospect Park, the most beautiful park in all of Brooklyn. Everybody from my kindergarten class was invited so nobody got their feelings hurt. Not everybody showed up yet, but it's time to get my party started. We're gonna play duck, duck, goose, pin the tail on the donkey, and I made a piñata all by myself out of papier-mâché that I filled with the best stuff I just know everybody is gonna love. My mommy is the cameraman and I love her so much for making my party dreams come true. Say hello to everybody in partyland, Mom."

The camera moves off Suzy and the image flips around like the camera almost fell. June's face comes into focus on a superclose close-up as she holds the camera on herself. "I love you, too, baby." June smiles and wipes away a big tear from underneath her giant-sized false eyelashes. Then the camera flips back around, but not before I've noted June and Suzy are wearing matching outfits again. June looks good in yellow.

"You're the best mommy. Make sure you tape as much as you can. I want to show my friends that weren't able to come."

I spend the next sixty minutes watching the most incredible five-year-old I've ever seen. She's a superstar. Not only is Suzy well-spoken, but she spends her whole party making sure everyone else is having a good time like a perfect little hostess.

The tape ends with Suzy standing in front of that big tree again. June's voice is heard. "I love you, baby!" The tape cuts off.

I'm numb. The girl in the tape was bright and engaging, filled with a love for life. The Suzy I know is retarded, as crude as that word may sound. Not to mention politically incorrect and insensitive. She's a severely compromised, brain-damaged, spastic quadriplegic capable of saying only three words.

After viewing that tape, I have the feeling that Suzy's hip to her situation. She's aware that what she is today is not what she once was. Somewhere in her consciousness she recognizes how her life has changed. There's a condition doctors call locked-in syndrome, and this resembles it in some small degree.

Two lives were lost when Suzy suffered her "complication." No amount of money will ever give her or her mother back their worlds, but their quality of life certainly can be improved. From my dealings with children like her who rely on Medicaid, I know they struggle daily just to get the necessaries. If I can make a difference here, I'm going to.

I hit the eject button and take the tape out while thinking how excited Suzy got when she saw it. She watches it every day. Yeah, she knows about her predicament.

Acute and Unpredictable

It's time to search the records. The entry I'm most concerned about in the Williams file is the one made right before Suzy's cardiorespiratory arrest or stroke. Or whatever it was.

I take out the records, place them in front of me, then put the empty file folder on the floor. The top two pages are the Discharge Summary. This narrative typically gets dictated and signed by the attending doctor just after the patient goes home or to the morgue, whichever the case may be. At the time of dictation the doctor is meant to go over the record to incorporate and summarize all the salient medical findings, treatments, and diagnoses. I know for sure that if a medical error has occurred, it is known at the time the Discharge Summary is created. However, by this point in time the doctor has had the opportunity to reflect upon the mistake and so dictates the Discharge Summary from hindsight rather than the initial reactive impulse to the event. Meaning, this lapse in time offers the possibility of creative medical thinking.

Before I actually begin to read Suzy's Discharge Summary, I scan it, looking for that configuration of letters that to me is the equivalent of a large pink elephant sitting on the side of a highway. The letters spell "iatrogenic." *Iatrogenic*, defined medically, means an injury sustained during the course of medical care.

Defined nonmedically, it means the doctor fucked up.

Complication, then, is the word doctors use to explain why the iatrogenic injury occurred. If I ever see either of these words—*iatrogenic* or *complication*—I can be sure a defense of the medical error has been set in motion by the doctor and/or the hospital's Risk Management office during the admission. Risk Management is that department of the hospital that is set up specifically to deal with medical mistakes in the appropriate manner, whatever that may be.

My scan of Suzy's Discharge Summary reveals a circus so populated by pink elephants that a cover-up would just be laughable. Starring in the role of top complication is her sickle cell disease. How convenient, but under the circumstances possibly true. I read the summary from beginning to end, noting the many defenses in the case, most of which I've heard already from my expert Dr. Laura Smith and that confirm the medical affidavit in defendant's motion to dismiss papers. Dr. Laura, I note, offers a complication not even referenced in the Discharge Summary—the blood infection.

The only good news, as far as the case is concerned, is the overall big picture: Suzy presented to the hospital in one condition and left in a vastly different one. She walked in with a fever and was wheeled out with massive brain damage. This is a major point, regardless of whatever complications may have occurred, because the injury claimed is seemingly unrelated to her presenting condition. Also, young people of relatively normal health tend to get better with hospital treatment, not worse.

The Discharge Summary indicates Suzy's condition deteriorated day to day, going into cardiopulmonary arrest on the morning of hospital day three. I finish reading it and place its two pages facedown. Then I begin going through the record page by page in a quick and methodical manner. The stack on the left begins to shrink as the pile on the right grows.

I get to a nurse's entry recorded at seven o'clock in the morning, but before I read it I take the next page off the stack, just to tease myself. Is it the one that documents the event? Yep. I'm excited to see how the moment is going to play out, but I'm willing to wait. You could call it record-reading foreplay.

The seven o'clock entry is a nurse's note with an illegible signature, the first letter of which is *B*. It reads in its entirety as follows:

Patient be restless. Temperature be up and down all night according to night nurse. Her blood pressure be high and she be breathing fast. See the girl's vitals chart. Patient says she has headache and sweating. She was comforted by me and mother is at bedside. Doctors on way doing their rounds.

The event entry is timed at 10:45 A.M. and is authored by the Dr. Valenti whom June spoke of. It was entered into the record by hand after Suzy met with her cardiopulmonary arrest at eight in the morning. It reads in perfectly clear and legible printed handwriting as follows:

Patient seen by myself (Dr. Gino Valenti) at eight o'clock this morning with hematology residents (Gold, Hassan, Guthrie, Peck, Lim) during rounds. I was the covering physician for Dr. Wise. After review of chart and physical examination continuous cardiac monitoring was ordered by me to monitor the patient's cardiac condition and vitals, which were of concern. At or about the time the patient was hooked up to the monitor she fell into cardiac arrest. The event was acute and unpredictable. Advanced cardiopulmonary resuscitation was initiated and a code 99 was called (see code sheet for further details). The patient's heart was electrically stimulated by defibrillation but she was without pulse for eleven continuous minutes (see code vitals chart). After being revived the patient was transferred to the pediatric ICU for further acute care. This author and residents did not witness the onset of the arrest. Cardiac monitoring was being initiated by the on-duty nurse, Nurse M. Braithwait.

The note is clear, concise, and without the flavor that sometimes can accompany an entry that follows a malpractice event. Dr. Valenti writes a tight motherfucking note. He even used the word *acute,* which, translated into English from medicalese, means there wasn't enough time to help this little girl. He should've ended his note by writing "defense verdict," to discourage would-be malpractice attorneys like Henry Benson from initiating legal action. But since Henry didn't have these records reviewed by a medical expert *before* he commenced a lawsuit, as the law requires, it wouldn't have made a difference here.

The only thing Valenti actually did wrong, as far as defending the case is concerned, was identify the only witness to the event: Nurse Braithwait.

I send an email to Lily telling her to serve defense counsel with a Notice of Deposition for this woman. She's the only one who can shed any light on the situation, as far as I'm concerned, and I want to hear what she has to say. The thing about nurses is they'll document someone else's mistakes but are skilled at covering up their own. It was pretty obviously Nurse Braithwait who made that seven o'clock entry with the *B* name, but there's no entry for her time with Suzy at eight o'clock when the event occurred, according to the timing of the Code sheet. Taking Nurse Braithwait's testimony is going to be a deep-sea expedition, but that's okay. I like to fish.

9

The streets down here at the tip of lower Manhattan are filled with hustle and bustle. And the dichotomy between the people is unavoidably obvious. The men and women in business suits are mostly in the financial fields and have a determined quickstep in their gait. As though if they got to work a minute later it would cost them millions. The people in plain clothes with a lesser pop in their step work for them. If they arrive late, they're out of a job. That's the feel I always sense when I come downtown for depositions at the law offices of defense counsel. Technically, these law firms are not in the financial field, but the insurance companies paying their billables indeed are.

The Staten Island Ferry has just let out a group of passengers and they're filing down the off-ramp. It's amazing to me that most of the women in the herd of people spilling out still wear their hair big, eighties style. And it's not like the airing of MTV's *Jersey Shore* brought that look back. On the island known as Staten, that hairdo never left. I by chance happen to see Jimmy Broderick falling behind from the pack as he slowly comes off the ramp. I know he's going to the same building as me on Whitehall Street, so I'm hoping to intercept him before he enters, purely for entertainment purposes.

Jimmy's what I call an old-timer in the legal defense industry. He's been at it so long and is so jaded, he no longer believes any plaintiff is actually really injured. He doesn't do medical malpractice defense work, though, because he's not smart enough, so I see him mostly on my construction accident cases, which are generally less intellectually challenging. He's in his early seventies, has scabs on his right cheek from treatment for sun overexposure, always smells like a bottle of whiskey, and is smoking as usual. He stops before going into the building, flicks his butt to the curb, and pulls out another cigarette. Excellent.

"Hey, Jimmy, how's it going?"

"Tug," he says in his raspy voice, "good to see ya, good to see ya." He lights and takes a draw of his cig, long, hard, and deep. He blows out a cloud, the way one does just before they're going to say something. "You know that guy don't have no brain injury on that case we have, you know the one, what's that guy's name?"

"My client's name is Montez, Julio Montez."

"Yeah, that's the ticket, Montez, Juan Montez."

"No, Julio Montez," I correct.

"Whatever, that guy ain't got no brain injury." You'd think practicing law all these decades Jimmy would've lost that "ain't got no" phrase.

"Really?" I respond. "Jimmy, the guy fell two stories, landed on his head, fractured his skull into pieces, had surgery because a collection of blood was compressing his frontal lobes, had a second surgery to place a shunt in his brain to drain out the cerebrospinal fluid that was causing massive intracranial pressure, spent three months in a coma, four months in a rehab center, and now he can't remember his own name. You took his testimony, you saw the guy. He couldn't remember the woman holding his hand during your questioning was his wife."

Jimmy takes a short puff, anxious to retort. "Tug, that ain't no brain damaged," he casually responds. "I'll tell you what brain damaged is. I once defended a case where a wrecking ball smashed a guy's head off clear across the street—that's brain damaged, ya see, that's brain damaged, Tug. And your client should be paying us for not being able to remember who his wife is. What do you call that there—oh yeah—mitigation of injuries." He takes another long, hard, deep puff, the way one does after having made their point in an important conversation.

"I always enjoy your perspective on damages, Jimmy. I got to go in. I got a depo at Goldman's office."

"Oh yeah, they got some fancy digs in here now." As I leave Jimmy, he's taking out another cigarette. He's probably the only guy down here in a suit who's not in any rush. But like most other defense lawyers around this area, he's in denial of his client's legal responsibility to pay out on their legitimate insurance claims. His smoking and wrecking ball comment remind me I got to check in with my mom before she calls me first and guilts me out.

I guess McGillicuddy has added value to the firm since partnering with Goldman & Goldberg. They've moved from the lower-rent district of the second floor to the thirty-ninth floor, and there's expensive brass lettering on the oversized mahogany door.

Before I get a chance to grab the handle, the door opens and out walks Michael Goldberg. "Hey, Mike," I say. "It's been a long time."

"Not long enough," Goldberg replies, then laughs at his stale old joke. "How's that case I sent you going, Tug?"

"Still in the works," I reply, "but it'll pay. Don't worry, I'll guard your referral fee."

"I'm not worried. That's one of the reasons I sent you the case in the first place."

I nod. "So who's this McGillicuddy you and Goldman made partner?"

"Winnie. We've known her for years. She's a nurse turned lawyer who's worked in hospital risk management for decades. A real tough egg."

I nod again. "She didn't work here the last case we had together and now she's your partner? You must've passed over a lot of next-in-line associates."

"Passed over and pissed off is a better way to put it, but Winnie brought with her new accounts—and money talks. She came here from her position as in-house counsel and chief of Risk Management at the Brownsville Hospital Center of Brooklyn, and she brought that account with her. She also brought a few other hospital accounts from the facilities she worked at over the years. Winnie pays for herself and lines our pockets. It was a no-brainer, and she's a damn good attorney, too."

"She's obviously got a lot of pull, because she got a witness here with just a few days' notice."

Goldberg smiles. "Then I'm sure this witness is just going to sink your case even more. Gotta go."

I love when lawyers say stuff without knowing. It can only lead to good.

After Goldberg walks away, I look at my watch. It's sixteen minutes after ten. The deposition was called for ten sharp so I'm one minute late. I like to keep my adversaries waiting exactly fifteen minutes for the main event. It's no different from the challenger in a boxing match anxiously waiting in the ring for the champ to make his grand entrance. The challenger has to pretend to keep himself occupied and focused by air jabbing and bouncing around the ring on his toes as the champion is announced and slowly makes his way, guided by the applause of the spectators. The slower the champ approaches, the more ridiculous the challenger looks and feels in center ring.

I check in with reception and am shown into the ring—I mean a large conference room with two surprises waiting. The first is a wall of windows on the far side of the room with incredible river views. I love water views and the Statue of Liberty is jutting up out of the water in all her glory. I put my bag down, stand at attention, salute Lady Liberty, who, frankly, I always felt looks like a transvestite. "God bless America, everybody," I announce.

My second surprise is the presence of June, Suzy, and Dog. June smiles at my entrance. She and Suzy are dressed in identical outfits as always. Today the boots are white.

Smiling back at June, I walk up to my adversary, Winnie McGillicuddy, and introduce myself. She shakes my hand. "I've heard a lot about you, Wyler," she offers perfunctorily.

"I hope all good," I say, opting for unoriginality.

"Not really."

I go for another cliché. "I've never been accused of winning any popularity contests."

"I can see why."

Here's the rule: if I just met you I'm allowed to make fun of myself but you're not. And don't call me Wyler. It's Mr. Wyler, unless of course you're a Disciplinary Committee judge.

Winnie is tall and thin like my expert Dr. Laura Smith. She's got to be in her late fifties, early sixties, and has a very distinct look to her face. You know how some people can resemble their pets or other animals? Winnie is one of these people. She looks exactly like a mammal in the genus *Mustela* of the Mustelidae family. The common weasel. Her dyed auburn hair color even resembles the fur of one. How fitting, given her occupation as defense counsel.

June, Suzy, and Dog are across the large oval table, which means if I let things stand, when the deposition begins we'll be facing into the room with the water view at our backs. No way. I'm going to have to fix this. If there's a water view to be seen, then I'm the one who's going to see it.

Kneeling down, giving love and attention to Suzy, is an older black woman with her hair wrapped up in a red, black, and green reggae swaddle. This seemingly harmless and heart-filled Caribbean lady perfectly fits June's description of Nurse Braithwait. Things are definitely going to spice up in here, because I know Nurse Braithwait could never in a million years connect with Winnie the Weasel the way I know she's going to connect with me.

I say across the table, "Good morning, June."

"Good morning, Tug," June replies.

I approach Suzy, placing my hand on her bony shoulder. I kneel down on the opposite side of the leg braces to Nurse Braithwait. "Good morning, Suzy."

Suzy responds by flipping her hands. "Sch-weet." Nurse Braithwait and I look at each other and exchange smiles.

"Oh, mon," Nurse Braithwait says, "I be tinking she know you, mon."

"I be tinking da same ting."

"Oh, you island accent be quite autentic, lawyer mon."

"Well dat be because I gots many clients from da Isle of Jamaica, mon. Was raised, in sorts, by a Jamaican woman, too, who worked in my home when I was a child."

"Oh, don't tell me dat, dat be just special, you know," she replies.

Before another word is said, I hear Winnie the Weasel. "Okay, that's enough talking to the witness," she barks.

"No problem," I tell her. "She be breaking up the get-ta-know-ya," I whisper to Braithwait. She grins.

"Ms. McGillicuddy," I say, "would you mind if I stepped into the hallway for a second with my clients so I can consult with them in private?"

"I'll step out so you can talk in here."

"No, I need to take Ms. Williams and her daughter out into the hall, if you don't mind." I begin wheeling Suzy toward the door.

Nurse Braithwait starts to follow us, but the Weasel is firm this time. "No, you stay there."

Steering Suzy out, I manage to bump the wheelchair into a couple of oak chairs, leaving gouge marks. Nice. As I close the door behind us June looks at me. "That was a big pain in the ass. She could have been the one to go out."

"Water views, baby," I answer. I glance down at Suzy. "Got that?" Suzy shoots me a look of understanding, or so I think. "June," I ask, "what are you, Suzy, and Dog doing here anyway? You already gave testimony in this case. I'm here to question the nurse."

"I wanted to see how you were going to fix things."

"I'm not sure I can do that. I have no idea what this nurse is going to say because she didn't make any entries in the hospital record referable to the event."

"I have only one thing to say to that."

"And that is?"

"Do your best."

I smile, and so does she. But her expression is fiercely determined.

We reenter the room, and the Weasel and Nurse Braithwait are seated facing the water, as anticipated. "Would you guys mind moving over to the other side?" I ask. "I had some problems negotiating this wheelchair around the table before."

"Sorry," replies Ms. McGillicuddy. "But yes, I mind. Defense counsel sits on this side of the table and your client obviously doesn't have the mental capacity to appreciate the view anyway."

Before I get the chance to blast this insensitivity, June goes all ghetto on her. "You listen to me. My baby knows the difference between looking at a damn wall and New York Harbor. I suggest you stop your minding and move your scrawny ass to the other side of the table before—"

I intervene. "June, settle down."

"Oh no. I don't take no shit like that. I got a little girl here with special needs and right now she needs to look out onto that water. You got me?"

Nurse Braithwait now speaks up. "Come, let's move across. Make da little girl happy. She has special needs, mind ya."

The Weasel reluctantly scuttles to the other side of the table and we take our seats. The view's all ours. Before I start my questioning, I lean over. "Damn, June," I whisper, "you made that lawyer your bitch."

The court reporter, who's been sitting quietly, does what she's there for and swears in Nurse Braithwait, who is very likable, to tell the truth. The floor is now mine.

At least I thought it was. Before I can pose my first question, defense counsel makes herself heard. "I'd like to place a statement on the record before you begin with this witness."

"Be my guest, counselor," I say.

"Let the record reflect that nurse Marsha Braithwait is being produced here today voluntarily by the hospital. However, although Nurse Braithwait was employed by the hospital at the time this occurrence arose, she is no longer so employed. It's our position that she's a nonparty witness. We produced her here today in the interest of justice to accommodate plaintiff's counsel, given the pending motion to dismiss."

"Anything else?"

"Nothing further," the Weasel replies. The striking fingers of the court reporter hit a few more keys, then stop.

"Off the record, please," I say, and the court reporter interlocks her digits and stretches them out away from her body. They often do this. I look to Nurse Braithwait. "Nurse, since you're technically here without counsel, I could ask that you leave the room with me and discuss your proposed testimony outside the presence of Ms. McGillicuddy before I even ask one question in here on the record. But I have faith you came here to be truthful and to tell us what you know. Am I right about that?"

She looks at me earnestly. "Tru dat, mon. I be coming to tell what I know."

"I believe you, so let's just begin. Before we do, though, I must ask, did you speak to Ms. McGillicuddy over here about this case?"

"I be talking to nobody until both side be here so it's be fair and square."

I turn to the Weasel. "You haven't spoken to this witness or know what she's going to testify to?"

"I tried," the Weasel answers, "but like she said, she wouldn't talk to me." Big mistake.

I look to the court reporter. "Back on the record, please. Let the record reflect that despite Nurse Braithwait's current nonparty status, the hospital is still vicariously responsible for her conduct. So stipulated, counsel?"

"So stipulated," replies the Weasel.

My laptop is connected to the court reporter's steno machine just like in court. I hate having the testimony in front of me as we go because it distracts from the job at hand. I know what I need to do and I like to just do it. But since defense counsel uses this new technology, I feel obligated to have it too. This is so I don't have to explain to my client why they had it and we didn't.

I Brought It for Ya, Mon

The first page up on my laptop's screen is the caption of the case. It starts filling up with my questions and Nurse Braithwait's answers as we go along. The court reporter also records the colloquy between myself, referred to as plaintiff's counsel, and defense counsel.

SUPREME COURT OF THE STATE OF NEW YORK
COUNTY OF NEW YORK
-- x
Suzy Williams, an infant by her mother and natural
Guardian, June Williams, and June Williams,
individually,

                              Plaintiffs,

            —against—

The Brooklyn Catholic Hospital Center and
Dr. Richard Wise,

                            Defendants.
-- x

EXAMINATION BEFORE TRIAL OF MARSHA BRAITHWAIT, a
nonparty witness, in the above-entitled action,
held at the law offices of Goldman, Goldberg &
McGillicuddy, 3 Whitehall Street, New York, New
York, taken before a Notary Public of the State of
New York, pursuant to stipulations between counsel.

Marsha Braithwait, a nonparty witness, having
first been duly sworn by the Notary Public, was
examined and testified as follows:

EXAMINATION BY COUNSEL ON BEHALF OF THE
PLAINTIFF(S):

Plaintiff's Counsel: Ms. McGillicuddy, Nurse
Braithwait has a Caribbean accent and pronounces
some of her words with such a flavor. Would you
stipulate to allowing the court reporter to record
the nurse's words exactly as she hears them,
phonetically, instead of interchanging
words she believes to be the traditional English
version, if such is the case?

Defense Counsel: So stipulated.

Plaintiff's Counsel: Thank you. I shall begin my questioning, then.

Q: Nurse Braithwait, how you doing this morning?

A: I be doing just fine. I tank ya for your asking.

Q: No problem. Did you hook Suzy Williams up to a heart monitor on the morning she met with some unfortunate event?

A: Yes, dat'd be me for sure.

Q: Had you ever hooked up a person, child or otherwise, to a heart monitor prior to that date?

A: No, dat would have been me first time doing dat.

Q: Did you ever receive any training by anybody at all on how to hook up a person to a heart monitor?

A: Well, nobody ever taught me dat, but I'd seen it a done a couple of time before dat day.

Q: Can you tell me where you saw that done?

A: Oh yeah, mon. I saw dat done during me training in Grenada. Went dere from Jamaica, ya know—for me training, dat is.

Q: Grenada. Is that the tiny island America invaded for a few hours back in the early eighties?

A: Yeah, dat be da Grenada.

Q: What school did you get your nursing degree from?

A: It's not exactly a nursing degree, mind ya.
     It's more like a certificate to be a nurse's
     aide. It took me two straight months of
     schooling to get it, ya know.

Q: Is two months of formal training all the
     training you ever had prior to hooking up
     Little Suzy to that heart monitor?

A: Dat would be all da training, mon.

Q: Can I ask you how you got a job as a nurse at
     the Brooklyn Catholic Hospital?

A: I answered an ad in a Caribbean newspaper. It
     said temporary nurses' positions be available
     because of da nursing strike at da hospital, ya
     know.

Q: How long had you worked at the hospital before
     you hooked Little Suzy up?

Defense Counsel: Objection.

Plaintiff's Counsel: Nature of objection, please?

Defense Counsel: I object to the form of your
                       question, Mr. Wyler.

Plaintiff's Counsel: What's the matter with my
                       form? I thought it was good
                       form.

Defense Counsel: You keep referring to the
                       plaintiff as "Little Suzy" and
                       that's not her name.

Plaintiff's Counsel: That's what I call her. Hey,
                       June, do you call Suzy "Little
                       Suzy" sometimes?

June Williams:	Yes, I do.
Plaintiff's Counsel:	Ms. McGillicuddy, her mother sometimes calls her Little Suzy. I would suggest that would be acceptable.
Defense Counsel:	It's not acceptable to me. My objection stands.
Plaintiff's Counsel:	Hey, Nurse Braithwait. Wouldn't you agree the name Little Suzy would be a perfect nickname for this adorable little girl over here?
Nurse Braithwait:	Oh ya, mon. She be just like, mon.
Plaintiff's Counsel:	Ms. McGillicuddy, we have a majority here, so I would suggest my form is acceptable.
Defense Counsel:	My objection stands.
Plaintiff's Counsel:	Okay. Can I continue?
Defense Counsel:	Please do.

Q: Now, Nurse Braithwait, again, can you tell me how long you worked at the hospital before you hooked up Little Suzy?

Defense Counsel:	Objection. I said I object to you referring to the plaintiff as Little Suzy.

Plaintiff's Counsel: Objection duly noted.

Defense Counsel: Then stop calling her Little
                         Suzy.

Plaintiff's Counsel: Why would I do that?

Defense Counsel: Because I'm objecting to it.

Plaintiff's Counsel: I appreciate and acknowledge
                         your right to object, but that
                         doesn't mean I have to listen
                         to you. If at trial the judge
                         agrees with your objection,
                         then the word *little* will be
                         stricken from the record. Now
                         can I continue?

Defense Counsel: You're an ass.

Plaintiff's Counsel: Well, that's quite
                         unprofessional of you, but
                         as an officer of the court I
                         support your right to free
                         speech. Now can I continue?

Defense Counsel: Go ahead.

Q: Nurse Braithwait, how long had you been
     working at the hospital before hooking up
     Little Suzy?

A: I be working at dat hospital almost two full
     weeks by dat time.

Q: And before that time, when was the last time
     you worked in the medical profession?

A: I gotten me my certificate 'bout ten years before dat, but only worked in a hospital fer three months at dat time.

Q: So you had a total of three months' experience in the nurse's aide profession, and that was ten years before you hooked up Little Suzy?

A: Yes. Dat would be 'bout right.

Q: Can you tell me why you left nursing for those ten years after getting your certificate?

A: Oh ya, mon. Because me jerk chicken recipe was in big demand, you know. I made da jerk chicken for some of da big hotels we be gotten down dere. Da jerk chicken money too good. Twice da money of nursing, ya know.

Q: Can you tell me, did someone tell you to hook Little Suzy up to that heart monitor?

A: Oh yeah, mon. Da doctor, mon. He be givin' me da order.

Q: Did you tell him that you only had limited experience with such a device?

A: I didn't tell dat man nothing, nohow. He be a firm man. I be no one to question his autority, mind ya. If he be needin' to ask me my qualifications, I would have told da mon, but he do more ordering den asking.

Q: Can you tell me exactly what you did when you hooked Little Suzy up to the heart monitor?

A: I stuck the first patch on her chest, you know, in da right place. Den I put dat wire into da hole on da top of da patch on one end, den plug

de other end of da wire into da plug coming
from da machine, mind ya.

Q: What happened next?

A: Da moment I be pluggin' in da wire Little Suzy
popped up out of da bed like if something hada
happened to her. Spooked she was, like da devil
hada taken her soul or ifin she'd been seen a
ghost, mind ya.

Q: What happened next?

A: She be screaming and I be screaming and da
doctor mon he come a-runnin' into da room and
threw da wire off Little Suzy at me, coverin'
up in da corner.

Q: And then?

A: Den dey be working dat poor little girl to get
the life back in her.

Q: What happened next?

A: After dey get her heart goin' again I was given
a talking-to and told to go home—fired, mind ya.

Q: Is that it?

A: That's about it.

Q: Is there anything else you'd like to tell me
that I wasn't smart enough to ask?

A: No, but I still be gotten da wire dat doctor
threw at me to this very day.

Q: Really?

A: Yes, really, mon.

Q: Why do you still have it?

A: Well, mon, dey be firing me and all dat and I just left with it in my pocket.

Q: Where is the wire now?

A: I be gettin' it right here in me purse. I brought it for ya, mon.

Plaintiff's Counsel: Let the record reflect Nurse Braithwait is taking her large woven canvas bag up from the floor and is looking in it. Let the record further reflect she's moving things all around and her hand is coming out of the bag holding a clear-plastic-coated wire that's attached to what looks like an electrode patch. Let the record further reflect Nurse Braithwait is offering plaintiff's counsel the wire and patch and that I am taking it from her.

Nurse Braithwait: Here ya go, mon. You can have it. I don't be needin' it no more.

Plaintiff's Counsel: Thank you, Nurse Braithwait, for your time and the information you gave us. I wish you well and hope we never meet again, and I say that with love and affection.

Nurse Braithwait: May God be with ya, mon.

I have the court reporter mark it as "Exhibit A," then quickly stuff the wire and electrode patch into my right front pants pocket. I look to Ms. McGillicuddy. "I have no further questions. I'll be seeing you on the flip-flop. Come on, June, we're done here."

The Weasel grimly sticks out her hand. "Wire, please?" It's an order not well disguised as a question.

"Of course not. Why would I give it to you?"

"Because it's hospital property."

"It was hospital property, then it was discarded and became the property of Nurse Braithwait. She has gifted it to me—on the record I might add—so now it's my property. If the hospital had any interest in this wire and patch they should've obtained it back from their former employee before discharging her. I'll keep it in a safe place so it's not lost, but for now it'll remain in my front right pocket." I pat my trousers for emphasis. "As a matter of fact, Ms. Reporter, please take this statement down for the record."

The reporter stretches out her hands and readies them over the steno keys. "Let the record reflect," I begin, "that the witness produced here today was categorized by defense counsel as a nonparty witness. As such there is no attorney-client relation between the two. Let the record further reflect that the witness gifted me a certain wire with an electrode patch that she has had in her possession since the date of the incident giving rise to this occurrence, and at no time prior to this moment has anyone asked Nurse Braithwait for them back. Is that accurate, Nurse Braithwait?"

"Dat would be da truth, mon."

"Given these undisputed facts relative to the wire and patch," I continue on the record, "I'll be keeping dem, mon."

The Weasel jumps in. "Off the record." She stares at me. "You're not leaving here with that, Wyler," she warns.

"I'm not looking for any trouble. I'd never be able to explain to my brothers of the bar how it was you physically took me down and relieved me of this wire and patch. So I would ask that you call into this room the biggest, baddest person you employ here to forcefully take them from me so that I'll at least sound heroic when

I tell my war story at the New York State Trial Lawyers conference."

The Weasel points her finger at me. "Stay here!" she orders. Getting up, she marches out of the room, slamming the door in apparent protest.

All is quiet in the conference room. Five seconds pass, then I count backward loudly and quickly. "Four, three, two, one. Come on, June. Put Suzy in high gear. We're going to make a run for it."

June releases the wheelchair brake and spins Suzy around, startling Dog, who loses her balance and falls to the floor. "Up, Dog," June commands. Dog jumps right back up onto Suzy's lap, giving a little doggy sneeze, while Suzy sways her head back and forth as if to say, "Spin me more."

I hold the door open as June wheels Suzy out, pulling a hard right toward the elevator.

"Sch-weet," says Suzy, in an excited utterance. We start running down the long hall with Suzy's relishing the thrill. "Sch-weet. Vegas. Sch-weet."

We reach the elevators and I hammer the button with my thumb. Let the waiting game begin. I take the lead wire and patch out of my pocket and hand it to June. "I have a plan. Just take these, no time to explain." She puts them in her oversized handbag. "If they get to us before the elevator comes, just follow my lead, no pun intended."

Five seconds pass and all three named partners turn the corner at the end of the hall, charging toward us. The fucking elevator is taking its sch-weet-ass time to arrive as they continue their rush. I know this Jewish lawyer can take out the two Jews rushing us, but if things get dirty June's got to handle McGillicuddy. "June," I tell her, "if we bang, you take out the Weasel, but that's a last resort. You hear me?"

"Who's the Weasel?"

"McGillicuddy, the lady lawyer." June starts laughing. I continue. "It's got to be self-defense. You got it?"

"Got it. Self-defense."

Waiting for the fucking elevator I feel like a bank robber with a faulty escape plan. I look at the doors. "Come on, come on," I urge out loud as the partners close in on us.

I hear the Weasel yell, "Stop right there! You have stolen property! Stop right there! I'm calling the police! I'm calling building security!" The lawyer lynch mob gets to us before the elevator. In all the movies I've ever seen the good guys get away, but not this time. The Weasel's all out of breath. "I'll take the wire and patch back, counselor." She looks pointedly at my hand, which is in my pocket. Dog starts barking in a protective manner. June hushes her.

"Let's at least go back in the conference room," I say, "so we can place a proper statement on the record about the exchange."

"Fine. Let's go," she says in cautious disbelief. "I appreciate your cooperation." She pats her hair.

"Think nothing of it. I mean, you guys are a force."

As we turn to head back, the elevator arrives. I say, "Hey, would you guys mind if my client and her brain-damaged daughter and poodle get out of here? They have a long journey back to Brooklyn, and I think Dog has to go wee-wee and I wouldn't risk staining your new carpet."

McGillicuddy looks to Goldman and Goldberg for the answer. They give her the nod. She turns back to me. "Sure, they can go."

"I appreciate your consent." I turn to June. "Okay, you go. I'll call you when I need you."

June perfectly employs reverse psychology. "We're willing to hang around if you need us for moral support?" She gives me a concerned look.

"No. You take Suzy home. She's had a big day." They step in the elevator. Boo-yah.

In the conference room the court reporter is in the process of packing her stuff away. "Can you set that back up again?" I request. "We need to place a statement on the record."

She gives us all a look and reluctantly sets up her machine. Moe, Larry, and Miss Curly are beaming with victory. "Did this guy really think he was going to leave here with that wire and patch?" I hear McGillicuddy whisper to Goldberg, shooting me the thumb.

"Ready," the court reporter announces.

I start. "Let the record reflect that Ms. McGillicuddy is standing to my right with Mr. Goldman and Mr. Goldberg. So stipulated, Ms. McGillicuddy?"

"So stipulated," she answers.

"Let the record further reflect that Ms. McGillicuddy, with the ratification of her two partners, consented to allowing my clients to leave here just a few minutes ago. So stipulated, Ms. McGillicuddy?"

"So stipulated."

"Let the record further reflect that Ms. McGillicuddy just made query to her partners, Goldman and Goldberg, as to whether I really thought I was going to leave here with a certain wire and electrode patch produced by nonparty witness Nurse Marsha Braithwait. So stipulated, counsel?"

McGillicuddy gives her partners a puzzled look. "Ah, okay, yes. So stipulated."

"Now, Ms. McGillicuddy, let me answer your question. No, I didn't think I was going to leave here with the lead wire and patch. That's why I gave them to June Williams, who left here with your permission and consent. Are we quite done?"

10

W hen I arrive back at my office and hit my voice mail, I hear my mom, who is at home now. "Is this thing recording? Hello? Is this recording? Son, it's me, your mother, Adele. Please call me. It's urgent. You and your sister must come to my apartment tonight. We have some planning to do. I'll explain it to you later. See you at seven sharp. It's urgent. And your sick mother shouldn't be the one calling *you*." There's the guilt.

I hate when my mom leaves messages like that. In fact, they're always urgent. She's been battling cancer for over two decades and every time I hear "It's urgent," I think it's the big one. I've asked her a million times to save it for when things really take a turn for the worse, but I know after seeing her in the hospital, this time may actually be truly urgent. In her last operation they removed the remainder of her left breast, and bits and pieces from various internal organs. They did some genetic studies and found she's a .38 Special.

I return some calls, push various papers around my desk, respond to several of Lily's emails, leave a message for June to come into the office tomorrow with the wire and patch so we can have them examined by a forensic electrical engineer, and then head uptown to my mother's apartment. She's long divorced from my father and lives with her horny little dog, Piero.

We're Jews, for Christ's Sake

I enter her apartment to see my sister, Rachael, sitting on a bronze Giacometti chair. Mom looks at me and smiles. "Good, you're here. Sit down. We have a lot of things to discuss."

"Okay, but how did you get out of the hospital so fast? You were just in ICU."

My sister answers for her. "She discharged herself against medical advice. Again."

"Good move, Mom," I tell her. "They've got to love you for doing that, giving them a complete defense, knowing I'm a malpractice lawyer. Now what are we here to discuss?"

"I called you children here so we can plan my funeral." My sister and I give each other a look and I crack a smile. "What's so funny?" Mom asks.

"Nothing's funny about you dying and all," I reply. "You just have a funny way of going about it."

"Well, I've finally accepted this is the end of the road for me and I want to make sure things go smoothly."

"Okay, we're listening."

"First of all, who do you think we should invite to the funeral?"

"Mom, it's not a bar mitzvah, for God's sake."

"I know, but I just think there should be a guest list. I can't tell you how many times I've been to a funeral and someone's not there who I know should be. I don't want that to happen to you. I want my children to know who snubbed their mother. I mean, I'm not asking you to make our guests RSVP. I just think sending out an invitation is enough."

"Um, okay, Mom. Just check the names of the people whom you want us to invite in your address book and we'll take care of the rest."

"Good," Mom says, satisfied. She turns to my sister. "Now, what do you think I should wear?"

I cut in. "Does it matter? We're Jews, for Christ's sake. The casket's going to be closed. What's the difference?"

"Of course it matters," Mom insists. "It's technically a formal occasion so black's appropriate. I want to be dressed in proper attire even if I'm not going to be seen. I'll know the difference."

"How will you know the difference? You'll be dead."

"If I don't pick out an outfit now, I'll know the difference while I'm still alive and that's the point. Well, honey? What should I wear?"

"Why don't you wear that black velvet jacket with the red Chinese embroidered flowers you love so much," Rachael suggests.

"Oh, I was thinking of that, too, but it's too good a piece to be buried in and I wanted you to have it. Maybe you guys can dress me in it for the service at the funeral home and then take it off my back before we head to the cemetery."

"You're kidding, right, Mom?" I ask.

"No, but I guess it does seem like it's too much trouble. Rachael, why don't you take it home with you tonight and then you can wear it to my funeral instead of me."

Rachael looks at me, then back at Mom. "Uh, good idea, Mom, I'll do that."

"Fine, then." Mom turns to me. "Are you free Friday?"

"I can try to be. Why?"

"I'll have recovered enough by then to leave the house and I want you to take me to Bergdorf's to get me something to wear to my funeral."

"Bergdorf Goodman's?"

"Of course. Where else would I go to get something to be buried in?"

"Fine. We'll go to Bergdorf's so we can bury you in a nice new outfit."

My phone rings and I look at the caller ID. It reads: PRIVATE CALLER, which is not private anymore but rather June Williams. I hit the ignore button despite my promise to be more sensitive to her situation. A few moments later, it rings again. She's stubborn. It happens twice more before I shut it off altogether. Client obligations or not, I don't want to interrupt my mom's funeral-planning session.

We don't have long to wait before she tackles the next item on her agenda. "Now, I'd like there to be a nice obituary written. Who's going to take care of that?"

"I'm really busy now," I offer, perhaps a tad too quickly, "investigating a case where a little girl went from perfectly healthy to perfectly brain damaged in a matter of minutes. I'm a little tight on time."

"Well, I'm tight, too," my sister says. "At least you work for yourself."

I look at my mother. "You have some time on your hands right now, Mom. How about you write a draft and I'll mark it up before it goes to press?"

"That's a great idea."

When it comes to her bio, we all know she prefers creativity to hard fact. Great art dealer, yes. But we all know she didn't discover Picasso as a child, despite her tale otherwise. The timing isn't even right. So even if I'm going to be the editor, it doesn't hurt to remind her. "Now, no fudging—"

Suddenly, the intercom rings. Mom grabs it. "Send it up."

"Send what up?" Rachael asks.

"I ordered in Thai. It just seemed the right kind of food for the occasion. Plus, I have no appetite these days, but for some reason was craving Thai."

"You can't eat," I advise her. "They just took out two pieces of your colon the other day. You'll perf yourself and end up with a colostomy bag."

"Oh, please. I'm not really going to eat. I'm just going to put the food in my mouth and absorb the flavor."

The bell rings. I answer the door and pay the guy. I hand my sister the two brown paper bags inside the two white plastic bags, and she carries them over to the table. I try to remember the last time the three of us had a meal together like a real family.

Just then the intercom rings again. I go to answer but Mom says, "I got it." She listens to the doorman. "No, I don't know who that is. Sorry." She listens a little more. "One moment," she says, turning to me. "Tug, are you expecting a June Williams?"

"Uh, no. Why?"

"Because she's here and claiming it's urgent she see you."

"Urgent? Sound familiar, Mom? Okay, tell him to tell her I'll be right down."

"Too late. She's on her way up. She gave Antonio the slip."

I sigh.

"Who's June Williams?"

"That's the case I'm working on. Right now I'm in the middle of trying to figure out whether there was malpractice or if her daughter's brain damage resulted from a sickle cell crisis."

"Treat her nicely. She's been through a lot."

"I intend to, Mom. But I'm allowed to feel irked about my situation, which I don't want to get into."

I peek out the door, waiting for the elevator. I hear a ding and June comes walking down the hall, looking hotter than ever.

I step out and close the door. "Uh, hi, June. Nice red, white, and blue outfit you're wearing. How patriotic."

"What can I say, I was inspired by Lady Liberty this morning."

"I am curious. Could you enlighten me as to how you knew I was at my mother's and how you knew where my mother lived?"

"Sure. I came into the city hoping I'd find you at your office because I wanted to talk to you about something. I thought you'd be there because your number came up on my missed call list. When I went up, your doors were locked. I thought you were still in there so I called your office number but the machine picked up. I hung up and tried again, still no luck. I was desperate to talk to you, so I called a third time, and when the machine answered, instead of leaving a message I entered your birthday for the security code. It worked and I listened to your messages and heard the one from your mother. And not that it's my business, but if she's sick, then you *should* be the one checking up on her, not the other way around. Anyway, so I called information and she was the only Adele with your last name. So here I am."

Wow, she's good. "How did you know my date of birth?"

"Well, when Mr. Benson told me he was transferring my file to you, the first thing I did was look you up in the New York State Bar Association directory to see when your birthday was so I could establish your zodiac sign. I need to know zodiacs. I'm just like that."

"You're something, June. Your resourcefulness is scaring me."

"I had to find you tonight because I got a man-genius who can look at the wire and patch for us except that he's leaving for South Carolina on an early-morning flight. So we have to see him tonight at his junkyard in Brooklyn."

"Unfortunately, I'm busy at this moment planning my mother's funeral with her."

"Oh, I'm so sorry about your mom. Is she going to die soon?"

"I couldn't tell you. According to her doctors, she should've been dead years ago. They can't give her a life expectancy because they've never seen a case like hers. She's basically living with bits and pieces of her vital organs."

"It's sweet of you to make the plans with her. I'll wait downstairs, and when you're finished we'll go."

"You're not going downstairs. You're coming inside or I haven't heard the last of it from my mother." We go inside. "Mom, Rachael, I present my favorite client, June Williams."

Mom yells to us from the table. "Hi, June. Come sit down. We waited for you two. There's plenty here for everybody."

"Thank you so much for your hospitality," June says courteously. "I'm so sorry I barged in like this. Your son told me in the hall. I hope things aren't too painful for you."

"Now, that's quite all right," Mom assures her. "How would you know we were planning my funeral? Unfortunately, things have become painful. I'm on the patch now—you know, morphine. It's the first step on your way out. Still, it's better than the pump, which I know is coming next."

"I'm so sorry. Yes, I know about the patch. My mother passed from cancer. She was an unusual case. She had both breast and ovarian cancer at the same time."

"I can't believe that!" Mom exclaims. "She was one of us! A Thirty-Eight Special!"

"A Thirty-Eight Special? You mean like—"

"Not the gun, although it's deadly. You see there's a group of thirty-eight women—most dead now—who have something wrong with a particular gene that triggers breast and ovarian cancer simultaneously."

"Oh my God. I never heard of that," responds June.

"It's a recent discovery. Who knows how many there were in the past. How old was she when she died?"

"Young, twenty-six. I was just a child. And as I understand it, breast and ovarian cancer were rare in a woman her age. But we stayed strong, my father and I. He was devoted to me, but fell victim to an act of violence, shot dead when I was twelve. My aunt took me in after that until I was old enough to be on my own. I know you didn't ask me all that, but I'm just saying. It came to mind," she finishes, glassy-eyed, with a tone of sorrow in her voice.

Mom turns to me. She's a champion of sorts in transitioning away from a sad moment given all she has gone through. "You better win the case for June's daughter or expect to hear from me! I'm going to stay alive as long as it takes to make sure you do your job right. By the way, June, I love your handbag, and the boots, too."

"Thank you so much, Adele," June tells her. They beam at each other. Mom dishes out pad Thai and basil chicken onto everybody's plate and we eat.

After dinner, my sister and I watch June and my mother bond. My mother gives June the recipe for her famous salmon mousse in exchange for June's cheddar-corn soufflé. All of the funeral planning stopped after June arrived, but for some reason the salmon mousse recipe brings us full circle.

"We still have to talk about what you're going to serve at my shiva," Mom says thoughtfully. "I'm going to make a couple of my salmon mousses just before the end so you can put them out with the buffet. I like the idea of cooking for my mourners."

CD Orange 45

June and I leave just after midnight. "May I get you a cab?" the white-gloved doorman asks.

"Yes, please," I say.

"No, thank you," June overrides me. "We don't need one."

I turn to her. "Okay, then. How are we going to get to Brooklyn?"

She responds with a wave. The 1962 black Impala bubble top with the checkered flag badge on the front grille comes roaring toward us from down the block. You can hear the cylinders scream through the stainless dual exhaust pipes as it accelerates. Its tires screech as it slides up to the curb and stops abruptly.

The doorman jumps back, eyeballing the plate. "What's 'the Fidge'?" he asks.

"The Fidge," I reply, "is not a what, it's a who. He takes care of things that need taking care of around the hood and keeps his peeps safe. Right, June?"

"Right, counselor," she confirms with a wink.

I hear superloud gangsta music emanating through the smoked-out windows of the Impala. Under the SS badge on the side fender the number 409 appears, signifying the cubic size of the engine. It has aftermarket Cragar mag wheels with redline tires flared by chromed curb feelers. I see the passenger-side window slowly descend into the doorframe, allowing the music to make a blasting escape. Passersby slow their pace and stare at the menacing piece of 1960s muscle.

A large black man with a shaved head and a full, neatly trimmed beard is leaning toward the passenger side. He speaks commandingly as he throws the door open of the Fidge's lowrider. "Get in." It's the same guy who picked June up after we ate our dogs in front of the courthouse.

June looks at me. "This is my friend Trace. He's going to take us to Fred's. It's safer to go with Trace in the neighborhoods we're going to travel through than in a taxi."

"Trace, like in Trace Adkins, the famous country singer?"

"Uh, no," June replies. "More like 'if anyone messes, they're gonna disappear without a trace' Trace."

"Hmm. I see." I look in at the colossus behind the wheel. "Good evening, Trace."

"It's morning," he informs me in a slow, deep voice.

"I stand corrected, Trace. Good morning." I reach down and pick up the chrome release lever allowing the front passenger seat to fold forward so I can get in the back, observing as I do that the interior is a sea of red. There are high-grade custom red leather seats stitched in the original pattern, red carpet, door panels, and dash. Even the fuzzy dice hanging from the rearview mirror are red.

June gets in the front. "Thanks for waiting, Trace."

He responds with a gentlemanly nod.

The doorman watches as we ready ourselves for takeoff. Trace catches his attention waving him over. He makes his way around to the driver's side and bends down. Trace shoots up two fingers with a twenty wedged between. "Compliments of the Fidge."

The doorman stops his nervous shaking and slowly takes the bill. "Please tell the Fidge I say thank you."

"Yeah," Trace says pleasantly, then peels away from the curb with the doorman standing street side.

"June, can I see the wire and patch, please?" I ask over the interior rumble.

Her hand disappears into her bag and she pulls out the wire. This has been one long-ass day, and it ain't over yet. I wish I were home right about now. Home! Crap! My wife. I forgot to call and tell her I had to go to my mother's and wouldn't be home for dinner. I'm in deep mud. If I call now and wake her from her precious sleep I'll be in deeper, waist high. But if I don't call and tell her of my whereabouts, the mud will act as quicksand. I pull out my phone.

"Who you calling?" June asks on the third ring.

"My wife."

"Hang up. You don't have to—"

"Shush," I say, putting my index finger to my lips.

"Did you just shush me? I know you didn't just shush me. Nobody shushes me—"

I hold my finger up to my lips. For a second or two this compounds her anger, but then June smiles. "Okay, be that way. Call your wife."

Tyler answers in a sleepy, annoyed voice, "What?"

"It's me. Sorry, honey. I've been running around and forgot to call you to say I wouldn't be home for dinner. I had to go to my mom's to plan her funeral and now I'm in a gangsta lowrider heading to the hood to meet an electrical expert at his junkyard."

As usual, she's full of questions. "Plan a funeral? Gangsta lowrider? Meet an expert? At a junkyard in the hood?" She pauses, but only briefly. "You're an asshole. Don't call here so late ever again!" *Click.*

"That didn't go over so well," I comment as I stuff my phone away. June laughs. "Domestic problems?"

"You might say that." She hands me the patch and wire.

"White girls. She's got to understand you're a hardworking man and you got the power to change people's lives. That's a big responsibility. If you don't win our case, me, Suzy, and Dog will be stuck forever, dependent on the system—and the system doesn't work."

"I really don't know how to respond to that, June. I'd like to believe my wife understands how important a lawsuit can be for a person in your circumstance."

"It's probably just another payday to her. I'm sure she just wants to know if you won. Bet she never asked you how winning your case changed somebody's life, did she?"

"I'm not really sure she has, but that doesn't mean she doesn't know or care."

"We'll see. After you win this one for us, we'll pay her a visit and set things straight if they need setting straight."

"That might not be a bad idea. On the other hand, it might be a really bad idea."

I look up at the bubble-shaped ceiling, which I know to be one of the unique design features of the 1962 Impala. Cool. I take in the red-and-white houndstooth pattern and see there's a courtesy light on the ceiling. I reach up and click it on, sending light into my lap right where I'm holding the stolen goods.

The stainless steel lead wire is three feet long, an eighth of an inch thick, and is covered with clear plastic coating. At one end there's an inch-long metal prong that I know from my visit to Dr. Vargas's office gets inserted into a housing attached to a cable that leads to the heart monitor. I bring the prong up to the light for closer inspection and see a bunch of black spots on the shiny steel wire inside the plastic right where the prong exits the coating. At the other end, there's a smaller prong still attached to the patch by being inserted into a tiny metal receptor that protrudes from the center of the patch. I look at its flip side, the part placed on Suzy's chest, and see some kind of substance residue. The residue on the patch at one end and the spots inside the plastic coating on the other are the only presumed abnormalities I see.

I take out a legal pad and jot down a few notes on the top sheet. I then rip off the page, fold it up, and stuff it in my front shirt pocket. I look up to notice June has been observing my very scientific inspection. I hand her the wire and patch. "Here, take this back. I want you to keep it in your possession at all times for issues surrounding chain of custody. Please don't lose them."

"Don't you worry. I have a feeling about this wire, and that's why I called Fred in on this."

"I have a feeling, too, but right now it's just that—a feeling." A few quiet minutes pass as I look out at parts of Brooklyn I never thought I'd visit. We're driving through Brownsville and it's one low-income housing project after another. Little kids who should be in bed asleep are out in the streets, some smoking, others drinking, some playing like, well, little kids. Groups of people are hanging out on street corners, some looking scary, at least from my perspective. And I would've said *gangs* of people if I weren't such an uptight nervous bald cracker from privileged beginnings cruising through a neighborhood I have no place being but for the task at hand. At least I admit it.

I know, however, despite the poverty, violent crime, and drug addiction and running that have been associated with Brownsville, Brooklyn, it also produced many talented and influential people. Rappers, boxers, basketball players, and entertainment personalities. I appreciate this neighborhood in eastern Brooklyn has given the world people who have had impact. Mike Tyson, Red Holzman, Larry King, Al Sharpton, and yes, the Three Stooges, among others. The thing that connects so many of Brownsville's notable natives is their ability to touch others in some way, shape, fashion, or form.

So now I ask, "June, who is this Fred we're going to see and what can you tell me about him?"

"His name is Fred Sanford. He owns a television repair shop as well as the junkyard next to the shop, which he operates with his son, Lenny."

"Hold on. You mean to tell me we're going to a junkyard owned by a guy named Fred Sanford and he operates it with his son, Lenny?"

"Yeah. Why you asking like that?"

"Doesn't that remind you of anything? Any television show from the seventies starring Redd Foxx?"

"You mean *Sanford and Son*?"

"Yes, June. *Sanford and Son*."

"In the TV show the son's name was Lamont, not Lenny. Plus, this Fred Sanford is educated and in the television repair business, unlike the Fred Sanford in the sitcom who seemed uneducated and strictly a junk dealer. So, what's your point?"

"Oh, no point, June. No point at all. Now that you've put it into proper perspective for me, I feel silly for bringing it up."

"I can sense sarcasm in your voice."

"That's because I'm being sarcastic. Now can you tell me why this Fred Sanford who does both television repair and deals junk is such a *genius*, as you've termed him?"

"He just is. Everybody knows it. And he's the Fidge's number one advisor on anything related to electronics or technology, among other things."

"Oh, well, why didn't you say so in the first place? If he's good enough for the Fidge, then he's good enough for me."

"Despite your continued sarcasm, Fred is the real deal. You'll see. He went to Yale undergrad and Harvard grad school for rocket science. And don't use the Fidge's name in vain. You never know when you might need him."

Trace, who's been scary-quiet, pipes up. "Yeah. Respect to the Fidge."

"My apologies to the Fidge," I tell them both. "So Fred Sanford, the junk dealer and television repairman, is also a rocket scientist?"

"Yes." She looks at me. "He was one of the principal engineers for the Apollo space missions in the 1960s. You know? 'One small step for man; one giant leap for mankind.' "

"I know the moon walk thing. I just find it interesting a Brooklyn television repairman and junk dealer was involved in the space mission."

"Would it change your mind any if you knew he owns miles of waterfront real estate in Red Hook, and has been offered hundreds of millions for it?"

"At this point, June, nothing surprises me. But why would he be living in this area if he owns land out in Red Hook and has so much money?"

"Fred's true to himself."

Trace pulls up to a three-story brownstone with a business at the street level. In the window hangs a red neon sign that reads: TELE-VISION REPAIR. A sign above the window reads: FRED'S FIX-IT AND JUNKYARD. FRED SANFORD AND SON, PROPRIETORS. To the left of the brownstone looms a large gated lot with all kinds of junk in it. It's too dark to make out what's in there, but it's most definitely a boatload of junk. The activity on the streets we just drove through is absent here, wherever we are, ten minutes from Brownsville.

Trace gets out. He's taller and wider than I projected, seeing him at a distance the other day. He looks up, down, and across the quiet street while June and I wait in the car. "Are we going to get out?" I ask.

"Of course. We just wait till Trace says so." He now does just that. It's weird how there's not one person in the street yet its emptiness is what's making me uneasy.

June hits the buzzer. A few seconds later, a light comes on and we hear a voice. "Wait a minute, I'm coming."

The door opens to reveal an elderly gray-haired black man with a pair of Ben Franklins resting on the end of his nose. He's wearing a multicolored Missoni bathrobe and a silk ascot perfectly knotted under his neck and neatly tucked into his robe. He's just shy of six feet, sports a distinguished gray mustache and goatee, has a small belly sticking out right where the robe is tied, and is wearing a pair of au-thentic leopard fur house slippers on his feet.

"June, you're beautiful, just like your mother," he tells her. "It's a shame you were deprived so young of knowing what a great woman she was. How long has it been since I've seen you, my dear? Ten years?"

"Maybe more," she replies. "Thank you for seeing us on such short notice. You know I wouldn't have bothered you if it wasn't so important. This is the lawyer I told you about."

Fred turns to me and extends his hand. "Pleased to meet you." We enter, but Fred looks back before closing the door. He sees Trace leaning on the side of the Impala. "Hey, Trace! Please be good enough to tell the Fidge his computer data is now being backed up on three different continents, as we discussed."

"On it!" Trace calls back.

Electrical equipment both vintage and state-of-the-art is strewn about all over the front of the shop. On the worktables are components disassembled into hundreds of pieces. There's just about every type of electronics in some stage of repair except for a TV.

We walk down a narrow hall into another large work area in the back. I see Lucite boxes containing spaceship parts with handwritten labels, and there are photos of guys in uniforms with Fred front and center in each one. There's also a signed picture of a familiar-looking guy in an astronaut's suit. He has his helmet under one arm and the other around Fred. The inscription says, WE COULDN'T HAVE TAKEN THAT WALK WITHOUT YOU, and the signature reads: NEIL ARMSTRONG.

"Please sit down and make yourselves comfortable," Fred says.

He leaves the room, and June turns to me. "He'll tell us what happened to Suzy. Don't worry."

"I'm cool."

Fred reappears holding a large sterling silver tray and sets it down on the table. He pours the tea, then reaches into the pocket of his robe and pulls out a sterling flask. "Try this," he suggests. "I blended it myself." He pours a shot of this secret elixir into our cups, then says to June, "Now, let me take a look at this wire and patch you spoke of. But please, don't say a word to me about anything. Just hand it over. I don't want my conclusions to be influenced."

"You mean you don't know anything about this wire and patch or why we're here in the first place?" I can't help asking him.

"Nothing other than that June has a wire attached to an electrode patch she wants me to look at. That's it."

"Don't you want to be pointed in the right direction?"

"These items will point me in the right direction. Please, just sit quietly and let me do what needs to be done."

"Will do," I respond obediently. I start humming "bump, bump ban nump; bump, bump ban nump dump dump dom . . . ," my best rendition of the *Sanford and Son* theme. By the look on Fred's face, he's named that tune. "Sorry. I couldn't help myself. That tea went to my head. What's in it?"

Fred smiles. "Ripple." I'm not sure if he's pulling my leg.

He holds the wire up for visual inspection. He twists his hand back and forth to catch the wire at different angles. "Um-hum," is all he says. He rests it on the table, then reaches into his right-hand pocket. He takes out a genuine corncob pipe with a yellow plastic mouthpiece and a vintage World War II lighter. He flashes the pipe. "Anybody mind?" We both shake our heads no and he sparks it, leaving butane residue in the air. The chemical smell quickly dissipates and a sweet floral aroma fills the room as the smoke mushrooms toward the overhead light.

Fred picks up the wire and walks a few feet away to an antiquated piece of machinery nailed into the top surface of a long, thin sawhorse. Once city property, it's light blue with white lettering that reads: NYPD. The left end of the device has a hand crank attached to a vertical metal cylinder about six inches high. The other end is some form of adjustable C-clamp attached at the bottom to a long track that runs the length of the sawhorse connecting both sides.

Fred plugs the wire's long prong into a receptor welded to the top of the cylinder and locks it in place using a paper clip he takes from his robe pocket, one I suspect he also uses to clean his pipe. He takes the patch off the other end, pulls the wire taut, then slides the C-clamp out some three feet underneath to where the wire extends. He inserts this end into an eyehole on the C-clamp and while holding it there, pulls open a makeshift drawer on the underside of the table and pushes things about until he finds what he's looking for. He takes out a metal grasping instrument and locks it onto the metal aspect of the prong coming out of the eyehole. The lead wire being held in place looks like a tightrope between the two contact points. All we need now is a few trained pigeons.

Fred cranks the handle with one hand as he pulls his pipe out of his mouth with the other. Continuing to turn the handle in a clockwise direction, he blows a cloud of smoke into the air. Sparks are flying out of the aeration slits of the cylinder housing the motor as electrical crackling noises—very Frankenstein—fill the air with each turn of the crank. There's a meter welded to the front of the cylinder, the only nod to modern technology.

Fred pushes a button and a little piece of paper spits halfway out from under the meter. He tears it off like a "now serving" numbered ticket from Zabar's and places it facedown on the table without looking at it. He measures the length of the wire with an old-fashioned yardstick, then picks up the ticket for a look. He murmurs something, tossing the ticket just as one does after being handed lox and whitefish by the counterman.

Fred releases the wire tension, then takes it out of the device. He walks it and the patch over to a counter running underneath a glass-paneled cabinet housing liquid-filled glass beakers. Out of a drawer he takes a metal tool similar to the gauze clamp used by dentists. He scrapes some of the residue off the patch into a shallow dish.

He opens up one of the glass doors. "No . . . no . . . no . . . no . . . no," he says aloud to himself as he scans the beakers. "Yes." He reaches up and pulls out a small bottle that's capped with a built-in dropper. Drawing in some clear solution, Fred squeezes it over the dish containing the particulate. The flecks of material turn a bright orange color. "Just as I thought," he remarks with a nod.

Walking back over, he sits down across from us and takes a long draw from his pipe. "Done. I'm certain of my conclusions." He looks thoughtfully at us.

The testing took less than three minutes. I'm both impressed and slightly confounded. "That's it?" I ask.

"There's nothing more to do. Yes, that's it."

June speaks the words I'm thinking. "Don't keep us wondering, Fred. Tell us what you found."

"The electrode patch," Fred explains, "is a receiver that picks up the heart's minute electrical impulses. It transfers them through the wire to a cardiac monitor that shows on a paper printout. This wire, along with this patch, is of great concern." He pauses.

Wow, good use of the pause to create suspense.

June can't outlast it. "Go on, Fred. Don't keep us waiting."

He continues. "The device over there, which I hooked the wire to, tested its integrity. I measured the wire's length, considered its circumference, and applied an established formula to determine how quickly electricity should travel from one end of the lead to its other end. The printout, however, indicated that the electricity I generated traveled in twice the amount of time it should have, which can only mean the wire has had a structural breakdown. This compromise is evidenced where you see charring or black flecks within the plastic coating near the prong that's received by a cable attached to the heart monitor. As a breakdown it's significant and has affected the impedance or conductivity of the wire, evidencing that there was an electrical force upon it in excess of its design tolerance or capacity."

June is spellbound by this narrative. "Go on. Don't stop."

"I scraped a foreign substance off the electrode patch, which you saw me deposit in the dish. I then put a few drops of a clear liquid protein on it known as CD Orange 45 to test its immunohistology. As you saw, the clear liquid turned the scrapings to an orange color. This confirmed my suspicions. The only thing CD Orange 45 can turn orange when applied to it is epithelial cells or human skin with fat lipids. This finding led to my conclusions."

"What are your conclusions, Fred?" asks June. "In plain English, please."

"Sure," Fred states. "Someone was electrocuted with that patch and wire. Who was it?"

"Oh my God! Oh my God! My baby was electrocuted!" June screams, starting to cry hysterically.

"Take it easy, June," I say. "Take a deep breath." But as I expected, my effort at consolation has little effect. One of the things I know about myself is my inability to provide helpful consolation in times of need or distress. I get up and give June a hug, but it's so fucking forced and unnatural I actually disgust myself. Here I am, at a time like this, thinking about one of my many shortcomings. Jesus. I can only hope June and Fred won't notice.

Fred's too smart, though, not to register my awkwardness. He comes and tactfully takes me off the hook. I move back and he sits down next to June. She immediately turns into him, resting her head on his chest. "Oh, my baby, my baby," she sobs repeatedly.

"There, there now, June. You go ahead and cry this one out," Fred reassures her every so often, his timing and sincerity both unimpeachable.

After ten long minutes of crying, June collects herself. "At least I know the truth now. I *knew* something happened in that room. I prayed it wasn't something I did and I knew it wasn't Suzy's sickle cell. They electrocuted my baby."

"I heard you had a daughter," Fred tells her. "I'm very sorry about this tragedy and sorry I had to be the one to give you the bad news. Did she pass away as a result of this?"

"Part of her did, but most of her is still alive. Only, her brain is severely damaged."

"I'm sorry, June. I feel deep sadness for you."

"Thank you, Fred. But how could this have happened?"

"A wire like this is designed to handle low-voltage current, but a high-voltage charge ran through it. The most common source would be an electrical outlet, a common wall socket. Someone put that prong into an electrical power source while the patch was on your daughter's chest."

June and I look at each other. "Nurse Braithwait," we say in unison.

Fred tilts his head in a questioning manner, then continues. "The shock stopped her heart. Most people don't survive such an event."

"June," I say, "I'm sure Nurse Braithwait didn't even know what she had done. She did it accidentally. Meaning, she probably intended to place the prong into the monitor's cable but accidentally put it into some extension cord. It was complete and utter incompetence and she didn't even realize it."

June shakes her head. "My poor baby."

"Tomorrow I'll buzz my expert, Dr. Smith—or Dr. Laura, as she likes to call herself—and let her know about these new developments. In addition to the affidavit I'll need from you, Fred, I'll want an affidavit from her laying this whole thing out in order to defeat defendant's motion to dismiss the case. More than that, June, we'll need to make a cross-motion seeking the court's permission to amend the claim to include an allegation of negligent nonlethal electrocution. This was no complication from sickle cell. Suzy was accidentally electrocuted by a caring but incompetent, unqualified nurse."

"Yes," June replies, "but she's as sweet as a candy cane. I don't want to get her in trouble."

"She won't get in trouble. It was an accident, but the hospital was negligent for employing a jerk chicken chef to perform the tasks required of a certified nurse practitioner that, if carried out improperly, could have disastrous results."

We gather ourselves to leave. Fred walks us back through the long hall with his arm around June. When we reach the front door he turns to me. "Look, I'm not the lawyer, you are, but something like this should never have happened. Even more so, it should have been impossible for such an event to occur."

"What are you saying here, Fred?"

"Machines with connecting wires that have inputs and receptor sites are generally designed in such a way that specifically prevents this kind of unintended occurrence."

"How so?"

"For one, the inch-long male prong was definitely plugged into either a wall outlet, which is unlikely, because I don't think anybody's that stupid, or, as you said, into an open extension cord that was left plugged into a wall outlet by the monitor, which seems more probable.

Design standards and specifications usually account for foreseeable misapplications and prevent them from happening. I'm not all that familiar with this technology, but I'm telling you an event like this should never have happened. You may want to consider a lawsuit against the manufacturer of the heart monitor for a design defect. They'd never be able to put forth a reasonable defense because the fact that the event happened made it a foreseeable misuse, wouldn't you agree?"

"Agreed. The manufacturer must always consider potential misuses that can cause harm before they put a product into the stream of commerce. I know what needs to be done in that regard. Thank you for all your time and help."

"Don't mention it. I've known June since she was born. I would do anything for her. I'll be in South Carolina for a short time, but I'll give you my contact information there so you can quickly arrange to get an affidavit to me for my signature. I can fly back on a moment's notice if need be." Fred gives June a hug and me a firm handshake.

As he closes the door, we see Trace leaning on the Impala. He looks at June. "Well?"

"Yeah." June nods and cries at the same time. Trace walks over and gives her a heartfelt and sustaining embrace. Damn, why can't I do that?

"Sorry, girl," Trace whispers. "You knew someone did your baby bad."

June looks at me. "Yeah, I knew, but my own lawyer over here didn't."

"June," I reply, "I made you a promise to investigate this case in more depth despite what our own expert advised, didn't I?"

"That's what you promised."

"Well, I'm in the process of keeping my promise." I say this softly, appreciating the delicate situation at hand.

"Yes, but I'm merely pointing out it was through my efforts that we found out what happened to Suzy."

"I appreciate that, but it's quite possible I would've come to this very same conclusion without Fred's involvement, isn't it?"

"We'll never know that, will we, counselor?"

"I disagree, June. You should have more faith in me."

"You disagree?" June questions. "How will we ever know if you would've figured out what happened to Suzy if we hadn't seen Fred?"

"Because I already figured it out," I answer confidently.

"Oh, really?"

"Yes, really."

"How do I know that? How could you ever prove that?"

"You remember, I made a note in the backseat of the Impala on our ride over here?"

"Yes, I saw you writing something."

"You also saw me fold up that note and put it in my shirt pocket, right?"

"You know I did."

"So, take it out." June opens my jacket lapel, reaches in, and pulls out the folded paper. "June, before you unfold that will you do me a favor?"

"Depends. What's the favor?"

"All I ask is that you read what I've written out loud nice and clear for Trace to hear."

"Why?"

"Since you questioned my commitment and ability in front of him, you should be the one to answer that question. Read for us, please." June unfolds the paper and I follow her eyes as they glance across the page. A smile appears on her face. "Out loud. Like you promised," I remind.

"Okay, okay. I'm sorry." She turns, faces her friend, and clears her throat before speaking. "Trace, the note authored by my lawyer over here, Tug, reads: 'Suzy was electrocuted. Game on.'"

White Boy, You So Naïve

Trace throws the Impala into gear and does his signature peel-out. Fifteen very quiet minutes later, we arrive in front of a dilapidated brownstone. June turns to Trace. "Thank you, baby. Now please take my lawyer home to Westchester so he can get some rest." She nods back at me.

"On it," Trace replies.

Before June opens the door, a thought occurs to me. "How'd you know I live in Westchester?"

"Oh, please," she says sarcastically, then opens the door with body language that says "Give me a break." June closes the door, turns, and leans down into the open window. "Counselor, you stay in the back. You'll be more comfortable."

Trace keeps his guarding eye on her as she walks toward her building. We both watch as she walks up seven entry steps to a landing, unlocks the exterior door to this five-story structure, enters into a vestibule, opens up an interior door, and begins walking up a flight of stairs that are clearly visible from our curbside position. As she disappears up, Trace puts the Impala in gear and races away in his standard fashion. The power of the low-gear torque throws me back into the red leather. As we cruise through the County of Kings, I'm uncomfortable being chauffeured, feeling as if I'm not worthy.

"Trace, can I ask you something?"

"Just did."

"Can I ask you something else?"

"Just did again."

"What floor does June live on?"

"Four."

"Is there an elevator in the building?"

Trace only chuckles.

"How long has June lived there?"

"Since her baby born."

"How does Suzy get up to the fourth floor?"

"June wheels her up to the front steps, then puts the brake on the chair. She takes Dog off of Suzy and walks Dog up the front steps and sets her down. She comes back down and lifts Suzy out and carries her up the front steps to the door and sets her down against the wall on the left side of the door. She walks back down to the street, folds up the wheelchair, and carries that up to the front door. She leans the chair against the railing, unlocks the door, opens it, and holds it open with her right foot as she leans down and picks up Suzy. She carries Suzy inside to the next door, goes through that, and sets Suzy down at the foot of the steps. She comes back outside, picks up the wheelchair while keeping that door open with her foot again, and brings it inside. She carries Suzy up the three flights of steps—taking a rest at the landing between the second and third flight—then carries her the rest of the way and brings her into the apartment. She belts Suzy in a chair in the kitchen, then goes back down the three flights to get the wheelchair. She carries it up into the apartment and transfers Suzy back. Dog knows the routine and makes it on her own. That's about it. I'm feeling her pain every time."

I feel awful just hearing. "Trace, how do you know that with such great detail?"

"Seen June do it twice a day, sometimes three times, ever since Suzy got hurt. I live on the fifth floor."

"Can't she move down to the first floor or find a place to live at street level?"

Trace snorts. The translation being "White boy, you so naïve." "Been on a waiting list for years."

"Suzy must weigh close to a hundred pounds. June's going to hurt herself if she keeps up that routine. I've seen it before."

"Suzy weighs a hundred seven and June won't let anybody help with the carrying. The good Lord and the Fidge both know I've tried. June says it's her baby and she's responsible. Never made one complaint, either. Just takes care of her motherly duties."

The next hour of the ride is silent except for Trace's GPS giving direction. The twenty-first-century technology in the '62 Impala makes for a disjunctive combo. As we near my home in the deep wooded sticks, Trace breaks the silence. "Got werewolves out here?"

"No, just coyotes and vampires."

Trace pulls into my driveway and I give him the gate code without thinking twice. My wife and I have an agreement never to give the code out to strangers for safety reasons, but Trace doesn't feel like a stranger. He feels more like the trusted sidekick of a mysterious super-hero. I envision the Fidge as the superhero who makes an appearance only when the need to save the day is at hand. At all other times, his faithful Boy Wonder, Trace, lowrides around the neighborhood in the Impala-mobile, deterring evildoers by the mere fact of his immense visible presence.

In addition to Trace's sidekick status, he's also June's personal guardian angel. I bet he keeps lots of other people safe, too. There's something about him being on your side that fosters a feeling of security. Ever since I got my first threat of bodily harm from one of Benson's HICs I've wished for a higher power watching over me. I never imagined it would be a guy like Trace.

Trace pulls up to my front door. "You can't even see your neighbors. Why would you want to live like that?"

"That's just the way it is in the country. That's what people move out here for, the privacy."

"Don't know why anyone would want to live out here when they could have a castle in Brooklyn for the kind of dough you musta paid for this place."

"To each his own, Trace."

"Heard that."

Trace now walks around to the passenger side, opens the door, lifts the lever, folds the seat forward, and takes my bag from my hand as I'm stepping out. I shake the pant leg that's caught behind my shoelace and stand up straight, face-to-chest with Trace. He's half a foot taller than I am and I'm six one.

I begin to offer a good-bye handshake. Trace steps past my out-stretched arm and gives me a firm hug, forcing the air up and out from my lung base. He takes a step away while sliding his giant-sized hands from around my back onto the sides of both my shoulders, which disappear into his palms. If he wanted to, he could squeeze his hands together and crumple me like an accordion. Instead, he gives me a little shoulder massage. "You got to win this shit for June and Suzy."

I nod. "I will."

Trace releases me, turns around, and gets back into the purring Impala. He grabs the brake release under the dash with his left hand, takes hold of the white shifter knob with his right, and puts the car into gear. Oh man! He's going to wake my wife with his spinout! Trace surprises me as he quietly pulls away using minimum gas feed. I didn't know he could move forward from a standstill without popping the clutch.

As I walk up to my front door, I realize Trace never took off those dark plastic wraparound sunglasses, not one time all evening. Yet I felt he and I saw eye to eye on everything, that we would be friends in another place and at another time. We're from different worlds—or should I say hoods?—brought together for the good of one cause.

A worthy cause, a cause of a wrong that needs to be put right so a loving mother can begin to recover. So a warm wonderful woman who has had more than her share of hardship can then move forward and live her life again. So June can be freed from the bondage of feeling responsible for something she has no accountability for. A horrible event that left her child severely brain damaged that she mistakenly allowed to become the core of her existence. This is the power of a mother's guilt.

Now that I know the truth about this circumstance, that little Suzy Williams was senselessly electrocuted, I can't fail June, and a money recovery, her share, my share, has nothing to do with it.

If I lose this case now, bad lawyering will be the cause of June's continued suffering and desolation, and *that* is something I just can't live with.

11

Today will be a breakthrough day. I can feel it. I have awakened with purpose and passion because of yesterday's developments.

Almost every case in my office has something about it that sparks me to win, including the HIC cases. Sometimes the fervor is obvious, like when you have to win enough money to take care of a catastrophically injured client who can no longer provide for his family. Sometimes the passion is hidden and must be flushed out until you find that one motivating factor.

In Suzy's case, I'm in a rage because they electrocuted her. I'm even thinking a cover-up's in play, but though I have the tingle, I'm not certain.

You'd think *someone* must know Suzy was electrocuted. On the other hand, Nurse Braithwait is the sole witness and doesn't even know what she herself has done. Furthermore, neither the doctor involved nor his attorneys have ever seen the wire and patch, which are the keys to the case.

The tingle I mention is real. I know it may sound crazy, but my anus has a way of tingling when I'm on the verge of exposing a cover-up. I don't yet know who it is this time or what they know, but my asshole's signaling suspicion. Someone knows something, or else I must be developing hemorrhoids.

I open my eyes and turn to look over at my wife. She's wearing a stack of two pillows signifying my snoring was heavy. That plus the fact I woke her after midnight will no doubt contribute to her kitchen disposition. I gotta make a preemptive strike to get even for what's to come. I have no choice. I'm gonna feel her wrath anyway so I might as well make the best of the situation and start one up. After taking a quick shower I ready myself to leave. But before I do, I reset her digital clock, advancing the time from 6:28 to 7:25, ten minutes after her wake-up time.

"Honey," I say, standing in the place I stood on Tuesday night, begging for the HJ. "Honey," I call out nice and loud, waking her.

"What? What's the matter?" she asks, removing the pillows off her head.

"You overslept and I know you time your morning schedule tight to the minute so you don't lose a second's sleep."

"What? What time is it?" I look toward her clock and back at her, theatrics. I turn the digital to face her so she can see for herself.

"Seven twenty-six! Oh no, the kids are going to miss their bus. Oh damn, I'll just have to drive them today."

"Sorry about that. Have a good night's sleep?" I ask, wishing I hadn't before finishing my question.

"Yes," she answers, which surprises me, "I did, but I had a weird dream about your mom working as an electrician at a junkyard."

"That sounds nutty," I respond, giggling to myself.

She changes topics and adopts a pleasant tone. "I really appreciate you having the new girl call me to say you'd be home late. That was so thoughtful of you."

"No problem," I say, searching my mind. "I got to go. Have a nice day."

"You too, honey."

Since I don't have any new girl working for me and since June was the only person who knew I was going to be home late, I conclude she took the liberty of calling my wife. That's probably why she tried to interrupt my call home in the Impala on the way to Fred's, when I shushed her. I wonder how she got my home number, since it's unobtainable from any source. Maybe she asked one of the Fidge's peeps to find out somehow. Whatever her method, she continually proves her resourcefulness.

I start up the Eldo. The music begins blasting so I follow the instructions Fred gave me last night before leaving him. I disconnect the power to the receiver, hit a reset button I never knew existed, then I reconnect the unit. It responds and my problem is fixed. I hit the off button to enjoy a quiet ride, after which I say out loud, "Thanks, Fred," just as my wife opens the garage door. Oh crap, she found me out and came down to give it to me. Deny, deny, deny.

"Who are you talking to?"

"Uh, just myself, honey."

"I think you've been working a little too hard lately. That's one of the signs."

"Thanks for your concern. Have a nice day." I put the Eldo in reverse to flee and roll two feet before she motions me to stop.

"Wait. I need more money. I had to buy tennis dresses yesterday at a cash-only sale at the club." I stop.

"I'm sorry you had to do that. No one should be forced to do anything so drastic."

"Very funny," she replies with a smile. "I need about fifteen hundred."

"What?" I say, crazed. "I gave you a thousand yesterday."

"I said tennis *dresses*. I bought six. One in every color. That tapped me out."

"Well what do you need fifteen hundred for, deli meat?"

"No, I'm going to the mall in White Plains. I need to buy socks and underwear."

"Fifteen hundred for that?"

"I may have to pick up a few other things."

"I see. Will another five hundred do ya for these very special socks and underwear?"

She counters. "How about a thousand? You said you didn't want me using my credit card anymore."

"Honey, you can't use your credit card anymore. You're at the limit and I only pay the monthly minimum."

"So what, I still haven't used it."

"You can't use it. Seven fifty, and I'll mark it settled," which is what lawyers say when they've made a final offer.

I surrender the cash to my garage hijacker. "Have a nice day, honey," I say for the third time, ecstatic she hasn't made a counterattack.

"I will. Where're you off to?"

"First to the office, then to my expert out in Brooklyn. I'll see what happens after that. With the case I'm working on now I could find myself just about anywhere. Have a nice day." Four times.

"You, too. Oh, can you pick me up a new alarm clock on your travels? Mine seems to be broken and you're better with the technical stuff." By "better," Tyler means it would be better if the money came out of my wallet to buy the clock rather than from the cash I just gave her, earmarked for more things she "has to buy."

"No worries, honey," I say, thinking I'll just reset her clock back to the right time later and tell her I fixed it, "I'm on it. Have a nice day." Five.

It's a fast top-down trip into the city. I get off the bridge at the 125th Street exit near Harlem Hospital. I drive slowly down Second Avenue, keeping an eye out for the sick, sore, lame, and disabled, hoping to pick up another case, but no such luck this time.

I enter my garage and see Oscar. "Don't bury it. I'll need access at a moment's notice."

As I walk out of the garage I get a call on my cell. Before I get to say hello, I hear an irate Lily. "Bert Beecher just called and wants to talk to you. He said it's important. When I told him you weren't in, he asked me where you were, but I didn't tell him."

"Good job. That HIC is a loose cannon."

"I know. He asked for your cell number, and I told him I couldn't give it out."

"Good job again."

"I know. He wasn't very happy about it. I had to spend a few minutes trying to calm him down. I told him you'd call him on his cell in ten minutes. Here's the number." She gives it to me.

"Try not to have much interaction with Bert Beecher. You never know what's going to set that guy off."

"I didn't sign up for this HIC shit," Lily notes, then hangs up.

I dial Beecher and he picks up. "What da ya want?"

"Bert, it's me, Tug Wyler, your new attorney. What's up?"

"Oh yeah, you. You're a motherfucker for doing what you did to me the other day."

I play innocent. "What're you talking about?"

"You know what the fuck I'm talking about! You know real well. I don't take kindly to humiliation."

"Bert, we were just dealing with what's in Betty's medical records. I didn't intend to humiliate you," I tell him in my defense.

"There's no other kind of humiliation but intentional, mother-fucker." The line goes dead.

Bert has busted me. I admit it and embrace my error. A slip I should not have made because Henry warned me about this guy's smarts. I promptly make a couple of mental notes: 1) Don't act superior to HICs or anyone else, and 2) If you're going to humiliate someone, be clear to whoever it is that you're trying to humiliate him because, as Bert correctly pointed out, there's no other kind. He'll calm down and come to his senses. I hope.

I arrive at my building and I detect a whiff of marijuana in the elevator on my ride up. The closer I get to my floor, the closer I feel I am to the source. I open the door to my office suite and sitting on the couch is a burnout puffing on a doobie. I thought those guys were away.

"Hey!" I scream at him. He's slow to react. "You can't smoke that in here! This is a law office."

"Sorry, dude, I thought this was *TOKE*—you know, the magazine."

"Well it is," I hesitate to admit, "but you still can't smoke that in here. It's illegal, especially within a law office."

"Dude, how we going to get weed legalized if we're so uptight about smoking it?"

"Put it out! Now!" He sees I mean business and complies.

As I pass Lily, I bark, "You got to enforce the 'no smoking' rule, and please bring a pad and follow me right now."

I enter my office, put my bag down, sit at the desk, and wait. One minute. Two minutes. Three minutes. No Lily.

I buzz her. "Lily, what's up? I need to dictate." I hang up the phone without waiting for a reply. I mean business. I've got a lot of things on the agenda. I've got purpose and passion running through my vessels.

I wait two more minutes, which seem like ten. Still no Lily. I get up and go out to her station and see she's on the phone. As I approach, she gives me the international sign for "wait a minute." I am not happy. "No. In my office, now!"

She speaks into the phone. "I got to go. My boss is being an ass." This comment is intended for me.

I shake my head, turn around, and walk back toward my office.

"I don't get it. What's with you?" I ask when she enters. "I told you to come in my office immediately."

"Yes, you did, but you didn't say 'good morning' first or give me any other type of appropriate greeting."

I am incredulous. "You're kidding, right?"

"I kid you not. I demand a proper greeting."

"Look, the Suzy Williams case has taken a turn in our direction, and I have a lot to do. I don't have time for pleasantries. I'm facing a motion to dismiss here."

Lily casually sits back like she couldn't care less. "I suggest you make the time for pleasantries or find another paralegal."

"Oh my God! Okay. Good morning, Lily. There, was that better?"

Lily comes back to attention. "That was fine, but don't make me ask next time. Now what do you want?"

"I'm going to dictate a list of things for you to do and it's critical that you do each task immediately. Ready?"

"Ready."

"Number one," I begin. "Letter to Judge Schneider requesting the pending motion to dismiss the Williams case be adjourned for an additional thirty days. Number two—"

Lily cuts in. "Hold on a minute. Slow down. Okay. Number o-n-e. Letter to who?"

"You're kidding me, right? You only got the first word down?"

"That's right. I told you when you hired me I hate taking dictation. I got a slow hand. You've known this for years."

"Just forget it, then. I'll send you an email."

"Good. Will that be all, sir?"

"No. Please don't say I'm an ass to other people even if you feel that way. It's very inappropriate."

"Don't be an ass and I won't say you're one." Lily sticks her pen behind her ear, gets up, and walks out. She's making my wife look good. I pull my keyboard over and begin typing:

1. Letter to Judge Leslie Schneider on the Williams matter requesting a thirty-day adjournment on defendant's motion to dismiss.

2. Call June Williams up immediately and tell her I'm hoping to see our medical expert today sometime after one. Ask her if she could please come to the office before then and bring the wire and patch with her so Dr. Laura Smith can look at them.

3. Do an Internet search and identify every single manufacturer, wholesaler, and retailer for cardiac-monitoring machines that did business in New York for the ten-year period prior to Suzy's date of occurrence. Send out the following letter, certified mail, to each one and direct it to the attention of their legal department. Dear Sir or Madam: Please be advised this law office represents a little girl who was electrocuted and sustained severe brain damage as a result of your negligence. The cause was a defective cardiac monitor you placed into the stream of commerce at the Brooklyn Catholic Hospital of New York. Your failure to respond within seven days from this date shall result in the formal institution of legal proceedings against you and negative media attention about your product and practices.

4. Do a Notice for Discovery & Inspection and serve it on Winnie McGillicuddy. I'm hoping to get some documentation on the hospital's use of heart monitors. It should read: Plaintiff hereby demands to discovery and will inspect any and all documentation, writings, charts, records, memoranda, inscriptions, notes, letters, notices, emails, interoffice communications, third-party communications, scratch pads, crib notes, Post-its, and any and all other writings heretofore not specifically delineated maintained in the ordinary course of business of the Brooklyn Catholic Hospital in general and the Engineering Department in particular that possess, contain, and/or allude to information relative to the proper and/or improper use, application, connection, disconnection, patient preparation, and otherwise general use of cardiac-monitoring machines and devices including, but not limited to, circumstances that may result in electric shock and/or electrocution of a hospital patient.

Before hitting the send button, I finish by writing, "Lily, I typed this really fast so clean it up and make it look lawyer-like." I send the email on its way.

My Hunch Is She's an *N* in the Making

I open my drawer and pull out a little blue address book with maroon trim. It contains contact information for all the medical experts I've ever used over the course of my career. They are the key to my success and have paid for enough tennis lessons to improve my wife from a 2.0 player to a 4.0 rank. The book is thumb-indexed for each letter, *A* to *Z*, so entries can easily be made alphabetically by last name. However, I've organized experts according to medical specialty.

I run my finger down the side tabs and stop at the letter *N* for neurology. I may need to call Dr. Mickey Mack, a rogue physician and my go-to guy. His license was suspended because of his drug problem, but it didn't cut into his income because he's a self-made millionaire. He developed ouchless medical tape, patented the idea, and sold it for a bundle. I enter his number into my cell phone just in case I need to call him later for guidance.

In my book the letter *S* appears next to Mick's name, which, according to my key code, stands for "suspended license." It's the only *S* in my book. I crossed out the letter *P* and the number 15 when I entered that *S*.

My code works like this: the letter *N* stands for a negative review on a case. The letter *P* stands for a positive review, meaning the expert doctor, on his evaluation of a matter I submitted, found malpractice took place. If a name has three *N*'s next to it, I'll never use that doctor again, on the assumption he's antimalpractice.

Next to the *N* or *P* is a number between 3 and 15 that signifies a rating assessing how well the doctor testified or performed in court. The number range of the point system is based on the Glasgow Coma Scale, or GCS. It's a neurological scoring system devised to give an objective way of recording the conscious state of a person after a head trauma. A GCS score of 3 means the expert was unconscious or completely sucked on the witness stand, and a score of 15 means the expert was alert, oriented, responsive, and an excellent court witness.

Using the tabs again, I stop at the letter *H,* for hematology. The last entry there is Dr. Laura Smith, whom I entered before I went to see her. I place a straight vertical line next to Dr. Laura's name. I hope to convert it into a *P* for positive review after our unscheduled meeting today but have an unsettling feeling that's not going to happen. My hunch is she's an *N* in the making.

After entering Dr. Laura into my cell, I dial her on my office line. On the third ring a familiar voice answers. "Smith Sickle Cell Pediatric Care Center. Steven Smith, director, speaking. How may I help you?"

"Hi. This is Tug Wyler, the lawyer on the Suzy Williams matter. The doctor reviewed the case, and I was in a few days ago."

"Yes, with your dog. How can I help you?"

"I need to meet with your wife again."

"It's my understanding she turned down the case."

"Yes, that's true, but—"

He interrupts. "Why don't you just accept that there's no case, Wyler?" Called by my last name, I hate that. "To my understanding, your client sustained a terrible complication from her sickle cell disease. That happens, you know."

"Yes, thank you for sharing, but I need to speak to your wife again. Her opinion was based on what she had before her and I have something new to add to the equation that I think might change her mind. She told me to let her know if there were any new developments, so that's why I'm calling."

"You can tell me," he says primly, "and I'll relay this new information to my wife—I mean the doctor."

"I'd be more comfortable discussing it directly with her, if you don't mind. And in person. I don't like to talk about important legal matters over the phone."

"Okay. But I just want you to know my wife shares everything with me. I suggest you tell me and I'll tell her. Then she can decide if she wants to see you, with my input, of course."

I am getting annoyed. "Maybe you didn't understand me. I don't want to talk about it over the phone."

"Oh, I understood you just fine. Please don't take that tone with me."

"Listen, your wife is my expert. I have some new information that will help my client. I need to see the doctor to discuss privileged matters. I sense you're being obstructive. Now, if there is a problem, just let me know and I'll act accordingly."

"It's just that she's had two looks at it, and I don't like pushy lawyers trying to take advantage of her helpful nature," Smith all but snarls.

"That's completely understandable," I say, keeping my temper. "But I assure you I just want to share the new information with her to see if it changes her opinion. That's all."

He takes a long pause. "Fine. She can see you tomorrow at five. Bring another check in the sum of one thousand seven hundred fifty dollars for the expedited appointment."

"I need to see her today."

"Are you saying it's a rush?" Smith asks. I know this is a loaded question but have no choice.

"If needing to see her today is a rush," I answer, "then yes, it's a rush."

"Hold on a second. Let me look in the book." I detect a hint of glee in his voice. "Okay. You can see her today at noon, but I'll have to charge you the rush fee."

"Is that something different from the five hundred extra you tacked on for the expedited fee?"

"Oh yes. *Expedited* means twenty-four hours' notice. *Rush* is a same-day appointment. That's five hundred dollars more so it's going to cost you one thousand for the rush, seven fifty for the hour of time, and another five hundred for my wife's—I mean the doctor's—time away from patients. That makes the total two thousand two hundred and fifty dollars for the hour. And just like an expedited appointment, that money is gone one minute into the meeting. If you're not here before noon, I'll consider you missed the appointment and you'll be billed anyway since I'm setting the time aside. Those terms are non-negotiable. Are they satisfactory?"

Absolutely not. No fucking way. "Pencil me in."

"See you at noon, then. Bring a certified check, Mr. Wyler."

"Certified check? Why do I have to get it certified?"

"Because this case has already been turned down once on initial review and then a second time when you came here before. I don't want to chase you for the money when it gets turned down for a third time. So, a certified check or no appointment." *Click.*

"Greedy fuck," I say aloud as I slam down my phone. I look up and see June standing within the frame of my office door. God, she looks amazing. "Hi. What's up? I just told Lily to call you to bring in the wire and patch so I can take them to my expert in a little bit. I hope you have them."

"I have them. Is my lawyer smoking weed? I can't have you smoking weed while working on my case."

"No, June, I'm not smoking weed. My subtenants are *TOKE*, the marijuana magazine, or should I say civil rights group. One of their people lit up in the entry. You probably passed the guy on the entry couch."

"No one was on that couch when I came in, but as long as it's not you, I'm fine. What time are we going?"

"There's no need for you to come along. I can handle it."

"You telling me you still don't realize how important this is?"

"I know, June. I'm sorry. I'd love to have you come with me."

"Now that's a good lawyer." She walks into my office, sits down, leans back, puts her boots up on my desk, folds her arms across her lean stomach, and smiles.

I nod at her feet. "Nice boots."

"Thanks." The conversation stops there.

It's my turn to talk, but I'm looking to avoid an uncomfortable pause situation just now.

"Can I ask you something?" I say quickly. "Did you call my wife yesterday and tell her you were a new girl in my office and that I'd be coming home late?"

"Sure did."

"Why didn't you tell me?"

"I tried, but you shushed me."

"That's what I thought."

"I guess you won't be shushing anyone again anytime soon now, will you?"

I shake my head in answer to her question. "Listen, at ten o'clock I have a witness coming here on another Henry Benson case. I need to take a statement, then we'll go right after."

"What kind of Benson case? Medical malpractice?"

"No. This one's an eight-year-old who was struck by a cop car while riding his bicycle. The officer said in the police report that the child rode out between parked cars and into the passenger side of the squad car and that there was nothing he could do to avoid the accident. My eight-year-old client says the officer went through a red light without any sirens on or lights flashing and hit him while he was in a cross-walk. I'm hoping this witness, who's listed on the back of the police report, can corroborate my client's version."

"Did the officer who hit the kid also make out the police report?"

"That's a very astute question. Yes, the officer who hit the kid also made out his own police report. I'm certain there must be some policy or procedure against such a practice."

"You're wasting your time. The officer wouldn't have listed the witness if the witness wasn't on his side."

"You're probably right, but I have to carry out my due diligence."

"Can I sit in?"

"Sure, but please, just observe. Don't say anything—and I mean it this time."

June raises her right hand as if swearing an oath. "I'll keep my mouth shut, I promise."

"Good. I have a particular approach when I'm meeting with a non-party witness who I believe is going to say something against my client's interest."

"What's that?"

"I try to appeal to their human side."

Lily buzzes. "The witness on the Taheem Thomas case just arrived. I put him in the conference room. He's waiting for you."

I look at June. "Time to work the witness. Come on."

We enter and find an elderly black man sitting at the far end of the conference table. He has a well-groomed white beard and mustache, which alone give him a dignified presence. He's in a three-piece suit I imagine he has worn to Sunday church for the last thirty years. A silver chain hangs flat against his vest ending in a pocket at the end of which no doubt is an antique watch that his father passed on to him. And he smells like the aftershave fragrance you smell when you walk the beauty aids aisle that runs through the center of Bloomingdale's. My take on this guy: he is elegant and respectful.

He stands up and takes a derby off his head. I introduce myself, identifying June as one of my associates, and we take seats. "Thank you for coming in, Mr. Jones," I say. "I appreciate that your time is valuable, so I'll get directly to the point. According to a police report I have here, you were a witness to an incident where a poor little boy riding his brand-new bicycle he got as his eighth birthday present was struck by a police car. Do you remember that?"

"I certainly do," Mr. Jones states.

"Great. My client is the unfortunate little boy, who sustained a bad injury to his leg. He may never fully recover, and I'm advised by his mother that the children at school make fun of his limp so much he comes home crying a few times a week. I can only get money for the child's life-changing and permanent injury if I can show the officer driving the police car did something wrong, like speeding, failing to yield the right of way, going through a red light without his sirens on, or failing to apply his brake mechanism in a timely manner. If he did nothing wrong, then I can't get this little boy, who happens to live in your community, any money. Do you understand me, Mr. Jones?"

"I sure do."

"Great. So what did the driver of the police car do wrong? Was he speeding, did he beat the red, or what?"

"Nothing. That boy caused the whole accident. He just rode right out into the street and into the passenger side of the police car as it was driving by."

"I see. I guess we really have nothing further to discuss, and I do appreciate you coming here. May I ask, did you tell the lawyers for the police department the same thing?"

"Yes, I did," he answers. "I also told them what someone at the accident scene yelled out."

"What was that?"

"After the boy rode into the side of the police car, the officer jumped out to see if he was all right. The boy looked at his mangled bike, then took a boxer's stance, saying he was going to kick the officer's f-ing ass for totaling his new bike. That's when someone at the scene screamed out something, causing the boy to fall to the ground and grab his leg."

"I'm following. What did the person scream out?"

"The man knew the boy by his first name," Mr. Jones says, "and he screamed out, 'Hey, Taheem, lay down, you just hit the jackpot!' "

I thank him politely, he makes a comment about the weed smell, then departs, leaving June and me in the conference room. "It appears Taheem isn't much different from Cornbread Connie," June comments.

"I guess not. What's worse is he's just a kid." I shake my head in disgust. "Before taking over these HICs, I never had to deal with this kind of bullshit."

"What's an HIC?"

"Did I just use the term *HIC*?"

"Yes, you did. What's an HIC?"

"An HIC is a client that was referred to me from Henry Benson. I call them Henry's Injured Criminals, or HICs."

She looks hurt. "So that's what I am to you? An HIC?"

"No, June. Your dead husband with the lengthy criminal record would've been the HIC. All I'm saying here is that with HICs I have to investigate my own clients to make sure they have legitimate cases. That's not why I became an attorney. Besides, it's frustrating and burdensome, and the worst of it is I'm continually doing a conflict shadow dance. I'm supposed to represent them zealously, but how can I do that when I confirm fraud, then am told by a judge I can't be relieved as counsel? In effect, I become an enabler for these clients. And then there's your case, June."

"I see what you're saying about the conflict, but why is my case different for you?"

"The verbal report from Henry on your case was, and I'll quote, 'There is no case.' Remember this is coming from the guy who goes forward on fraudulent cases. So what am I supposed to believe or do?"

"You want the answer?" she asks.

"Sure. What's the answer?"

"The answer is you're a good man at heart. As each situation presents itself, you'll somehow end up doing the right thing, just the way you've agreed to further investigate Suzy's case. So give it no more thought."

"Thank you, June. Now it's time to see if Dr. Laura, our expert, is going to do the right thing. Come on. We've got to get to Brooklyn before noon or we're going to have a problem."

12

June and I enter my garage, and I wave down Oscar. "Yo, I got to fly. How 'bout it?"

"*Oye, amigo, momentito,*" he replies. "The keys are in the visor." He points back behind us. We turn around and see that the Eldo has its own private parking spot with no cars next to it, an unusual visual for a city garage.

"Oh my God, that car is beautiful!" exclaims June. "Trace and the Fidge would love to cruise that."

"Thanks, June. It takes a particular kind of person to appreciate it."

Making good time, we cross the Manhattan Bridge, right onto Flatbush Avenue, the most direct route. A little bit down, the traffic is backed up, way congested for this time of day. "Damn," I say as we come to a stop for a red light. I realize this is the first word spoken since we turned out of my garage.

"What's the matter?" June asks. I look to her. She has a wide smile, ear to ear, the same one she has been wearing this whole trip.

"Traffic," I answer. "What's the big smile for?"

"This is my first time in a convertible. I love it. Suzy would love it, too. Look around, everybody is staring at us, pointing and smiling. I'm not used to that—the smiling, that is. With Suzy, everybody stares and points, but nobody smiles, ever. It's just the opposite. This is a nice change."

"I can appreciate that, June." The light turns green and we slowly cruise down Flatbush toward increasing congestion. Storefront after storefront lines the avenue, with a bodega on every other corner. People are moving in the street, on the sidewalk, everywhere, none of them in a suit, other than me, the bald guy in the Eldo with a sweet cup of hot chocolate in the passenger seat. We stop at another red and the obvious source of the traffic jam is the commotion on the corner. Not a disorderly one—rather it has the type of energy you feel in a casino, where people surround a player who's hot at a gambling table.

"A big game of three-card monte," June says, looking over.

"What?"

"Those boys over there got a game of three-card monte going on—you know, a money scam, a short con, where a plant pretends to buddy up with a guy they've marked to cheat the dealer while really conspiring with the dealer to cheat the mark."

"Thanks for the definition, June. I'm familiar with the card game. I just couldn't see the box from my vantage point." I pull up a few feet more to catch a better look.

"Check the boy with the bills slipped between his fingers. That's done to cover up his hand tricks with the cards." I look over and as I do, nothing short of a police raid breaks out initiated by two uniformed cops who snuck around the corner. The kids running the game go flying, as does the dispersing crowd, and the one with the money in his hand heads in our direction, hobbling on a cast.

It's none other than Barton Jackson III—Mile High.

"Yo, yo, yo, it's my lawyer," he says, opening June's door, to her surprise.

"Yo, scooch over, hurry, scooch over." June reluctantly complies, the door slams shut, and Barton yells, "Go, go, go, the light's green." I make the getaway. The legal term is *aiding and abetting*.

"Hello, Barton Jackson the Third," I say. He looks to June and his brows rise high.

"Yeah-ya," I say, "she's a great-looking woman." June smiles. Mile High gives a nod of approval.

"I didn't know you had a thing for the Nubian princess. This girl's got it going on," he says, looking at June with intentions, as if he had a chance. It's clear she's not into talk like that.

"Barton," I say before June cuts him down, "remember that respect thing we discussed in my office concerning my paralegal, Lily?"

"Oh yeah, man. She has it going on, too. My lawyer's a ladies' man and smokes weed, too," he says, laughing it up.

"I don't smoke pot, Barton! I rent space to . . . oh, never mind. Anyway, the same respect rule applies here and with every girl you encounter, and you shouldn't be using your cast as a walking boot. Why don't you go back to the hospital orthopedic clinic and ask them to change it into one?"

"'Cause I got no ride," he answers, suggesting. I look at my watch.

"You're lucky, we're heading near there anyway."

It turns out Barton Jackson III is a really smart young man. That's not an observation, that's a cold hard fact that June surfaced. He'll be going to college next year, the first in his family to attend, on full academic scholarship. He was running the monte game to raise funds for "uncovered expenses." That kid, another product from Brownsville, is going to be somebody. He already is. And he and June are hitting it off well. It seems Barton's little cousin has cerebral palsy and he's well aware of and sensitive to June's struggles, which she greatly appreciates. I pull up to his stop.

"Out you go, Barton." He and June are exchanging numbers.

"Now, Barton," June cautions, "don't be abusing the privilege. I can't be getting any late-night calls from an overzealous youth."

"Oh, snap, June, nice try. Being the betting man that I am, I'd wager you'll be the one calling my hotline before I'll be calling your precious digits."

How Did You End Up with a Creep Like Him?

We arrive at the Smith Pavilion at eleven-fifty-five. I park illegally right in front of the entrance in a space reserved for emergency vehicles instead of in the underground garage. The thirty-five-dollar parking ticket will be a lot cheaper than the two-thousand-dollar-plus loss if we're a minute late.

I close the Eldo's weighty door. "Let's go, June. We've got to roll." We fast-walk into the building. I hit the button and again my elevator waiting time has potential consequences. The doors open to an empty compartment and I pull June in. She didn't realize I was going to grab her so as a result loses her balance. She ends up falling into my arms. As she looks up into my eyes there's what I believe to be a romantic pause, which is ranked way up there in the world of pauses. I lift her up and she shoves me backward.

"Don't handle the merchandise," she cautions. She smoothes out the imaginary wrinkles in her clothing caused by the dip. When she's done, she looks back over and smiles.

"We'll flirt later," I tell her. "There's no time for that now." I hit the fourth-floor button.

The elevator door opens on four. Directly ahead is the HEMATOL-OGY DIVISION, SMITH SICKLE CELL PEDIATRIC CARE CENTER sign with an arrow underneath pointing to the right. We hit the hall floor running. I gain the lead and come to a sliding halt at the entry doors to Hematology. I pull the right door open and we enter.

Humpty Dumpty is sitting behind the reception desk on his high chair again. "We're here, Mr. Smith," I announce.

He looks at his watch. He cocks his neck around 180 degrees to see the clock hanging on the wall behind him. It reads: 11:59. "You just made it." Then he nods at June. "Who's this?"

"This is my client, the child's mother, June Williams."

"She can't go in. She'll have to stay in the waiting area."

"I don't think so," I tell him firmly. "It's her case and she has a right to sit in. There's a Court of Appeals decision on this point. It's the matter of Homer Simpson, formally cited as 45 New York Supp. Second 419, affirmed 1978 by the Court of Appeals. I'll have to charge you a hefty cancellation fee for violating June's right to be present if you don't let her in."

Smith gives way. "She can go in, if my wife does not object, but I need your check before either of you take another step."

"Sure." I pull the check out from my wallet and hand it to him.

He grabs it like a four-year-old getting a lollipop and inspects it for spelling, grammar, and punctuation. He looks up. "Two thousand two hundred fifty. Very good."

He takes leave of us now, clutching the check and scooting down the corridor to his wife's office.

June laughs. "Homer Simpson? You got to be kidding me. You could've blown the whole thing."

"There's no way a guy like that would know of *The Simpsons*. He's too busy counting his nickels."

The patient waiting area to our right is filled with little kids presumably with sickle cell. The place does a good business. Smith comes out of his wife's office and waves us over. "It's great that your wife is helping all these children," I say. "And I bet you're not doing too badly on the receivables, either, judging by the crowd in your waiting area."

"We're the most profitable sickle cell center in the nation," Smith tells us smugly. "People come from all over to consult with my wife. We have numerous contracts with major institutions to provide hematological services related to sickle cell disease. Plus, we receive grants for the research we do here."

"Dr. Laura must be quite a good physician."

"Yes, that's true, but she owes all this to me. I'm her business partner. We own this building. This whole operation, including its high profitability, was my brainchild. Medicine is a business just like anything else, and, done right, it can be a lucrative one."

"I see. You're quite the entrepreneur. I bet you're the one who developed the distinction between the expedited fee and the rush fee."

He beams proudly.

From inside her room I hear Dr. Laura's voice. You have to wonder why she settled for this character. Opening her door, she stands there waiting for us. They must have had a fight over something because she looks visibly upset.

I do the introductions. "Dr. Laura Smith, June Williams."

"Please, call me Dr. Laura. Everybody else does." She extends her hand. As they shake, she places her other hand over June's and holds it there. "I'm so sorry about the terrible injury your little girl sustained. Sickle cell can be crippling when a crisis gets out of control. If I understand correctly what my husband has told me, your attorney has something new for me to consider that may change my opinion. I hope it does. I want to help."

Dr. Laura slowly lets go of June's hand. "Please, be seated, and let's get to work. My husband has carved out an hour for us and I mustn't run over." She turns to him. "Dear, will you be good enough to close the door, please?"

He follows her instruction, but to my displeasure remains on the wrong side of the door. "Mr. Smith, please take no offense, but I'll be divulging confidential communications to your wife. If a third person is present, husband or otherwise, it'll be considered publishing, which, in effect, makes it lose its privileged status, so I'll have to ask you to leave."

"I thought I told you my wife tells me everything."

"You did, but her telling you something and you hearing it come from my mouth are two different things."

"I don't see any difference. I don't want anybody intimidating her into changing her opinions. I think it best I stay."

"I can assure you we're not here to do that. Again, I must ask you to leave."

I peek over at Dr. Laura. She knows I'm right but doesn't dare call her husband wrong. He's got her number, that's for sure. Just as I'm about to cave, June, who has been looking intently at Dr. Laura, turns to Smith and speaks up. "Mr. Smith, you're obviously a very important person around here, and I appreciate the concern you have for your wife. Men as devoted to the marital bond as you are hard to come by. I understand that by leaving the room you feel that you are giving up your ability to care for your wife, so I'm going to promise to keep watch over her. In addition, my lawyer's going to give you an extra three hundred dollars to compensate you for what you feel you'll be giving up. Would cash be acceptable?"

"I'd feel better about it if the compensation were four hundred." Smith sniffs. "I feel I'm really giving up a lot here."

June turns to me. "Give him the money."

"June," I say quietly, "can I talk to you outside for a moment?"

"Sure, after you give him the money."

"Fine," I reply. I reach for my wallet and pull out whatever bills are in there. They add up to three hundred eighty-two dollars. I look at Smith. "Give me a moment. I always keep some emergency funds in my bag." I search six different compartments and come up with another six dollars and forty-seven cents. I turn back to him. "Would you accept three hundred eighty-eight dollars and forty-seven cents as payment in full?"

"I'll accept that now as partial payment," he says in an officious manner, "but you'll have to promise to promptly make up the difference."

"I promise."

He takes the money out of my hand and looks at his wife. "Laura, I'll be back at reception if you need me. Remember, don't go over the hour, or should I say the fifty minutes you have left."

Dr. Laura looks back at him affectionately. "I won't, dear. Thank you for your concern." Smith departs, still reluctant but clutching my money. During their exchange I note that her diplomas are still on the floor leaning against the wall face forward. As I'm thus prevented from ascertaining her medical training, I remind myself to ask for her CV again.

"I must apologize," she tells us. "My husband is very protective of me. Sometimes I feel honored, and sometimes I feel like he's protecting his investment. Either way, I wouldn't be where I am today without his business skills and the way Steven manages my life so I can concentrate on my patients."

"He manages your life?" I ask. That she admits this seems a little odd.

"Actually, it's okay with me. It's best for both of us. Anyway, we're not here to talk about me. Let's get to your case. What's this new information you have for me?"

"Before we start, would you like me to hang your diplomas back on the wall?" I offer. "I'm the product of generations of art dealers, and I enjoy the exercise of hanging a picture in a perfectly even manner."

"Oh no. Thank you. I'm having them reissued in my married name. The new ones should be here soon. These are going to storage. Steven thought it would be a good idea for them to read Smith instead of my maiden name. Since this is the Smith Sickle Cell Pediatric Care Center in the Smith Pavilion, it seemed fitting the diplomas of the doctor-in-chief should read Smith. Now, shall we begin?"

I ask June for the wire and patch. She removes them from her bag and hands them to me. "Dr. Laura," I begin, "these are the actual lead wire and patch that were connected to Suzy Williams at the moment she went into her cardiopulmonary arrest. The nurse who hooked her up to the cardiac monitor had them in her possession all this time and just recently gave them to us. We had them analyzed by a well-qualified electrical expert and they told an unbelievable story. Suzy Williams was electrocuted. We believe the inch-long prong end of the lead wire was mistakenly plugged into an extension cord near the monitor that must have been connected to a wall outlet at the other end instead of the appropriate heart monitor cable connected to the machine, and a charge was sent through the wire, causing Suzy to sustain a nonlethal electrocution." I pause because of what I see. Dr. Laura has a look of fright on her face. She goes completely white, ghost white, and looks like she's going to faint.

"Dr. Laura, are you all right?" I ask. "You don't look too good. Is something the matter?"

"No, no, I'm okay," she assures me. "I just need a moment. That's the most horrible thing I've ever heard happen to a child. How do you know this? Did the nurse confess to doing such a horrible thing?"

"The nurse has no idea what she did," I say. "As far as I know, nobody except our electrical expert and we three in this room knows what really happened. And I believe that includes the hospital and its attorney. Our electrical expert established that the charring seen inside the wire could only have been caused by the high voltage of a wall outlet, and there were traces of burned skin on the electrode patch. I should also tell you, since you never had the opportunity to examine Suzy, that she has a round scar on her chest just left of midline in the exact shape and size of this patch, conclusively establishing the event. Here, take this wire and patch and see for yourself." As I move toward her she jumps back the way a vampire does when a crucifix is displayed. "What's the matter? Don't you want to see for yourself?"

"No, please," Dr. Laura's voice cracks. "I, I . . . Things like that I'm not good with. Please. Move it away from me!"

She is turning even whiter, so I move my hand back. "Okay. I'm sorry. I didn't know it would have such an effect on you." My compliance seems to help, as she immediately looks less agitated. Still, she's not completely regained her composure. So I pause—the kind where you allow someone to collect themselves. "Doctor, if you accept this as being the truth of the matter, isn't it possible Suzy's cardiopulmonary arrest was induced by electric shock rather than her sickle cell crisis?"

"Yes, that's a possibility, but this scenario seems highly unlikely."

"Why is that, Doctor?" I ask.

"For one, who would lack the common sense enough to plug a child into a wall outlet?"

"An uneducated, untrained, and inexperienced temporary nurse who's only qualified to cook jerk chicken." June supplies the answer unhesitatingly. "She mixed up the cables. She didn't actually insert the prong into a wall outlet, but rather into an extension cord that was plugged into a wall outlet rather than the cable for the machine."

"Okay," Dr. Laura says. "Then it's possible, but before I could commit to such a theory, I'd have to be relatively certain that your electrical expert is right. I must also point out Suzy's acute arrest is also consistent with a sickle cell crisis, unrelated to being electrocuted. It would be hard to distinguish between the two as the causative agent."

"I'll get you our electrical expert's affidavit," I offer. "If you agree with it, will you support our position on this for now? I need to submit a medical affidavit to the court to prevent the case from being dismissed at this point. If you change your mind later and wish to withdraw from the case, I'll understand, but for now I just want to avoid the dismissal. Are you open to that?"

Before Dr. Laura can respond, the door unexpectedly flies open.

The momentum and its weight cause her husband to lose hold of his grip, with the door slamming into the doorstop.

"Don't answer that question, Laura!" he exclaims.

I look at June. "So much for confidentiality." I turn my attention to the intruder. "Mr. Smith, since you're in breech of our oral contract, I would like my three hundred eighty-eight dollars and forty-seven cents back, please."

"I just happened to hear what you were talking about as I was walking by. It's not like I was eavesdropping or anything."

"Of course you weren't. Who would've thought that?"

But all of a sudden he changes gear. "Listen, maybe I can be of some help here," Smith suggests. "Can I see that wire and patch, please?"

"Sure," I say as I hand it to him, knowing, if need be, I can kick his fat little ass to get it back.

He inspects it. "I know a lot of people in the electrical industry. I used to work for an electrical contractor and engineer before Laura and I met. I'll have this wire examined by one of my confidants at your cost. If they confirm what you're saying, then Laura will come forward on your behalf. But I'm not going to let her sign a statement under oath, based on the findings of an electrical expert retained by a plaintiff's lawyer."

"Are you questioning my veracity?"

"I'd like this to be looked at by a person with integrity and credibility before Laura changes her position and signs an affidavit, that's all."

"Fine. You designate whom you want to look at this and I'll bring it there personally. But, I might add, our expert does have integrity and credibility. And just make sure your guy's prepared to perform an impedance test and make sure he has an immunohistological chemical known as CD Orange 45 available, to test the electrode patch for Suzy's charred flesh. When he's done, we'll be in business."

"Oh no. I'll take it there myself. I see how you operate. I don't want my engineer to be intimidated by your presence, similar to what happened here."

"Mr. Smith, stop fulfilling your own prophecies. No one put

pressure on Dr. Laura. In fact, she didn't even commit to changing her opinion. As for your taking possession of this wire and patch, that's not going to happen. I've placed a statement on a judicial record indicating I'd keep it in my possession and that's what I intend to do."

I get up and take a commanding step toward him. By the look on his face he senses my urgency. As I take my second step, he offers back the wire and patch, palm up. My third step would've been up in his pint-sized grill and he knew it.

"I don't know what's going on here, Mr. Smith," I say firmly, "but it's very unprofessional. I'll send you a copy of my electrical expert's affidavit, and after reading it, along with his impeccable qualifications, you can decide if you want your wife to be a part of this case. You'll have it within the next day or so. I'll expect an answer immediately." I turn to Dr. Laura. "By agreeing to be an expert to evaluate this case, you have a duty to June over here and her brain-damaged daughter, Suzy, to carry out your highly compensated obligation in a reasonable and fair manner. Can I count on you to do that?"

Dr. Laura has tears gathering in her eyes, and I have no idea why. I certainly didn't say anything to induce them. I turn my attention back to her husband without giving Dr. Laura a chance to answer, in hopes of preventing her from breaking down completely. "Mr. Smith," I continue, "time is not on my side here. If you want out, let me know now and I'll scramble around for another expert. So what's it going to be? Do you want to read what my electrical expert has to say, or are you and Dr. Laura bowing out?"

"You're right," he concedes. "I've been a little overbearing. I don't want you to take this case away from us if you feel there's more we need to see to make a proper and educated decision. Please send us the affidavit from your electrical expert and give Laura the chance to evaluate it. There will be no further charges on the matter, either."

"That's more like it. Thank you. Come on, June."

June stands up and looks directly at Dr. Laura. "You're such a nice woman. How did you end up with a creep like him?" This causes Dr. Laura's floodgates to open. June steps over and gives her a comforting embrace much the same way Fred comforted her. Dr. Laura is weeping heavily on June's shoulders. "There, there. Everything's okay." I've got to learn how to do that.

Dr. Laura welcomes the embrace as if she'd been in bad need of a hug. After a moment, she gathers herself. "I'm okay now," she says.

"June's just emotional about this whole thing," I tell Smith. "I'm sure you can understand. Please accept her apologies. She didn't mean it when she called you a creep."

"I understand," he responds graciously.

"Thanks." As I walk by him, I whisper some advice. "Go comfort your wife." He nods. Then, when June and I reach the door, I stop and turn around. I see Smith holding his wife. It's an odd visual, since she has to bend down into an awkward position to accept his comfort. "One last thing," I say, "this should've never happened—Suzy being electrocuted, that is. We intend to sue the manufacturer of the cardiac-monitoring machine for putting a dangerous apparatus on the market. Our engineer said this type of foreseeable misuse should've been considered and the machine should have been designed in such a way so as to have prevented someone from plugging the prong of the lead wire into a source of live current such as the female receptor of a common extension cord. The prong should have been designed so that it could only fit into the housing for the cable leading into the cardiac monitor itself."

This manages to open Dr. Laura's floodgates again. Her husband whispers something in her ear, then releases her with a pat on her back. He looks at us. "Come on. I'll walk you out." We leave Dr. Laura's office and start our journey down the hall as Smith apologizes for his wife's emotionality.

"We can't have a breakdown like that occur in court," I caution, "no matter how sympathetic she is to what happened to Suzy Williams."

"I assure you it won't happen. She's a great witness. I've seen her on the stand." We walk the remainder of the hall in silence until we reach the elevator, then he asks a question. "How does suing the manufacturer of the cardiac monitor work? Do you have to bring a whole other lawsuit?"

"No," I answer. "I intend to add them as a party to this lawsuit since the claim arose out of the same operative facts. Why do you ask?"

"Just curious as to how it works, that's all."

"How do you feel about that? Are you going to have any problems with my suing the manufacturer for any reason? If you are, I want to know about it before we go any further."

"If it happened the way you say, and if your engineer says it could've been prevented but wasn't because of a design flaw, then I'm fine with it, since they would bear some responsibility."

"Good answer," I tell him. I push the down button. "I have a question for you, Mr. Smith. How did your wife get involved in this case as an expert?"

He makes a quizzical face. "I'm not really sure. I'd have to look it up. I had signed my wife up to be a member of a medical-legal review company and it's possible that was the connection, but I really can't say for sure."

"I see. Oh," I add, "I really need a copy of your wife's curriculum vitae so I can put down her qualifications in her affidavit should she agree with my engineer."

"I'll get that to you and you get to me my eleven dollars and fifty-three cents. Good-bye."

As we walk toward the car, I reprimand June for insulting the man in front his wife, our would-be expert. "We don't choose the people we fall in love with. Most of us don't know what's good for us in the love department. That's why we choose what's familiar or someone we perceive as giving us a sense of security, even if everything else about them is wrong."

"I guess you're right," admits June. "Look at me. My father, even though he loved and cared for me after my mother died, was a badass who got murdered, and I married a man who ended up being a dangerous felon."

I switch from the love topic. "Dr. Laura was a little too emotional for me."

"I like the fact she feels for what my baby has been through. She's a compassionate woman. That's probably why she works with children.

But there's something about her that's familiar that I can't put my finger on."

I open the passenger door for her. "Let's go. Get in."

"I can get home on my own from here. I want to walk a little and take some time to myself."

"You sure?" I ask, knowing we're not too close to her home.

"Certain."

Without saying a word I shut the door and June starts to walk off. But not with the confident, determined gait I'm used to seeing. She's kind of wandering in a pensive mode, off on a tangent, deep in thought. Maybe June's rethinking what she herself just said about our expert—that Dr. Laura "feels" for what Suzy has been through. Maybe she's thinking about Dr. Laura's tears and having to give *her* comfort, not the other way around.

I know I am.

ily's packing up to leave when I arrive back at my office. I note the time aloud. "It's four-thirty."

"Thanks for the time. Will I need an umbrella?"

"Very funny."

"You know the deal. Babysitter issues. Got to leave a little early."

"Fine. Did you do those things I emailed you about earlier?"

"What things?"

"Lily, tell me you're kidding," I say testily.

"I am. Did it. On your desk for review. Bye."

I know after all these years her work needs no review, but I look at it anyway. It's perfect like always, which is one of the reasons why I put up with her attitude. I also put up with it because it keeps things spicy around here. Besides, she's the sexiest woman on Park Avenue South and I love to look at her. At least I admit it.

When I handled my first HIC case, Henry was intimately involved in the matter all along the way. I guess he wanted to make sure he'd chosen the right guy to take over his injured criminals. Since then we've rarely had contact. He simply expects me to do what I do best and to send him a check for 50 percent of the attorney's fee. When I do call him, it's mostly to find out information that should be contained in a file but isn't and that he may remember.

I had Lily go through Suzy's files to see how contact was first made with Dr. Laura Smith. She left me a Post-it, the gist of which is that the file's silent on the issue and to go through it myself next time. I need to call Henry to see if he remembers, because I find it odd that a doctor would agree to review a medical malpractice case against a hospital three blocks from her office.

I dial Henry's cell. He picks up on the third ring. "Benson here," he answers casually. He's the poster boy for men over sixty who haven't lost their cool. I'm certain he and Fred Sanford would hit it off big.

"Henry, it's me."

"Me who?" I attempt a response but am cut off. "Oh, that me. Make it quick. I'm eating a piece of pumpkin pie at the diner on 125th Street. Go ahead. I'm listening. Do we have an offer on one of my cases? Remember, I have the last say on the money."

"Henry, I know you have the last say, and no, I don't have an offer on any of your cases. Won't the big fee from the nine fifty I told you about on Cornbread Connie be enough to hold you over?"

"Cornbread? I'm eating pumpkin pie, not cornbread."

"Never mind. Look, I'm calling to discuss the Suzy Williams case."

"Give me a few facts to refresh my recollection."

"Henry, you're pulling my leg, right? This is the case of the little girl with sickle cell disease you handed me the other day. Your verbal was that there is no case, remember?"

"Recollection refreshed when you said the word *sickle*. Are you getting us out gracefully yet? I don't want any more complaints against me with the Office of Professional Conduct."

I give a long pause before answering, the kind of pause you give someone on the other end of the phone line where you want to trick them into thinking the connection's been broken. A few seconds in I hear Henry's voice. "Hello, hello. You there?"

"We're not getting out so fast," I inform him.

"I thought I got a negative review from my expert."

"That's what I'm calling about, our expert and the merits of the case. Let me explain."

"Hold on a second," Benson says shortly. Despite his applying the phone muffle, I hear him in the background. "Moisha, darling, would you be a dear and put my pumpkin pie in the warmer until I'm off the phone?" Then a faint sound of clattering comes over the line.

"Go on. I'm listening," he says, rejoining our conversation.

"I think there's a case here, Henry, just not the kind of case you thought there was. You thought it was for mismanaging Suzy's sickle cell crisis, which I agree could have been managed better, but I concur with our expert that there's no malpractice based on that theory. Meaning, if Suzy did have an acute sickle cell crisis resulting in a cardiopulmonary arrest and stroke, there was little anyone could have done to change the outcome of things."

"Are you going to tell me something I don't already know? What's our theory of recovery, then, if not that?"

"I believe this unfortunate little girl was electrocuted by an inexperienced nurse. She placed an electrode patch on Suzy's chest, connected the lead wire to that, then plugged the child into an extension cord connected to a wall outlet she mistook for the monitor's cable." There's silence, and I'm actually not certain if it's a pause or not.

I'm about to do the "Hello, hello?" thing myself when Benson finally speaks.

"What the devil are you talking about? I don't recall anything like that in the hospital records."

"That's because it's not *in* the hospital records. It's nowhere to be found, but I have the mechanism of electrocution in my possession, which is a cardiac-monitoring lead wire and electrode patch. I had them tested by an electrical expert named Fred Sanford and he was the one who came up with this conclusion. It's based on hard evidence. That's the best kind, although everything else surrounding this theory is still circumstantial at this point."

Benson is confused. "Fred Sanford? Isn't that the name of that comedian on that show with the junkyard?"

"The character, not the comedian. Anyway, my Fred Sanford owns a junkyard, too."

Benson shifts from confused to concerned. "Are you feeling all right? This sounds ridiculous."

"Oh, I'm fine, perfectly fine. Your instincts were right about there being a malpractice case here but wrong about what the malpractice was."

"What did I tell you about pointing out to me when I was wrong?" Benson asks, although it seems like a command in question form.

"Never to do it?" I answer.

"That's right. So don't do it again. I'm glad you found a case here. That's why I hired you. Is there anything else? I want to get back to my pumpkin pie."

"Yes, there's something else. I need to know how you found the expert on the case, Dr. Laura Smith."

"Why is that important?"

"Because I discussed the wire, the patch, the electrical expert, and the scar on Suzy's chest with Dr. Laura, as she likes to call herself, and she and her control freak husband weren't receptive in the way I'd expect an expert for the plaintiff to be. Before I continue with her, I just want to know a little more about her. The place to start is how she got involved in the case."

Benson pauses, but I've lost count of the pauses by now. "My recollection is that she was referred to me by another doctor."

"Who was this other doctor?"

"After the girl sustained her injury, the mom switched her care to another hospital and a different group of doctors. I believe it was one of her subsequent treating doctors that made the referral to this expert. In fact, I'm sure it was, but I don't recall the doctor's name."

"Hm, okay. Got to go. Enjoy your pie."

Henry Benson is so good at keeping criminals out of jail and so bad at understanding the dos and don'ts of handling a medical malpractice case. Although the rule is not absolute, you never want to rely on a subsequent treating doctor or a referral from a subsequent treater to be your expert in a malpractice case. First of all, many patients are referred to a subsequent treating doctor by their prior doctor or group who is the malpractice offender. If this is the case, then obviously the two know each other and the bias is inherent. Second, the prior and subsequent treaters are likely to know each other if their specialty is the same—especially if they're practicing within a close geographic proximity—and that influences things as well. Moreover, if the subsequent treater commits malpractice during the patient's care, the only reason the subsequent treater would point the finger at the prior treater would be to transfer responsibility away from his own mistake.

Furthermore, at the time of trial the subsequent treating doctor will be cautious not to say something on the record that one day could come back to bite him in the ass if a similar act of malpractice is committed in the future. Last, by hiring such a doctor or a referral from such a doctor as your expert, you may find there's a high probability that he is unfamiliar with the medical-legal process, and there's no room for inexperience in this game.

It's possible Dr. Laura Smith falls into one of these categories. Or maybe she's hesitant for other reasons not yet known. The fact of the matter is that when I told Dr. Laura I had hard proof that Suzy Williams was electrocuted, she should've been all over it. Instead, she hesitated, resisted, and then her obnoxious husband made his play to get their own electrical expert's review. This all makes no sense to me, even given the guy's control-freakism. In addition, Dr. Laura found more complications from the sickle cell crisis than are documented in the hospital record or even in defendant's expert's affidavit in support of the motion to dismiss, which I also find curious.

Stay Conscious

I leave the office and stop in a newsstand downstairs. I pick up two six-inch Avo cigars, one for the journey home and one just to keep on hand. As I'm walking down the garage ramp, Oscar sees me and heads in the opposite direction to retrieve the Eldo. He pulls it up and the two other people before me waiting for their cars start acting out. Oscar disarms them. "You're right. You were here first. I'm sorry," he tells his confronters, who, of course, are disappointed they won so easily. He's a smart guy, and we travel on the same path of life.

I pull out of the garage and head toward East Thirty-Fourth where I intend to take the FDR Drive to the Thruway to the Saw Mill to home. I cross East Thirty-Fourth Street and turn into a parking area underneath the FDR overpass where people are let off for the heliport. I put the column shift into park and retrieve one of my cigars from my inside pocket. It's not that easy to light a cigar while trying to keep the Eldo between the lines.

As I lower my window, I see a homeless guy lying there by the little building with an overflowing shopping cart. He's registering my presence. I hold my cigar out of the car and clip the butt, which begins its journey down. The nonmedical term would be *gravity*. After I've lit it, I think the guy's going to say something, and he does. In a cultured voice.

"Is that Eldorado a 'seventy-six?"

"You nailed it." I puff carefully.

"I had one of those in another life."

"What happened to your Eldo?"

"Lost it with everything else."

"Sorry to hear it."

"No worries," he says with a shrug. "When I'm ready, I'll have it all again. For now, I'm too busy being happy without a dime of money or a penny of responsibility. Life was too complicated when I had everything."

I think about that for a second. "There's something to be said for that. How'd you make your money?"

"I worked for a law firm."

"I'm a lawyer, too."

"Oh no. I'm not a lawyer," my new friend corrects. "I was a mailroom clerk."

"How'd you make money doing that?"

"Inside stock information."

"Huh. How'd you get the inside information?"

"By copying confidential documents. I also happen to like to read, so as fate would have it, I was privy to a lot of info on new issues and put it to good use—or so I thought at the time."

I acknowledge this and then there's a break in the conversation, which I'm pretty sure is a "crime doesn't pay" pause.

"You're a resourceful guy," I tell him. "I'm working on a case right now, and my client has proven to be pretty resourceful, too. I misjudged both of you on appearances alone. I'm kind of in the profiling business, and whoever coined the maxim 'You can't judge a book by its cover' knew what he was talking about."

"Benjamin Franklin, and he did. Is that an Avo you're smoking?"

"It is, actually."

"You wouldn't happen to have a spare one, would you?"

"I certainly do. Do you want to smoke it now?"

"That would be a treat." He gives me a broad smile.

He gets up and walks over to the Eldo. Even in a torn suit that probably hasn't seen the inside of a dry cleaner in years, he still looks pretty respectable. He has a full head of long brown slicked-back hair, further confirming my theory that the homeless have a genetic predisposition against male-pattern baldness. He can't be older than fifty.

I cut the butt off the cigar. I hand it to him with my windproof lighter. He thanks me, then runs the cigar under his nose while taking in a big inhale. "Ahhh. This is going to be good. It may even motivate me to go back to work." He sparks it up like a pro, then takes a few puffs. The way he holds the cigar, brings it to his mouth, and draws on it all are pretty sharp. I have everything in the world going for me and I'm envious of a guy down on his luck because he has a full head of hair and looks cooler than I do when he smokes a cigar. What does that tell ya?

The man extends his hand to formalize our meeting. "My name is Horatio Cohen. What's yours?"

"Rockwell, Trevor Rockwell," I say. It's the one I keep in reserve. No need to give him my real name.

"I like the way you say it, although I question whether it's your actual name. No matter. So, tell me about this case of yours."

"It's a long story. The short version is, I represent a little girl who got electrocuted by a nurse who misapplied a cardiac monitor by

220 / ANDY SIEGEL

plugging her into a wall outlet. The only people who believe in the fact of this unwitnessed and undocumented event are the little girl's mother, a junkyard dealer name Fred Sanford, who's a friend of Neil Armstrong the astronaut, and myself. My own medical expert is giving me resistance, and I'm facing dismissal if she doesn't change her mind real soon."

Horatio Cohen takes in what I said. It's clear he's of a very high intellect, probably much higher than mine. "How certain are you this is what really happened?"

"Positive."

"Then get a new expert."

"That may sound easy, but time's a factor. This expert is familiar with the case, and it's not so easy to get a new one just like that. You know how doctors stick together and don't like to finger-point."

"Get a new expert," Horatio repeats in a clear and convincing tone. "Go do what you know needs to be done and do it now."

"Now?"

"When you're done smoking your Avo. Don't waste time. Follow your instincts. Trust yourself and align with others who believe in you, trust you, and who share your passion. Move away from the nonbelievers. There can be no conviction regarding your cause absent belief."

"You know what? That's really sound advice. I appreciate it, Horatio." We blow sizable clouds into the air, cementing this agreeable mutuality.

Horatio puts his right hand on my left shoulder. "Always know who is for you and who is against you. Always be conscious of each. You hear me? Always be conscious of who your ally is and who your enemy is, and never confuse the two. Stay conscious to this fact, you hear me? Stay conscious, conscious, conscious . . ."

How Does This Feel?

. . . *conscious, conscious.* "Is he conscious? I think he's coming around. He's conscious!" I hear June's voice scream. "Get a nurse! Get a doctor!

He's conscious! Get someone! Go get somebody, damn it! He's coming out of it! His eyes are open! He's awake!" June pleads with enthusiasm as she pushes on Trace, who doesn't budge. That's because he wants to watch a guy—me—come out of a coma and arise from near death. Who could blame him?

I open my eyes a little more and take in my full surroundings. June, Trace, and Fred are standing over me. I look past them and see Suzy in her wheelchair jerking back and forth in excitement while staring up at the ceiling as Dog tries to balance herself on her lap. "Sch-weet, sch-weet, sch-weet!"

I'm lying down with my upper body slightly elevated, which I know for a fact from the angle of my view. My head is pounding. I feel like every bone in my body is broken. I look toward my feet to see my left leg has a cast on it. I look around and, for sure, I'm in a hospital. I'm a patient. I look at my left hand and there's an IV infusing. I look up at the IV bag and note I'm getting lactated Ringer's solution for hydration. The last time I was hospitalized, I was being infused with the same solution, but that hydration therapy was for a diagnosis of dehydration. It's clear to me my condition this time is one of a traumatic nature and so the IV's about maintenance.

Maybe Horatio Cohen assaulted me and stole my Eldo, but I kind of remember giving him a hug good-bye. But what else could have happened? My last conscious memory is him telling me I must always know who's on my side. I also vaguely remember someone chasing me. A car chase. Maybe more will come back to me over time. I've seen it happen with many of my head trauma clients.

June takes a step closer, bends over, and puts her beautiful face in my face. "Can you hear me?" she says, slightly louder than necessary.

My throat and lips are so dry I don't even think I can talk. I can hardly get my mouth and throat to a place where I can swallow, but I force some saliva down, which burns my esophagus. I must've had an airway tube put in so I must've had surgery. I struggle to speak. "J-J-June, what's up? What am I doing in a hospital? What hospital am I in? What happened? What day is it? I need a drink. What . . ."

She caresses my forehead. "Settle down. Just settle down." She pulls a spoon out of a cup with something on it. "Here, suck on this," she directs, putting a few ice chips in my mouth. Despite all the pain I'm feeling during this postcoma awakening, when June said, "Suck on this," I briefly thought she just might pop her tittie in my mouth. I want to blame the thought on the delusional effects of the pain medications, but I know better. I'm a pig. At least I admit it.

"Be quiet. Just relax. You were in an accident," she tells me.

"An accident?" I question whether my head trauma has caused me to suffer from echolalia, a medical condition where you immediately repeat a word or phrase you've just heard someone say to you. I promptly dismiss the notion. "When? Where? With who? . . ."

"You were run off the road by someone with a severe case of road rage, at least according to the cops. The guy in the other car crashed and died. We're supposed to call them if and when you woke up, when you're well enough to talk. They have some questions for you."

"How long have I been here?"

"Ten days. This all happened the same day we went out to see Dr. Laura."

"You're kidding me, right?" I ask. I honestly don't know if I said that or just looked as if it were what I was thinking.

June responds in either event. "I promise you, I'm not kidding. You've been in and out of semiconsciousness for the last eight days. The first two you were in a deep coma."

Holy shit! "Is there a chart hanging on the end of my bed?" This time I hear my own voice.

"Yes, right over there."

"Hand it to me, please."

June complies. I read the entries under the heading "Impression." It's written in scribble-scratch, which I am an expert at reading:

1. Status post left ankle fracture with open reduction and internal fixation

2. Blunt head trauma with loss of consciousness, negative for skull fracture or mass effect on brain

3. Testicular trauma and torsion requiring operative intervention without complication

Shit! My boys were injured! I need to undertake an immediate accounting. I reach under the covers to check on my testicles. I feel one, two, and . . . three. Yep, they're all there. What the fuck? What the fuck? I check again. On the recount it's only two but my left nut is so swollen it feels like a third. Odd numbers would be fine as long as it's not one. I also feel a whole lot of stitches with the tip of my finger running the length of my sac. I want to jerk myself off this instant to make sure my mechanics are in check, but I suppose that'll have to wait.

I hand June the chart back. I take another big swallow to coat my scratchy throat. "The last thing I remember I was smoking a cigar with a well-dressed homeless guy named Horatio Cohen and we were discussing your case." June looks to her left at Trace and then to her right at Fred with an expression that translates as "My lawyer's gone crazy." I continue. "No, really. I shared an Avo with a thick-haired, good-looking bum at the East Thirty-Fourth Street Heliport. That's the last thing I remember clearly. I must have posttraumatic amnesia. Where did the accident happen anyway?"

June looks to Trace. "On the Saw Mill River near Pleasantville," he discloses. "Didn't they make a movie about that town?"

"Trace, please." June, annoyed, shakes her head.

"What hospital am I in?"

"Northern Westchester."

"Oh God! My wife! Does she . . . ?"

"Relax," June tells me, "she's been by your bedside around the clock since you were admitted. That is, in between her yoga, tennis, and kickboxing. She left about an hour ago at our insistence, to get some rest and see the kids. I promised we'd stay right by your side and told her not to worry."

"Apparently, that means you met Tyler?"

"That's what it means. Tyler Wyler, I love that name. It has a ring to it and she carries it well."

"I see."

June turns to her posse. "Trace, Fred, I need to speak to my lawyer alone, please. I'll meet you in the waiting area when I'm done. Take Suzy with you." Trace grabs Suzy's handgrips and begins to wheel her.

"Feel better," Fred wishes me, then follows behind as June watches them make their way out of the room.

Just as June turns back to me and smiles, worry fills my head. "Man, I feel like I got worked over. The case! We got a deadline! I've got to get out of here. I have papers to prepare." The energy of my excitement has the effect of a piano falling on my head from ten stories up.

June tries to calm me. "Relax. Please, just relax. We have two weeks from your discharge date to put in opposing papers—the judge insists on seeing a copy of your discharge documents, by the way."

"That was nice of Judge Schneider to give me more time, given my coma and all."

"You think? I went to court on my own and had a little talk with Judge Leslie myself."

"June," I advise her, "it's inappropriate for you to talk to the assigned judge, especially in the absence of opposing counsel."

"I told you to relax. I called up Winnie 'the Weasel' McGillicuddy myself, and she was present for the conference. It wasn't ex parte, as you lawyers like to call it."

"Good job, June, and good use of legalese." Then another thought comes to mind. "What about the Eldo?"

"Barely a scratch. That thing's a tank. It saved your life."

A nurse comes in carrying a deep metal pan and doesn't even look at me. She goes to the sink, filling it with water and a soapy solution. She turns around, looks at me, and jumps back. "Oh my God! You're up!"

"Yes I am." I make an attempt at a smile.

"I'm Nurse Rena. When did you wake? How are we feeling?"

"A few minutes ago, and I don't know how 'we' are feeling, but I'm feeling like I got hit by a truck."

"That's understandable, but it's wonderful that you're awake and talking." She turns to June. "Has he gotten excited yet? When patients come out of a coma it's not unusual that they become keyed up and a bit agitated."

"Those are all good words to describe his behavior," answers June.

"Just as I suspected. Listen, it's standard care that I give you a little pain medication to ease you back into reality, especially with all your other injuries. Do I have your consent?"

"Give me the pills. I can't wait."

"No pills for you, not in your condition." Nurse Rena walks out of the room and back in just as fast. She has a syringe in her hand. She walks over to my IV line and injects the solution through a port. I feel instant warmth all over my body, which now seems a bit heavier.

"The doctors will be in just as soon as I report that you're back in the world of consciousness. Would you like me to do that now?" Nurse Rena asks. "Or after I give you a sponge bath?"

"After, please. I'm in no mood to talk. In fact, could you make sure that no one comes in here for at least an hour after my sponge bath? I just want to relax. That stuff you injected is a miracle drug. I'm floating."

"Fine, that's actually a good idea." The nurse looks at June. "Miss, would you mind leaving the room?"

"Oh, I'll do that for you. I'm a nurse of sorts, too, and take care of a much less compliant patient for a living."

Nurse Rena tilts her head. "Is that all right with you?" she asks me.

"Yeah. That's perfectly fine. Thank you."

Nurse Rena puts the pan down on my side table, hands June the sponge, steps out of my bed area, and draws the curtain for privacy.

June opens my hospital-issue pajama top, one button at a time. "Nice chest." She dips the sponge into the basin and fills it with water. She lets the excess drip out, then moves it over my chest. She puts a little pressure on the sponge so that warm water trickles out down onto my chest. "Take your time and get better," she softly admonishes. "The case isn't going anywhere. We've waited this long. We can wait a little longer." She dips and drips a few more times, then applies the sponge directly to my chest and starts moving it in a slow circular fashion.

"So, what do you think of my w-wife?" I mumble, taking note my speech is slurred from the painkiller.

"She's a beautiful woman and tough as nails."

"You're m-money, June. You got her p-pegged," I burble. "That sponge feels g-good can you keep doing it that w-way?"

June smiles slightly. "Sure. How does this feel?" she asks as she moves the sponge gradually downward onto my belly, keeping a slow circular motion.

"Feels g-good," I murmur, struggling to keep my eyes open, then realize, looking down, I got a pop tent going. I draw attention to it to save myself the embarrassment of June mentioning it first. "Oh shit. The Governor's come to town," I say, weights on my lids, realizing I didn't stutter there, strange.

"The Governor?"

"Pet name from an ex-girlfriend," I explain.

"Is that normal?"

"Is what normal?"

"To have an erection after coming out of a coma, with a broken ankle and recovering from surgery on your testicle?"

"It's obviously normal for me."

June dips and drips again, but this time she targets the Governor, making him look like a participant in a wet T-shirt contest. Nice.

June puts the sponge down, then slides her hand into a sensitive spot. I realize I haven't gone ten days without an orgasm since discovering myself during the summer of eighth grade.

"June," I point out, "I had surgery down there. You've now established I can get hard. Taking it any further may not be such a good idea."

"Your chart doesn't have any orders to the contrary," she teases.

"Listen, I'm pretty sure the surgeon wouldn't write an order *not* to jerk the patient off."

June looks me in the eye. "Just relax and let June practice a little nursing magic."

For the next five or so minutes not a word is spoken. Finally, after working me over with the sponge—dip and drip, then dip and drip again—the Governor is close in color to June's handbag, which today is dark purple. Producing from its depths a travel-sized bottle of moisturizer, June takes hold of the Governor just under his helmet and applies circumferential cream coverage. No pulling or tugging, however. Next June wraps her left hand around the bottom of my cock just above the first stitch and pulls down, making things skin tight, though still without tugging. Now with her creamed right hand she makes an okay sign just under the head. With the perfect amount of tension she slowly motions up, then down.

I spontaneously erupt. The unofficial tug count is two. "Tug count"—that's a funny double entendre.

June wipes me clean, just the way Tyler does. Oh, Tyler, I crossed the line. I didn't think I had it in me. "I'll leave you alone for now, but I expect to be the first call you make after discharge." I don't say a word. She turns, opens the curtain, and leaves.

The next morning, I'm awakened by Nurse Rena. "The police are here to see you."

"Send them . . ." Before I get out the word *in* two officers enter and approach.

"Good morning," the older guy with the name badge that reads PATEL says. They are from the Westchester County Police Department. "So what happened?" Officer Patel asks. I see his partner is called O'Malley.

"I'm told I was a victim of road rage," I answer, displaying my uncertainty.

"I want to know what you remember, not what you were told," says the officer.

"The last thing I remember clearly is smoking a cigar with a homeless man named Horatio Cohen at the East Thirty-Fourth Street

Heliport. The guy gave me some sound legal advice. After that, my memory is a little fuzzy."

"Tell me the fuzzy stuff," Patel urges.

"I kind of remember being hit from behind on the Parkway. Then I felt another ram, clearly indicating someone was trying to run me off the road. But I have some memory, a really fuzzy one, of there being an extra vehicle. Like, if it hadn't been there, I wouldn't be talking to you now."

"Are you saying three cars were involved in this incident?" asks Patel.

"Yeah." I wait a moment for Patel to finish jotting down his note in his memo pad. "Are you going to tell me who the guy trying to kill me was?"

"What do you mean?"

"I know he crashed and died. So who the fuck was he?"

Patel looks at O'Malley, then back at me. "Got any enemies?"

"None that I know of."

"Are you sure?"

"Well, I had a disgruntled client with a criminal record that wasn't so happy about the news I shared with him. He was in my office not so long ago."

Then I realize it was longer ago than I think. As I'm trying to assimilate this, Patel asks, "What news?"

It seems Patel is short on answers but full of questions.

"I had to tell him his wife thought he was a shitty lover and things of that nature, trying to force him to take a settlement, which, if I recall correctly, he still hasn't taken."

"You were involved with her?"

"If you're asking if his wife was cheating on him with me, the answer is no. I'm familiar with their marital sexual history from her medical records."

"What's your client's name?"

"That's privileged," I say, firmly hoping it will prompt the officer to be gratuitous.

Patel bites. "Is it Bert Beecher?"

"You said it, not me. Privilege preserved. That's the guy."

Patel looks at his partner, then back at me. "Then you did have an enemy, but you don't anymore. He's the dead guy who ran you off the road."

"Why didn't you say so in the first place? Privilege dies with the client." After an angry pause, I can't contain myself. "Fucking Henry Benson!" I yell. I know what's on Patel's mind, so I beat him to the punch. "Henry Benson is the attorney who referred Beecher to me. I've had a lot of problems with his clients, but this is the first guy who tried to kill me with premeditation."

"Can you give us any information on the other vehicle you think you remember?"

"I got nothing for you. Zero."

"You know how you got from the accident scene to this hospital?"

I shrug my shoulders and pose my own question. "Ambulance?"

Patel shakes his head. "Nope. You were found unconscious on the sidewalk right outside. Someone rendered first aid to you at the scene of the accident, which stopped your bleeding and saved your life, transported you here, and left you on the curb in front of the emergency room entrance. My guess would be the driver of the mystery vehicle. Looks like we're going to close the case. You can't charge a dead guy with a crime." Patel and O'Malley turn and leave.

Within moments Nurse Rena runs in. "Well? What happened?"

"Not much. Why are you so interested?"

"I don't mean to be nosy, but we don't get a lot of police activity in this hospital, so it's exciting. Who's the guy who tried to kill you and ended up dead?"

"He was a secret agent," I whisper conspiratorially.

"For real?" Nurse Rena asks.

"For real. He was Siegfried, one of the top guys from KAOS, a secret crime organization at the center of the Axis of Evil. More dangerous than Al Qaeda and the Taliban."

"Wow! Why was he trying to kill you?"

"If I tell you, you'll be at risk."

"Then don't tell me. Come on, you're getting out of bed. I'm taking you down to rehab for your initial evaluation so they can set up a course of treatment for you."

"Sounds like a plan," I respond. I struggle to move, then look to the nurse for an answer.

"You haven't used those muscles in a while. It's going to take a little to get your strength back." I nod, but didn't realize when I did it would take me near three minutes to transfer from the bed to the wheelchair. It's not just muscle stiffness from disuse, but also the delicate tomatoes in my stitched-up cinch sack.

We arrive down at the rehab facility of this smallish Westchester hospital and Nurse Rena stops pushing me at the closed double doors. She walks around and pulls the handle of the right one, which locks into an open position. Before me is one large, empty, rectangular room, with all its rehab equipment set out around the perimeter with a large blue gym mat in the middle.

Nurse Rena has wheeled me two feet forward when a young child on crutches glides by us from behind, saying, "Excuse me, mister." He pulls the other door open with his left hand while balancing on the crutch under his right pit as the other stick leans against his body. That kid has skill. He quick-crutches in and over to the light panel, flicking six switches on in rapid-fire succession. He rests the crutches against the wall and hops to the mat on his left leg, the right one having been amputated.

"That's Charlie," Nurse Rena says. "He lost his leg to a bone cancer," which I had assumed given his hairlessness. I feel her grab the handgrips of my wheelchair and I say, "I got it," preferring to wheel myself in. I'm pretty sure that's the first thing I've done for myself since awakening. I stop a few feet in to watch Charlie. He has a below-the-knee amputation of his right leg but that ain't stopping this rascal. He's jumping around on the mat like he's some kind of gifted gymnast. The kid is incredible, hopping along, then throwing himself into a one-handed cartwheel, then into some kind of tumble. My amazement is interrupted by a minor startle from behind.

"How do you feel today, Mr. Wyler?" asks a deep male voice I don't recognize. The source comes around and his tag reads: WINSTON FOREMAN, PHYSICAL THERAPIST. "I'm here to evaluate you for purposes of setting up a course of physical therapy. I'm also going to teach you how to most efficiently perform your adult daily living tasks such as wheelchair transfers, using crutches, negotiating stairs, showering, and things of that nature."

"Thanks," I respond. "Could you step to the side, please?" I ask, giving Winston the hand motion to move out of my way. He looks behind at Charlie, now doing one-legged jump rope, with double jumps and hand crossover's.

"That boy is amazing," Winston Foreman says. "Nothing will ever stop that child, certainly not cancer. Sad case, he's only seven."

Nurse Rena chimes in, "Yes, there's something inside of him that just won't let the obstacles of life slow him down." That statement struck a nerve—not a peripheral one, my cord.

"Winston," I say, "when do you think I'll be ready for discharge?"

"I have no idea. I haven't evaluated you yet."

"How about you, Nurse Rena—when?"

"I'd project two weeks at the minimum."

"I see," I answer, knowing instantly what must be done. "Winston," I say, "I appreciate you coming down here, but I won't be needing your services. What I would like you to do for me, though, is call an orthopedist to meet me in the area where they apply casts."

"But—"

"No buts about it, Winston. If you want to help me, that's how you can help." He shrugs, then turns and leaves as I keep watching this boy, Charlie. This amazing boy, Charlie, who won't let the loss of his leg get in his way.

"Nurse Rena, I'm going to get myself to the casting area, what floor is that on?"

"Two. But—"

"Please, no buts, I have some unfinished business that cannot wait. I want you to meet me there and bring some papers for me to sign. Do you know what papers I'm talking about?"

"Discharge documents, AMA?"

"That's right, Nurse Rena, I'm leaving here against medical advice. By the way, what day is today?"

"Saturday."

"Thanks. I'll be going to my home, then. Could you arrange for a cab? My address is in my chart."

"You're crazy, Mr. Wyler."

"No, not crazy, I just have purpose and passion that was run off the parkway, so to speak. But I'm on the road again," I say, admiring Charlie. She turns to look, following the line of my sight. He's on a stationary bike, pumping his leg, spinning a million miles an hour with determination on his face.

arrive in the city bright and early Monday morning to make up for lost time. The projected two weeks of hospitalization is totally ridiculous in light of the fact that I already spent ten days running the course of my coma. The weekend at my highly mortgaged boot camp was just the kind of rehab I might have expected. Tyler had me organizing the basement and moving the backyard furniture around, the better to be viewed from the kitchen window. I'm surprised how mobile I am in the walking boot I had the orthopedists put on me before leaving the hospital so I wouldn't have to mess with crutches. By Sunday evening my wife was making out a list of chores for me to accomplish while at home so I thought my chances of recovering were greater at work.

As I enter my office, I'm just as surprised by Lily's early presence as she is by mine. She looks up and freezes as if Casper the Friendly Ghost were paying a visit. She's staring at me with those big brown eyes, and they're now forming puddles. "You're alive! I mean, out of the hospital! I mean, here. *¡Dios mío! ¡Dios mío!*"

"Correct on all four accounts. Say what you mean. You work for a lawyer, you know. Our words are our stock-in-trade."

"What are you doing here? I mean, when did you—?"

"I work here. Remember? My name is on the door, the letterhead, the business cards, the website, and on the signature portion of your paycheck, just to mention a few."

She gives me a look. "I see you've *recovered,* so I'll drop my false act of concern."

"Say what you want, but I saw genuine worry in your eyes. The tears forming, the glassiness, and your lip—that began to quiver, too."

"I was faking. When did you regain consciousness? When were you discharged?"

"Conscious on Friday, discharged on Saturday, completed home work release on Sunday, and here I am. Let that be a lesson to you."

"Yeah, you're fully recovered."

I look at her desk. "What's been going on around here?"

"The cops investigating your accident came by. As per your standing instructions, I dummied up on every question. I settled three cases you had been negotiating, and the clients all came in and signed their releases. Best of all, I think you're going to love the responses we got from the attorney defending the hospital on the June Williams case and from one of the cardiac monitor manufacturers I sent the claim letter to."

"Don't say anything. I want to see for myself."

"They're on your chair."

"Perfect. Thanks for holding down the fort in my absence."

"That's what I do when you're around anyway," remarks Lily. "Hey, did they catch the guy who ran you off the road?"

"You mean you don't know?"

"Obviously not."

"It was that Bert Beecher. The best part is he killed himself trying to kill me."

"*¡Increíble!*" Lily exclaims. "I told you no good would come out of taking over those HICs."

"What do you mean? We couldn't settle Betty Beecher's case with Bert alive, so he did us a favor. Have her come in to sign the release of settlement and I'll call Benson up and tell him I closed the case—and the coffin. Otherwise, hold all my calls."

"I told you—" Lily starts in.

"This is no time for a lecture and you know my position on 'I told you so's.'"

"Well, I told you so anyway. We need security around here."

My left ankle begins to throb, and not just a little throb but a massive one. I move two chairs over. I sit my big ass down on one. The other I use to elevate my leg. The walking boot is heavy and I need a break. I also need to address a certain issue with Lily right now, before it gets out of control.

I look at her and pause, the kind of pause that occupies time when one doesn't know where to begin. "Lily, please. Don't you think you may be overreacting?"

She is clearly upset. "I'm not overreacting, *idiota*! I'm reacting. There's a difference, you know. Overreacting is an excited response in disproportion to the stimulus provoking the reaction in the first place. This isn't a disproportionate reaction. It's a normal and appropriate reaction under the circumstances, which is to say, when one of our clients tries to kill you."

"Good definition of *overreacting*, but please, settle down. It was an isolated incident."

"An isolated incident?" Lily isn't buying this. "An isolated incident is a onetime occurrence that happens outside the normal course of ordinary events."

"I have to commend you on your ability to define terms, but please, just take it in stride. We've made a lot of money off Henry's injured criminals and risk is always associated with financial return."

Lily looks at me and takes a big swallow. She's all choked up and holding back tears. I sense this whole megillah is because I got hurt and not necessarily because she feels like she's in danger. Nonetheless, she's going to take it further anyway. She blurts out, "I'm a mother and . . ."

"Lily! Enough! I want you to understand I'm fine except for a broken ankle and a couple of twisted nuts that have been surgically untwisted. You have my consent to take any measures you deem necessary to make yourself feel more secure around here, but I'm telling you this was a freak incident. I assure you, nothing like it will ever happen again."

"Okay. But I'm still going to hire a big black security guard who can also do filing and light typing. Is that okay with you?"

"Fine, but you sounded a little racist the way you put that. When I speak to June Williams, I'll ask her if she knows anybody who fits your criteria. She's rather resourceful. Now, kindly hold my calls."

"I heard you the first time," she responds.

It takes great effort to get out of the chair and mosey into my office. I'm mentally fatigued, developing a postconcussion headache, and dizzy as a carousel. My scrotal stitches are itching like crazy, but if there ever was a time not to scratch my balls it would be now. To top it off, I'm craving tequila and asparagus. Why, I cannot say. I've never yearned for the combination before. I can't explain it, but I badly need a shot of Patrón Silver tequila together with a plate of grilled asparagus—and I need it *now*. The asparagus, I should add, has to be topped with a sprinkling of large-crystal kosher salt.

Notice and Remedy

My office is exactly as I left it except for the intense smell of floral air fresheners and two pieces of correspondence I see on my chair. I limp around the desk, pick up the letters, replace them with my buttocks, elevate my ankle on the edge of my desk, and recline. The document on top is a formal legal response to my Notice for Discovery & Inspection from the office of Goldman, Goldberg & McGillicuddy. It reads:

Dear Sirs:

In response to your recent Notice for Discovery & Inspection, please be advised that our client, the Brooklyn Catholic Hospital, in general and by their Department of Engineering in particular, does *NOT* have any documentation, writings, charts, records, memoranda, inscriptions, notes, letters, notices, emails, interoffice communications, third-party communications, scratch pads, crib notes, Post-its, or any other writings heretofore not specifically delineated maintained in the ordinary course of business that possess, contain, and/or allude to information relative to the proper and/or improper use, application, connection, disconnection, patient preparation, and otherwise general use of cardiac-monitoring machines and devices including, but not limited to, circumstances that may result in electric shock and/or electrocution of a hospital patient.

This Discovery & Inspection response is signed by Winnie "the Weasel" McGillicuddy. Attorneys in New York are required to sign discovery responses. The signature is a verification that the contents of the response are truthful and accurate. In short, you'd better not lie or you're exposing yourself to a license suspension.

My anus is tingling big-time, so my conclusion is that the hospital or its attorneys or both are perpetrating a cover-up. And by this written answer they've now committed themselves to the lie to the very end. They'll need to be exposed for this, on meat hooks, by the very anatomy that defines them as defense attorneys. It's unbelievable that a hospital and, more specifically, their Engineering Department, would have no written documentation concerning the use and operation of a heart monitor.

I turn my attention to the correspondence received from the only cardiac monitor manufacturer that responded to my threatening claim letter.

It's from the Toledo Patient Monitor Manufacturing Company.

Dear Attorney:

Pursuant to contract, Toledo was the manufacturer and direct seller of all the cardiac-monitoring devices sold to the Brooklyn Catholic Hospital for the time period in question. Please be advised that approximately three years prior to your date of incident, in a hospital facility in Missouri, one of our older-model devices was misapplied to a patient who was electrocuted and died from his injuries. Please be advised the misapplication occurred when the medical professional applying the cardiac monitor accidentally plugged the male end of an electrode lead wire into the female receptor site of a live electric extension cord rather than into the monitor's receptor cable. Although we did not foresee such an occurrence at the time of manufacture, the fact that it did happen made it a foreseeable and dangerous misuse of our device. We could not possibly recall all of our machines and, in light of only one single event of this nature, same would be an unreasonable and undue financial hardship.

However, Toledo, at the advice of legal counsel, felt the situation needed to be addressed and remedied immediately. Accordingly, we retained the services of an independent safety engineering company known as Engineersafe, Incorporated. Enclosed please find a copy of their recommendations and a sample plastic adapter they designed to prevent a future occurrence of this kind.

By serial number tracking we identified that one of our "defective" machines was in use at the Brooklyn Catholic Hospital. It was the only Toledo monitor they had with a manufacturer identification number beginning with the letters CBE.

Enclosed also please find a copy of the correspondence and signed certified return receipt for same of our "Notification of Defect" to the Brooklyn Catholic Hospital's Risk Management Department. Please note we advised the hospital of the potential misuse; provided them with Engineersafe's recommendations; and provided them with a plastic adapter, serial number 23890873, to be placed on the monitor with the CBE manufacture number.

It is our position that the Toledo Patient Monitor Manufacturing Company provided the hospital in question with both actual notice and remedy to the potentially dangerous circumstance two years, nine months prior to the date of your client's injury and, as such, bears no responsibility for same.

Last, if the adapter had been applied to our machine as instructed, the event outlined in your claim letter could not have occurred. We hope this correspondence proves valuable, and we wish a satisfactory outcome for your client.

Very truly yours,
Ari Haimovic, Chief Engineer

"Holy Toledo!" I say out loud, giving literal meaning to the phrase. They had told the hospital almost three years earlier that this could happen and had provided them with a ten-cent plastic adapter to prevent it from occurring. All the hospital had to do was attach it and Suzy Williams would still be the bubbly little girl she'd been in the video. On top of it all, the hospital is denying it has any such documentation, despite Toledo's letter with certified receipt to Risk Management, which I have in my very hand. This is big, real big. I also might add I've never seen corporate America come forward like this. I guess since Toledo managed to insulate itself from liability by taking a reasonable corrective measure, they must feel they have nothing to lose—and I agree.

I dial up Dr. Laura. "Smith Sickle Cell Pediatric Care Center, Steven Smith, director, speaking. How may I help you?"

"Hi. It's your favorite attorney."

"I thought it was you from the caller ID. How can I help you?"

"More new developments," I answer. "In addition to the patch and wire, I now have further proof my client was electrocuted. I'm coming out there this afternoon to speak to your wife and to have her sign an affidavit, to attach to my opposition papers."

"When I didn't hear from you or receive your engineer's affidavit, I thought you gave up on us. I'm glad you didn't. Congratulations on your new proof. You wouldn't want to share it with me now, would you?"

"You know the deal, Mr. Smith. I only divulge confidential communications in person, not over the phone."

"That's what I thought." He quickly adds, "And mine is that you bring a certified check in the rush amount, with all the i's dotted and t's crossed.

"Hey, you said there'd be no further charge."

"I don't remember that."

"Oh, okay. I'll be glad to bring another check. I might even throw in a little bonus just because I know how happy it'd make you."

"Bonuses are always welcome. Please tack it onto the eleven dollars and fifty-three cents you still owe me."

"Will do. See you later."

As I go to place the receiver down, I hear him say suddenly, "Wait! Don't hang up."

I wonder how much this is going to cost me. "I'm still here. What's going on?"

"My only request is that you come after hours, and after hours today means nine-thirty this evening."

"Nine-thirty? Isn't that a bit late?"

"Better late than never," he responds cryptically. "See you then. Don't forget the check and your engineer's affidavit." *Click.*

I hate that guy. June was right when she called him a creep. There's something about him that just rubs me the wrong way over and above his blatant greed, his faulty recollections, and his arrogance in taking credit for the success of the care center. His wife's the head physician, so I'd imagine the center's achievement has at least a little something to do with her. Or maybe I hate him because of the way he controls his wife.

That's definitely part of it, and a reason I resent him. It seems Dr. Laura and I are connected by virtue of our spousal domination issues. I mean, he even had her diplomas reissued so his last name would appear on them. What's up with that?

Before I head out to the Smith Pavilion in Brooklyn tonight I need to set myself up with a closer just in case. The information from Toledo together with wire, patch, and Fred Sanford should make getting a backup expert not too difficult. I confess I even hope Dr. Laura sticks with her "no case" opinion, as I've come to question whether she has it in her to come to court and implicate a fellow member of the medical community.

I call Dr. Mickey Mack, my guy with the suspended license. This should be right up his alley because his medical specialty used to be neurology.

Mick picks up on the second ring and I greet him. "How goes it, friend?"

"You know, never happy," he replies. "I got some hot ass twice in the last three days, and afterward I felt all deflated and depressed both times. Maybe I shouldn't have gotten divorced."

"Mick, I know I promised to always listen and give advice, but I got a situation here and I need your direction."

"Okay, but you better reserve some time for me after your situation ends. So, let's have it."

I tell Mick all about the case, incorporating the view of my Avo-smoking mystery man, and then say, "So I'm thinking I want you to find me a backup expert just in case Dr. Laura still won't commit."

"I got to tell ya, I agree with the homeless guy. What did you say his name was?"

"Horatio Cohen."

"Yeah, Horatio Cohen. You need a new expert, not a backup. Forget about Dr. Laura."

"I can't. Call me crazy, but I have this loyalty thing running through my blood and I want to give her the first right of refusal. In fairness to her, I didn't have the Toledo information at the time she last reviewed the case so I want to present this change of circumstance to her first because she's been involved since the beginning. Lastly, given her reluctance, I feel if she does commit, she'll commit hard to the cause once she becomes a believer."

It's Mick's turn to talk but he doesn't. I suspect it's the pause of disapproval. "I'll try to find you a backup," he finally says, "but you're wrong on this one. You need a new expert. The husband's just going to extort more of your money."

"I hear you, Mick, but I'm deep in with this Dr. Laura and time is not on my side. Let me know as soon as you find my backup. Bye."

I put my cell away and fall victim to a "phone trail," which is that series of thoughts that spontaneously pops into your head immediately after hanging up. For the next few seconds I question whether I want to bring the Toledo development to Dr. Laura in an effort to sway her opinion out of loyalty to her or because of my own self-righteousness. As a trial lawyer, persuading those around me and being right is everything. It's a flaw in my personality that results in large jury verdicts, but tends at times to compromise my personal relationships. If I think I'm always right, then someone has to be wrong. This character short-coming can turn people off and push them away.

I spend a good part of the day finalizing my legal papers in opposition to defendant's dismissal motion where they're asking the judge to throw Suzy's case out. My Affirmation in Opposition, which details the lawyer's argument against the motion, acknowledges Suzy was in sickle cell crisis but clearly states the crisis was not the cause of the cardiopulmonary arrest and its resultant brain damage. I lay out the information that supports the electrocution in terms most persuasively supporting Suzy's claim. I discuss her chest scar, attaching a photograph; the internal charring of the wire; the skin residue on the patch; the unqualified substitute nurse; Fred Sanford's analysis and findings. I also include the affidavit I prepared for Dr. Laura that posits Suzy's cardiopulmonary arrest was from a nonlethal electrocution causing her heart to stop, the Toledo letter, and the hospital's answer to my Discovery & Inspection, which directly contradicts the Toledo letter. I clearly state to the court that a cover-up is in play, but leave out the part about my anal tingle.

In addition to opposing the hospital's motion, I also construct a cross-motion of my own seeking to amend my pleading. Amendment of a legal pleading is where you seek the court's permission to add something to the claim that has recently come to light. Amendments to pleadings are freely given as long as there is no prejudice to the opposing party in defending the case on the merits.

I craft my cross-motion to claim that the Brooklyn Catholic Hospital was negligent in the ownership, operation, maintenance, inspection, supervision, and control of the hospital and its facilities inclusive of, but not limited to, its cardiac-monitoring equipment by its servants, agents, licensees, and/or employees of the Departments of Engineering and Risk Management.

I lay the case right out and explain how a ten-cent plastic adapter provided by Toledo could've prevented the whole occurrence. I argue the new claim could not have been known or made at an earlier point in time as the hospital records are silent on such an occurrence and that it came to the surface only after Nurse Braithwait provided the charred lead wire and electrode patch bearing the cells of burned human flesh. Suzy's flesh.

I also cross-move the court to add a claim for punitive damages, which are not intended to compensate the injured victim but rather to punish the hospital for its grossly negligent conduct. Punitive damages are not covered by insurance. Courts permit such a claim only if it can be shown the defendant was not just negligent but grossly negligent. If I can prove what I've laid out in my affidavit, the conduct of the hospital by its Engineering and Risk Management Departments arguably ascends to the level of gross negligence, which, simply defined, is a reckless disregard for someone's safety.

I Can Tell When Someone's Lying

I spend the rest of the afternoon returning calls and putting an end to the rumors swirling around the legal community that I'm brain damaged from my auto accident. I mean, who would hire a brain-damaged lawyer? After quashing the rumors, I send a copy of my Discharge Instructions to Judge Schneider and then sit back in my chair to take a rest. I think the postcoma thing is catching up with me, and I'm still craving tequila and asparagus.

I put my leg back up on my desk for the thirty-second time and unbuckle and unzip and stick my hand down my pants to check on the twins for the fifteenth time. The swelling has gone down, and they're just about their usual size again. Still, the way the stitches feel is disturbing. I pull my elastic band out with one hand and take a peek. The black sutures look horrific. Just as I begin to pull my hand out of my pants, June appears at my office door.

"Take your hand out of your pants, counselor. I'm mad at you. You promised I'd be the first call when you left the hospital and you were discharged at two-thirty-seven in the afternoon on Saturday. That shit ain't right."

I quickly zip and buckle. "June, for real, I don't even remember that promise. I barely escaped death, remember? I don't want to hear it now. I got a broken ankle, my testicles just got out of the repair shop, I'm suffering from postconcussion syndrome, my butt knuckles hurt from sitting with my legs up all day, and I got a bizarre craving for tequila and asparagus that I haven't had the time to satisfy yet. Cut me some slack."

"Not happening, Tug. You made a promise I'd be your first call. I've been staring at my cell since two-thirty-eight on Saturday. I have it in me to call your mom, or maybe I should send the Fidge over here to give you some guidance."

"June, you're going to tell my mommy on me? I'm in my fourth decade of life, not fourth grade, despite my juvenile behavior, for Christ's sake. Give me a break. What's the Fidge going to do? Put a hurting on me? Too late for that."

"You're right about the Fidge," she admits, "but say you're sorry or I will call your mom."

"June, really—"

"Say it or I'm calling her right now. I've got her number, you know."

"Okay, okay. I'm sorry I didn't call you first thing after I was discharged."

"Good. See, that didn't hurt too much, now, did it?"

"No, June, the apology didn't hurt too much, but that may be because the rest of my body is chock-full of throbbing pain." I take a deep breath. "I have some updates for you I think you're going to be happy about." I spend the next half hour detailing the latest developments. I conclude, "A cover-up is what I think happened here, given the conflicting versions told by Toledo and the hospital."

June looks shell-shocked. "You mean to tell me my baby was electrocuted because someone didn't plug in a ten-cent adapter?"

"That's what I'm saying."

June begins to cry uncontrollably, as expected. I start limping around my desk and go to comfort her. "Sit back down. I know you care," June says. I take this as her way of saying I suck at the comfort thing. I comply with her demand.

"When you collect yourself, I suggest you go home and relax for the rest of the day. I'm going out to Dr. Laura's office later to firm things up, and no, you're not coming, so spare me the argument."

"I won't argue if we can do one thing. I want you to call up Winnie

McGillicuddy and probe her about her response where she claimed the hospital has no documents. Put her on speaker 'cause I want to hear every word she has to say."

"There's only one thing wrong with that idea, June."

"What's that?"

"That I didn't think of it first," I confess. "Tell me why you want me to do this."

"Because I can tell when someone's lying by the tone of their voice."

I dial. "Goldman, Goldberg and McGillicuddy. Hold, please," the receptionist sings. I need to take another painkiller, but I've taken three times the recommended dosage already.

The receptionist picks back up. "How may I direct your call?"

"The Weasel, please."

"Excuse me?"

"Winnie McGillicuddy, please."

She giggles with understanding. "One moment. I'll transfer your call."

A moment later, I hear, "Attorney McGillicuddy speaking."

"How goes it, counselor?"

There's a long pause, of the "I didn't think I'd be hearing from this guy so soon" variety. "Oh, you took me by surprise," she replies. "I thought you were in a coma and brain dead. Goldberg was getting nervous about his fee on the case he sent you. He was going to pull his client out of your office."

"Please don't get all gushy on me. I was comatose, not brain dead. Tell Goldberg to relax and feel free to spread the good word of my full recovery."

"I see," she sniffs. And she didn't buy me a get-well card, either.

"Anyway, I got your response to my D and I. Frankly, I'm a little perplexed."

"Really? Why is that?"

"Because in a major institution like the one you represent there are generally files and files of documentation maintained in the ordinary course of business concerning important equipment like cardiac-monitoring machines."

"I went to the hospital and did the search myself with a member of the Engineering Department. We came up with nothing."

"Nothing at all?" I question.

"Nothing at all."

"Absolutely nothing?"

"Absolutely nothing."

If she were Pinocchio she'd be looking for rhinoplasty by now. "You know your response is verified, meaning it's a sworn statement subject to the laws of perjury."

Ms. McGillicuddy takes a tone. "I resent what you're implying."

"Okay, resent me. My feelings won't be hurt. But why don't you check one more time and maybe you'll come up with something."

"I tell you what," she says, "I'll check again and you arrange to have the wire and patch available for the hospital's engineering expert to inspect."

"That sounds reasonable. The wires will be available for you to inspect at my office with twenty-four hours' notice."

"Consider this your notice."

I put my hand over the receiver and silently mouth words to June. "You good for tomorrow?" She nods. "Winnie," I say, "June Williams and I will be here tomorrow and you can bring your engineering expert over. You can even do testing on the patch and wire if you want. I invite it. I'll even tell you what kind of testing I think you should do."

"I'll be there in the morning with my expert at nine sharp. He'll decide what testing, if any, is appropriate."

"You got it. Will you have completed your recheck for records by that time?"

"Definitely. By the way, as per Judge Schneider's instructions, I hope you notified the court you're out of the hospital."

"Don't worry, I did. You should be getting a CC of the letter for your files."

"Good. In two weeks this case will be dismissed."

"We'll just see about that." *Click.* I look at June and she's got a smirk on her face. "Why the grin?"

"She's not even a good liar. We need to call Trace."

June puts the call through on my phone. She hits speaker and on the second ring a deep voice answers. "Trace."

"Hey, Trace," June says.

"Hey, baby. Things secure?"

"All is well. Trace, do we have peeps in the Brooklyn Catholic Hospital?"

"The Fidge got peeps everywhere in seven-one-eight. What do you need?"

"I'm gonna give you a copy of a letter from the Toledo Company addressed to the hospital. I want you to find out if the hospital got it, responded to it, knows of it, or any which other way. Have the Fidge's people start looking in the Engineering Department, then in Risk Management."

"On it."

She hangs up. I smile. "This should be interesting."

June walks around the desk, bends down, and gives me a heartfelt hug. "I'm glad to see you out of that hospital," she says, sighing while holding me.

"Me, too." I enjoy the comforting hug, which I didn't realize until this exact moment I so desperately needed.

She lets go and stands back up. "I got to be going now."

"Okay. On your way out, ask Lily for a copy of the Toledo letter to give to Fidge's peeps. Travel safely, and by the way," I add, "I really enjoyed that sponge bath."

She gives me a quizzical eye. "What are you talking about?"

I nod at her. "You know. The dripping-water bit in the hospital."

"Really. I have no idea what you're talking about."

"You know, the cream? Come on, June, don't embarrass me by making me say it."

She shakes her head. "You were pretty much out of it. I have no idea what you're talking about." I was out of it, heavily medicated, but wasn't that too good to have imagined?

"You know. When you told Trace, Fred, Suzy, and Dog to leave the room?"

She shakes her head again. "Suzy and Fred weren't at the hospital,"

June informs me. "Only Trace was with me, and we left together." I thought it was too good to be true.

Coma Foreplay

I have about an hour to burn before I have to hail a cab to Brooklyn. I'm not in good shape, having worked a full day against medical advice. I'm also a little stressed about seeing Dr. Laura, and without good reason because if she's not on board, I'm confident Dr. Mickey Mack will get me another expert.

I leave my building and cross the street to the Gansevoort Park Avenue Hotel on Twenty-Ninth and Park Avenue South. It has a really nice bar, and I know the kitchen does special orders. I go in, sit on the only open stool, and catch the attention of the sexy bartender. From experience, I know Ginger is truly dedicated to getting me the drink she knows I need in an expeditious manner.

Ginger comes over. "What can I get ya?"

"Tequila and asparagus, please." She looks confused. "I'll have a shot of Patrón Silver with an order of grilled asparagus, lightly salted with kosher salt, if you have it."

Ginger shrugs. "I'll put the order in. What happened to your ankle?"

"Broke it in a car accident. Had surgery."

"Sorry to hear it. That sounds pretty bad."

"Not as bad as my coma."

The coma comment causes her eyebrows to raise. Ginger's interest is clearly piqued. "Were you *really* in a coma?"

"Yep. For ten days. Caught a glimpse of the other side."

"Wow. I never met anybody who was in a coma before. That's really cool. What was it like?"

"Very peaceful. Like the kind of peace you'd expect when you're between the universes of here and there."

"Way cool. Can I tell Margo?"

"Sure, if you think she'll care."

"Oh, she'll care. She's *into* the coma thing. First it was tarot cards, then it was the Ouija board, now it's coma victims."

"I didn't know we had a following."

Ginger turns to her right and makes a bullhorn with her hands. "Hey, Margo! Margo!"

The hottest woman I've ever seen is filling mixed nuts dishes at the other end of the bar. "What? I'm nutting bowls over here," she says without looking up.

"This guy was in a coma," Ginger yells as she points at me.

The entire bar crowd is now looking at yours truly as she continues her pointing gesture. "A true-to-life real coma or, like, a semicoma?" Margo yells back, as if screening me for participation in some coma study group.

Ginger turns to me for the answer. I say, "Full coma with complete unconsciousness and no responsiveness to painful stimuli."

Ginger shouts in reply, "Real full-blown coma with no stimuli to painful responsiveness." I smile.

Margo makes a gesture with her hand that (although there is no generally recognized international signal for it) would seem to indicate "Tell him to stay right there." Moments later, she's standing next to me at the bar. As soon as we connect, her right eye flashes a sparkle, bursting like a shooting star. I've never seen that before absent some reflection, but this lighting is inadequate for that. I'd describe the twinkle as a distinctive flicker of radiant beauty. Fitting, too, for this dark-skinned, dark-eyed, heart-shaped-faced girl. She looks like a Brazilian beauty queen.

"So, did they scale you?"

A more traditional hi would've been nice, but given her gorgeousness I overlook the omission. "You mean Glasgow Coma Scale?" I ask.

"What other kind of scale is there?" she quips.

The Glasgow Coma Scale—which I also use to rate my experts—designed and intended to be used to objectively evaluate the level of consciousness of head trauma victims. It ranges from 3—complete unconsciousness—to 15, or full consciousness. "Yes, I had a GCS."

"What was it?"

I think I'm going to like this inquisition. "The ER doctor initially scored me a seven." Her jaw drops. "The repeat evaluation ten minutes later was a fiver." She's in awe. She's about as turned on as any woman I've ever met, and I haven't even touched her.

"Wow! I never met anybody below an eight before. You're the worst coma victim I've ever had contact with!" She gives me a look of excitement mixed with concern. "Do you mind talking about it, or is it still too fresh?"

I give her my best sincere look. "No. I can talk about it. I think it would even be healthy if I did."

"Don't make a move," Margo commands. "I'm putting in for a break right now."

"How far could I get with this boot on my leg? Would you mind checking on my order of tequila and asparagus?"

"No problemo. But a quick question—say the first thing that pops into your mind. How would you describe your coma experience in one sentence?"

"Like I told Ginger, in between the universes of here and there." She nods with satisfaction and disappears again, this time behind the kitchen's swinging doors. A moment later, they're flung open like a new sheriff is in town and Margo puts a plate of perfectly grilled asparagus down in front of me. Next she heads to the rows of bottles behind the bar and stretches prettily to reach the Patrón tequila. Pouring a double-sized shot, she places the glass in front of me.

I spend the next forty-five minutes making up all kinds of coma fantasies for the sole benefit and entertainment of Margo. The more bizarre the twist I come up with, the more worked up she gets. For the last ten minutes my testicular stitches have been badly itching, but I can't think of a clever way to connect a scrotal scratch to a coma chronicle. I want to parlay this coma foreplay into something more but it's getting late and I have to get out to Brooklyn. Besides, it seems the furthest I ever get is fantasizing, or dreaming, about extramarital adventures, but I can live with that.

"Listen, Margo, I've told you about, I don't know, maybe five percent of my coma experience. Unfortunately, I just don't have enough time now to get to the good stuff."

"Having coma sex with Marilyn Monroe wasn't the good stuff?"

"Just the beginning." I look at her earnestly. "You've been a great audience. I mean, I can't imagine a better. We'll just have to have a rain check."

"When?"

"Sometime soon."

"That's not good enough. I need a place and a time," she says, pouting.

"Look, I appreciate how important this is to you. At the end of the week I'll be back to share all the little-known facts and high excitement of coma living. But unfortunately, right now I got to go."

"See you at the end of the week, then."

"Yes, see you then." I push my empty plate forward.

Margo looks at me, then down at my dish. "Tequila and asparagus. Coma food. I like that. I think I'll have an order myself."

"You do that," I say, when all of a sudden I feel like a knife was jabbed into my gut. It was no blade, however, just the prospect of venturing into Brooklyn, in pain, groggy from drugs, physically injured, handicapped, if you will, and alone. And why? To see my resisting expert and her greed-driven husband, strangely, way after hours, in the face of an all-hotted-up Margo, so I can prove to my expert the merits of Suzy's case.

t's impossible to elevate your leg while sitting on a bar stool, so the cab ride into Brooklyn is a welcome rest. Not coma restful, but restful enough.

The driver comes off the Manhattan Bridge and pulls up to the red light at the corner of Tillary Street. I hear the sound of basketballs spanking the pavement with authority coming from the courts just to my right. Men from the hard side, setting stiff picks and committing fouls with intent, and barking smack at one another so sharply I can feel the edge of competition a block away inside the cab. You win, you stay on, you lose, you sit, yelling "Next!" as you walk off the court, only to be corrected by the guys on the sideline in a challenging way. "We got next."

The light turns green and I feel a sense of relief that we're moving away from the conflict on the courts. I played one game there when I was a first-year law student and quickly realized I was out of my league and out of my element.

We pull up and the Smith Pavilion looks closed. I struggle out of the taxi and hobble toward the entrance, thinking how fortunate I am to have a walking boot instead of crutches. I enter the deserted building, noting for the first time the sting of a pressure blister on my heel.

The place looks completely different from the last time I was here, but I realize it's the absence of human activity making the difference.

There's no one around, not one single person, not even the security guard who appreciated I had to bring Otis because of my wife's commitment to her Brazilian hair removal therapist. I find it odd in this part of Brooklyn not to have twenty-four-hour security, but that Smith is tight isn't a matter for debate.

Before pushing the up button, a flickering light on the elevator tracking panel catches my eye. The light is marking the elevator's progress down. But when the door opens in front of me there's no one there. That's weird. I always thought motion had to be initiated by the press of a button. I get in and press 4.

Stepping out into the dark hallway, I know the sign in front of me reads: HEMATOLOGY DIVISION, SMITH SICKLE CELL PEDIATRIC CARE CENTER, with an arrow underneath pointing to my right, but I can hardly make it out. I begin walking down the corridor toward the fluorescent light escaping from underneath the Hematology Division doors ahead of me. The iridescent time on my watch reads nine-thirty. Where is everybody? Anybody?

When I'm about twenty feet away, the right-hand door slowly opens outward. I see Smith's silhouette image holding the door open. His shadow looks like a big black egg with a short arm popping out of the shell.

"Great. You're right on time," he greets me as I slowly move toward him.

"I know your rules. I can't afford to be late."

"Follow me," he directs. "My wife's waiting for you in her office."

I follow, but he's trotting faster than I can hobble. He stops at Dr. Laura's office, then looks back at me. He seems annoyed the journey is taking me so long, but the stingy little control freak can go shove it, having me come out here at this time of night. I shamble past him and see the doctor is seated behind her desk. The next thing I notice is that all her diplomas are back on the wall, the name Laura Smith on each one.

She smiles. "Hi. I'm glad you could make it at this late hour."

"No problem at all. This is an important case and an important meeting."

"Yes, it is. Please have a seat." She looks at me curiously. "What happened to you?"

"Car accident, but I'm okay."

Before I can get my next word out, a loud throat-clearing is heard. I look over. "Let me guess. The check?"

"Yes, the check." Smith confirms my hunch.

"Here it is," I reply, plucking it from my wallet.

He examines it, wrinkling his nose but making no comment.

I turn back to Dr. Laura, sitting attentively behind her desk, as Smith voluntarily leaves without protesting to stay. A deviation from his normal behavior. Interesting.

"First order of business. I need your CV, or whatever you use as a summation of your medical education, training, board certifications, awards, hospital affiliations, and the like."

"My husband mailed it to you per your request just after you left here last time."

"I don't doubt he did, but it's just that I never got it. Do you have another?"

"I'll have my husband get it for you before you leave."

"Do you think I could have it now? I'm postcoma, and my short-term memory likes to play hide-and-seek. I don't want to forget."

"If you insist." She looks out into the hall, calling in a loud but apologetic voice, "Dear, I'm sorry to trouble you!" She pauses, the type one employs when waiting for someone to turn around and respond. "Would you bring in a copy of my CV, please? He never received the one you mailed!" She sits back down. "He'll bring it."

"I see you got your reissued diplomas."

"Yes, we put them up just yesterday."

I briefly admire them, complimenting her on the presentation and framing, then get to the point of my visit. "Let me bring you up to speed. I've confirmed that what happened to Suzy was indeed an electrocution."

"Oh?" At least she doesn't turn white this time.

"Yes. What was a strong theory supported by physical evidence when I last met with you is now a certainty."

"How so?" Dr. Laura looks interested. Just not as interested as I'd like.

"I received a letter from a representative of a company named Toledo, which manufactured and supplied heart monitors to the defendant hospital. He told me a patient had been electrocuted in the same exact manner three years before Suzy's event. More important, he said Brooklyn Catholic Hospital had been informed of this event by written letter. Toledo, in fact, sent the hospital an adapter that would have wholly prevented Suzy's electrocution, but obviously the hospital never placed it on the defective machine."

Dr. Laura still doesn't look as excited as I thought she would. Maybe Horatio Cohen and Dr. Mickey Mack were right.

"I brought for your review a copy of the Toledo letter, together with a statement made by the hospital attorney saying in effect they don't have the Toledo letter. This is despite a certified return receipt establishing otherwise. I also brought my expert engineer's affidavit, and crafted a proposed affidavit for you to read—and, I hope sign—which will likely defeat the hospital's dismissal motion. You might note certain contents in your affidavit are also in support of my cross-motion to add a new claim, which basically states the hospital was negligent by failing to utilize the adapter. I am also making a claim for punitive damages."

Dr. Laura once again has suddenly lost all color. "Can I see the Toledo letter and everything else?" she requests.

"Sure. That's why I brought it." I hand her the documents, and she begins to read.

A few minutes in I interrupt her reading. "Doctor, would you mind if I elevated my broken leg on the edge of your desk? It's throbbing pretty badly."

She nods distractedly.

A moment later, I hear Smith's approaching footsteps. He enters with a sheet of paper in hand and places it on the desk in front of her.

Dr. Laura looks up at her husband. "Dear, it's confirmed. Suzy Williams apparently *was* electrocuted. According to these documents, one can conclude the hospital knew of the danger and failed to place an adapter on the monitor that would've prevented the occurrence of this unfortunate tragedy."

"That's horrible," he responds. "Can I see those papers?" He points to the documents in her hand.

Dr. Laura looks to me for permission. "Is it okay?"

"Sure. Meanwhile, why don't you hand me your CV so I can look it over while your husband is reading that stuff?"

Dr. Laura looks to him for approval. "Is that okay, dear?"

He hesitates. "Fine." She hands her husband my documents and me her CV. What a weak person she is, having to ask permission before making almost any move. It sure seems odd for someone in the medical profession, since they daily must make life-or-death decisions. I gaze over her CV without absorbing any of it because I'm too distracted thinking about Smith's reaction to what I handed him. He controls Dr. Laura's every move. He's the one who has to be convinced about Suzy's case, not her. Besides, I'm also too beat up, drugged, and exhausted right now to examine the minutiae of Dr. Laura's life anyway. I fold it up into a neat little rectangle and submerge it in the inside pocket of my suit jacket for safekeeping.

As it disappears from view, I realize something seemed familiar on that quick glance I gave it, but I can't place what. I hate my head-trauma-acquired inability to access information from my brain in the snap of a synapse. It's frustrating in the extreme. Smith motions toward the desk, setting down my documents in front of his wife. They look at each other with a strangely complicitous air. What's that all about?

"Well?"

"This is sad," he says. I have to note, though, he doesn't look convincingly affected.

"V-v-very sad," Dr. Laura chimes in.

"It's more than sad, it's criminal," I tell them. "The hospital had nearly three years to plug a ten-cent adapter into that machine and failed to do so. There's no reasonable excuse for such gross misconduct. Someone's going to go down for this criminal act of neglect, and the hospital's going to pay big-time."

Instead of responding to what I thought was a rather impassioned statement, Smith chooses to gaze at the diplomas on the wall. "Laura, the end one's a little off. Did someone touch it?"

"No it's not. It's perfectly even," I say, confirming what I saw earlier.

On the word *even,* he makes a quick move at me.

"Steven, no! You promised!" Dr. Laura screams.

He kills the bee that just stung my shoulder with a hand smack. Only there's no bee, I wasn't stung, and that was no hand smack. As he withdraws his arm I see a needle attached to a syringe.

I know the answer given how I'm feeling—unable to rise—but I ask him anyway, "Did you just stick me with that after distracting me to look away?"

"Yes, I did."

"I can't believe I fell for that. That's the maneuver I use to steal food off my kids' plates. What the hell? Why did you inject me?"

"You mean you don't know?"

"No, I *don't* know why the husband of my expert has apparently drugged me."

"Huh. I gave you too much credit. How are you feeling?"

"Queasy, just about to pass out. What did you stick me with?"

"A narcotic. You'll be asleep in a few moments, but at least it should take care of the pain from your injuries."

As I descend into this new coma, I think how this will give rise to another story line for Margo. If I live. The thought brings a smile to my face, which I quickly lose as my walking boot slides off the edge of the desk. I watch helplessly as it crashes to the floor, shattering the heel into a few large pieces. Meanwhile, I'm dimly aware they're arguing and that they stop to see what the bang was, then pick up where they left off.

It's the first time I've ever heard her speak to him sharply, but I can hardly make out what the dispute is about as I fall deeper and deeper into an unconscious state. The one thing I distinctly hear her say, because of its repetition and distinct tone of disappointment, is, "You promised nobody would get hurt."

The room begins to swirl around me. The medical term would be *vertigo*. I must admit, though, I feel no ankle pain, like Smith promised.

The Smiths finally stop their heated bickering, the content of which I am unable to fully register, but the argument is far from over. Now he moves in front of me, peering into my face in an evaluating kind of way. His own looks are distorted, fun-house-style, and suddenly Dr. Laura appears next to him. She bends down to see if I'm still awake by checking the reactivity of my pupils with a beam of light. I'm still awake, Dr. Laura, but paralyzed from the drug your motherfucking husband stuck me with. If she were doing a Glasgow Coma Scale evaluation, I'd score a 12, but in serious rapid decline. Margo, Margo, *Margo*!

I have enough strength to say something. I want to say something. I want to appeal to Dr. Laura's sense of reason. I know she's good at heart. I don't know why that evil husband of hers did this, but it's definitely not worth it. She feels my carotid for a pulse, then flashes her penlight into my eyes again, back and forth, back and forth. I always wanted one of those lights when I was a kid, but never got one.

"He's still awake, but his pupil reaction is very sluggish. What did you give him and how much?" Dr. Laura says in a slow and garbled voice.

I muster enough strength to raise my chin off my chest. I can tell Dr. Laura is surprised by my neck control. I want to appeal to her better nature and good sense. But I can't even stay upright. Next thing I know I've hit the floor and something's moving my feet around. Moments later, I sense Smith dragging me down the dark hall. He's pulling a rope tied to my ankles and dragging me one wobbly backward step at a time. He has the other end of the rope tied around his waist, with some four feet of slack between us. As we reach the elevator he gives one last strong tug on the rope, sliding my heavy structure a good two feet. By the nature of that dehumanizing last yank, I feel like a body heading for disposal.

This Shit Never Happened. Understood?

I somehow sense I am about to awaken, but before I regain consciousness I want to acknowledge how much I hate Henry Benson. I don't want to waste a single wakeful thought on that arrogant ass, so I'm gonna get it done now as I climb the Glasgow Coma Scale back into consciousness.

Life before Benson started referring his HICs to me was quiet and safe. Life after Benson has been a big fucking hassle. Now I'm drugged, tied up, dragged on my ass down a very long corridor by a psychopathic midget, and locked up in what feels like the trunk of a car. Kidnapped! For what or why I have no idea. I'm a *lawyer*, goddamn it. What could I possibly have done to land myself in this predicament?

There, that's better. Bitching about your circumstance can do that. It's time to wake up and attempt escape. I open my eyes to darkness. The nonmedical term would be *pitch-black*. My ankles are still tied together, and my hands are secured in back of me. The hair is being ripped out of my wrists, leading me to believe that some form of adhesive tape has been used to bind me. Most likely medical tape, but definitely not ouchless. It's obvious I'm not escaping from this easily, if at all. Time to pray for another divine intervention. I'm definitely in the trunk of a car—and it's akin to a soundproof chamber. I can't hear a thing. Maybe my ears are taped, although I don't recall seeing anyone's ears taped in any of the kidnap movies I've ever seen. Maybe I'm just parked in some desolate area only to be found as a cadaver years from now when the car is towed to a junkyard for crushing. News of my finding solves "The Case of the Missing Lawyer." The insurance companies will have to pay my wife the proceeds of my life policies since the rumor I ran away to Bali with an underage girl has by now been disproved. With the money, she purchases our local tennis club and ups her court hours from five a day to seven, and hires two more handsome pros from Argentina. The unsuspecting junkyard owner will get his fifteen minutes of fame. I hope it's not Fred Sanford, because he'll be traumatized if he is the one to find me.

Wait. I hear something. It sounds like footsteps, thereby demonstrating the trunk's not as soundproof as I thought. Someone is approaching. I'm able to move my legs into position, and I kick the trunk lid hard three times. *Bam! Bam! Bam!* The sound echoes as I nail it with what's left of my walking boot. The footsteps continue and stop behind the trunk. I'm not sure if I should kick again. If it's Smith coming to finish the job, I'll want him to think I'm still out cold.

Suddenly there's a male saying, "I know you're in there. I'm here to get you out. Move to the back of the trunk. I'm going to bust it open." I shimmy as far back as I can, which is about seven inches. I hear the clanking of metal hitting metal, strike after strike. After the sixth wallop, I hear the sound of metal being wedged between metal. A metal bending sound picks up where the wedging left off, then the trunk bursts open with the energy of a cork popping out of champagne.

The first thing I realize is that I can't see a thing: I'm blindfolded. The next thing I realize is how good it is to take in fresh air. Nice. I take three deep breaths in through my nose and out through my nose. I have no other option. I hear the voice again. "I'm going to take the tape off your mouth, but keep quiet."

I feel him trying to peel the edge of the tape. He finally gets the corner up and rips it off with one swift pull, the way my mom used to take off my Band-Aids. I take in a huge gasp of air. I realize I can inhale twice the volume of air through my mouth than I can through my nose. Even nicer.

"Let me help you out of there," my rescuer firmly states, "but like I said, keep quiet. No questions." Somehow I take his meaning as "I want to help you, but I'll hurt you if you don't comply." I feel him curl one arm underneath my knees and the other under my back, the way a groom carries a bride. How romantic. I note his arm and hand size are tiny and wonder if he's really strong enough to lift out my two-hundred-thirty-four-pound body. I am lifted up and out and stood against the car in one swift efficient motion. He's strong. I feel myself being steadied with hands at my shoulders.

"You good?"

"I'm good," I reply. He lets go. I realize from the direction of his voice I must be much taller than him. I also realize at this moment that my rescuer's disguising his voice. "Thanks," I say in his direction. "Can you take my blindfold off now, please?"

"I told you, no questions! Can't do that."

"For the same reason you're disguising your voice and ordering me to keep quiet?"

"Exactly."

Despite my instructions otherwise, I pose another question. "What now?"

To my surprise, he answers me. "What now? I'll tell you what now. I'm gonna cut your hands and ankles free, then I'm walking out of here. You're gonna count down from a hundred so I can hear you. If I see you take that rag off your eyes before you're done, you're gonna get capped, making this rescue shit very counterproductive." He sticks what feels like, and what I imagine tastes like, the barrel of a gun into my mouth. "Got it?"

"Got it." I garble. He withdraws the gun, leaving my mouth filled with a grimy metal residue and oily aftertaste. "Then?" I ask.

"Then? Then you're gonna take your rescued, broken ass home, rest up, and after that go about your business. This shit never happened. Understood?"

"Understood."

"So start counting."

I commence counting backward as I hear his footsteps vanish into the distance. I realize as I make my way down through the eighties that it's difficult to think of other things while in the midst of a countdown, or maybe my recent experiences have compromised my ability to mentally multitask. As soon as I hit zero, I know exactly what my first thought's going to be, even if I lack the ability to think it while counting down.

I get to three . . . two . . . one, and here's what my first thought is: I bet I'm the first person in history to be rescued and threatened with death by my rescuer simultaneously. I take off the blindfold and see I'm in a parking garage leaning on the back of a silver Mercedes-Benz with a mangled trunk lid and MD plates that read HCT HGB. Those are the abbreviations for *hematocrit* and *hemoglobin*. No doubt it belongs to my friends, the Smiths. I recognize the garage as the one where I parked that first time, with Otis.

I gimp for the brightly lit EXIT sign and feel anxious, like I'm not going to make it. I walk up the stairs, trying not to bear weight on my bad ankle, and out onto the street. I experience an immediate rush of freedom. It quickly dissipates when I see the Smith Pavilion directly in front of me.

I have a decision to make, but before I do, I better call home. I reach into my suit jacket pocket and my cell phone is exactly where it's supposed to be. I look at the date and time and realize I've been kidnapped for only about three hours. It's one in the morning. According to my call log I've missed three calls, all from my wife, five minutes apart. Tyler also sent me a text message and an email, which I read, then I listen to my three voice mails, also from Tyler. They all communicate the same thing: don't forget to take the dogs out when you get home and, second, where are you?

I hit my speed dial. On the tenth ring she picks up. "Don't forget to take the dogs out!"

"I won't."

"Now, where the fuck are you and why didn't you call?" she barks.

"Honey, I'll give you the details later, but in short, I was drugged, kidnapped, and locked in the trunk of my expert's car, then was rescued by some unknown hero who disguised his voice and threatened to kill me."

She pauses. "You expect me to believe that? Just don't forget to take the dogs out!" *Click.* I'll deal with her later.

Back to the decision of what now. I can call the police and get the authorities involved, which is the obvious option. I can go home and call the cops in the morning. I can go back upstairs and confront my abductor, in the spirit of a caped crusader. Or, as my rescuer advised, I can take my broken ass home, rest up, then go about my business like this shit never happened. This last option is against my nature and would be the most difficult thing for me to do.

Before I get a chance to decide, my decision is made for me by the sound of a loud bang. A gunshot. From somewhere close by. I instinc-tually begin running, thinking maybe my rescuer has morphed into a killer. By the time I've run two blocks my ankle boot has completely crumbled to pieces under my foot and fallen off. The only piece left looks like a big plastic ankle bracelet. As I finish my third block, I feel like a criminal fleeing from a crime scene—from which flight a jury would be inclined to impute guilt. This, despite having done nothing wrong and, in fact, having been the victim of a crime myself. Blame my upbringing.

I duck into the first open establishment I come by on block four. I sit, exhausted, on the first bar stool near the door and suck in air. I'm facing the street and watch as a police car races by the window, its siren blasting. "Bartender, two shots of tequila, please. One for me and one for my friend." I point to the lost soul sitting next to me. Aside from us, the place is empty.

"Coming right up," the bartender replies.

The guy beside me raises an almost empty glass in my direction. "Thanks for the drink, buddy. I wonder what the police activity is all about."

"Search me."

The bartender puts our shots down. "No last call tonight. We're closing now. These are on the house."

I throw back my shot, ignore my craving for asparagus, pick myself up, and limp into the takeout next door with the immediate intention of getting home. There's only one customer in here, too. He's a sumo-sized Asian, just paying for whatever's in his brown paper bag.

"I'm sorry to bother you, but is that your cab parked outside?"

"Off duty," he replies in a surly fashion.

I'm not deterred. "I'll pay you two hundred fifty dollars cash and pick up the tab you've got there if you take me to Westchester, how's that sound?"

"Good idea." I like the way he likes my suggestion. I respect flex-ibility.

16

After taking the dogs out, which was an event I had to cut short due to increasing ankle pain, I get three hours of sleep on the couch downstairs. I didn't attempt sleeping in our bedroom and chancing waking Tyler. Plus, the stairway to my distorted heaven looked a mile long with my bum leg.

All joy is lost when I put my foot down on the floor from a seated position. The minor pressure rockets the pain from my ankle throughout my body as I realize the fracture is now unstable. I guess the endorphins running through my body last night masked the seriousness of my situation. I dread standing up, so attempt it slowly. And unsuccessfully.

Before I attempt to get up again I take an accounting of my mental state. I conclude I'm completely wasted, among other mental disabilities. But I already knew that. I'll just have to suck it up, though, because I've got a lot of decisions to make this morning and need to stay focused.

I gingerly walk through the kitchen toward the mudroom to let the dogs out for their morning business, only to see a large lump of poop front and center. Otis is the culprit by the size of it. He never does that. The prospect of bending down to clean it at this moment sends pain to my ankle, but I'll have to get rid of the evidence before Tyler sees it or she'll have it in for me. I turn the corner where the mudroom and kitchen intersect, I open the door, and the dogs, two Yorkies and

Otis, escape into the beautiful morning. I stand there a few moments enjoying the gentle morning wind. Possibly there'll be genuine calm to follow as the day proceeds. Frankly, however, I'm skeptical.

I slowly snake my way back to the kitchen using the mudroom sidewall for balance, intending to clean the poop and sip some coffee. I grab my cell off its charging station as I turn the corner into the kitchen to see I have two missed calls from Dr. Mickey Mack, both within the last hour. Maybe he's anxious to tell me he found an alternate expert for Dr. Laura, which expert will now be my primary one, given the events of last night. The only way I can defeat defendant's motion to dismiss Suzy's case is by getting a new expert on board immediately, so I'm happy to see his calls. I hit Mick's speed dial and he picks up on ring two.

"Crazy, huh?"

"Crazy, huh, what, Mick?"

"You don't know?"

"Apparently not," I say as the events of last night soar through my brain. "Out with it."

"Your expert, the one we spoke about yesterday, the one you were going to see, Dr. Smith—her husband was found shot dead." Wonderful. Now I'm a suspect! Place, time, opportunity, and motive can all be clearly established by some young DA who wants to make a name for himself on his first murder prosecution. And I got no alibi! I was locked up in the trunk of a car. Did I say wonderful? "You still there?" Mick asks.

"Yep, sure am. I think I should go, Mick. I'm considering calling the police. They may be looking for me and I don't want them coming here. It would piss Tyler off."

"Why would they be looking for you?"

"For questioning, I imagine."

"Why would they question you? This Dr. Laura of yours confessed to putting a bullet into her husband's head." He stops talking and waits for my response. I am numb, surprised, and yet not surprised all at the same time. I heard that gunshot but never would have concluded this. He continues in light of my silence. "She ended her marriage the easy way. No messy divorce, no asset allocation, no sale of home, no business valuation, and no mudslinging. Best of all, no scummy divorce lawyers. The one drawback—jail time."

The implications of all this flood my brain. "I got to go, Mick. I have to find out where she is and go talk to her."

"Easy does it," Mick says, responding to the anxiousness in my voice, "she's being held at Brooklyn House of Detention awaiting arraignment. Her attorney has suggested she may be a victim of battered wife syndrome, have suffered temporary insanity, and acted in self-defense."

"Thanks, Mick, I got to hop, literally. Oh, Jesus," I say, having momentarily lost sight of the target, "any headway on finding me a new expert? That's why I thought you were calling in the first place. This has to be a priority now. Find me an expert!" I say in a firm and desperate manner.

"On this case? Forget it," he responds in a tone of certainty. "No one's gonna touch this thing. This is a major problem for you. I don't think you're getting it. This case is tainted with murder, so no one, and I mean no doctor in his right mind, is going to want to get involved once they find out who they're replacing as the expert and why."

"I don't see the reasoning, one thing has nothing to do with the other," I say, not believing my own words. "Dr. Laura had a crappy marriage, that's all."

"I'll make more calls, but until this thing cools down I don't know why any doctor would want to get involved. Give it six months, we'll have a better chance then."

"I don't have six months, Mick. I have a motion to dismiss pending now. Find me an expert!" I bark, inappropriately, at a friend who is doing me a favor. "I gotta go." I hang up. I am run-down. I'm not thinking straight. I'm in a state of disbelief. I need to pull it together before I crack.

I realize it's time to get ready for my nine o'clock meeting with June, Winnie the Weasel, and her engineer to inspect the patch and lead wire. I turn the corner into the mudroom, place my cell down, and let the dogs in. I hobble back toward the kitchen with intentions of cleaning that poop. I'll have to sit down on the floor next to it to clean it up so as to take the pressure off my ankle, which is now throbbing with pain. I turn the corner into the kitchen and standing there over the poop, waiting to pounce, is Tyler. Uh-oh. And she's up fifteen minutes before it's time, too. Not good.

"Morning, honey," I say timidly.

"Don't 'morning, honey' me," she rumbles. "Did you take the dogs out last night when you got home like I told you to?"

"Yes, honey."

"I said don't 'honey' me. Then why is there a big pile of dried-up shit on the floor? Otis never poops inside. You didn't take the dogs out, did you?"

"No, I did take the dogs out."

"Then why is there poop on the floor?" I look to Otis sitting there. He knows I'm taking one for him. He gets up and leaves the kitchen knowing he's done bad. Thanks, buddy.

"I don't know why," I say, thinking I didn't let them stay out long enough.

"Because you didn't take them out like I asked, that's why. And why didn't you clean it up when you saw it this morning?" Choice A, I was just about to, or choice B. Neither will fly. I go with B.

"Because I didn't see it, that's why."

"Bologna," she screeches. "You saw it. It's in the middle of the kitchen. You were just leaving it there for me to clean up." She places her hands on her hips for emphasis. This is the last thing I need right now. "You look terrible," she adds.

"I know. What I'd like for you to consider is that I'm lucky to be alive. You might even want to think again about your warm greeting. According to the morning news, the guy who drugged and kidnapped me last night was shot in the head by his wife. His wife is, or was, my medical expert, so I'm rather certain I just lost said expert in the face of a pending motion to dismiss. I'm sure it's on all the news stations, so if you have any doubts, please go see for yourself."

"Don't you think you're taking this lie a little too far?" she questions. "What I see for myself is poop on the floor that you left for me to clean up. Now stop with your stories. Save it for your jurors."

I can't deal with this now. Take the path of least resistance. "I'll explain everything in detail to you later," I say in surrender. "I got to get out of here and be in my office by nine. When this case is over I'll guarantee you two more years of prepaid tennis lessons with any pro you want."

"Really? Can I increase my lessons from two to four times per week?"

"Would you settle on three if—and only if—I can set June Williams free?"

"I met June in the hospital. Why didn't you tell me about her?"

"Why would I?"

"Because she's gorgeous," my wife replies.

"So you only want me to tell you about my cases if the client involved is a babe?"

She ignores the question. "I'm reserving that extra day now. Just win your case."

"I'll try, I gotta get going."

"What happened to your ankle boot?"

"Got destroyed during my kidnapping."

"Kidnapping," she repeats in a sarcastic tone, "please," as in "Give me a break."

"Really, I got to go get ready."

"Not yet."

"Why not?"

"Clean the poop up first."

She Thinks I'm Bluffing

I arrive at my office at ten after nine. Sitting in my reception area is Winnie the Weasel and her expert engineer. I don't recognize the expert, which means he's not on the circuit and may actually give an honest evaluation, although I doubt it.

"You look terrible," she says as I approach.

"Thanks. We have a consensus on the issue. Good morning to you, too. We'll get started once I settle myself and all are present and accounted for."

I move past them, doing the best I can to pretend I'm not hobbling. "Morning, Lily," I say as I pass her.

"You look horrible."

"Is that better or worse than *terrible*?"

"What?"

"Never mind," I say, in an effort to conserve energy.

"Did you see the news?"

"Yes, I saw the news. We'll discuss it later. Come into my office with a steno pad, please. I have to dictate something to you."

"Are we going down that road again?"

"It's one sentence. Just come in."

"Give me a minute. I got my sitter on hold." I have a witty smart-ass reply in mind but just don't have the strength to voice it. I make it down the hall and into my office, one faltering step at a time. I have my eyes closed because it somehow helps me bear the pain. I drag my head up, level my chin, and open my eyes to see June sitting in my desk chair. Nearby, Suzy with Dog on her lap. Dog gives a little yap.

"I know, Dog. I look terrible. Good morning, June," I say, then turn to her daughter. "Good morning, Suzy."

"Not sch-weet, not sch-weet, no Vegas, not sch-weet," Suzy says. June hushes her, but Suzy continues with her "not sch-weets" until June hands her the light-up plastic globe.

"What's happening to you? Where's your ankle boot? You need to be more together than that to lawyer for Suzy and me. Come on now."

"June, a lot went down last night. By any chance did you see the morning news?"

"Had no time, with getting Suzy ready and coming here and all. Why? What's in the news that concerns us?"

"June, we got a boatload to discuss, but not right now. The Weasel's out there with her expert forensic engineer to look at the wire and patch, which I assume you've brought with you, correct?"

"Correct. But you're not hearing me. I like to be well informed, so out with it. Now!"

"After their inspection, I'll bring you up to snuff. Right now I need a moment to put something into the works. Just sit tight."

By the look on her face I can tell she's not happy. Suzy senses it, too. "Not sch-weet, not sch-weet, no Vegas," she resumes saying. June hushes her into stillness, as I note for the second time now that Suzy can say the words *not* and *no* in proper context to *sch-weet* and *Vegas* to voice her displeasure.

I hit my intercom. "Lily, where are you?"

"Right here," Lily replies as she walks through the door. "Oh, hi, June. I didn't know you were here. When did you come in?"

I speak before June can. "Lily, how could you not know June and Suzy and Dog were here? They have to walk right past you."

"Well, they didn't!"

June joins in. "She's right. We didn't."

"I don't get it. Can someone please explain?"

"Me, Suzy, and Dog got here before Lily, so we let ourselves in and came into your office to make ourselves comfortable."

"Let yourselves in? How did you let yourselves in past a double-locked door?"

"I unlocked it."

"Who gave you the keys?"

"Um, no one."

"Then how'd you get in?"

"If you must know," she says, as if offended, "I picked the locks with one of the Fidge's lock-picking sets. The kind the police and fire department have. What's the problem? I didn't think you'd mind. You're my lawyer."

"Picked them? June, I'm too tired to deal with this right now. Just resist breaking in and entering the next time you get here early, okay?"

I switch my focus back to Lily. "Take this down."

"Slow," Lily cautions, "and it wouldn't hurt to say please."

"I'm in a slow mode. Don't worry. Ready? Uh, please."

"Ready," Lily replies, flashing her steno pad and pencil.

"Put the lawsuit caption of the Suzy Williams case on this document and title it 'Exchange of Nonparty Witness.' The body of the document should read as follows and I'll go slowly: 'Dear Sirs: In response to defendants' continuing demand for the names of witnesses, please be advised that the plaintiff intends to call Dr. Laura Smith at the time of trial as a nonparty witness to give testimony on behalf of and in support of the plaintiff, Suzy Williams. Very truly yours,' etc., etc., etc."

"Nonparty witness?" Lily questions. "I thought she was your expert witness. For that matter, she's not going to be any kind of witness, since she'll be in jail for killing her husband."

"What!" June exclaims, startling Suzy into a litany of "not schweets." "What are you talking about, killing her husband?"

"It's on all the news," Lily tells her.

"June," I say, "Dr. Laura committed mariticide last night. I was there, kind of."

"You were there? Kind of?" Lily asks.

I look at her. "I'll tell you all about it, both of you, just not right this second." They both look at me in exactly the same demanding way. "The bottom line is, she and her husband didn't want this case to go forward for some reason. Reason enough to kill, although I would've expected Smith to have been the killer, not Dr. Laura. I don't know why yet, but right now that doesn't matter. All I can assume is they were somehow aligned or connected with the hospital, which I'll remind you is only three blocks away from the Smith Pavilion. If my assumption is right and I get the Weasel to think Dr. Laura's a turncoat on murderers' row with nothing left to lose, it may change things. But this is just based on deductive reasoning. However, when we go into the conference room, just keep quiet about it. You got that?"

June wants more. "Can you explain something to—?"

I cut her off. "Not now. We have a hand to play, so let's go play it."

"Okay. I'm with you."

"Do the Exchange of Nonparty Witness for Dr. Laura," I instruct Lily, "and put together in final form my Affirmation in Opposition and cross-motion amending the claim to add the electrocution and punitive damages. Make sure to attach Fred Sanford's affidavit and be certain to redact the name of Dr. Laura from the medical affidavit in support and in my affirmation, wherever it appears."

"Can you do that?" June asks. "Hand over papers without names?"

"In the state of New York the defendants are not entitled to know the name of the plaintiff's expert in a medical malpractice case by provision of 3101(d) of the Civil Practice Law and Rules, nor do we get the name of their expert."

I turn back to Lily. "This is important. Five minutes after we go into the conference room, bring in the Exchange of Nonparty Witness and my opposition/motion papers and hand them to Winnie McGillicuddy. Ask her to sign our copy, acknowledging personal service of the documents. You got that?"

Lily gives me a furrowed brow. "What do you think? I'm a dummy? I got it."

"Sorry. Okay, ladies, it's time to initiate the plan."

June wheels Suzy and Dog into the conference room. There are no windows so there'll be no jockeying for water-view positions. However, I do have a seating plan for the Weasel and her expert.

"June, stay here," I direct, then continue around to the far side of the oval table to the two guest chairs, side by side. I pull out the closest chair, sit in it, then reach underneath, fishing for the adjustment handle. I pull the handle up and hear the sound of a pneumatic device release the air pressure as the chair lowers itself until it bottoms out. I move to the next chair and do the same thing. Next, I bend down, unscrewing and removing the two handles so the chairs can't be readjusted back up.

"Why'd you do that?" June wants to know.

"To set the tone of things." I move back around to our side. "Sit and rise, please." We giggle as our own seats move, this time upward. "June, go sit over in one of those lowriders, I want to see our height differential." She complies. I look across and down at her. "Hmm. We need more elevation."

I hobble back around and flip one of the guest chairs over. I grab a black plastic wheel and give it a hard tug, causing it to disengage and come off. I pull all the other wheels off, giving our side two inches more of height. I flip the chairs back over. "Okay, that's taken care of. Good guys high, bad guys low. We'll let them sit first. And, June, please, put all eight of these wheels in a spot where they can see them from their seated position."

June smiles. "Good idea." I go down the hall to get our guests.

"Ms. McGillicuddy, would you and your expert follow me please to the conference room?" They get up. "First door on the right, please," I say as I limp behind them.

The Weasel turns in and I hear Suzy. "Not sch-weet! Not sch-weet!" I enter on the fifth "not sch-weet" to see June taking out the light globe. She hands it to Suzy and presses the magic button and things begin to spin as the light flickers, giving Suzy comfort and us silence.

June looks at the Weasel. "Sorry about that, Ms. McGillicuddy. Please don't take it personally. Suzy sometimes reacts that way to strangers." Just as the Weasel is about to respond Suzy looks off her light toy and up at the Weasel, giving one last perfectly timed "not sch-weet." "Sorry again," June offers.

"You two move around to the other side of the table and we'll stay here," I say. "That way I don't have to struggle with moving Suzy. Besides, she's kind of calm and I don't want to interfere with her moment of peace." They move around and struggle with pulling their wheel-less chairs out because of the carpet friction. Naturally, June and I are patient.

They move in front of their chairs, sit down, then struggle with pulling them forward. Once they reach the table, I look at June and we sit down together. I'd estimate we're a foot and a half above them. The Weasel gets it.

"Hey," she says, looking over at the floor beyond. Aren't those the wheels to these chairs in the corner there?"

"Nope. Those aren't them."

She gives me a disbelieving look. Game on.

"June, give them what they came here to see, please." June reaches into her big leather bag and produces the wire and patch. She slaps them down on the table with authority, the noise catching Suzy's attention. She drops her light toy and starts yelling out an uncontrolled frenzy of "not sch-weets" again and again. June quickly picks the spinning light globe up and puts it directly in front of her eyes while Suzy looks past it, trying to see the patch and wire. It's almost like she knows. After a few moments, the light ball gains the upper hand. Suzy quiets again.

The expert engineer, who to this minute has remained mute, is a small, unassuming guy in his late fifties. McGillicuddy introduces him as Oleg Krauss.

"Would you like me to give you some guidance here?" I ask him. "Do you want me to point out to you what my expert found on his inspection?"

"No need," he replies. "I'm done."

"You're done?" I ask incredulously.

"Yes, I'm done." He looks over at the Weasel. "We can go."

"That wasn't very thorough," I tell him. "You hardly looked at it."

"Please don't speak to my expert about the case," admonishes his companion. "It's improper and you know that."

"Sorry, you're right," I admit as I gaze down on them. I've seen this kind of inspection before. It's not an inspection at all, but rather a formality so as to have a basis to come to court and tell the jury nothing wrong or unusual with regard to the wire or patch has been found. His testimony will be "I saw it and it was normal." This sucks, but SOP when dealing with an unscrupulous defense attorney.

"Ms. McGillicuddy, before you leave, I have something for you. Since you've only been in this room two minutes, I'll have to go get it. I planned on springing it on you at the five-minute mark but we obviously never got there. Hold on a second."

I hobble out and hobble back, just as quickly as it took me to make the round-trip to Lily's desk, fifteen feet away. Not very quickly, in other words.

"It's not five minutes," Lily tells me when I picked the papers up from the edge of her desk.

"I'm well aware," I reply.

Back in the conference room, I lean across the table and hand the documents over to the Weasel, who reluctantly accepts them. "These are my opposition papers to your motion to dismiss; a cross-motion to add a claim that your engineering department failed to put a ten-cent adapter on a heart-monitoring machine known to be danger-ous—which, I might add, would've prevented Suzy's electrocution by your inexperienced jerk chicken chef nurse—and a nonparty witness response." I pause and with perfect timing Suzy yells, "Sch-weet!" to punctuate the exchange.

"It's self-explanatory," I continue. "You may want to read it now, before you go and communicate its contents to your expert over here. It may prompt him to reinspect the wire and patch."

Defense counsel is not fazed. She ignores my advice and looks at her expert. "Okay, we're done. Let's go."

"Travel safely," I say, opening the door for them. Ms. McGillicuddy has to fight gravity to get out of her chair but she manages on the sec-ond try.

"Prepare for battle," I warn as she walks by.

She makes it halfway down the hall, then stops and turns as if something's just registered. "Did you say these papers contain an exchange of nonparty witness?"

"That's what I said."

"Is this a new witness or someone known to both sides?"

"I know her and I have reliable information you know her, too."

"Her? Who is she?"

"Dr. Laura Smith."

"Isn't that the one who's all over the news this morning? Who killed her husband last night?"

"That'd be the one."

"Well, I don't know her, so you've been misinformed. What does she have to do with this case anyway?"

"Something."

The Weasel gives me a look, one that says she thinks I'm bluffing. "Did you talk to her?"

"I did."

"What did she say?"

"Stuff."

She looks annoyed. "What kind of stuff?"

"Stuff about the patch and wire. The kind of stuff that's going to help the good guys. Stuff she's willing to come to court for and stuff she was willing to kill her husband over. This is no longer a medical malpractice case. This is a cover-up turned murder, with my client the innocent little girl victim of hospital neglect caught in the middle. You know what I'm talking about, and it's all going to come out. This shit's going down, and so are the players. I'd give some thought to amending your response to my Discovery and Inspection, but it's probably too late for that now anyway, and you know what I mean."

"I can only say you're delusional," she replies, "and you better watch what you say about me or you'll end up being slapped with a lawsuit. Libel, slander, defamation of character, and whatever else applies. I would suggest that maybe the head trauma you sustained in your car accident is interfering with your ability to think rationally and exercise good judgment. Maybe you should go home and get some rest. I'm sorry your client has to witness you in this condition, but in your defense, irrational behavior and compromised thought are not uncommon in such cases as yours."

The Weasel's pause fills the hallway with silence. It's the kind of pause one revels in after having made a winning argument that's difficult to refute. All eyes are on me, waiting for a return of synapse fire. Unfortunately, my neurons are shooting axonal blanks. This woman has me doubting myself—and why shouldn't she? I made all that up, kind of. Still, my philosophy on coincidences is that there are no such things. If a connection can be drawn between two seemingly unrelated events, then they are somehow related. I have to maintain my position if for no other reason than to save face in front of June, who's waiting for my snappy rebuttal as interestedly as my opponent is.

"Dr. Smith has agreed to cooperate," I announce. "I'm going to the Brooklyn House of Detention, the holding facility, to take her statement. Once she's committed what she knows to writing under oath, the punitive damages I'll be asking for will bankrupt the hospital. You run along and continue with your sham defense of a sickle cell crisis. What Dr. Smith will soon corroborate is all there in my opposition papers and cross-motion. After my visit with her, I'll be filing those documents with the court. Once it's a matter of public record, we'll be at the moment of no return."

Now McGillicuddy's staring at me like I'm crazy. June, however, seems to be giving points.

"All I want to do here is get my client fairly compensated. I haven't been retained to expose the hospital for criminal negligence or anything else unrelated to improving my client's quality of life. It's up to you to get this case resolved before the lives of more people are altered forever, including your own. You know the way out. Now run along."

Only You Know

June and I watch defense counsel and expert make their exit from the conference room. When they're out of hearing range, June demands, "What's going on here? You're not going nutty on me like she said, are you?" She looks anxious.

"No way. Relax." I change the subject. "How did you get here?"

"Trace. Why?"

"Is he downstairs somewhere?"

"He's a phone call away. He had some business in the area to take care of for the Fidge."

"Make the call. We're going to the Brooklyn House of Detention to speak with Dr. Laura. I'll fill you in on everything that's happened on the ride there."

A few minutes later, Trace pulls up to the curb. June insists on carrying Suzy out of her wheelchair and into the car. She buckles her into the backseat as Trace puts the chair in the trunk. June gets in the back next to Suzy and I sit next to Trace. As expected, he peels away from the curb leaving the smell of burned rubber behind. The scent brings to mind what Suzy's room must've smelled like at the moment of her flesh-charring electrocution.

I update June on the events of the last twenty-four hours. She listens intently, rolling her eyes at the sheer implausibility of it all. She laughs when I tell her how I fell for Smith's look-over-there trick. More practically, Trace instructs me how to jimmy my way out should I be kidnapped and stuffed in a trunk again.

As we arrive June is still trying to get a handle on the whole thing. "I don't understand why you told that woman—"

I interrupt. "The Weasel."

"Yeah, the Weasel. Why is Dr. Laura our witness if she's been an accomplice to drugging and kidnapping you? God knows where you'd be now without that mystery rescuer. That part, by the way, I don't get at all."

"It was her husband who started to play rough and so she went and killed him. I have a hunch about her, though. Plus we're making a big play with no downside. As for my rescuer, I can't explain anything about him other than that maybe he's some kind of vigilante like Charles Bronson." He was a pretty small guy, too, I suddenly recall.

We enter the building and are pointed in the right direction. We arrive at the area we need to be when we spot the person we need to speak to. She's on the other side of a security wall, sitting behind a bulletproof teller's window.

I walk up to the tiny window that's framing her large body. Her badge reads: SERGEANT ROOSEVELT, and she reminds me of a big black girl I grew up with whom everybody was scared of. "Excuse me, Sergeant," I say through the little vents in the security window, giving her a friendly smile.

"How can I help you?" Sergeant Roosevelt inquires.

"I'd like to see Dr. Laura Smith, please. She's probably waiting arraignment."

"That she is. Only her lawyer and family members can visit. You either?"

"Well, I'm a lawyer."

Sergeant Roosevelt raises an eyebrow at me. "You *her* lawyer?" she asks sternly. "Because you don't look like her lawyer that was here earlier." The jovial tone of our previous exchange is now a thing of the past.

I'm about to conjure up a response when, to my surprise, June appears from behind me. "Sergeant, can we speak privately? It's about my little girl." June steps to the side, pointing out poor Suzy, who's staring into space.

Roosevelt looks past us at Suzy, and the hardness in her face vanishes. She purses her lips. "Affirmative," she responds in a very official way. "When you hear a buzz, pull open that metal door to your right. I'll meet you in there."

June turns to me. "Watch Suzy."

As she reaches the metal door fifteen feet away, there's a loud buzz and a click. She pulls open the door, then disappears behind it. I wink at Suzy. "Let's hope your mom keeps that resourceful streak of hers going."

Suzy doesn't reply. But I believe she hears me.

Ten minutes later, there's another loud buzz, then a click, and the metal door swings outward. June and Sergeant Roosevelt appear from behind it, continuing their conversation in the hall as the door shuts tight behind them. The tone of their exchange is friendly. Superfriendly, in fact. June opens up her big leather bag and takes out an old-style Filofax. Finding a piece of paper, she writes down what I assume to be her phone number and gives it to the sergeant. They start walking toward us, then stop a few steps later, continuing their absorbing conversation. The sergeant then puts her arms around June and they hug. "Now, don't you forget to call me, Rosie!" I hear June tell her as they let go of each other.

Rosie smiles. "Speak to you soon, girlfriend," she says, "and give my best to the Fidge. Don't you worry, that doctor in there will help you out. She's got nothing else to lose."

Rosie now looks at me, and her tone quickly changes back. "I'm going to buzz you in. Once inside, you'll be escorted to where Dr. Smith is being held so you can speak to her."

After being metal-detected by a machine and a hand wand, I then am frisked by a pretty corrections officer, whom I ask to be gentle due to my ball sutures. After placing all my worldly possessions in a safe, the aforesaid pretty officer locks it, giving me the key along with a written itemization.

The next thing I know, I find myself sitting in a tiny, barren room with two cheap metal chairs facing each other. They're the same kind of chairs the City of New York Department of Law has in the Tort Division reception area. Bright white light emanates from the fluorescent overhead lighting, triggered by motion detection when I entered the room. I take a deep breath. I feel like crap. I'm nauseous, tired, and have a pounding headache. Did I mention severe ankle pain?

After I have waited five minutes, the door opens and the pretty corrections officer who lightly patted my testicles escorts Dr. Laura into the room. As bad as I may feel and look at this moment, the doctor is obviously much worse off. Way, way worse.

The officer walks the doctor over to the chair opposing me and helps her sit down. "I'll be stationed right outside the door," she explains to me. "You must be a pretty important person to have gotten yourself back here, but please be quick."

"As far as I know, I'm only important to my dogs and children, but thanks anyway." I watch as she leaves. When I hear the latch click, I turn to Dr. Laura, who's just sitting there quietly with her head down. "Hi, Doctor. I'd ask you how things are, but I think the question is inappropriate right about now."

Dr. Laura slowly brings her head up. "I appreciate your consideration," she says, bit by bit, a syllable at a time, with the weight of the world on her. "What are you doing here?"

"The answer is that I still have a job to do. I have to get a little girl whose life has been ruined enough money so she won't need to wait three years to get a new wheelchair from Medicaid when hers breaks down."

"I hope my attorney's as committed as you, but it wouldn't make a difference. I already confessed to killing Steven." She looks and sounds childlike, despite being in very adult circumstances.

"Just because you killed him doesn't mean you did anything wrong—under the law, that is. This state recognizes justifications for murder, and your attorney is already putting those defenses forth."

"My attorney?" Dr. Laura asks sarcastically. "You mean the guy who showed up here unsolicited and told me he'd represent me for free in exchange for the media attention?"

"I guess that would be him. If you're not happy with that guy, I could find someone else for you."

"No, that's not necessary," she says in a defeated tone. "I really don't care anymore. What do you want from me?"

"I want you to connect the dots. To start, I'd appreciate if you'd explain the relation between your husband's kidnapping of me and Suzy's case."

She looks at me. It's the kind of look someone gives you when she is contemplating whether or not she should give you information. She begins pulling out the lashes of her top right eyelid. She grips them by the bunch, yanks, then her arm comes down, releasing them. They flutter to the floor, landing there by her government-issue laceless right shoe. After a few more grabs she runs the lid with her finger, then moves down to the bottom lid and starts the de-lashing process.

I put my voice into the empty space. "I mean, your husband kidnapped me and made a comment implying he was surprised I didn't know why. That can only mean it relates to Suzy's case in some manner."

"I'm really sorry about that." She begins working on the lashes of her top left lid. "We had an agreement that nobody else would get hurt and he broke his promise. That's why I killed him. There are rare instances in life when a person has to kill the one they love to protect the innocent. No different from putting a beloved family pet down when the dog has become vicious."

"Doctor," I say, not really feeling her analogy, "I'm no psychiatrist, but there was a lot going on between the two of you from what I saw. I mean, it was like he controlled your every move."

She agrees with me. "I had no life. I just did what I was told and asked no questions." Yet I remember clearly, brain damaged or not, that she had once pronounced herself grateful for his authority over her and the secure environment it created. His attention to all the details of their business affairs, along with his unabashed greed, meant she could devote her time to ministering medically to the young patients at their clinic. Still, I figured it might be rude to point this out now, so I change tack.

"Can you explain all this to me? I need you to tell me what I need to know to get Suzy Williams fairly compensated. That's all I want to do here, get my client the money she needs to live her life more comfortably, to take care of her financially so that her future is assured. I truly believe you're the key to my doing that, but only you know. I should also say that instead of going straight to the police last night after your husband kidnapped me, I went home after my escape—and I use that word loosely. I'd hoped that by not turning you in maybe you'd find it within yourself to help me out here. I heard you arguing with your husband after he drugged me. Was I wrong? It seemed to me you were struggling and wanted to help."

Dr. Laura stares at me, her face now softened somewhat. She starts feeling the tips of her hair, searching for brittle ends as she continues to gaze at me. Every time she identifies one, she snaps it off and drops it on top of the pile of lashes. After seven or so split-end snaps, she yanks a handful of hair out by the root.

"Doctor," I urge, "stay with me here. You're pulling your hair right out of your head."

She looks startled. "Am I? I'm sorry. What was it you were asking me?" She returns to the hair-ripping routine.

"I need to know your connection to my case. Tell me, please."

All of a sudden she stops and focuses. "My connection—okay, I'll tell you. It all began a long time ago. I was never very popular growing up. I guess you'd say I never really fit in. I only ever wanted two things for myself as I struggled through high school like many other unpopular kids. I wanted a boyfriend and I wanted to be a physician."

"Listen, Doc, we don't need to start back in high school—"

"You said you wanted to know my connection. This is all part of it.

Do you wish to know or not?" Given we're pressed for time, I quickly apologize.

She continues. "My mother was so supportive. She often told me the story about the ugly duckling that grew up to be a beautiful swan, but I always knew there was no swan inside of me. I'm ugly. I've always been ugly. Only one person in the world ever made me feel beautiful and that was my husband, Steven."

I cut in and try to speak with sincerity. "Doctor, you're not ugly."

She ignores me. "Steven and I met on Valentine's Day when I was a first-year resident. We met early one morning and he swept me off my feet by noon. Did I say we met on Valentine's Day?"

"Yes, Doctor, you did. Valentine's Day. Very romantic."

"On that Valentine's Day we bonded on every human level, emotional and otherwise. We realized we both had tormented childhoods because of our appearances. Steven was the victim of vicious teasing as a child. You met him, so you know he had an unusual body type. He was bottom-heavy—buoy-shaped, I guess you'd call it. Children can be cruel, and they teased him about it." She pauses. The pause of someone fast losing touch with reality. "They called him 'the Weeble' after a child's toy."

I now realize I have no choice but to play along, to encourage her to keep going until the story reaches the conclusion she's building toward.

"Steven and I spent hours together that Valentine's Day. By three in the afternoon, we realized we were a match made in heaven and had to get married. It was not that we merely had to get married, but that we had to get married that day, Valentine's Day . . ." She trails off, and I clear my throat.

She gets the hint. "Anyway, that very afternoon we rushed to Borough Hall so we could get married. On the way, we went into a cheap jewelry store to pick up our wedding bands because, you know, you can't get married without a wedding band. We made it there with time enough to get our license, and our civil service was the last one of that afternoon. I recall you making a comment about the picture on my desk when we first met. Our wedding photo, on the steps."

She stops again, but despite feeling panicky now, with the hourglass running out, I make myself nod kindly.

Suddenly, her expression changes. Looking at me, she says, "I need to go to the bathroom. I need to tell the guard."

I get up and knock on the door. The pretty officer opens it. "Done?"

"Not yet. She's just getting to the heart of it all. But she needs to pee." The officer walks past me. "Come on, Doctor."

The officer gently takes her by the elbow. On their way out, the officer turns to me. "Be right back. You stay here. I'm not allowed to leave anybody unattended, so lie low."

So now I'm sitting alone in the middle of the tiny room with my ankle swollen like a melon. I can feel that a stitch or two has come loose inside my jockeys and my head hurts and the walls are spinning around me. All this, and I still don't have any fucking answers, despite listening to the most boring tale of ugly love I've ever heard.

I spend the next seven minutes resting my foot up on Dr. Laura's chair and readjusting my stitch-popped balls. Each time I withdraw my hand I run my finger under my nose to whiff my nut juice for any tinge of infection. I'm willing to do whatever it takes to win for June, but I draw the line at partial testicular resection from uncontrolled infection. On my last dip and whiff I look up to discover I'm on *Candid Camera,* the mother of modern-day reality shows. Great. The next thing I know, bells and sirens go off. Real loud bells and sirens.

Fire alarm. What the . . .

I get up to hobble to the door to see what's going on. *Wham!* All of a sudden I'm staring up at the ceiling wondering why I'm lying on my back. I've gone down, and gone down *hard.* My balance isn't that good, but somehow I can't remember that. My ankle's throbbing beyond belief and I'm too scared to check inside my pants. I manage to get up, stumble over to the door, and slowly open it. The deafening sound of the alarm rushes in.

I limp out of the room and head toward where I came from, knowing it's the fire escape route. Everyone else in the hall is rushing past me in the opposite direction in plain violation of the IN CASE OF FIRE guidance sign up on the wall. I make it to the door that leads to the hall where I left June and Suzy without one corrections officer stopping me. I push the button on the wall. I hear a buzz and a click, then hobble out.

June's talking to Rosie through the little vents in the security window. Suzy seems entertained by the alarms and bells, although Dog is shaking with fright. I drag my leg over to them. "Don't we have to get out of here, or is this just a fire drill?"

"No, no, no," Rosie says. "It's no fire alarm. Something's going down back where you came from, a prisoner fight or some other type of disruption. Don't give it no attention. Did you get what you came for from Dr. Smith? I've been a notary for two years, I do some private investigations on the side, but nobody needs to know that. Anyway, the point is I never got a chance to use my stamp. Can I notarize her written statement for you?" She holds up her self-inking notary public stamp. "Got it right here," she says with delight.

At that instant her walkie-talkie interrupts and a staticky female voice starts blaring out. "Come in, Budding Rose, come in, Budding Rose. This is Man Eater, over."

"Budding Rose, over."

"We got us a situation here, over," Man Eater reports.

"Open ears, over."

"It's Dr. Smith," Man Eater says. "Suicide."

June, Rosie, and I look at one another in disbelief. Before that moment I'd have said it was physically impossible for three people to look into one another's eyes all at the same time. "No!" I yell.

Suzy reacts to my scream. "Not sch-weet, not sch-weet, no Vegas, no Vegas."

I kneel down next to her. "Don't worry, little one. We'll figure this out." I stand back up. "How could this happen?" I ask Rosie.

"Which list you want, the short or long?"

I nod, understanding that if someone wants to check out, they find a way to get the deed done.

"How you gonna *figure* this one out, counselor?" June asks. "She's dead."

"I don't know for sure, but I have an idea. Just keep the faith." The enemy right now is time. I turn to Rosie. "What kind of control do you have here?"

"I'm second in command."

"Really? No offense, but why are you working the window like a ticket taker at the movies, then?"

"I'm covering, we're shorthanded today. No offense taken."

"I see. Listen, can you keep Smith's suicide quiet for twenty-four hours?"

"Affirmative. That's a maybe affirmative. The trouble is it's the age of the iPhone, counselor. Mega pix could already be out there going viral on YouTube. The opportunists get slipped fast cash from the vultures at the tabs for those kinds of shots. And I said I was second in command, so the number one guy calls the shots. But if her death warrants investigation, and suicides always do, I could keep it quiet until the internal is done. That could be as little as twelve hours, but I'll try to stretch things out. Lucky for you, Smith don't have no next of kin to notify."

"Well do your best to keep it on the down-low for twenty-four, and give me your stamp."

"My stamp?" Rosie asks nervously. "Why do you want my notary stamp?"

"Just trust me, it's all for the cause, Rosie. All for the cause." She reluctantly slides it under the glass window.

I take a legal pad from my bag. "Rosie, may I have your autograph, please? Press down firmly on the paper." She gives me an inquiring look, but I'd never tell her it's to trace it onto the notary line of the sworn statement Dr. Laura Smith gave me just prior to killing herself. Of course, there is no such statement. But when a notary puts his or her signature on the line next to the words that read "Sworn before me on this day," *poof*, like magic, one can be created. She may conclude this, though, after I give her instructions.

"Here ya go." She slides the pad back to me.

"One last thing."

"Ears still open," she replies in her walkie-talkie lingo.

"I'll be giving your cell number out. To the attorney we all hate, the one defending the hospital against Suzy's case. All you have to do is tell her you have an envelope in your possession with the inscription 'Statement Number Two' on the outside of it, and that Dr. Smith gave it to you after you notarized two separate things for her, and that she instructed you to give it to the press here in the building tonight at seven unless you are directed otherwise from me. Got it?"

"Got it, but let me repeat that. I'm holding an envelope labeled 'Statement Number Two' that came from Dr. Smith. I'm to give it to the media people in the basement here at seven tonight unless I hear from you."

"Perfect. I'll have the envelope delivered here within the hour." I turn to June and Suzy. "Let's go, guys. We got things to do."

My Lawyer Is Clever

When everybody's buckled in to the Impala, I say, "June, get Barton Jackson the Third on the phone for me right now. I need him to do something for us." I give Barton his marching orders to be carried out stat and Mile High couldn't be happier to help. We screech away and head back to Manhattan as I tell June about Dr. Laura's peculiar love story.

"Okay, now what?" she asks.

"Well, it's kind of an 'as we go' plan. But I have a direction."

"As we go?" She looks more troubled than I've seen her to date, but then before, a murder-suicide hadn't entered the picture.

"Listen," I say carefully. "I have no direct evidence here. No medical professional or medical record has stated or even alluded to the fact that Suzy was electrocuted. What I have is a lot of circumstantial evidence, which is a distant second to direct evidence. Circumstantial evidence requires reasonable inferences to fill in the blanks. I'm super-uncomfortable with that as a trial lawyer because you can be faced with legal obstacles, ones that are beyond the scope of this conversation. What I'm trying to do here is tie the circumstances together and present them to defense counsel in a neat little box beautifully tied up with ribbon and bow. The charred wire is my ribbon and the patch is my bow. They're the only tangible pieces of evidence we have giving our claim substance. Just keep the faith. That's all I ask. You with me?"

"I'm with you. I'm just kind of nervous."

Surprising to me, Trace has something to say. "June, give the man the support he deserves, yo. Look what he's been through for you." It's the first time I ever heard him initiate a sentence instead of just responding.

"Thanks, Trace," I say. "And, June, your apprehension is understandable." I look at my watch: twelve-thirty-five.

"June, listen carefully to the conversation I'm about to have. You'll understand better where I'm going with this then." I dial Goldman, Goldberg & McGillicuddy. "May I speak to the Weasel, please?" I ask the receptionist.

"Oh, you again. Transferring to Ms. McGillicuddy."

She picks up. "Winnie McGillicuddy here."

"Hey, it's Tug Wyler. I'm sitting on the red leather seat of a 'sixty-two Impala bubble top coming from the Brooklyn House of Detention, where Dr. Laura Smith is being held. She sends her regards. She told me everything. She even put it in writing."

"What's everything?"

"Stop playing games. Once I bring myself to say it there'll be no going back and you, your new law firm, and the hospital will all be exposed. The headline of the *Post* is gonna read 'The Shocking Truth' and Suzy's going to be the cover girl."

"I don't know what you're talking about," she insists.

"Yes you do."

"No I don't. Really."

"You want proof as any good attorney would under the circumstances so I'm gonna give it to you the way the good doctor has instructed. She put some thought into it, which makes sense given how her circumstances have changed." It's quiet on the other end of the line. "Are you listening?"

"I'm listening."

"Dr. Smith insisted on handwriting out two sworn statements under oath and duly signed them before a jailhouse notary public, who also happens to be a decorated corrections officer with the rank of sergeant. She calls them Statement Number One and Statement Number Two. Statement Number One I have in my possession, and it's only a couple words long. It's Greek to me, but she said you'd understand. She's no longer interested in being a part of this, as a result of her circumstances, but she has made a commitment she'd come forward as a witness for my case if need be, to right a wrong. She asked that I give you Statement Number One as soon as I left her, in hopes you'll do what needs to be done to get Suzy Williams's case settled. Dr. Laura—I mean Dr. Smith—wants the case settled today. No extenuating conditions. If I don't call a certain number by seven tonight and tell a certain sergeant the case has been settled, the publication of Statement Number Two will go forward. I don't have a copy of Statement Number Two, but Sergeant Roosevelt at the Brooklyn House of Detention does." Dead silence. "Ms. McGillicuddy?"

"Still listening. Go on."

"To my understanding, Statement Number Two lays everybody involved out for dead. However, Dr. Smith doesn't wish to see anybody else get taken down over this, including you. It's why she made the two statements with these precise instructions. She refused to give me Statement Number Two specifically so I wouldn't use it in an unintended manner should the case settle this afternoon. Moreover, Dr. Smith has instructed me to give you Sergeant Roosevelt's cell phone number so you can verify with her that she has an envelope in her possession marked Statement Number Two. The sergeant has specific instructions from Dr. Smith to give it to the jailhouse press unit at seven this evening, telling them also that the doctor agreed to be interviewed so her story could break on the evening news if the case hasn't resolved. Now, do you want me to read Statement Number One to you, or would you like to continue your charade of innocence?"

"You can read it to me," the Weasel responds, "but don't infer from my curiosity any credibility with regard to your case."

"Whatever you say. Statement Number One reads and I quote: 'Valentine's Day.' End quote. That's it. That's all it says. I'll fax it to you when I get back to the office. You still there? Hello? You still there?"

"I'm here. Fax it to me." *Click.*

"Clever, my lawyer is clever," June says. "I hope it works."

"Me, too, June. I have no idea why Smith drugged and kidnapped me, but it was right after he read my papers laying out what happened here. He wanted to keep the truth buried, and now it is, literally, with the Smiths. We'll probably never know their connection, but if this works, who cares?"

Trace pulls to the curb in front of my building. "You guys stay here in the car," I say. "I have some things I need to do in private. When I'm done, I'll come back down."

I go up to my office as quick as I can hobble. You never want a witness to a crime, and what I'm set on doing is a crime. All I can hope is I'll never be tried and convicted. What I need to do now is look at Suzy's file for something very specific to my intended malfeasance. *Bingo.* I find and take out Dr. Smith's rejection letter, along with the three handwritten pages she attached to it.

I take out my orange highlighter and start highlighting the letters and numbers. I have every letter except for a capital *V.* Good enough. I open up my middle drawer and start fishing around. Next, I pick up a black fine-point marker. I take the cap off and test it to see if it still has juice. It does. I write over the highlighted letters and numbers, making them as dark as possible. Before capping my fine-point, I write over Dr. Smith's signature at the bottom of her typewritten rejection letter. I open the paper compartment of my printer and take a clean white piece of paper, in order to start the tracing process. The *V* is my original, but the rest of the letters are an authentic forgery. I love it: authentic forgery.

When I'm done, the paper reads: "Valentine's Day," with Dr. Smith's signature traced underneath the message and Rosie's signature, likewise under that. I take out the notary stamp and press it down between the two signatures and the "sworn before me" language and date I entered. This means that Dr. Smith's signature was, in fact, legally, made before a notary public of the state of New York.

I fax my forgery to the Weasel with a handwritten cover note that reads: "June, Suzy, and I are going to Judge Leslie Schneider's courtroom. We will see you there to place the settlement on the record. Come with big authority. I will not take a penny less. But don't worry, I won't shake you down, despite our disproportionate bargaining positions. I only want that justice be served and my client be compensated fairly. If you're a no-show, that'll be okay, too. It's your career."

Before walking out, I get the text I've been waiting for from Barton. It reads: MISSION ACCOMPLISHED. ENVELOPE DROP MADE. I WANT ALL MY VISITS TO THAT DETENTION HOUSE TO BE VOLUNTARY. PEACE.

The Game Is Afoot

Trace takes us downtown. On the way there's a call from someone I assume to be the Fidge. Trace's side of the conversation is "Uh-huh . . . uh-huh . . . uh-huh . . . yeah . . . see you in fifty." He pulls up in front of the Supreme Court building at 60 Centre Street and says to June, "Baby, can you make it on your own? I got a matter to attend to."

"You know I can." They share a smile. They're really good friends with an amazing relationship, and I remind myself they're not married.

I look out at the court building and curse Henry Benson. This case could have been brought in Kings County instead of a New York County venue, the latter being much worse for the plaintiff because of a more conservative jury pool. The thing is, Henry's office is right across the street from 60 Centre, so he's more concerned with his own convenience than the best interests of the client.

I direct June to take Suzy around to the back of the building, where the handicap-accessible ramp is, and I go up the front stairs. I want to get to the courtroom as soon as possible to make the necessary arrangements.

I enter Judge Schneider's courtroom and check the wall clock. It's three-forty-five. Every single person who works in this building is part of one union or another, so four-fifty is the deadline time for the Weasel's arrival. Five minutes later, June enters pushing Suzy.

There's not much going on except for a conference between five attorneys. Toby Wasserman, the judge's law secretary, is ruling on the argument. After they clear the courtroom, she comes over to June, Suzy, and me. Dog is hidden in June's big bag. "Can I help you?"

"I'm the attorney on the Suzy Williams matter, and these are my clients."

Toby Wasserman turns to June. "Nice to meet you. I know you were here recently when your lawyer was in the hospital. Your handbag left quite an impression on the judge. She's been talking about it ever since."

"Thank you," June says. She looks pleased at the compliment, but distracted. Then, unexpectedly, she adds, "I design them."

"You've got talent." Toby turns back to me. "Yes, we got a call from Lily at your office. If you need to put a settlement on the record, the judge will come down from chambers and we'll call in a court reporter. By the way, how are you feeling?"

"Fine, thank you for asking."

"What was it like being in a coma?"

"Surreal and peaceful. Why do you ask?"

"It's not every day you meet someone who's been through something like that." She heads back to the judge's chambers.

This coma thing is definitely a whole new social platform.

An hour goes by and no Weasel. We continue to sit and wait. When the wall clock reaches almost five, Toby comes out from behind the wooden door. "I'm sorry. We have to close up shop. You can always come back tomorrow or the next day or at any time during normal hours if you need to put a settlement on the record, but we can't keep a court officer, a court reporter, a court clerk, a law secretary, a judge, and the rest of the crew it takes to run a courtroom after hours. It's against the terms of certain bargaining agreements."

I look at June. She looks at Suzy. "Not sch-weet, not sch-weet, no Vegas," Suzy says.

"Time to go," I tell them. "No worries, June," I say in the most convincing manner I can. "I have Dr. Mickey Mack finding us a new expert as we speak. Once we defeat the motion to dismiss and the judge grants us permission to make the electrocution and punitive damages claims, we'll have momentum again. If it doesn't resolve after that, we'll win before a jury and receive the largest jury verdict in history based on circumstantial evidence. I promise, everything's going to be just fine."

June looks deep into my eyes. "Those are the very words Dr. Valenti used outside Suzy's hospital room just before she was electrocuted."

Grabbing the handgrips on the back of Suzy's wheelchair, she turns her toward the door. Toby, sensing June's disappointment, speaks to us again. "We're here if you need us during normal hours to place a settlement on the record. Have a pleasant evening."

June pushes Suzy down the narrow aisle. "I got the door," I tell them. I hobble around the wheelchair and pull the brass handle. Just at that second, in stomps the Weasel.

She is trailed by two people who also walk by me as I hold open the door. They come to a halt, being blocked by the leg braces jutting out from Suzy's wheelchair. They look down. She looks up. "Sch-weet."

The Weasel squeezes angrily around Suzy toward the bench, the pair of stooges following in tow. As they make it to the wooden fence known as the "bar" that separates the people involved in the litigation from the general public, the Weasel looks back at me. "Well, are you coming? Let's do this."

As I drag my leg forward, my adversary points to her colleagues. "This is Joel Glendale, the hospital's independent counsel, and this is Sean McClain from Evergreen Structured Settlements, whom I brought to run some numbers if need be."

Toby Wasserman, having made an about-face from her attempted exit, approaches. "Sorry, people. This part is shut down. Come back in the morning."

"Not before we put a settlement on the record," the Weasel says. "Call the judge down and get a reporter in here."

"No can do," Toby replies.

"Yes can do," McGillicuddy counters. "I formally request that you make a call to chambers and tell the judge we're in the courtroom waiting for her and a reporter to place a settlement on the record. It's five minutes to five and none of the union agreements will be violated. Pursuant to article 3B, if all counsel are present and ready to proceed before five, which they are, we're permitted to place a settlement on the record in the interest of judicial economy, even if we run past the hour. I'll have you know I'm on the state's Judiciary Committee, and if the judge doesn't come down, this matter will be reviewed, as will her practice of keeping her courtroom clock set ten minutes fast."

Toby walks over to the desk next to Judge Schneider's bench, sits down, and picks up the phone.

June tugs on my jacket. "What's going on?" she whispers. "Why can't we just settle the case? Everybody's here."

"In order for a settlement to be legally binding on both sides without there being a chance of one party backing out," I explain, "it has to be settled in open court, on the record, before a judge. The committee the Weasel spoke about is a group of lawyers who review the conduct of judges. They wouldn't look favorably on a judge not being available during working hours when the attorneys, independent counsel, and a structured-settlement guy were all in the courtroom waiting to put a settlement on the record. Let's take a seat and see what happens."

Toby's still on the phone, presumably with the judge. When she finishes, she makes two more calls. Then, addressing us, she says, "Everyone who needs to be here is on their way."

As the judge enters, she finishes zipping up her robe. "All parties please note their appearance for the record." When she speaks, the mood of the room changes. The game is afoot.

Since I represent the plaintiff, and the plaintiff has the burden of proof, most anything that has to be done or said in the courtroom starts with me. I give my appearance as such in the appropriate dignified manner.

The Weasel places her appearance on the record and the appearances of the hospital's independent attorney and the money person as well.

The judge addresses all of us. "Counsel for both sides, we're going to go off the record for a moment."

The reporter ostentatiously raises her hands after striking the last key. "Thank God," she murmurs. Quite the complainer. I mean, we gave only our names. If she thinks this little exercise is painful, she wouldn't exactly have cherished my last few days.

The Weasel and I approach the bench and step up on the little platform. "So, what do we have going on here that brought me from chambers at this late hour?"

The Weasel responds by addressing the bench. "Judge, we're here to settle the case. By settling this case we are not admitting, conceding, or confirming anything was done wrong or that liability attaches. We're settling it for reasons that may have no relation to the claims made by plaintiff's counsel. Simply stated, we just want the case done, to eliminate the uncertain conclusion of a jury trial."

"As long as it's off my docket," the judge informs us, "I don't care why you're settling the case—that is, as long as the child is fairly compensated. I won't sign an Infant's Compromise Order otherwise. So, what's the settlement number? Present value, of course."

It's at this very moment I realize I've never given the Weasel a settlement demand, which is how such negotiations normally begin, but this is no normal case. "Counsel knows the value of this type of injury," I state. "I'm listening."

"We took the numbers from your Life Care Plan," the Weasel says, "and intend to pay it to the penny, four-point-two million."

"Perfect. Now Suzy's future medical care and special needs will be covered and she can go off Medicaid. What are you adding for her past and future pain and suffering and loss of enjoyment of life?"

The Weasel sighs. "We're prepared to offer another three million for the pain and suffering, for a package of seven-point-two."

"You're low and you know it," I tell her.

"I'm here to close the case and save where I can. What were you thinking?"

"Five million, not a penny less, for her pain and suffering. It's not negotiable. We close Suzy's case at nine-point-two. I'd suggest your structure guy can take this up-front lump sum, place it in a conservative annuity, and project a thirty-five-million-dollar payout over the course of her expected life. I'll be using Brian Levine from Structure Solutions as my settlements consultant to check on Evergreen's numbers. I also insist on having the payments guaranteed for thirty years in the event of Suzy's premature death."

"As tragic as this little girl's condition is, that sounds awfully high," Judge Schneider comments.

"Judge, my client seems to have some understanding of her unfortunate imprisonment and what's going on around her. In a strange way that I cannot put into words, she has a jovial acceptance of her life predicament. She's happy and excited and sad and down at just the right moments in response to her environment. The number's nine-point-two without getting more into the specifics of this matter—and counsel knows what I mean."

"Judge," the defense now requests, "may I have a moment to confer with the hospital's private counsel and the structured-settlement representative?"

"Go ahead."

The Weasel walks away and begins her discussions. I turn and give June an affirmative nod and she responds with a smile.

"You may join your client, counselor." That's the judge's way of saying go away. We sit and wait, and neither of us says anything. I see Dog's little nose poking through June's bag. After ten minutes of corner whispering, the henchmen break their huddle. We approach the bench.

"We have a settled case," the Weasel declares. "I'll forward you the appropriate closing documents and included in the package will be a nondisclosure agreement. This will be a sealed settlement, or no settlement at all. Let's place this on the record."

"I hate being a part of the medical community's continued suppression of their malpracticing ways, but the interests of my client outweigh my personal beliefs, so fine, nondisclosure it will be."

The judge bangs her gavel twice. In a loud clear voice, she pronounces, "Mazel tov, people. We have a settled case."

"Judge," I say, "I can't step on the glass yet."

"What do you mean?" McGillicuddy asks.

"Well, June Williams has a claim for the loss of Suzy's services and she has just about given up her individual existence to take care of her daughter twenty-four/seven."

Judge Schneider nods in agreement. "That's very true. Toby tells me she designed her fabulous bag I admired so much last time she was here. She might well have made a career out of that."

The Weasel is furious. "Why didn't you bring up Ms. Williams's claim for loss of services when we were negotiating?"

"Well, I was addressing Suzy's claim first." I pause, then motion for her to come a little closer for privacy. "You're not going to take the position in front of the hospital's lead counsel that you forgot about June's claim, are you?" I whisper. "I mean, that's the guy who hired you and your law firm to save them money. I would suggest that'd be a foolish position."

The Weasel knows I'm right. I can see it in her face, along with her anger.

I glance back at the judge, who's not paying attention. But then she says, unexpectedly, "It would look pretty bad if you took issue, like you forgot about her claim."

The Weasel is pissed. "What do you need to close June's case?" she demands.

I put my pinky up to the corner of my mouth in Dr. Evil style. "One million dollars."

"Yeah, baby." The judge can't resist making an Austin Powers reference of her own. The Weasel is not entertained.

"The Appellate Division has never sustained more than five hundred thousand dollars for a loss-of-services claim," the Weasel declares.

"We're settling the case, not litigating it subject to appellate review. One million is fair under the circumstances."

The Weasel shakes her head. "Give me a moment," she mutters, stalking back to her cohorts.

I look back at June again, who mouths, *What's going on?* I mouth back, *Sch-weet, Vegas, sch-weet.* She smiles.

The Weasel's at my side again. "They won't pay a penny more than seven hundred fifty thousand."

The judge looks down at me like I'd be crazy not to take it. "Can I bang my gavel now?"

"Bang away, Your Honor."

She does. "Mazel tov again, for sure, everybody. Who wants to place the settlement on the record?"

Whenever I settle a case that was hotly contested by defense counsel, big or small, I make them place the settlement on the record. It's like rubbing their face in it so they should remember for the next time we meet. "Ms. McGillicuddy can place the settlement on the record," I suggest.

"No, you can."

"Oh no. You do it."

The Weasel gives me her hundredth or so maddened look of the afternoon, then takes a step off the platform and looks at the court reporter. "You ready?"

"Ready," the reporter replies.

"It is hereby stipulated, agreed, and consented to by and between the lawyers for the respective parties in the within action that this matter is hereby settled, with prejudice and without costs, in the sum of nine-point-two million dollars for the cause of action on behalf of the infant plaintiff, Suzy Williams, and in the sum of seven hundred fifty thousand dollars for the cause of action brought by the mother and natural guardian, June Williams, so stipulated, counsel?"

"So stipulated." Right after, she takes a moment to whisper in my ear, off the record. *"Don't forget to make a call to a certain crooked sergeant."*

"So stipulated," I softly reply, although I have to question in my mind why she called Rosie "crooked."

Just then, the courtroom doors burst open and an excited, sweaty little guy comes running in. "Hold it!" he yells, as I think, *Too late sch-weaty boy.* He stops next to the Weasel and puts his iPhone in front of her face. She reaches for it, scanning the screen, then gasps.

"What's up?" I ask, though I already know.

"Dr. Smith," she says, then pauses, struggling to arrange her features. It doesn't work. She looks like she's just been flattened by the Brooklyn-bound 4 train, in this instance also known as the Wyler express.

"Dr. Smith what?" I ask. That's right, I need her to say it for the same reason I just had her put the settlement on the record.

"Dead. She's dead," she mutters.

"Dead?" I repeat, putting on my most surprised expression. "Dead how?" I ask, loving now more than ever the binding and irreversible effect of open-court settlements. I'm not too sure she feels the same way.

"The headline reads, 'suicide,'" she says, shaking her head in disbelief. I step toward her as she turns the screen so I can see. On it is a gruesome picture of Dr. Smith. She's flat on her back sprawled on a tile floor, eyes rolled inside her head, but the telling part of the photo is her hair. It's standing on end, spiked, the way you see in the movies when a person is electrocuted. Well lookie there—isn't that fitting?

"How could that happen to a prisoner in custody?" she asks.

"Which list you want, the short or long?" I reply. She stares at me, not a kind one. "Gotta hop," I say, cheery as a motherfucker. "Good doing business with ya, say hello to the boys back at the office for me, see ya on the flip-flop."

"Clear the courtroom," the judge declares, "and have a nice evening, counselors. We're adjourned."

I step off the platform and walk over to June and Suzy. They're all smiles. "Sch-weet, sch-weet, Vegas, Vegas," Suzy exclaims.

I bend down to her. "That's right, sweet Suzy. You're going to Vegas for the light show of your life."

June embraces me. I return the favor. "Wow, now that's how you hug with feeling!" she says.

"Yeah, I really felt that one."

"That's because you've changed our lives and you're happy for us. What was that seven hundred fifty thousand dollars for?"

"You don't know?"

"No."

"It's for you, for all you've done for Suzy over the years."

"I don't want any money for that. She's my daughter."

"Okay, then you can use it on her if you want. It's yours to do with what you want. I'd suggest you create your own line of handbags. Everybody loves your stuff—the judge and Toby are ready to be your first customers."

We leave the courtroom and make our way out of the building, using the basement ramp. The settlement is just now hitting June. She can't contain herself and is literally jumping for joy. I push Suzy up the ramp one labored and painful hobble at a time. I think I've popped a few more stitches from the effort as we make our way up, but it's worth it to see the smile on Suzy's face and to hear her exuberant cries of joy. "Sch-weet! Vegas!"

When we get outside, I begin to feel an overwhelming sense of accomplishment. My awareness of this great achievement doubles for every limping step I take farther away from that big, cold stone building. The open air fills my lungs, and I sense victory running through my vessels as my endorphins release. I'm superhappy about the humongous fee I'm going to make, but that happiness is dwarfed by the feelings associated with the good deed I've done. I just changed the lives of June and Suzy. I've made their daily struggles easier to manage, and that's a big, big deal.

Was It You Who Saved Me?

Not a word is said during the long walk from the back door exit to the roadway curb line. We are all silently and independently immersed in our victory.

I stop wheeling Suzy. "June, you got two calls to make. One to Rosie and one to Trace."

"Done," June says, then smiles.

" 'Done' meaning you're going to make the calls or 'done' meaning you made them already?"

"I called and left messages for both of them. Neither picked up."

"When did you make the calls?"

Just as she's about to respond, her cell rings a familiar song. June says hi and listens for a moment. "Uh-huh, uh-huh. Rosie wants to talk to you." She hands me the phone.

The first thing I want to know is whether the Weasel contacted her, which would give credibility to our theory. I put the phone to my ear. "Hi, Rosie. What can you tell me, over." I listen to what she has to say for the next several minutes without interrupting. "Okay. I'll tell June, and yes, I'll tell her to call you tomorrow. Bye." *Click.*

June tilts her head. "What's up?"

"You ready for this? The Weasel herself called Rosie to confirm the existence of Statement Number Two. Fifteen minutes after her call, a lawyer affiliated with her office showed up to physically see the envelope, which Rosie only *showed* him through the guard window. Ten minutes after that, another guy arrived whom Rosie described as sweaty and nervous, most likely the guy who just ran into the courtroom. He offered Rosie ten thousand big ones for the envelope, which she declined. Then he upped it to twenty-five thou cash. Rosie jumped on the deal, taking the money for the envelope."

"Rosie wouldn't give us up like that. I heard you tell Barton to just put two blank pieces of paper in that 'Statement Number Two' envelope when you were instructing him on what to do. And if she gave them an envelope with blank papers in it, then why'd they pay? I can't believe it."

"You don't have to." June stares at me. "On her way out to make the exchange, she quickly scribbled a fake Statement Number Two envelope and stuffed some blank papers in it, leaving the real one—I mean the real fake—under her counter. She made the swap for the briefcase filled with the cash right then and there in the hall, handing him the fake-fake envelope, not realizing it wouldn't have made a difference. After doing the exchange, she told the creep to wait a minute, that she had something else for him at her window. When she got back behind it, she told him he was holding a fake envelope, flashing the real one, I mean the real fake. She explained to him that he'd been videotaped, pointing out the security cam in the ceiling. She told me she didn't think a little extortion would hurt none, since we were in the process of a blackmail, fraud, forgery, and bribery anyway."

"I knew Rosie wouldn't give us up."

"Yes you did, June. I knew it, too."

June and Suzy come back to my office to wait for Trace to take them home. I begin to explain the terms of the settlement in plain English. This is something I normally do beforehand, but I wasn't sure the Weasel was going to show. "First of all, the monies that both you and Suzy are going to receive are tax-free. You see, this is not income. You're being compensated for a loss sustained, so technically there's no gain, capital or otherwise. Most of Suzy's money is going to be placed in a financial vehicle known as a structured settlement. It's like an annuity. The hospital is going to purchase a payment plan that will make monthly payments directly into an account for Suzy's benefit, maintained jointly by you and an officer of the bank. She'll receive great big lump sums scattered throughout the payment schedule, which will also be placed in this same account. The first big lump will occur when the initial settlement check is issued and the others will be paid at time periods throughout the rest of Suzy's life. Usually, the schedule correlates with an expected event such as college, which is clearly inapplicable here."

"I always thought my baby would be smart enough to go to college, but I'd be unable to afford it. Now, just the opposite is true. I guess this money will make our lives easier, but it really doesn't change things. I'll never have my baby back."

"June, that's the bittersweet reality of what I do. None of my clients are ever made whole." I quickly continue my explanation of the settlement to avoid June's final realization of this merciless truth. "One reason we use structured settlements is because there's guaranteed return over the life of the payout, with annual built-in three percent adjustments for cost-of-living increases. Another reason we use a structure is so Suzy receives her money plus the money she *earns* on her money tax-free. If we took her settlement all at once in one big lump sum and invested it, reaping the same return as a structure, we'd only receive half that money because our profits would be taxable. You follow?"

"Yep." She sighs. Who can blame her?

"The last thing you need to know is that this money is guaranteed for the next thirty years, even in the event Suzy has a premature death. I hate to talk about anyone dying, especially someone I've come to care about like Suzy, but you have to know about this provision. In the event she predeceases you, they still must make all the payments over the next thirty years. That means, God forbid, if she dies six months from now, they still have to make payments for the next twenty-nine and a half years directly to you, June, as her sole heir and beneficiary under the Trusts and Estates laws of New York."

"I understand completely." Her cell rings. "It's Trace." She flips it open. "Yeah, baby . . . okay, baby . . . the case settled, baby . . . we don't need it anymore, baby . . ."

"We don't need what anymore, June?" I ask.

"Hold on, Trace," she tells him, then looks at me. "Trace got some documents from the Fidge's people inside the hospital."

"Tell him to bring them up! Tell him to bring them up!" I yell twice for good measure.

"Chill, chill. You don't have to scream." She turns her attention back to Trace. "Heard that? Good. See you soon." She flips shut her phone. "He's around the corner and will be right up."

In ten minutes, I hear my office entry door bang closed with authority. Trace enters and I reach for the beaten-up folder he hands me. I open it and there are two pieces of paper. The top one is just as I expected. It's a copy of the letter from Toledo to the hospital. The same exact one Toledo sent me a copy of, identifying the dangerous condition, with Engineersafe's instructions to apply the enclosed adapter as a remedy. Only this copy is date-stamped RECEIVED: HOSPITAL RISK MANAGEMENT DEPARTMENT. I hand it over to June and she looks at it.

"That's the date for which Toledo has the certified signed receipt from the hospital, as described in the letter they sent to me. The

Weasel'd be in big trouble if I let this out, since she verified in her D and I response the hospital had no documentation."

"Let her slide," June says. "She did the right thing in the end."

"That's the proper attitude. It's of no consequence to us now. We knew the Weasel was attempting to pervert the course of justice. Here we have concrete proof."

The other piece of paper in the folder is a document titled "Work Order" on a preprinted form. The heading reads: "Brooklyn Catholic Hospital, Department of Risk Management." It's dated February 14, two days after the receipt of Engineersafe's "Notification of Defect" letter and instruction to apply the adapter. The body reads:

To: Department of Cardiology; Department of Engineering, Maintenance Division

From: Brooklyn Catholic Hospital, Department of Risk Management

Work Order Number: 00139

Purpose of Work Order: Our contract heart monitor vendor, Toledo, has identified a potentially dangerous condition with a heart-monitoring machine we have in the hospital bearing a manufacture identification number beginning CBE. We have only one of these "defective" machines from Toledo, which is a replacement monitor. The male pins on the end of the electrode lead wires have been misapplied by a medical professional into the female receptor socket of an extension cord connected with live current, causing bodily harm to a patient in another hospital facility. Toledo has provided the Department of Risk Management with a plastic adapter to remedy the potentially dangerous condition. See copy of Toledo letter attached hereto with schematic diagram instructing how to place the adapter.

Action Required: A member of the Engineering Department, Maintenance Division, together with a member of the Cardiology

Department are to place the male ends (prongs) of the lead wires used with that machine into the provided adapter to prevent the potential danger to a patient from an accidental misapplication.

Deadline for Completion: Within twenty-four hours from the date of this Work Order.

Verification of Work Order Completion: I, _____ , am a member of the Department of Engineering, Maintenance Division, and hereby affirm I have completed the "Action Required" by this Work Order.

Date: _____ Signature: _____

Verification of Work Order Completion: I, _____ , am a member of the Department of Cardiology, and hereby affirm I have completed the "Action Required" by this Work Order.

Date: _____ Signature: _____

Verification of Work Order Completion: I, _____ , am the Risk Manager of the Brooklyn Catholic Hospital, and hereby affirm I have verified that the above members of the Department of Engineering and the Department of Cardiology have successfully completed the "Action Required" by this Work Order by personally inspecting the work performed.

Date: _____ Signature: _____

I take the Work Order and hold it up to June, Suzy, and Trace. "This paper is a Work Order requiring two people from the hospital to put the Toledo adapter on and for a third person to make sure the work was performed. It's dated two years and nine months prior to Suzy's injury. I'm not surprised it's not signed by anyone in the "Verification of Work Order Completion" sections because had the adapter been plugged on, Suzy never would've been electrocuted."

"So what are you going to do with *this* information?" asks June.

"Nothing."

"But this shit ain't right."

"It's criminal negligence, if you ask me."

"So what are you going to do?" June eggs me on.

"I told you already. Nothing. There's nothing to gain from it. We can't give Suzy her life back and we've accomplished the only thing we can by getting her money for an improved quality of life. You and Suzy are now taken care of and can live each day without a financial care in the world. There's great value in that, I promise, and Suzy definitely likes to have fun. You guys deserve to enjoy each minute after what you've been through since Suzy's injury."

June is quiet for several seconds. "I think you're right. Suzy may be brain damaged, but she definitely does enjoy doing fun things. I think the first stop is that trip to Vegas."

"That's wise, June. Some scholar whose name I'm having difficulty retrieving from my long-term memory once said, 'The art of being wise is the art of knowing what to overlook.' If we seek action based on this, it'll just put us right smack back into the middle of things. Stuck in the system again. Overlook it, I say, and move forward with your new life."

I turn to Trace. "Thank you for all you've done. You're a good friend to June and Suzy, and you've helped me out greatly on this case. There's something I've got to ask you, though. Was it you who saved me when I was run off the road? And was it you, again, who saved me from inside the trunk of that car?"

"Na, man. Wasn't me," Trace answers in his deep voice.

"You sure you're not just being humble about taking credit for your good deeds?"

"Na, man. I'm telling you. It wasn't me."

"Okay. I thought it might have been you who saved me at the crash, although I had my doubts about you being my rescuer from the trunk because he didn't have your giant arms. Was it the Fidge that rescued me?"

"Wasn't the Fidge, either, I'm certain," Trace answers. This makes no sense.

I address the group. "I guess we're done here. Trace, please get my favorite clients home safely and take it easy on those rubber-burning peel-outs. Suzy, after her money is placed in a structured settlement, is now the thirty-five-million-dollar girl. My next stop is the emergency room uptown."

A Piece of Folded Paper

I walk into the ER at Lenox Hill Hospital and immediately begin arguing with the chief of emergency medicine to call the chief of plastic. "Sir," he tells me, "you don't need the chief of plastic and reconstructive surgery to come here to close your scrotum. It's not an anatomical area requiring the aesthetic skill of the chief of the department."

"Says you. I'll have you know I have the balls of a twenty-year-old, and I don't want anything done to compromise their youthful appearance. It's not like I want him to Botox the wrinkles out of my sac. My condition is a medically necessary procedure and I just want your most qualified doctor." I settle for the one with the second-most seniority in plastic.

As far as my ankle is concerned, I allow a second-year resident to do the closed reduction and recasting, but I experience a brief encounter with the attending after seeing the postreduction X-ray films. With the films up on the view box, I make myself heard. "Your resident hasn't achieved satisfactory anatomical alignment of my medial malleolus," I tell him. "There's some external rotation of the fracture fragment." I point to the spot.

The attending, being protective of his resident, initially resists. "When ossification begins, it'll mold itself into proper alignment as it heals."

"Why should I rely on chance when you can get it right now with a little more effort? Besides, you know as well as I do the healing process can't remedy rotation. What's wrong is wrong. Just cut this cast off and re-reduce it." That is exactly what happens.

Just before discharge the attending finds me and apologizes for what he called "an error in judgment" concerning the rotated fragment.

"At least you didn't assert risk or complication," I tell him, but it only makes him smile uncertainly.

I take a car service home and sleep like a baby during the ride. Having been given crutches this time despite my pleading for a walking boot, I crutch my way into my house at close to four in the morning.

I quietly make my way upstairs, feeling woozy from the Percocets. I stumble into my smallish walk-in closet, which was three times bigger on the blueprints but was downsized by my wife's intervention between framing and drywall. The secret change order made her adjoining closet 50 percent bigger, but the builder's profit ten thousand less for his indiscretion.

All I can think about as I slowly get undressed is taking tomorrow off and smoking a cigar. I cautiously take down my underwear, then inspect my intact sutures. Next I take my watch off and set it on the shelf where it always goes. To my surprise, on this same shelf is a piece of folded paper.

The only time paper makes its way there is when our housekeeper, the New Marcolina, finds it during a pre–dry cleaning pocket frisk. The neatly folded rectangle looks familiar. I decide to play the "I'm not going to look at it until I remember what it is" game, but a few seconds later it hits me. It's Dr. Laura Smith's curriculum vitae.

Instead of dropping the CV into the wastebasket, I allow my curiosity to compel me to unfold it. Reading it, I quickly get to the part that lays out her education. And there it is.

Dr. Laura was a first-year resident at the Brooklyn Catholic Hospital when Toledo sent the adapter to Risk Management and a third-year resident when Suzy got electrocuted. She undoubtedly didn't want the case to go forward because it was being brought against the hospital at which she trained.

I go to the last page of her CV. It gives her maiden name. How do I know it? I've seen that name before. It suddenly occurs to me where. So much for a day of cigar smoking. There's more to this, and I need to know.

n the morning, I call the office to check in with Lily. She repri-
mands me for not picking up my cell or house phone, then tells
me a man is sitting in our reception area who wants to speak with
me. He's refused to give her his name but said he was a client. Lily
doesn't recognize him as one of our clients, nor has she pegged him
as an HIC. I tell her if he isn't causing any problems just to let him sit
there. If he wants to talk to me, I'll be in around four and could see
him at four-thirty. Lily says he's no problem, and that because of his
size, she's sure she can handle him if he becomes one.

At four sharp, I find myself standing outside my office entry door. I
take my right crutch out from under my pit and steady myself on my
left one. I grab the handle, press it down, and try to fling the door open.
It opens about two feet, then begins slowly to come back at me. This
makes me appreciate how truly skilled that one-legged boy, Charlie, was
when I saw him down at rehab. I hope that kid lives a long life. Anyway,
during my attempt I glimpse the guy waiting for me in reception.

He's a smallish black man in his late thirties who's very well dressed
and very good-looking. He's wearing a gray pinstriped suit that feels
more gangsta than banka, but it's definitely cut from fine Italian stock.
As I make my way slowly through the door, he stands up. He measures
no taller than five foot six. Despite his slight size he gives off an air of
importance in a mildly threatening kind of way. I don't know whether
to respect him or be apprehensive.

He sees me struggling, so pulls the door open to allow me more room to maneuver.

"Thank you," I reply as I pass him and look directly into his hollow eyes. Not an ounce of human emotion. What was Lily thinking? If I've ever seen that look before it's been in the orbs of hardened HICs who've developed their empty eyes in the solitary areas of jail confinement. I stop and balance myself on the crutches. "Can I help you? I understand you've been here quite a while waiting for me."

"Yes, you can. But I see you're getting used to using your crutches, which I'm sure can be tiring. Why don't you get settled? Then, when you're ready to see me, we'll talk."

"I appreciate that. What's your name, may I ask?"

"My name is Carlton Williams Junior. I'm Suzy's father and June's husband."

He'll Find Out Anyway

I'm obviously shocked because June told me her husband was dead, but I don't want to show any signs of reaction. "Oh, great to meet you. You have a special little girl there." I try to extend my hand, which is kind of restricted by the crutch.

He reaches to make the shake. "I wouldn't know. Haven't been around too much." We shake, and by the squeeze of things, he makes sure I know who's boss. I crutch forward and he kindly opens the inner office door for me.

"Give me half an hour or so."

"Take however long you need."

By the time my duff smacks my office chair, I've got June's number connecting from hitting speed dial.

"Hello," she greets, then pauses.

"June, it's me," I reply, only to realize it was a fake-out hello. Her voice message continues. "June, Suzy, and Dog are a little busy right now but leave a message and we'll call you back as soon as we can."

After the beep I begin with my message. "It's your lawyer. Your dead husband is sitting in my reception area waiting to talk to me. Call me back as soon as you get this." *Click.*

I'm nervous and tense. Something's up. I'm feeling a little helpless, too, because of my physical condition. I start to do what I came here to do and open Suzy's records.

I go directly to the progress note made on the date of the incident and there it is, just as I thought. It reads: "Patient seen by myself (Dr. Gino Valenti) at eight o'clock this morning with hematology residents (Gold, Hassan, Guthrie, Peck, Lim) during rounds." Dr. Laura, who changed the name on her diplomas from Guthrie, her maiden name, was *actually there the moment Suzy was electrocuted.* Still, that doesn't explain why I got kidnapped by her crazy husband.

My cell rings and scares the living daylights out of me. The caller ID reads: PRIVATE CALLER, and I pick up. "You got some explaining to do here, June," I assert.

"It's not June. It's me, Rosie," the caller says.

"Oh, hey, Rosie. To what do I owe this surprise?"

"There's a note in an envelope addressed to you in the doctor's belongings. I'm responsible for the disposition of her arriving inventory. I thought you'd like it if I disposed of Statement Number Three to you. You want me to mail it?"

"No, Rosie. I want you to open it up and fax it to me right this second."

Rosie resists. "Right this second? I'm on break. Can't I get it to you when I'm back on duty?"

"Rosie, you made a cool twenty-five Gs here. Won't you do me that favor?"

"All right. I'll fax it now, but I'm not writing a cover sheet so stand by your fax."

"No problem. Please keep the original safe for me." *Click.* I buzz Lily.

"What?" I hear this through the phone as if I'm some kind of annoyance.

"There's going to be a fax coming in the next few minutes. When it gets here, I want you to bring it right in."

Lily mocks me. " 'There's going to be a fax coming in the next few minutes and when it gets here bring it right in.' Give me a break!"

"Lily," I say firmly, "I'm in no joking mood." Her response is a *click*.

A few minutes later, she enters my office unannounced, holding the *Post* open in her hands. She puts it down in front of me, place mat style. "Look here."

"Where's the fax?"

"Not here yet. Look here! Now!"

I look down and start scanning the stories. I see nothing of interest. "And your point is?"

"Does the guy in that picture look familiar to you?" She points. Come to think of it, he does look familiar. He's next to a headline that reads: "Killer Freed." I look at the picture again with a scrutinizing eye and realize it's Carlton Williams Jr., the guy sitting in my waiting area: June's husband and Suzy's father.

"Did you read the article?" I ask.

"Sure did, and I'm going home now. This shit was not in the job description."

"You mean the verbal?"

"Right, the verbal."

"There's a lot of that going around. Travel safely. Just check for that fax one more time before you leave, okay?" She departs without a response.

I speed-read the article. It seems Carlton Williams Jr. comes from a well-known, successful Brooklyn family, and is one of three sons of Carlton Williams Sr., who apparently made a ton of money as a roofer turned real estate baron. He filed mechanic's liens on the buildings he roofed and ended up owning about thirty of them. However, Carlton Senior lost his fortune investing everything in the development and manufacture of a bagless vacuum system before the technology was advanced enough to work properly. Carlton Williams Jr. was his father's financial advisor and so was primarily responsible for the loss of the family fortune. Carlton Junior then had to go to work and ended up becoming a sales rep for a law enforcement uniform and apparel supply company. The article goes on to say Carlton made big bucks supplying police uniforms to the most ruthless gang in the city. Among his other criminal designations, he is also a murderer.

After Carlton and his gang were busted, he turned state's evidence against his gang, putting many of his accomplices behind bars for life. In exchange for his testimony, he was accepted in the witness protection program. After a number of years in the program, the authorities discovered Carlton was responsible for criminal activities related to a drug-running operation unconnected to his plea bargain. The government agreed to drop all new charges in exchange for expelling him from its protection program. He was recently released, but the article doesn't say exactly when.

I'm sure he can't be too happy about his picture being in the papers for those he testified against and their families to read about. The next thought that comes to mind is "Benson!"

I dial up Henry in a huff. After the third ring I hear his voice. "Benson here."

"Henry, it's me, and I'm really pissed."

"I'm listening if you need to vent," says Henry casually.

"I've been through a bunch of shit with your injured criminals, especially in the last several weeks. Right now I got Carlton Williams Junior sitting out in my waiting area. You've heard of him, haven't you?"

"Calm down, calm down. Yes, I've heard of him. You're not dead yet, are you?"

"No, Henry, I'm not dead yet, but this wasn't in the verbal. It definitely was not in the verbal."

"I understand, but we're making money, aren't we?"

"Yeah, Henry, we're making money—but at what cost? This has gone too far."

"I understand. Relax, will you? Just relax. Things will settle down. They always do. By the way, did you gracefully get us out of his kid's case or are you going forward or what? Maybe that's why Williams is there in the first place."

"No, Henry. I didn't get us gracefully out of the case. What was your verbal? Oh yeah, the verbal on the Suzy Williams case was 'There is no case.' You really have no idea what you're doing when it comes to injury law, do you?"

"Relax, please relax. To answer your question, no, I don't know what I'm doing when it comes to personal injury. That's why I gave you all my injured criminals. Now, how come we're not out of it?"

"Henry, are you sitting down?"

"Yes, I'm sitting. Why, did I fuck up?"

"You might say you fucked up, but I fixed things. I just settled Suzy's case for close to ten million dollars." There is silence on the other end of the line. The "I just hit it big" pause that has rendered the person pausing speechless. "Did you hear me, Henry? Ten million dollars, and that little girl is going to get a payout from a structure to the tune of thirty-five million. Do you hear me?"

"Great. I knew I made the right decision when I chose you to take over my injury practice. I'm right again."

"Henry, is that how you see it? You were about to throw a case worth ten million dollars right out the window and would have destroyed this family in the process."

"That may be how you see it, but I brought you in on these cases for that exact reason. I think I made a good decision. If not for my decision, you never would've been in the position to make any money on Suzy's case and save the day for this family."

"There's just no getting through to you, is there?"

"Now if there's nothing else," Henry says dismissively, "I have to get over to the Four Seasons for an early dinner."

"There is something else. What's the story with junior, the guy sitting out in my waiting area?"

"There is no story. He's your typical uniform supply salesman gone bad. He's also a killer, but only if he has reason to kill. I was his attorney when he was pinched and I got him into witness protection. He's been a client of the public defender ever since. He doesn't like to pay his legal bills. I heard he was being kicked out of protection. Must've been released in the last several weeks."

"You carry a gun. Why don't you get down here and protect my ass? This little guy scares the crap out of me."

"I told you, I'm having an early dinner and have to get going," replies Henry. "Carlton's not a cold-blooded killer. He doesn't kill for sport. He needs motive. Don't worry about anything. Like I told you, he's only a danger if he has reason to kill, and he has no reason to kill you, so relax. You don't need protection." *Click.*

I can't believe he hung up on me. I hit my redial button and get Henry's voice mail. Damn it! Just then Lily marches into my office and slams the fax from Rosie down on top of the *Post,* which is on top of Suzy's records. She snaps her fingers twice in my face and says, "Bye." She performs her patented catwalk turn and prances out like a commando swimsuit model. An instant later, she sticks her head back in. "By the way, lock up. You're the last one here."

I look at my watch and see it's five to five. My heart's racing and I'm not happy about being here alone with a known killer. I take out a few ER-issue Percocets and mix them up with a few Xanax as a rescue dose. Down the hatch they go. I take five deep breaths, repeating my calming chant, then remind myself what Henry said: that he only kills when he has motive to kill and there's no motive for him to kill me. In fact, he should want to send my ass to Vegas with June and Suzy for getting his daughter millions of dollars.

Carlton has been waiting for me an hour now, and that's on top of all the other hours before I arrived. I better go out there and tell him I need thirty more minutes, suggesting he may want to come back. I crutch my way there and take a peek at him through the spy door. He looks like a tiny harmless little man and then he quickly turns his head in my direction, catching me in midspy. Busted.

I quickly open the door to save face. "Mr. Williams, I need another half hour or so. Do you want to wait or come back tomorrow sometime?" I pray for the latter.

"Take your time. I assure you, I'm in no rush. Take your time. I'll be right here," he answers in a most pleasant manner.

"Thank you for understanding."

"No problem."

What a nice guy Carlton is—a ruthless murderer, I think to myself. Never be fooled by smiling faces.

Back at my desk, I pick up the fax of Dr. Laura's letter. It reads:

Dear Mr. Wyler:

I hope this note finds you alive and well. The fact you are reading it means I'm most likely dead. I write this to finish the cleansing of my soul you began when you first walked into my office. Please share its contents with your client as she has a right to know after all these years.

I went to the hospital on February 14 and this Valentine's Day started out just like any other day in the life of a first-year resident except that morning a man from the hospital's Engineering Department came up to the cardiology suite and had a conversation with the attending in charge. The attending called me over and introduced me. From that introduction I fell in love with and married Steven Smith.

The attending said Steven needed someone from cardiology to accompany him to satisfy a work order issued by Risk Management. We were to find a specific cardiac machine and attach a little plastic device. You know what I'm talking about. Steven and I had so much fun looking for the machine all over the hospital, much like an Easter egg hunt.

After searching for hours, Steven called Engineering and was informed the machine we were looking for was actually there in the basement for a wheel repair. We were hungry by that time so Steven suggested we eat, then complete the work order, so we left the hospital for lunch. We ended up spending the day together and were together ever after. We got married late that afternoon and took the next several days off for our honeymoon.

We never completed the work order and I didn't realize this until the day Suzy was electrocuted years later. I was there with the hematology residents when it happened, having switched my residency out of cardiology. I was there when the nurse wheeled that machine down the hall. I heard a broken wheel as she pushed it toward us, and that clicking sound was the first time I remembered we never put the adapter on. Since it was almost three years later, I dismissed the thought that the machine this nurse was wheeling could be the one in question because I remembered it was having its wheel fixed.

I thought it couldn't be the same machine but I was wrong. We weren't in the room at the time Suzy was electrocuted, but right after you could tell something bad had happened by the smell of seared flesh wafting out into the hall. I was in a state of disbelief and Suzy's mother was frozen, sitting up against that wall in shock. I tried to comfort her but I'm pretty sure she didn't even know I was there.

When things settled down, I went into her room. I don't know why, I just did. On the floor was a book Suzy had been reading, *Old Yeller*. I recall her saying she hoped it had a happy ending. And I remember praying in the hall she wouldn't have the same fate when the code team carried her by me. Funny how life is, I had to do to Steven what that boy had to do to Old Yeller, and for a similar reason.

When I collected myself I went directly to Risk Management. I explained to Winnie McGillicuddy, the chief of Risk Management, exactly what happened. I told her how we forgot to place the adapter and I wanted to know if this was the same machine.

I stop reading to take a break. I can hardly believe I have it in me to take a break at this moment. But I'm tired, achy, and drugged out. Nonetheless, I need to assess my thoughts.

The Weasel was the chief of Risk Management at the defendant hospital; the Weasel knew exactly what went down; and the fucking Weasel was the person from Risk Management who assigned the work order in the first place and who was supposed to verify its completion. I continue reading the note:

I never got an answer from Ms. McGillicuddy but Steven confirmed the bad news. That little girl was injured because we put our selfish needs before the welfare and safety of innocent hospital patients. This always overshadowed our marriage. My guilt was immense and growing, especially because I had a second chance to save Suzy.

Unfortunately, the same could not be said for my husband, Steven. He was an opportunist. He figured he could take what had happened and turn it into money. He went to Ms. McGillicuddy after getting word the hospital had been sued and cut a deal. He knew she would be open to it because it was she who was ultimately responsible for seeing the adapter was placed. Steven also found out the hospital didn't have independent insurance coverage during that time and any payout would be directly from the hospital's self-insured pocket. Their agreement took place after I had already left the hospital and was working at a public clinic making very little money. The terms were we would keep silent about the mishap if the hospital would refer their pediatric sickle cell patients to my care in a private practice that Steven was to set up for me. This allowed me to pursue my passion, which was pediatric sickle cell research and treatment, and simultaneously allowed Steven to achieve his goal, which was to be rich.

The hospital stopped treating sickle cell children and their referrals made us the biggest treatment center in Brooklyn. We received hospital grants as part of the deal. Steven applied for and received federal grants independent of our agreement with the hospital. We became rich beyond our wildest dreams all because we neglected to plug an adapter on a machine that electrocuted Suzy Williams, then blackmailed the hospital over that terrible error.

I set the papers down again in disbelief. Smith hadn't been kidding when he said he was responsible for the success of the center. I can't believe the Weasel was able to orchestrate such a deal, but it was a win-win arrangement all around. I keep reading:

When you came to see me the first time, Steven knew things were going to heat up. That other attorney, Benson, knew nothing and suspected nothing. I told him there was no case and he said okay. When you figured out what happened, Steven used that to attempt to extort more money from the hospital with threats of exposure but it backfired. McGillicuddy immediately had our hospital grants revoked and the referral of patients was stopped cold. Over the last number of days alone we lost hundreds of thousands of dollars. McGillicuddy told Steven that you were onto the truth and that given what we had built up with our center, we were now the ones who stood to lose the most, and she was right. At the rate things were going, we were heading for bankruptcy in six months. McGillicuddy said she'd put things back to normal if we were able to convince you to drop the matter. We tried, but you just kept coming and coming and pushing and pushing.

When you insisted on my CV and read it in front of us, Steven was certain you'd figured things out and, well, you know the rest. I made Steven promise me that no one else would get hurt over all this, that Suzy's injury and its effect on her loved ones was enough. I was so upset when he drugged you. When I asked what he was intending to do with you he didn't answer. I knew his greed would lead him into darkness. That's why I had to stop him. It all went too far. That's about it. I am so sorry for what I have done.

Dr. Laura Smith

Just as I'm setting the note down for a third and final time, my cell rings, startling the fuck out of me again. The caller ID reads: PRIVATE CALLER. I hope and pray it's June. "June?" I ask.

"It's me, counselor. How you feeling today, Tug?"

"Not so hot, June. Can you guess why?"

"Carlton?"

"Bingo, June. You told me your husband was dead. What's going on here?"

"Well, technically, I told you he was 'no longer with us.' You just inferred he was dead."

"Whatever the exchange, you left me with the belief that your husband was dead, and you compounded that sentiment yesterday by your silence when I said you were Suzy's sole heir and beneficiary to her millions should she die before you. Now I find out your husband is alive, a uniform supplier turned murderer, and was exiled from the witness protection program. Are you going to tell me next that you're still married?"

"By 'married,' do you mean that we weren't officially divorced, with papers and all?"

"That's great! So you're still married to a killer. I'm not happy, June. What's more, I feel totally threatened by him, despite his overly polite demeanor and slight stature."

"Just relax. He's harmless without a motive."

"You know what, June? That's exactly what Henry Benson said to me. You know what else? I really don't care. The guy scares me, motive or no motive. What is he doing here anyway?"

"He probably wants information on Suzy's case," June says matter-of-factly. "So give it to him."

"Give it to him?"

"Yes, give it to him. He'll find out what he wants anyway. So just tell him whatever he wants to know and you'll be safe. Don't hold back. Do you understand me? Don't hold back anything. He'll find out anyway, and then you'll have given him a motive and you won't be safe. Understand?"

"Yes, June, I understand. Now, before we hang up, did we have this conversation?"

"Stick with the truth and you'll be safe," she instructs. "So yes. If he asks if we spoke, tell him we did. Give him the time we spoke, what we spoke about, and anything else he asks. Like I said, he'll find out anyway. I learned my resourcefulness from him."

"Okay, June. Let me go and speak to him now. Later we'll talk."

"Just stick with the truth, and you'll be safe." Then she's gone.

Our Conversation
Never Happened

I can't get the fucking Weasel off my mind, and I'm debating on whether or not to tell her what I know from Dr. Laura's letter, just so she knows I know. Being right is everything when you're a litigator. Anything less is crap. Didn't I have that thought already today?

I crack open the door. "Come on in, Mr. Williams."

"Call me Carlton, please." He follows me back into my office. I navigate around the desk, resting my crutches behind me.

"So, Carlton, uh, how can I be of assistance to you?"

"I understand my daughter's case has settled."

"That's an accurate statement of fact."

"What was the number?"

Technically, he's not my client, and normally I wouldn't share privileged information with him, but June has given me the go-ahead to do so. "Hers settled for nine-point-two million and June received seven hundred fifty thousand for her claim, both to be reduced by the attorney fee, which percentage is fixed by statute."

"That June deserves every penny. She's one devoted mother. She was a devoted wife, too, before this unfortunate circumstance changed all of us and wrecked my family."

"I imagine June to have been a good wife. If the way she cares for Suzy is any indication. And I'm sure it must be."

"So what happens with Suzy's money?"

"The money goes into a financial vehicle known as a structured settlement and she'll get paid out over her lifetime."

"How much is the payout?"

"Approximately thirty-five million over the course of her expected life. It's an annuity, so they take the client share and invest it, producing thirty-five, guaranteed."

He ponders the large number. I can tell he's happy with the result. "That's a lot of money," he says, supporting my observation.

"It is," I agree.

"Who controls it?" he asks after a few seconds.

"It's initially invested directly by the defendant into an annuity fund of an A++-rated insurance company and then reinsured by another A++ company, with a schedule of payments that automatically deposit money into a joint bank account in the name of Suzy, June, and an officer of the bank on a monthly basis to cover Suzy's necessaries with lump sum payments at different intervals during Suzy's life."

"I understand, but now that I'm back in the picture I want to get to know my daughter again. So how does that work? You know, custody and getting some of that money released to me so I can do things with Suzy?"

"Things like custody are not within the realm of what I do. I'm an injury lawyer, not a matrimonial or family lawyer. You and June will have to work that out between yourselves or with lawyers that do that kind of work. As for releasing Suzy's money to you, once you've established your rights of visitation I'd be happy to make application to the court on your behalf for the release of money to you to spend on your daughter. We have to give the judge supporting documentation as to where you're going to spend the money, then evidence that you did, in fact, spend it there. The key in getting the money released is showing the judge it's in the best interests of Suzy."

Carlton's pleasant demeanor takes a quick turn. "Are you saying spending time with me wouldn't be in Suzy's best interests?" he asks suspiciously.

"I'm not saying that at all. I was just laying out for you the legal criteria for the release of funds. The best interests of the child are that legal criteria."

"There, you did it again! What are you trying to say here?"

At this moment, I realize Carlton's looking to make an issue of things. It reminds me of Bert Beecher's misinterpretation of the divorce laws where he was insisting on 50 percent of the settlement, thinking it was marital property. Like Bert, Carlton is one of those angry people who look for opportunities to create a combative exchange. I imagine his life experiences have caused him to develop this negative mannerism.

"Carlton, this is all good. Suzy's case is over and she's well taken care of financially. You are now available to be the father you weren't able to be when you weren't around. It's a whole new beginning for you and your family. I'm proud I was a part of it and was able to help."

Carlton first responds with calm and an appearance of agreement, which quickly and surprisingly turns to rage. I have no idea what in my last statement could possibly be making him angry, but I'm sure I'm going to find out. He is one irate fellow. "Help me? Help me? You didn't help me, motherfucker! I helped you! I helped you, motherfucker!"

"Please calm down, Carlton. There's nothing to be upset or angry about." I wonder to myself, How does this murderous lowlife think he helped me?

"Yeah, I'm calm, but you should be thanking me, motherfucker, not the other way around."

Instead of placating Carlton, which I know I should do in an effort to calm him, I take another tack. "Carlton, can you explain to me just how it is you helped me? I'm not sure I understand."

"Yeah, I'll tell you, motherfucker, since you don't seem to know shit about it. Who the fuck you think saved your ass when that guy ran you off the parkway, gave you first aid to stop your bleeding, carried you out of the woods from that old Cadillac, and drove you to the hospital, leaving you on the sidewalk? That was *me*, motherfucker! Who the fuck you think broke you out of the trunk of that car? That was me, too, motherfucker. You'd be dead two times if it weren't for me. You got that, motherfucker?"

I have to agree with him there. "I had no idea that was you, Carlton. How was I supposed to know it was you? I didn't even know you existed until you showed up here. So yes, I owe you a thank-you. No, two thank-you's for saving my life twice."

"Damn right, motherfucker," Carlton fumes. "I also finished the job on that piece of white trash who tried to run you off the road. He wasn't dead from the crash, but I made sure he wouldn't come after you again."

"Please, Carlton, I appreciate you saving my life, but please don't give me any information about your criminal wrongdoings. I don't want to know any of that, okay?"

We sit there looking at each other for what must be half a minute. He finally decides he's going to tell me what he's been thinking about during his pause. "I did it for me, not you."

"Did what for you?"

"I saved your life for me, not for you."

"Carlton, I'm not following you here. Can you explain?"

"Yeah, I'll explain. I was protecting my interests by saving your ass."

"Can you explain that to me?" But I'm afraid I think I understand.

"Naw, man, I can't. I can't explain it to you, but you can explain something to me. What happens to that thirty-five million if Suzy dies? You know, if she dies from a complication of her medical condition or if she dies some other way?"

"Under the intestate laws of the state of New York," I tell him without hesitation, "both you and your wife would get that money in equal shares." Holy shit! Motive.

To kill Suzy, not me.

"Does June know I'm here?"

"Yes, she does."

"We're done talking. Good job on getting my daughter that money, lawyer. You and I, we helped each other. That's good. About this conversation, we never had it. No one, I mean no one, and that includes June, is to know anything. Not that I intend to get back into Suzy's life, not that I saved your life, and not about our conversation about what happens to the money if Suzy dies. You got that?"

"Got it," I say. Meanwhile, I'm thinking that as soon as my office door hits this guy in the ass, I'm calling June to warn her.

"It's late. You going home?"

"Uh, yeah," I reply.

"I'll walk you out and put you in a cab. It's hard to do that with crutches. Come on."

"Thanks, but I'm good. Need to tie up some loose ends. Been out of the office a lot lately."

Carlton turns insistent. "Come on. Let's go." In the spirit of taking the path of least resistance I stand up to leave. But immediately I feel dizzy and shoot my hands down onto the desk for balance. The various drugs I've taken are respiratory and cardiac depressants, and I just had an episode of postural hypotension.

"Are you okay?" he asks with seemingly genuine concern.

"I'm fine. I'm on some medication that interferes with the vasoconstriction ability of my arterial system to compensate for changes in gravity. The blood wasn't forced to my brain fast enough when I stood up." He's unimpressed with my medical knowledge.

"I'll carry that for you," he offers. He takes my bag, which I'd been struggling to hold on to while also gripping my crutch. I hobble forward toward the door. "I got that," he says.

After the elevator levels, Carlton holds open the door as I struggle my way from the deserted lobby toward the refuge of the busy street. Carlton, still being helpful, holds open the building door. Out on the sidewalk, I feel the relief of the street's safe haven. People are everywhere.

"Let me put you in a cab," he proposes.

"Thanks, but I'm going to pick up a bite and talk to a young woman named Margo. Former coma victims turn her on."

"I figured you for a ladies' man." Carlton gives me an acknowledging nod.

I dissuade him of the notion. "Not really. Married, kids, you know the deal. I seem to strike out a lot anyway."

"Yeah, right."

I put my hand out for a shake while balancing on my right crutch. "Good night, Carlton. If you need anything else, just call."

Carlton takes my hand and gives it a seriously firm squeeze. "Just remember, our conversation never happened. I believe you lawyers like to call it privileged communication."

"My lips are sealed," I respond. Of course, I haven't changed my mind about warning June as soon as he's out of range.

He smiles. "Later." I detect a hint of cautious reserve in his completely buying my commitment to silence.

"Yeah, later," I respond.

I make it to the Gansevoort Park and lean against the outside of the building to catch my breath. I don't want Margo to think I'm too out of shape and have her thus infer it's reflective of my sexual prowess. The inference would be accurate, but I have great stamina when it comes to receiving oral favors.

I also want to reach June before I go inside, so I can have a clear conscience when I mesmerize and moisten Margo with my coma tales. That I can still think of engaging Margo after my exchange with Carlton is no doubt a flaw in my character, which admission makes the thought no more justified or acceptable.

I lean there for another ten minutes, just taking in the scene. I'm watching everything around me. Nothing is slipping by without being assessed and accounted for. I'm looking for anything that even resembles Carlton Williams Jr., and if I see his brother from a different mother who lives in South Dakota, I'm not making the warning call to June, for both our benefits. I'm not even going to motion toward my inside lapel pocket where my cell rests until I'm certain the coast is clear.

I've had my law office in this neighborhood for over eighteen years and never took notice during all that time of local sights I've seen in the last ten minutes. For example, I never knew I could try a Chinese hair-straightening, have my back waxed, eat a buffalo burger, have the skin of my cracked heels shaved off with a complimentary green tea footbath, sit for a palm reading, join Jews for Jesus, get my vision surgically corrected to 20/20 without a blade and without making a payment for twelve months, or ask that my wife's G-string be analyzed by a professional lab for evidence of extramarital semen.

I've never smelled the roses, and I'm just this moment realizing what that saying really means. What a shame.

I take a far look uptown, a far look downtown, and survey the entire square-block radius from where I'm standing. I take three deep breaths in through my nose and out through my mouth, repeating my calming chant. To the best of my knowledge, Carlton Williams Jr. is nowhere in sight.

I take out my cell and press the button that needs to be pressed to get June on the phone. I'm looking back and forth, scrutinizing, examining, checking, scanning, inspecting, and searching my environment for signs of danger as her cell rings once . . . twice . . . three times.

During this three-ring period, I recount that both Henry and June said Carlton was only murderous if he had a motive. He definitely has a motive to kill his daughter. I realize he gave himself a motive to kill me. I'm not safe.

June picks up midway into ring four. "Hey, counselor. Things go all right with Mr. Witness Protection flunk-out?"

"June, no time for jokes. Listen carefully. You got me? No kidding. Listen to me carefully." Before I get my next word out—*bang, bang*—explodes and echoes from behind me. It's a gunshot, point-blank, to the back right of my head. I lose voluntary control and find myself falling forward toward the roadway, vaulting over my crutches, and crash-landing onto the pavement. I sense I've been shot in the back of my head, but I've somehow miraculously survived. So far.

My head is hanging off the curb, face downward, between two parked cars. I can't believe I'm still conscious. The GCS numbers 15, 14, 13, and 12 flash on my brain's coma counter, reflective of my decreasing level of consciousness. Margo's gonna love this shit.

I feel something running down my cheek like warm water. I want to wipe it away, but I can't lift my arms. I see bright red blood, my blood, and a tiny piece of my shattered scalp floating downstream.

The turmoil around and above me sounds like white noise. It's hard to make out what any one person is saying. I hear screaming, yelling, crying, arguing, directing, all with a common purpose: get help for the guy in the gutter with the back of his head shot off. The only thing I hear clearly is the voice coming from my cell resting on the concrete near what remains of my right ear. It's June. "No! Oh my God! No!" Over and over again.

I watch the stream turn to a red river polluted with bits of ear cartilage. I love my wife. I love my children. I love my dogs. I also love Lily, who's been such a big part of my life. I admit to myself she was right that the dangers of handling HIC cases are not a mere matter of isolated incidents, as she so perfectly defined that term.

Crap, I forgot to call my mom. I've been watching her die one cell at a time with dignity and courage over all these years, and now I've gone and got myself shot in the back of the head. I've now forced her to have to deal with the loss of a child after all she's been through—and that ain't right. This leads me to my next thought.

I hate Henry Benson and I hate Carlton Williams Jr., who are jointly responsible for my more-than-likely impending death. But I have to take responsibility here. Once I realized what these HICs were all about, I made a business decision to keep on representing them for the money.

I slowly feel myself falling into Glasgow Coma Scale 11, then 10, as I make my way down, hoping to avoid GCS level 3.

"You're going to be fine, I promise," I hear a sympathetic little girl's voice say, or so I think as I slip deeper into nothingness. It's a sweet voice, a kind voice, a caring voice. A voice I have heard before. I search for the source of this familiar voice. Rummaging about with my mind's eye, which is slowly losing its acuity.

"Just relax, you're going to be just fine, no worries," the soothing voice reinforces. My jaw drops in surprise—no, bewilderment. There, kneeling over me, as I lie with blood trickling out of my head, is Suzy. Is my brain playing tricks on me? She looks like a perfectly normal, healthy, and thriving twelve-year-old child. As if nothing ever happened to her. Wearing that yellow party dress she wore in the video of her fifth birthday party. And she is beautiful, just like her mother.

"Is that you, Suzy?" I ask now, somehow face-to-face.

"Yes, it's me."

"You can talk?"

"Yes, in this place I can talk."

"What place is this?"

"Between the universes of here and there. The place you told Ginger and Margo about at the Gansevoort bar."

"How do you know about that?"

She smiles, as if it were a naïve question.

"So, I'm not going to die?"

"No, Mr. Wyler, you're not going to die. Like I said, you're going to be just fine."

"Please, Suzy, call me Tug."

"That would be disrespectful, you're an adult. My mother always told me to address adults in a proper way."

"I could see her telling you that." She smiles again. "Can I ask you something, Suzy?"

"Of course, that's why I'm here. And to comfort you the way Nurse Braithwait consoled my mother and me early that morning before she electrocuted me. She's a caring lady. Please make sure she never finds out what she did to me. She would never be able to recover from it if she knew."

"I'll never tell her, Suzy. I promise. And I'll call the Weasel and make sure she doesn't, either."

"Good. We don't need any more unnecessary suffering, now, do we?"

"No, no we don't."

"So, what is it that you want to ask me, Mr. Wyler?"

"Well, in my law practice I represent many victims of traumatic brain injury. Do you know what that means?"

"Yes, Mr. Wyler, I most certainly do—you know, given my condition. Go on."

"Just checking, sorry." She smiles. "Anyway, one of the items of damage that I get money for, to compensate the injured, is known as *conscious* pain and suffering." I pause to see if she needs explaining.

"Yes, go on, Mr. Wyler, I understand. Go on."

"Well, I just wanted to know, when you're as brain damaged as you are, stuck there in a wheelchair, staring out into space, with no control over the movement of your body, drooling, seemingly unaware of what is going on around you, with the whole world assuming you can't understand a thing—well, is that really the case? Or are you *conscious* of your environment and aware of the fact that you have been severely injured and permanently compromised? I always wanted to know the answer to that question. And more so in a case like yours, where you seem to respond to things with the appropriate *sch-weets* and *not sch-weets.*"

Suzy smiles, the kind one gives when asked an intelligent question particular to the circumstance. She folds in half the napkin that somehow materialized in her hand and dabs the sweat off my forehead in a caring way. Just as she is about to answer, I slip further into unconsciousness, leveling at GCS 9. As I do, Suzy, in a snap, disappears, vanishing into thin air.

fter an undetermined period of time suspended at GCS 9, I start to become consciously aware of my surroundings. I've ascended back to a GCS 14 and see a paramedic on my left. He's finishing his work on me with the skill and expertise of a tenured veteran. I'm still on the ground, but they've turned me over so I'm facing up at a circular line of very interested New York City bystanders who are surrounding me.

I know there are rows of people behind the front line, but I can't see them because of my fixed position. My body is secured on a restraining board and my neck is in a plastic brace. My head is wrapped in what I'm certain is a red-soaked bandage. From his movements and the soft sound of cloth sliding against cloth, I decide the paramedic must've just finished tying and securing my head to the board for immobilization.

After a good-luck last tug, ensuring the knot is taut and my head fixed, the paramedic moves his face over mine and we lock eyes. He has a kind and familiar face, perfect for a lifesaver. "I'm paramedic Jim Henson. You were shot in your head. The bullet went in the back on an angle and out the side, tearing part of your right ear off, but you're going to be fine. You're a lucky man."

I ignore the great news and instead ask a question. "Did you say your name was Jim Henson?"

"Yes, I did." I can tell by his apprehensive expression he knows I know that's the name of the guy who invented the Muppets. Maybe that's why he looks familiar; the Muppet guy has joined the celebrity-turned-paramedic fad. Wait a second. Jim Henson's dead. I somehow recall seeing a tribute show to his life and genius. My paramedic just looks like the real Jim Henson and shares his name, that's all.

Jim Henson responds to my thank-you. "Just doing my job." Then he speaks to one of several other paramedics that have crossed my view. "This one's alert, stable, and ready for transport."

Now I hear another paramedic, who by the sound of things is only a few feet away, say something startling. "This other one's gone. I'm calling his unofficial time of death at nineteen-twenty-four. We should bag him."

"We can't," Jim Henson replies. "This is now a crime scene for a murder investigation. I don't know what's taking the detectives so long, but they have work to do before you can take your transport to the morgue."

Oh, man. Some poor unfortunate bystander took the bullet that went through my head and was killed. Damn you, Henry!

Two more paramedics come over. By the angle of their approach I know they are neither Jim nor the guy he just spoke to. They kneel in the same spot Jim kneeled. One of them moves his face directly over mine. "We're gonna take you to Bellevue. You need medical care."

"If I need medical care, then why would you take me to Bellevue? No city hospitals for me! You're taking me to NYU Langone Medical Center on Thirty-Fourth Street or you can just leave me here." He moves out of my face. He conferences with his colleague, then leans over me again. "No can do. Gunshot to the head requires a level-1 trauma center."

I start yelling. "Get Jim Henson over here! I want to speak to Henson now!" The paramedic who said "No can do" looks at me questioningly. "Jim Henson? The Muppet guy?"

"No, not that Jim Henson. That Jim Henson is dead. I want to speak to Jim Henson the paramedic. The guy who fixed me up and restrained my head."

"That's me," he states. "I'm the guy who fixed you up. My name's Steve Bruckner. There's no paramedic here named Jim Henson. Listen, you sustained severe head trauma. Take it easy. We'll take you to NYU Langone. Just calm yourself down, or we'll do it for you."

Now I'm really scared. I hallucinated the guy who invented the Muppets was the paramedic who fixed me up. I'm not sure how Margo's gonna take this. Maybe Bellevue's the right destination after all.

"I'm sorry. I'm just a little stressed out. It's been a tough couple of weeks, even without getting shot in the head."

"Understandable. Just take it easy. We're gonna get you out of here."

"Okay, but tell me something. Is there a dead guy next to me? Or did I hallucinate that, too?"

"No, you didn't hallucinate that. There's a dead guy three feet from you. He took one in the head, too."

"The bullet that left my head caught the guy?"

"Separate shooting," Bruckner responds. "According to the crime scene detectives—"

"I thought the detectives didn't get here yet," I interrupt.

"The detectives were here before we arrived and our response time was six minutes."

"Sorry, I thought I overheard Jim . . . I mean, uh . . . never mind. Go on."

"Anyway, according to the crime scene detectives, five people heard two separate and distinct gunshots." That explains the gunshot echo I heard, which was no echo at all. But who's the dead guy? I guess Carlton silenced a nearby eyewitness who happened to be in the wrong place at the wrong time.

An instant later, a mobile stretcher is parked between me and the dead guy. Paramedic Bruckner puts his face over mine again. "We're gonna pick you up and put you on this stretcher on the count of three."

"Fine, but I want to see who the dead guy is lying next to me."

"No can do," he responds in knee-jerk fashion. He apparently likes that phrase.

"Listen, Bruckner," I plead, "if, God forbid, you were the survivor of an attempted double homicide, you'd want to see who the actual dead guy was before being taken away, wouldn't you?"

"Let me ask the detectives," he says, then moves out of my sight.

A moment later, Bruckner's face is above mine again. Next to him is a detective. You could tell this guy's a cop from a mile away, and here he is, about six inches from the tip of my nose. "We were gonna talk to you at the hospital, Mr. Wyler," the detective tells me, "but since you and I want the same question answered, we're gonna accommodate your request."

"Thanks, detective," I respond, "but please, call me Tug." He nods.

"Okay," Bruckner informs me, "we're going to pick you up by the board and tilt you to your left so you can get a glimpse. Then we're gonna set you on the stretcher for transport. Listen, I've got to warn you. The guy's a mess. A large-caliber bullet came out the front."

"Just let me see."

The two paramedics lift and tilt as the detective pulls the tarp off the dead guy in a way so as to curtain him off from the surrounding crowd. I see Carlton Williams Jr. sprawled out in a twisted and very unnatural position with a giant hole in the side of his head. I'm confused. Why would someone try to kill both him and me?

"Had enough?" Bruckner asks. "You're kind of heavy."

"Not so fast," the detective interjects. "You know the guy?"

"Yeah, I know him," I confirm.

"Name?"

"Carlton Williams Junior."

"Relation to you?"

"He's the father of one of my clients. I'm a lawyer."

"Do you know why he tried to kill you?" the detective asks.

Now I am more confused. "How do you know he tried to kill me? It seems like someone tried to kill us both."

"No. He was your shooter."

"How do you know?"

The detective pauses—the kind when someone's trying to decide whether to tell someone something or how much of that something to tell someone—then gives a small sigh. "By his positioning relative to yours, by the discharged gun found in his hand, by the rough field ballistics match between his gun and your wound, and by the witness standing right over there who told us he saw the whole thing."

"That sounds reliable," I conclude. After using a pause of my own to collect myself, I take a deep breath. "What did the witness say?"

"The witness said your Carlton Williams Junior got the trigger pulled on him just as he was pulling the trigger on you; like someone was trying to protect you. Why'd he want you dead?"

"Because I was going to tell his wife that he was going to kill their daughter."

"That's a different motive," the detective comments. "Usually, it's money."

"Did the witness say anything about Carlton's shooter?" I ask.

"Black male, average height, fast runner. That narrows things down," the detective answers in a sarcastic tone. He looks to Bruckner. "You can take him now." He looks back at me as if to finish a thought. "We're going to have more questions for you, Tug," he apprises me as if I didn't know, then walks away.

The stretcher pops up and they begin wheeling me toward the flashing lights. The bystanders are all vying for position to get their glimpses of me. I can see them jockeying their heads up, down, back, and forth to grab a good look. Everybody in the crowd—black, white, Hispanic, Asian—meshes into a sea of bobbleheads as they move in all directions to catch a glance. All I see is head motion except for two people whose stillness sets them apart from the throng.

One flashes a twinkle out of her right eye, a distinctive flicker of radiant beauty. Margo. She's standing motionless with her arms at her sides. When we approach, she gives me a sympathetic smile and slowly waves. I smile back as I'm being rolled past her and closer to the other motionless person whom I definitely don't know.

He's a black guy wearing a black baseball cap, which somehow accentuates his stillness. He has an unobstructed view from three rows deep, and that seems odd since everyone else is jockeying for position. I'm wheeled toward him and observe the slow swivel of his head as he follows the path of my stretcher. As we pass him I can see the raised embroidery gold lettering of the insignia on his baseball cap. It reads: THE FIDGE.

I'm surprised. But I should've figured it out. I mean, given what's been happening and all. I'm just not that smart, I guess.

At least I admit it.

ACKNOWLEDGMENTS

Michele Slung, thank you for everything—for changing the course of my life. Colin Harrison, my editor, I thank you for embracing *Suzy's Case* and taking the time to teach me how to bring it to a higher level. Sterling Lord, my agent, my favorite movie growing up was *One Flew Over the Cuckoo's Nest*, and while I sat in remedial reading class, I never would have imagined that one day I would share the same literary agent as Ken Kesey. In fact, I didn't even know they made the movie into a book.

Victor Greco, thank you for beating me at trial. That defense verdict was the best defeat that was ever handed to me. From it, you have become a referring attorney, a writing instructor, a book reviewer, and, most important, a trusted friend. My cousin Danny Green, thank you for taking the time to read my book and sharing your wisdom and insights. Deborah Purcell, thank you for telling me to write thirty-five pages, the start of it all. Kim White, thank you for directing me to look at a picture frame and to describe what I saw.

There are many other people who have influenced my creation in some way, shape, or form, even if only through support. Sanford Preizler, Holly Singer, Scott Mesnick, Brian Schachter, Davena Levine, Simon Sinek, Maura Cohen, Josh Silber, Matthew Weiss, and James LePore, to name a few.

On a personal note, I would like to thank my lifelong best friend, Evan Davis. Your support, encouragement, and guidance are valued and cherished. To my cousin Andres, *¿Qué pasa, primo?* Dad, I love you. And to my mother, Adele, rest in peace, finally. No one ever could have taken on cancer in a braver manner than you did.

To my children, Blake, Cooper, and Phoebe: Thank you for loving me, inspiring me, and entertaining me. I love you guys so much. And to my wife, Randi: I knew it would piss you off to be the last person acknowledged. That's why I did it. Consider it foreplay. You inspire me, incite me, annoy me, put up with me, and everything else that provokes the intense energy that makes our marriage work. I love you dearly.

ABOUT THE AUTHOR

Andrew W. Siegel is a personal injury and medical malpractice lawyer in New York City and serves on the board of directors of the New York State Trial Lawyers Association. He lives with his wife, Randi, and three children, Blake, Cooper, and Phoebe, in Bedford Hills, New York.